Death Becomes Her

Stephanie appeared to be sleeping, crumpled on the bed, lying on her side, her arm flung over her head, the lights in the adjoining bathroom illuminating the bottom of the bed, and then the walls shouted color at Natalie, bright red walls above the white and gold headboard.

"Stephanie . . . oh God!" Natalie cried. Her knees buckled, and with tears streaming down her face, she knelt by the end of the bed. She put her face in her hands. She didn't approach her sister – wanting too – *needing* to – but she knew it wouldn't do any good, because she had seen dead people before. Lots of them. Natalie Collins was a detective sergeant in the homicide unit of the Portland Police Bureau.

But this was family, and she couldn't move . . .

Praise for Enes Smith and *Fatal Flowers*

"A CHILLINGLY AUTHENTIC LOOK INTO THE BLACKEST DEPTHS OF A PSYCHOPATH'S FANTASIES . . READ THIS ONE ON A NIGHT WHEN YOU DON'T NEED TO SLEEP!"

Ann Rule, bestselling author of *Small Sacrifices*

Also by Enes Smith

Fatal Flowers
Cold River Rising
Cold River Resurrection

DEAR DEPARTED

ENES SMITH

Enes Smith Productions Edition

DEAR DEPARTED

Printing History

The Berkley Publishing Group
Diamond Edition
December 1994

Enes Smith Productions Edition
December 2010

Cover design by Kent Wright

For additional copies, go to Amazon.com

ISBN-13: 978-1456390051
ISBN-10: 1456390058

Printed in the United States of America

FOR MY MOTHER

MARJORIE BERYL SMITH

AUTHOR'S NOTE

Dear Departed was my second novel, and there were many people who contributed to this story and the novel seeing the light of day: Ann Rule, with constant encouragement; literary agents Joe and Joan Foley; and my editor at Berkley, Melinda Metz.

Dear Departed was first released in December, 1994 by the Berkley Publishing Group, with their Diamond imprint.

This new edition reflects changes in technology and society since I wrote the story; other than that, the story remains unchanged.

ACKNOWLEDGEMENTS

There have been many people who have contributed time and effort to get this new edition of Dear Departed on its way:

Nancy Spreier, friend, consummate researcher, and constant believer, owed more than I can write, a person with unlimited knowledge of the works of fiction; Barbara Lambert, for typing and work on the manuscript; Annie Hausinger, for typing, editing, and copyediting, and most of all, encouragement and friendship; Kent Wright, for technical advice and cover design; and Deb Walker for manuscript assistance.

Part One

"I never got married until I was sixty-five years old, that's why I lived until I was one hundred sixty-five."

SHIRALI MISLIMOV 1805-1973
Caucasian Mountains
Russia, Hamlet of Barzavu

And all the days of Methuselah were nine hundred sixty-nine years, and he died.

THE BIBLE
Genesis
Chapter 26

Prologue

He could smell the night smells from the room down the darkened hall. A room he moved easily in, even though this was his first visit. Cold cream. A bath powder. The smell of sleep.

He heard the sounds of slow, deep breathing. Sleep sounds. Two women lived here, and he was comfortable with their odors, their sounds, their . . . things.

Two women. One was gone. One was sleeping.

But not long.

It was time for her to awaken.

He moved slowly, the covering on his shoes whispering softly to him as he moved across the carpet. He walked to the large windows and looked at the water below, smoothing his face as he glided quietly across the room and into the hallway. He walked to the end and stopped at the open doorway where the sleep sounds were, his pulse and breathing quickening. He looked at the sleeping form on the bed and then moved past, unhurried, relaxed here, and entered the second bedroom.

He moved to the dresser, the odor of the powder biting, tickling the mask. This one might be home soon, but he had time to move slowly. A dim, diffused light came from the half-open bathroom door down the hall, and with the lights from the far bank of the river shining through the bedroom window, he could see the photos on the dresser.

A man in a blue police uniform, a veteran with stripes.

A woman with the same uniform, younger, youthful, athletic with short blond hair.

This was her room.

He carefully reached out and took the picture in his hands, reassured by the slow, even breathing coming from the next bedroom. There were small figurines on the dresser, children's toys, he thought, but there had been no mention of a child.

They were Disneyland artifacts, old ones, Mickey and Minnie Mouse, an orange dog with long ears and a stupid expression, some ducks. Molded plastic. He picked up a small figure with big black ears and a polka-dot dress.

A mouse.

He put it in his mouth and took it with him. He held the picture of the woman up, squinting, staring at her eyes, trying to know her, looking for what she knew. He carried the picture with him to the other bedroom and watched the sleeping form.

She's not the one, but she might know something of what I need.

He woke her up to inquire, and when it was done . . . he waited.

Friday, September 15 and Saturday, September 16

Minnie Mouse

One

On the night Stephanie died, Natalie Collins had the cab drop her off up on Front Avenue, two blocks from her riverfront apartment. She loved to walk the last few blocks of the hill down to the river. The buildings and skyline of downtown Portland rose up behind her, the upper floors of the buildings a bright halo in the dark rain.

She walked a few steps and then stopped as the cab pulled away. The broad expanse of the Willamette River was in front of her, lined with condos and apartments. The double-decked Marquam Bridge was upriver and to her right, up high in the rain and mist, lighted with streetlights and cars. Down river, she could make out the top of the steel bridge, a black grid framework from another era.

The rain fell softly, almost a mist, and she pulled the hood up on her trench coat, watching the way the lights from the marina made glistening halos, silent and alone. The river was dark, broken only by the lights on the east shore and on the bridges. The street going down to the river was busy, with people leaving the floating restaurant and the seafood restaurants on the waterfront. The BMW's, Mercedes, and cabs passed her on the street, but she had the sidewalk to herself. The street scene was a small community, reminding her of a European village. There were shops on each side of the street, ending at the river in a circular drive. She walked past a microbrewery, with northwest beers and ales advertised in the window on colorful banners. The yeast smell of the beer followed her for a few steps.

Natalie walked under a canvas awning, and once she was out of the rain, she threw the hood of her glistening, black trench coat to her shoulders. She pulled the belt loose, letting the coat fall open, warmer now as she walked toward the river. Natalie wore a sleeveless black evening dress that fell to mid-calf, with a front slit, black nylons, and black high heels. She looked alluring and sophisticated tonight, and when she thought about it, she knew it.

Natalie walked the last block down the hill to her apartment, pausing to look in the windows of the small shops she passed. A door opened in front of her, a small figure leaning over the lock to secure the door. She slowed when she saw who it was.

"Hi, Mr. Barker."

The figure rose suddenly and stepped back, fear in his face, an aging shopkeeper wearing a hat and overcoat, vulnerable, locking up late at night.

"Natalie?"

"Yeah." She grinned at him.

"You're out late in the rain, young lady." He leaned closer, relieved, and smiled. He was equal to Natalie's height at five feet four. She was five feet four when she was wearing heels.

"Hey, big date, all dressed up to kill," he said.

Natalie laughed. "No date, symphony tonight with friends."

Mr. Barker shook his head. "Boy, those young guys you work with, they don't see you like this. You should grab one of them."

"Yeah, any day now." They both laughed.

"Hey, saw your sister today. She came in for a sandwich."

"Stephanie."

"Yeah, Stephanie. Hey, you hungry, I can open and fix a sandwich, open a bottle of wine."

"I'd better not." Natalie laughed. "I've had enough chardonnay, and you feed me too much as it is. I'm already running three miles a day so I don't blow up." She put her hand on his arm. She had an easy friendship with Mr. Barker, who was forty years older.

"Come in tomorrow, try my new soup." Mr. Barker looked around, his grin fading. "You get home and lock your door, what with all that goes on these days. But I guess you know that, what with the work you do."

"You're on about the soup, and I'm fine, Mr. Barker," Natalie reassured him. He stepped off the curb and turned to wave, taking careful steps across the street to his car. Natalie continued down the sidewalk, her heels clicking on the wet surface. Her right heel came down and she lurched forward, took a quick step, caught her balance, and stopped, looking down at the black heels. Natalie hummed the melodic line of Tchaikovsky's 1812 Overture, feeling better than she had in months. A major case had finally sifted together today, and tonight had been the opening night of the symphony season at the Arlene Schnitzer Concert Hall. Natalie had dined and wined with friends downtown. She laughed aloud and then looked around to see if anyone heard.

"Need to wear these heels more often," she said, and then laughed again, feeling a little giddy with the wine. Kirby had remarked about her black high heels when she changed at work today, grinning at her and telling the others that the boss had a hot date. She laughed again and looked up at her reflection in the window of a pastry shop. Not bad for an old woman of thirty-six, she thought. Blond hair, cut short, stylish, like Princess Di. Natalie had a small nose with a hint of freckles that she had hated until it didn't matter anymore, a few small wrinkles at the corners of her eyes that her dad said she got from squinting up at him and always asking, "Why?" She was called cute, but she supposed it was more for her size than for her face. In truth, she knew it was for her attitude, her personality, her way of looking at things with humor, even when things got bad, really bad, as they sometimes did at work. Natalie winked at her reflection and tried a couple of poses. She stuck her tongue out at herself and laughed again.

The street ended at the riverbank in a circular drive, above the small marina and floating restaurant. Up the street behind her, the lighted skyline of Portland glistened through the rain. When she reached the circular drive, Natalie turned to her left and walked on sidewalk amid the tables and chairs of the delis and shops.

She saw movement in front of her then, a shadow in the shape of a man, a shadow leaning against the railing. As she approached the gate to her sidewalk, she shifted her purse to her left hand and dug out her keys. A worn figure of Minnie Mouse dangled from the ring. She glanced down the sidewalk at the shadow, and shivered. The shadow was wearing a sweatshirt in the rain, a soaked sweatshirt from what she could see, and a thought hit her that he was not from here, a stranger, with no raincoat or a jacket with a hood. He appeared to be waiting, as a father might wait for a child, but more nervous somehow, waiting, knowing *that something's going to happen.*

She'd seen it before, other times and places, the lone figure – a lookout.

Oh yeah. I've seen it before, once at a bank when everything turned to hell. It's my job; it's what I do.

You could tell a lot about people if you looked – though most people didn't look. That's how they got into so much trouble.

No obvious tattoos, beard trimmed a month ago, alert, confident stance; yeah, he's waiting.

The second thought Natalie had about the shadow person, a man with a beard to hide his face and age, was that he was looking up at her apartment.

But my apartment is hard to see from the sidewalk. She punched the security numbers on the gate and shut it quickly as she walked through, feeling safer as she started up the steps to her door, two and a half stories above the sidewalk. The apartment complex was terraced above the river, with outside entrances to each apartment, with private decks and a view of the river. She passed doors sheltered by hanging plants, the walk often reminding her of trekking through a miniature jungle.

Natalie paused at her door and looked down, looking for the shadow figure on the sidewalk, but from where she was, all she could see was the marina. She shook off her uneasiness, put the key in the lock, and turned it quietly, thinking that Stephanie would be sleeping.

Damn! Stephanie hadn't locked it. The door opened as she turned the knob. She entered and kicked the door closed and stood looking out at the stunning view, a ritual she'd faithfully observed since the first time she saw the apartment. She had rented the apartment for this, and it hadn't failed to thrill her in the past three years.

The apartment was furnished with a mixture of new things and antiques, an eclectic collection that displayed her tastes and impulsive nature. She had a Japanese painting on the living room wall that she had spent a month's salary on. She had worried about the cost for the next six months.

As she started across the living room, she pulled her trench coat off and kicked one of her heels toward the kitchen. A faint odor came to her then: *gunpowder and blood.*

Natalie just as quickly dismissed it, her heart picking up a beat, and then slowing, as she reasoned that it was just an olfactory memory of odors she'd picked up from one of the many crime scenes she had visited.

Can't be gunpowder and blood, not here in my home, and I've smelled them before, oh, yeah, I have.

To Natalie's right, the floor-to-ceiling windows that made up the east wall of the living room overlooked the river and east Portland. In the daylight, snow-covered Mount Hood rose up close enough for her to touch in the clean air. For many months the river was full of small boats with bright sails. She never tired of the view.

Natalie kicked off the other shoe and walked across the room, laying the trench coat and her small purse on the counter that separated the kitchen from the living room. She walked to the windows and stood with her back to the room. She heard a sound from hallway and smiled. It was good to have Stephanie home.

Stephanie, my beautiful, elegant Stephanie, running to me from her third broken marriage . . . now she's beginning to heal.

Steph must be up to go to the bathroom. Footsteps whispered on the carpet from the bedroom. Natalie turned around to see how Stephanie's day had been.

Dan McClellan Harris shifted, uncomfortable in his wet clothes, watching the apartments from the sidewalk, the water dripping off his beard. He moved down the sidewalk toward the gate the woman had entered, and looked up at the terraced apartments. A light came on, two and a half stories above the sidewalk, and he thought it must be the woman who just walked up.

I know there's a man in an apartment up there – a man looking to kill someone. I know him. I don't know which apartment, maybe it's the one the woman went to, but I will find him.

Dan moved closer to the wrought iron gate, knowing that he had to find the man. He had to get inside the security gate, but it wouldn't be easy. The gate was at least eight feet tall, with sharpened iron spears on the top. He shook the gate and looked behind him at the seawall and then up and down the sidewalk.

No one was on the sidewalk.

The gate was locked. He took one more look around and began to climb.

Natalie stared at the river. From her window, she could see the tops of the masts of the sailboats moored at the dock below. The marina was directly beneath her apartment, a sheltered docking area with the floating restaurant at one end.

I need to move, to find the energy to make hot chocolate with a drop of brandy, and take a hot bath with a book.

She heard a soft *thump* from Stephanie's bedroom, and she smiled, thinking that Stephanie might join her for some chocolate. She walked through the living room and entered the hallway. She stopped there, at the entrance to the hallway from the living room, a pungent odor stronger here, and she stood looking at Stephanie's open bedroom doorway at the end of the hall, and then she knew what it was.

Gunpowder and blood. Oh, dear God – Stephie – gunpowder and blood.

There was something else Natalie couldn't quite place. She jerked around, looking at the counter where her purse with her gun lay. Her heart pounded.

Don't be stupid, this is your apartment.

That decided it for her. She started down the hallway, the light from the living room giving the walls a soft glow, her black nylons a mere whisper on the carpet.

Another *thump* came from the room at the end.

"Stephie?"

Natalie's voice came out as a croak, and she called to her younger sister again.

Nothing.

Quiet.

You're being stupid, Nat old girl, really stupid, still thinking of work, and she's fine.

But Natalie had done this before, getting her gun and wandering around her apartment, the curse of paranoia of a police officer, chasing ghosts of the past, usually a night or two after a particularly bad murder case, and she knew that she was just being paranoid, extra paranoid during those times, but being paranoid could also keep you alive.

This is stupid.

Steph, she thought, and then she said it, the silence greeting her call.

My purse is on the counter.

She looked back at the living room, the lights from the marina far below winking up at her in the rain. Natalie moved forward, slowly, creeping, and then stopped again just outside her sister's door, the smell of gunpowder and blood stronger than ever. Her knees trembled and her hand shook and the fear for her sister rose up to meet her like a fist.

This is stupid. Stephanie just burned something on the stove, that's all. That's not gunpowder – not blood.

She almost went back for her gun then, but she heard a noise in the bedroom, and she remembered later that she thought it was Stephanie.

But it wasn't.

She pushed the door farther open with her left hand, looking.

The odor – omigod – the odor.

Stephanie appeared to be sleeping, crumpled on the bed, lying on her side, her arm flung over her head, the lights in the adjoining bathroom lighting the bottom of the bed, and then the walls shouted color at Natalie, red walls above the white and gold headboard.

"Stephanie . . . oh, God!" Natalie cried. Her knees buckled, and with tears streaming down her face, she knelt by the end of the bed. She put her face in her hands. She didn't approach her sister – wanting to, needing to – but she knew it wouldn't do any good, because she had seen dead people before. Lots of them. Natalie Collins was a detective sergeant in the homicide unit of the Portland Police Bureau.

This was family, and she couldn't move.

Minutes later, in her grief, she went to her thirty-two-year-old sister. She stayed there with her, touching her, the emotions pushing away the intellectual part of her brain that screamed to stay away, to let others do the job of piecing it together. Another person would have run screaming from the bedroom, calling medics, calling for someone to breathe life into a loved one beyond caring or repair. It was the curse of Natalie's job that made her know with a certainty that this was Stephanie's last day on earth.

She stayed there, not really knowing how long, sitting on the bed with her sister, sobbing, thinking then that she should have been here for Stephanie, to help her so she wouldn't do this . . . this thing to herself.

Natalie heard a soft cough from the doorway just to her right, the doorway to Stephanie's bathroom, and suddenly she was aware that she and Stephanie were not alone. She slowly swung her feet away from the bed and reached for her gun, knowing before her hand reached out that her off-duty gun was on the kitchen counter in her handbag, and with her ears ringing with her mistake, she felt a shadow rush toward her, a shadow framed in the bathroom light.

Oh, God, Natalie, you didn't check the house. You didn't check the bathroom!

She lunged for the end of the bed, the motion bouncing Stephanie in an eerie parody of living movement, and she knew it wouldn't be soon enough, she wasn't close enough, and the shadow fell on her, as she scrambled for the door, for the kitchen and her gun, as much to avenge Stephie as to protect herself, screaming, "Nooooooo!"

As she fell off the end of the bed, she twisted around, and a knee slammed into her back.

The blow drove the wind out of Natalie's lungs, her face mashed into the carpet, paralyzed, trying to scream, trying to move, pushing her knees up, grunting, crawling toward the open doorway of the bedroom, a crablike, painful movement.

Gotta get out, oh God, gotta get out!

And she had the wildest thought that her front door was opening, crashing, when powerful hands caught her. She kicked and gasped for air as she was flipped over to face her attacker. A face loomed over hers, a face shadowed by the backlight from the bathroom. She slammed her right arm straight up into the face, the blow glancing off a cheekbone, the flesh feeling cold, tenebrous.

A face with dead flesh, a rubber face, a . . . a mask!

The rubber face flinched, and an arm raised, blocking the light, raising to strike, and Natalie's skin tightened painfully, waiting for the blow, and her head was slammed back against the bed frame, her eyes watering, her vision dim, and suddenly the face was gone, the rubber face lifted up and away, almost as if her attacker had reached the bottom of a bungee cord and was springing upward on the elastic band. There was an arm around his neck.

Natalie watched, stunned, trying to breathe, the breaths coming ragged and weak. She struggled to sit up against the bed and then pushed herself across the carpet and away from the man with the mask and the figure that was now struggling with him.

My gun – gotta get my gun. They killed her, she didn't do it to herself.

Then she glimpsed the man who had pulled her attacker away, a bearded man.

The bearded man on the sidewalk, the man with no raincoat.

The two men crashed against the dresser, fighting, struggling in a silent, evil choreography, the bearded man swinging at the rubber face, trying to hit the mask, his beard wet with rain, his face a contorted twist of hatred. The man in the rubber mask broke free and swung at the bearded man, striking him on the cheek, drawing instant blood, knocking him back against the bed, and Natalie threw herself at the man in the rubber mask, knowing then with a horrible certainty that Stephanie hadn't shot herself, that the man in the rubber mask had killed her little sister. Natalie was quick, an athlete with a daily regimen of weight lifting and running, but the man in the rubber mask was as quick and hit Natalie with a forearm, knocking her backward. She fell against the dresser, bright lights exploding in her head.

Natalie crumpled on the floor as the masked man jumped over her and went out the bedroom door. She felt rather than saw the bearded man launch his body over hers, yelling, trying to reach the assailant as he ran out of the room. Natalie shook her head as she heard a crash in the living room. She listened to the struggle, unable to move. She heard yelling coming from her living room.

"Caught you . . . Gonna kill you!"

The voice was so matter-of-fact, yet it was a voice of rage, and Natalie had a sudden wild thought that the two men knew each other.

And one of them killed my Stephanie. The son of a bitch killed my Stephanie, and they know each other!

Natalie pushed herself up and got her knees under her and then stood, holding onto the bed, her body swaying, and she lurched out the door and into the hallway. She heard what sounded like a chair slam into the wall in the living room, and she lurched down the hallway.

This can't be happening. This isn't real.

For an insane moment, the child in Natalie wanted to run to her bathroom and lock the door and hide.

Natalie entered the living room and put her hand out to the wall to steady herself, seeing movement on the floor by the front door, the door open, splintered door frame lying on the carpet, two dark figures struggling, swinging, punching.

Natalie lunged for the counter and grabbed her purse as she went by, throwing her body around the counter and into the kitchen, her cheek bouncing on the cold tile floor. She tore at the flap of her purse, jerking the small pistol out in one motion, and then she was up from behind the counter, holding the Beretta in a two-handed grip and she saw the man in the rubber mask stand up, moving now along the wall toward her. The bearded man was on the floor. Natalie fired three shots in quick succession.

A shot hit a lamp and the ceramic exploded in a white shower. The shade bounced crazily across the carpet and then the man in the rubber mask lunged for the open doorway, twisting, throwing his body outside.

Natalie knew as she pulled the trigger again that her last shot was through the empty doorway.

The man in the rubber mask was gone.

She stood there, holding her gun, her ears roaring, watching, her finger so tight on the trigger that the slightest twitch would touch it off. She saw movement on the floor by the door. The bearded man tried to sit up. Natalie moved her hand down slightly, until her gun was lined up on the gray sweatshirt. She squinted through the smoke from the rounds she had fired, her ears still ringing.

The man turned his head toward Natalie. He looked defeated. His wet, brown hair was plastered to his head, and blood oozed from the corner of his mouth.

The bearded man pushed himself up from the carpet.

"Don't move!" Natalie said, holding her gun steady on his chest, and he stopped moving, remaining in a crouch. He spoke for the first time.

"He's getting away," the bearded man said quietly, "and I'm going after him." He stood up slowly, his shoulders slumped in defeat, the gun following his movements, and they watched each other from across the room. They stood like that, the bearded man wet and bleeding, with Natalie holding her gun on him from the kitchen.

"My name's Dan," he said, "and I saved your life." He spoke quietly, his voice breaking at the end. "I'm going to leave now to get him. So . . . shoot me if you have to."

"What about my Stephanie?" Natalie asked quietly, talking more to herself than to him, the tears starting again.

The bearded man shrugged and then said something, something she remembered later: "I'm the only one who knows who he is." He said it as he was turning for the door, and then he was gone, running wildly down the steps. She caught a glimpse of him as he passed the window by the door, and she tracked the running figure with her gun.

"I'm the only one who knows who he is."

Natalie slowly lowered her gun and let the automatic pistol slide from her fingers. She slumped to her knees and sobbed, her body shaking, the pain in the back of her head roaring now, her face in her hands with tears spilling out between her fingers.

"Oh, Daddy," she sobbed. "Oh, Daddy, now who's gonna be my sister?"

After a while, she heard sirens.

Two

Sometimes when Natalie dreamed, she knew she was in a dreamworld, that sleepy place in time just before waking. She smiled, drifting, not wanting to leave the dream, sleepily floating to the rhythm of a steady booming sound.

The sound grew louder, and it comforted her, something she had heard before, at some other place. It was a bass drum.

Bright colors and happy faces flashed before her – a parade.

And there was Stephanie, little Steph, laughing and bouncing, her excitement vibrant, electric. She was beautiful even then, at age seven, holding onto Mickey Mouse's large hand, her ponytail bouncing up and down as if she were a proud, golden horse.

Natalie felt the reassuring squeeze of her dad's hand. She frowned, wincing at the bass drumbeat as it grew louder.

It hurts, oh, stop.

The Disneyland parade rounded the corner on Main Street, U.S.A., and Natalie pushed forward for a closer look. Natalie, the oldest by four years, was a real grown-up at age eleven. Mickey Mouse started to move out onto the street, with Steph trailing after the bouncing giant mouse. He was joined by Minnie Mouse, their frozen smiles and happy expressions a beacon for kids and a symbol for the good things in this pretend world.

Steph was running now, reaching for her favorite Disneyland animal, and then she was blocked from Natalie's view by the crowd.

"Dad, she's going too fast."

Her dad just increased the pressure on her hand, and Natalie floated in the whiteness, the drum louder now, the happy kids still blocking her view of her sister.

```
      The    drum    began    beating   closer,   faster,
closer,  as  if  the  drummer  was  hitting  the  back
of her head with his padded drumstick.
      The kids were crying, and Natalie cried with
them.
      "Where's Steph?"
      "Oh, Daddy, she's – gone."
```

The tears came harder now, streaming down the sides of her face, wetting her pillow, and Natalie floated in the whiteness.

But my daddy's here, holding my hand, squeezing.

Natalie opened her eyes, the pain and the whiteness causing her to jerk them shut. She opened them slowly now, feeling the drum at the back of her head, and the other dream, the nice one, faded away.

Steph's dead.

The pressure increased on Natalie's hand.

My daddy –

Her eyes were open all the way now, looking at the white ceiling with a large, round light bracketed high above her. She lay on tight sheets next to a chrome railing.

Hospital.

I'm in a hospital emergency room, with a curtained partition around the bed.

Her eyes still wide, she looked around for her daddy. Only it wasn't her daddy holding her hand.

Couldn't have been. Dad died years ago.

Grant Birnam squeezed tighter, the worry adding wrinkles to his already large and wrinkled face. Grant was her closest friend, her confidant and mentor. He was a senior detective in the homicide unit, a man who had known her dad.

"Stephanie," Natalie croaked.

"Easy, Minnie Mouse," Grant said. "Just you lie back down." From the pain in his large face, she knew it was true—Stephanie was dead. Grant was a bear of a man in his in his fifties, tall and getting larger, at a dangerous age for a homicide detective. He was ready for retirement with memories of too much death to leave the bureau and quietly wait for his own time. He loved Natalie like a daughter.

She looked at him as pieces of the evening came back to her and closed out the dream of the Happiest Place on Earth.

Stephanie, oh, God, my Steph.

The memory came back all at once: the fight, Stephanie's body, the sirens, the uniformed police coming, and an ambulance ride with the siren working again.

"Stephanie," Natalie said. "Oh, Grant, is it true?"

She stared at his face, watching.

Grant finally nodded, the tears forming in the corners of his eyes, and Natalie sobbed as Grant leaned over and took her into his arms.

They stayed like that, Grant awkwardly bending over the bed, Natalie letting herself go limp, vaguely aware of other people around her bed. She nodded, and Grant gently lowered her back to the bed. She struggled to sit up, and a uniformed officer on her left brought his arm up to steady her. She smiled at him, trying to think of his name, a Mike something.

He's guarding you. What the hell did you get yourself into, Minnie Mouse?

Looking behind Grant, Natalie could see other members of her homicide team crowding into the curtained enclosure. Thompson and Eldredge were there, and Kirby, her youngest detective (and possibly one of the best) standing in the back wearing blue sweats and an Oakland A's baseball cap, his young/old face framed by the curtain. She could hear others behind them, talking quietly on the other side of the curtain.

She didn't want to get up and face them, these men she'd shared so much with—so much death.

Natalie's movements were slow, exaggerated, and she couldn't concentrate, and with the numbness, she had a feeling of déjà vu, like she had been here before. And she had—she had seen the apathy and inability to function in people many times. Natalie had watched as people collapsed when they learned of the sudden death of a loved one, their bodies shutting down in protection, the brain not wanting to believe, letting the pain in slowly.

And now she, too, was a victim.

Lieutenant Derry from Internal Affairs was standing at the foot of the bed, his head above the others, holding a notepad and recorder, a gray suit hanging on his lanky frame, matching the usual dour expression on his face. It was customary, she knew, for Internal Affairs to take over the case investigation when a detective was involved, but it hurt. She wanted her people to conduct the investigation. Natalie reached out for Grant and swung her legs off the bed, sitting there, holding Grant's hand, her dress hiking up over her thighs.

"I'm cold."

Grant turned, and Kirby's face disappeared. He returned in seconds with a blanket, handing it to Grant.

"I'm all right," she said, and looked at the men crowded around her bed. She tried to smile, then stopped, looking at Grant. A doctor pushed his way through, ordering them out, giving Natalie the harried look of an emergency room doctor on a Friday night. Grant stayed as Natalie was poked and prodded with quick movements, and the doctor checked the bump on her head. Her pupils her okay, he said, and he signed her release, telling Grant that someone should stay with her. When the doctor left, his space was immediately filled by the officers waiting outside the curtain.

"Natalie, we need to talk, and right away," Grant said gently.

She nodded and pulled the blanket around her. She stepped down onto the floor, the tile cool on her nylons. Eldredge and Thompson backed out and held he curtain as Grant led her through the emergency room, past quickly moving nurses and orderlies. A team working with sudden efficiency was on her right, putting paddles on the chest of a young woman, her bare breasts slack and twitching with the movements around her, embarrassment for her forgotten as strangers fought to save her life. A doctor emerged with bloody gloves from a curtained area to her left, and then they were out in a hallway. Grant led Natalie to a couch in a private room and sat down heavily beside her.

There was a commotion at the door, and Lieutenant Derry entered with another detective from Internal Affairs, Sergeant Nichols. Derry shut the door behind them and moved a chair to a spot directly in front of Natalie. Nichols, a short, bald counterpoint to Derry, sat at a small table.

Derry jerked up as the door opened again, and Kirby came in with a clipboard. Derry looked at him and shook his head no.

"He stays," Grant said, his voice a deep rumble, an ominous message to everyone. Derry nodded, and Kirby placed a folding chair by the door. It seemed to Natalie that Kirby was there as a guard as well as a detective. She gave him a small smile and he winked at her.

Natalie told the story then, talking about the symphony, her trip home in the cab, crying when she got to the part about seeing

Stephanie, and then blinking back her tears when she told about seeing the man who killed her sister, seeing him again and again in her house. Kirby got up suddenly and left the room, his notepad full of scribbling.

Derry took her through her story again, getting more detail, asking about times, descriptions, and guns.

"Natalie." Lieutenant Derry leaned forward. "How many guns were in your house?"

"Two, one in my bedroom . . . my duty gun . . . a Glock 17, and, and uh . . ."

"Where was it?"

"In my bedroom, in the closet."

"And the other?"

"A Beretta .380 I use for off duty, in my purse in the kitchen, the one I shot." She looked up at Derry. "Was my Glock used to kill Stephanie?"

"There was a Glock on the carpet, partially under Stephanie's bed."

Natalie put her face in her hands.

The son of a bitch used my gun.

Lieutenant Derry stopped while he changed the tape in his recorder, and Natalie leaned her head against Grant's shoulder, his arm around her, and Natalie started into her narrative of the evening again. As she ended the story for the third time, Kirby came back into the room and quietly stood by the door.

"And this bearded guy, the one who came in later," Lieutenant Derry asked, "what do you thing he was after?"

Natalie shook her head. "I don't know . . . it was really strange, as if he knew the guy with the rubber mask. At one point he said, 'Caught you, gonna kill you.'" Natalie shuddered at the memory of the fight.

"Caught you . . . gonna kill you!"

The lieutenant nodded. He leaned forward and spoke to Natalie quietly, as if he didn't want to share his question with the others in the room. "Natalie," he said softly, "who do you think they were after?"

And for the first time, she wasn't sure. Stephanie? No, it wasn't possible.

"It must be me," she said.

I've killed her, ohmigod, I've killed Steph with my job because someone was after me.

She put her hands over her face, with Grant holding on.

"Natalie . . . can you think of anything else that might help us?"

She pulled her hands away and looked at Lieutenant Derry.

"No."

Derry turned to the others in the room. "Anyone else have anything to add?" He was greeted with silence, and started to get up.

"No . . . wait!" Natalie reached for him.

"The man, the bearded man," she said in a rush, "he wasn't from here. When I saw him on the sidewalk, he looked out of place, and later in my apartment there was something else, and I don't know how I know, maybe an accent or something, but I don't think either one of them were from Portland."

Lieutenant Derry nodded and left the room.

Natalie could see the bearded man again, the rain-soaked sweatshirt, the wild eyes, and she realized for the first time that the bearded man hadn't paid any attention to her or the fact that Stephanie was on the bed. The bearded man wanted one thing; to kill the man with the rubber face. She could feel his hatred. And who were they after. . . . Stephanie or her? Natalie had told Lieutenant Derry that the killer must have been after her, but now she wasn't sure. Steph'd been married three times. Maybe an ex-husband or boyfriend . . .

It didn't really matter. It didn't matter where they were, the man with the rubber mask and the bearded man, or who they were. Natalie was going to find them, no matter where they might have gone.

As it turned out, both men were still in Portland.

But not for very long.

Three

Dan's right eye was swelling shut badly, and he knew he was going to have to get some ice on it soon or he wouldn't be able to see. He also knew that it was noticeable. Damned noticeable. He stopped and turned to look into a shop window where the latest fashion in men's suits was displayed. He used the window as a mirror and a hiding place, his back to any passerby.

People swirled around him, behind him, not interested or looking, rushing to catch the late-night shuttles to San Francisco, Seattle, or Denver. Dan was in a concourse in the Portland International Airport. His reflection startled him, and at first he wondered who the stranger was glaring back at him in the window. The face was hidden by a full beard, a brown beard that hadn't been trimmed for weeks, a beard that was just starting to show gray hair. His right eye was indeed red and swollen, and he knew that in another day it would be very black and swollen. His left eye was green, cloudy and dark with blood. The cut on his cheek had stopped bleeding, and was mostly hidden by his beard. His face, what there was to be seen, was pleasant, with a pug nose that had once been broken. His brown hair was thinning— thinning, hell, it was vanishing—and long on the sides, to match his beard.

Dammit!

Dan would have punched the glass until his hand was a bloody stump if he thought it would do any good. To be so close after all this time! Not for the first time he wondered if he hadn't been the object of some kind of sick joke. There were times when he thought his life a bizarre and demented thing, spent running around the country trying to kill a man. It seemed sometimes as if he were a stranger with no past or future.

He took my life away.

The corners of Dan's mouth turned down, and he knew he shouldn't be thinking about this, couldn't be thinking about a time in the past when he was a whole person. He had to stay with the task at hand. He shook his head, trying to clear the pain, knowing that with pain medication his eye would be fine, but for the other pain, the pain in his heart, there was nothing that could be done.

Two Port of Portland Police officers approached and walked behind him, and Dan saw them after they passed. He stared more intently at the suits, hoping to pass for an early-morning window-shopper, his heart hammering in his chest. He knew that the police might have his description and be looking for him, and he couldn't be taken into custody for questioning . . . even for a few minutes. They walked on past, talking, showing no interest in the bearded man.

Dan forced himself to breathe, to relax.

Damn. The man's been here and gone, and it won't do any good to stay here at the airport.

Dan looked for the escalator down to the baggage area and parking level. He needed a room downtown and then time to find the woman. As he stepped onto the escalator, he heard a commotion behind him and saw two police officers questioning a man with a beard next to the restroom. Two more officers were approaching them, with grim expressions.

They know who I am. They're looking for me.

Dan froze in place, letting the escalator carry him down. In front of him he saw security officers guarding the doorways, officers who usually examined baggage claims, but they might have his description.

I can't be caught. I have to catch him first.

Except for a few people gathered around a carousel at the far end of the room, the baggage area was empty. *I have to walk right past the guard,* Dan thought, and he knew that he had no other choice. He couldn't go back upstairs and try another exit. As he stepped off at the bottom, he walked straight to the gate where the guard was standing.

The guard held the gate open for Dan and nodded as he went through. Dan walked outside, his legs feeling weak and rubbery, and moved at a steady pace along the sidewalk. There was a line of cabs off to his left, and he walked in that direction, expecting to be grabbed at any second. The rain had stopped, and the street glistened in the bright lights.

He told the driver to take him downtown and slumped in the backseat, feeling the fatigue settle in. He was now beyond the point of caring if the cab driver had heard a description of him on the news and would turn him in.

During the wild chase from the riverfront apartment, Dan was sure that he had committed several crimes and at the very least, had driven recklessly. But he knew that really didn't matter to him anymore, and during the past year, he had held one thought: kill the man and avenge the death . . .

Dan had the cab drop him off downtown, at Tenth and Burnside, in an area where he would blend in wearing a sweatshirt and jeans. He turned in to the lobby of the Imperial Hotel and walked to the elevators, facing away from the desk clerk. He went to the seventh floor, two floors past his room on five. He walked down the stairwell to the fifth floor, cautiously looking down the deserted hallway at the door to his room.

No one near five oh five, or in the hallway.

He cut the beard first and then shaved. The face wasn't too bad with the blood wiped off. He stopped and looked longingly at the bed, but he couldn't stay. He could sleep later. He dressed in beige slacks, a navy cashmere sweater, and brown leather jacket. He added a black baseball cap to hide his face. He wiped the room down, knowing where he had touched, where his prints might be.

Twenty minutes later, Dan took the elevator down and walked with a group of people past the front desk and out onto the street. He carried a small leather bag. His face felt naked, the cool air touching skin that hadn't been exposed for almost a year. He had a Band-Aid up high on his cheek, and he wore the baseball cap pulled down low. He walked four blocks and entered the lobby of the downtown Hilton. He picked the youngest clerk behind the counter, a kid barely out of his teens, looking uncomfortable in his gray suit. Dan waited for the kid to look up from his computer, the kid's helpful smile in place.

"May I help you, sir?"

"I'd like a suite," Dan said, knowing that the less-expensive rooms would be rented on a weekend. He put his bag down.

"Sir . . . and what is . . ."

"McDaniel," Dan looked around carefully: no cops were in sight, and the lobby was active, with people going to the restaurant and lounge at the top.

"I'm sorry, sir, but I can't seem to find your registration."

"My friends must have forgotten," Dan said with a smile, and placed a bill on the counter. The kid looked around carefully, and placed the bill behind the counter.

"Yes, sir. I think I might have something." He began typing, his movements lively, animated. Dan took another look at the lobby.

". . . bad about the team," the kid was saying, looking at his computer screen.

"What?"

He pointed to Dan's baseball cap, with the local NBA team logo on front. "The Trailblazers, or after last year, maybe we should call them the 'Failblazers.'"

"Oh."

Dan paid for the room, hoping the kid would remember the smooth face, the Trailblazers hat, the Band-Aid, the large tip, and nothing else.

In his room, Dan tried to relax, feeling safe for the first time since he had arrived in Portland. But he knew this was temporary. He stripped off his clothes and lay on the top of the covers.

What does the man want with the woman, with either one of them? The woman on the bed was dead. The other one, the one with the gun, she knows something about the man, but what? Why her? And what the hell does she have to do with me?

Natalie sat at her desk and closed her eyes. Grant brought her a cup of coffee and left, closing the door quietly. She didn't have the energy to reach out for the cup. Police artist Steve Poole entered and put his arm around Natalie. She had worked with Steve on several other cases. He talked her through a likeness of the bearded man, and then she talked about the man in the rubber mask. When Grant came to get her, the sky was getting light on the south side of Mount Hood. The day would be gray, dismal. It was 9:30 when they walked to the parking garage and started for Grant's house. He drove quietly, his shoulders slumped with fatigue. They entered the Sunset Highway tunnel under an overcast sky, but the rain had stopped sometime during the night. Grant drove up the hill past the entrance to the Washington Park Zoo, driving fast now in the light Saturday morning traffic. The hillside was a jumble of green, with red, white, pink and yellow rhododendrons and azaleas in bloom. Natalie closed her eyes and willed herself to not think, to not feel. She dozed with the motion of the quickly moving car, hearing Grant's occasional curse at other drivers. She opened her eyes again as they pulled into Grant's driveway in Beaverton.

Aimee was waiting in the doorway of their two-story house. She was a striking contrast to Grant. She was trim, athletic, and constantly moving with an energy that surprised those who knew her, the wrinkles around her eyes and her long gray hair the only reminders of her age. At sixty, Aimee was six years older than her husband. She ran to the car and opened Natalie's door and put her arms around the younger woman, drawing her out, leading her into the house. They stood in the hallway and hugged, their tears mixing together as they both cried. Aimee had been everything to Natalie for over a decade: mother, sister, aunt. They sat on the couch, the room darkened with the drapes pulled.

Grant held a large glass filled with a brown liquid in front of Natalie. His wife looked up and pushed his hand away, glaring at him, but Natalie reached out and took it, taking a gulp of the whiskey, feeling its warmth jolt down her throat. She sipped and talked about Stephanie and their life, their family, and their dad.

Thirty minutes later, the whiskey gone, Natalie nodded, her head bouncing down and jerking up.

"Come," Aimee said, "I'll take you to your room."

Natalie allowed herself to be led down the hall to the stairway, and she and Aimee walked upstairs to a spare room. She undressed slowly, with Aimee helping. Natalie suddenly noticed with a shock that she had on her black evening dress, and then remembered the long night again. She let Aimee tuck her under the covers.

Aimee lay on top of the comforter, stroking Natalie's face. Although she hadn't known Stephanie well, she felt Natalie's pain as if it were her own. She heard the shower running, and then Grant came to the door, wearing one of his best suits.

"Get some sleep," he whispered. "Eldredge is in the living room and he's not to let anyone in."

Aimee nodded and mouthed, "Be careful . . . I love you."

Grant closed the door, and Aimee laid her head on the pillow next to Natalie, holding her friend as she jerked in her sleep, Aimee's long gray hair mixing with Natalie's short blond hair. Aimee cradled the daughter she never had.

Grant walked past Eldredge in the kitchen and poured a cup of coffee.

"We got us a dual investigation going, Boss," Eldredge said, "and we are the black sheep on this one. The Internal will be the one with all the big guns, overtime, and extra help."

"*Fuck* the internal investigation," Grant yelled, the loudness surprising both of them, and they both looked to the ceiling and waited for noises upstairs.

"Fuck the internal," Grant repeated fiercely, his voice a whisper, "and the investigation, the overtime, the extra bodies. We don't need 'm."

"Right, Boss." Eldredge went on drinking his coffee.

Grant left his neighborhood, picking up speed as he gave cryptic orders on his cell phone.

Dual investigation? Maybe, but I'm sure as hell gonna run one of them.

What Grant Birnam didn't know—couldn't know—was that Natalie would soon be caught up in her own investigation, a bizarre and far more deadly and frightening journey than they could ever imagine.

Four

"Police are looking for two suspects in the shooting death of a Portland woman. The shooting is believed to have occurred last night at about midnight at a fashionable riverfront apartment." The newscaster, a woman in her thirties, with short brown hair, told of other stories that would follow a commercial break.

Suspect, hell, Dan McClellan Harris thought as he waited for the local morning news to come on. He opened a desk drawer and made notes on hotel stationery as the lead story continued. The deceased woman's name was Stephanie Walker, a sister and roommate of the woman who fought.

The survivor is a Natalie Collins.

Natalie Collins is a detective sergeant with the Portland Police Bureau, a supervisor in the homicide unit.

Christ! I should have known, Dan thought. *That's why the woman held the gun like she did. Why didn't she shoot me?*

They showed cut-away clips of the apartment complex, with crime scene tape and police cars, a shot of the river and the marina. He scribbled furiously and then stopped as the artist's pictures of him with his beard were shown.

"Suspect, hell—I saved her life," Dan grumbled, staring at the screen.

The chief of police gave a brief statement, saying that the entire resources of the department would be used, declining to say whether or not the killing was motivated by Sergeant Collins's assignment.

Dan studied the picture of Sergeant Natalie Collins, a studio picture of her in uniform. He learned that she was a fourteen-year police veteran, with four years as a homicide investigator and supervisor. A decorated veteran, who looked to Dan as if she were in her mid-twenties.

I have to find her.

Dan decided he could stay at the hotel one more day. He washed his hands, his reflection in the mirror startling him, the smooth face making him look far younger than he had, younger than his forty-one years. He took the elevator to the lobby and walked out onto the sidewalk. He stood in front of the hotel for a moment, knowing that he should be moving, that a person who walks with a purpose doesn't attract attention. He started off down Broadway Street, looking for a

place to get a professional haircut. *The picture of me on television looks good,* he thought, *too good. I'll change my hair and get some information. Information about a Portland Police Bureau sergeant.*
  I have to find her.

The Boeing 767 came up through the dark evening sky, leaving Chicago's O'Hare International on a heading that took it northeast, out over Lake Erie, and then began a slow turn to the southeast for its trip to the Gulf of Mexico.

The Freedom Airlines Flight 2484 from Chicago to Tampa was on time, and on this early fall weekend evening, there were only a hundred or so passengers to roam around in an airplane designed to carry over two hundred fifty.

The man in 26A leaned his head back and closed his eyes, letting images of the last evening's events come to him randomly, not trying to place them in any order. That would come later. He sensed movement beside him and his eyes flicked open and then shut again just as quickly. A flight attendant was walking down the aisle, taking orders from passengers, smiling, approaching. He was seated in the middle of the plane, on the left side, with only one passenger wholly visible, a frail, elderly lady across the aisle. She was busy making her nest as the flight was getting up to cruising altitude.

During the few times when he had to make a quick, prudent exit from a city, he hadn't panicked and sought to take the quickest flight available. He studied, planned, and always reduced his immediate problem.

He let himself drift, thinking about the woman, and then he was back in the apartment above the river, standing in the living room by the green chairs, looking at the lights of the bridges, the reflections on the water.

He wandered through the rooms, a detached observer of what was to come.

The smells of a woman sleeping came to him as he watched the hallway, and now he was moving down the hall and into the empty bedroom. Disneyland artifacts, the miniature Mickey Mouse figurines and the large stuffed Disneyland figures of Pluto, Tigger, Mickey Mouse and several of Minnie Mouse were on the dresser. He entered the small walk-in closet and examined clothes until he found what he wanted. He took one more look at the stuffed animals, and then shuffled into the adjacent bedroom, and watched the sleeping woman, looking at the last minutes of her life.

He awakened her then, so she would know that she had to die, and then watched as she entered the first minutes of death. He was content to stay with her like this, a companion to her first minutes of death. The front door opened and closed, and after a time, the other woman entered the bedroom.

He was ready for her.

His forehead creased in a frown and he moved, squirming in his seat as he again saw the bearded man burst into the bedroom, an intruder into his work.

He moaned, twisting in his seat as he watched the bearded man fight him in the woman's apartment, and then he broke free, fear giving him strength.

Before he left the bedroom, he looked at the one he had left behind, and she wore a death's head, a skeleton of empty eye sockets and exposed teeth grinning back at him.

"Sir?"

Then he was on his way to the airport to catch—

"Sir."

The voice was calm, more insistent, and he left his dream and jerked his head up and heard the background whine of jet engines and saw the flight attendant above him, a show of concern on her face.

"Sir, can I get you anything? You . . . uh, you must have been dreaming."

"Uh, sorry, I—"

"Would you like something to drink, a soda?"

"No, really, I'm fine." He looked up at her then, at her dark blue uniform and bright scarf. He imagined her dead, the uniform covering the vertebrae of the neck, the lower mandible clicking with speech.

He grinned up at her.

The attendant, a tall, dark-haired woman in her early forties, blinked her eyes and fought against her instinct to recoil from him. *I'm getting too old for this*, she thought, the frozen smile on her face losing ground to the disgust she felt. *His skin is as white and as thin as old parchment.*

She shook her head. "Can I get you anything at all?" she asked shakily.

"No thanks, I'm really fine."

She nodded and straightened up, shuddering as if she had passed an open grave. She walked quickly toward the front of the plane, feeling his eyes on her back.

He watched the attendant until she disappeared, and glanced over at the old woman across from him and saw that her nest was complete with pillow and blanket pulled up tight, her aged skull lying over at an angle next to the window. She appeared to be awake, but he knew that it was just an illusion, her eyelids half shut over aging eyes.

Oh, the things I could show you, as I have shown so many people your age. Yeah, you will all die before me.

He closed his eyes and could see the man with the beard again, frightening in his wholeness, the flesh on his face.

It can't be, he can't have a face. I can tell if they die before me. I can tell by looking. He must have a skeleton head—and he will.

He held his hand up in the dim light of the cabin, held it up in front of his face, looking with satisfaction at the flesh on the hand.

I am destined to live, but they will all die.

He smiled.

A skeletonized head bobbed up from a seat two up from his, a man adjusting his pillow, and then the head disappeared, hidden by the seat back.

He carefully flexed his legs, his arms, his fingers. He probed his head gently, feeling for bumps, for tears in his skin. Nothing. Satisfied that he was not injured, he methodically opened an attaché case, clicking each latch with the precision of a concert pianist. He reached inside with long, tapered fingers and withdrew a cloth headband. He turned the combination wheel on first one side and then the other, dialing in a different number, and then pressed the latches closed. He leaned over at the waist, lowering the case to the floor. He unfolded the headband slowly, looking at it as if there were a surprise inside, and covered his eyes. He sat upright in the seat in the darkness, his hands aligned on his thighs.

The Japanese are getting closer. Dr. Kiri Yamaguchi at the University of Tokyo is very good, but not good enough. The French, well, they have gone in a promising direction, haven't they, but they really haven't a clue yet. The Institute of Longevity in Chicago was publishing some exciting work. The next century has possibilities.

You will all die before me.

The plane flew on through the night, the ninety-eight passengers and crew of eight unaware of the monster in their midst.

The Evidence

One

Natalie stood in front of the window in Grant and Aimee's spare bedroom, looking down at the backyard, a yard that ran out thirty yards from the house and ended in a thick blackberry bramble. Beyond that, the trunks of tall fir trees stood mute in a fine rain.

Rain's coming early this year.

She stood with her hands at her sides, wanting to make some sense out of the past few days. Part of the healing process, she realized later, was despair giving way to exhaustion. When she had tried to sleep, she was struck with images of Stephanie, of their life, of growing up as kids. She had gone through the three days following Stephanie's death in a sleepwalk. She let Grant and Aimee take care of most of the details, answering their questions about what she wanted for Stephanie.

"Casket? Who gives a damn, Grant. Stephanie? Hell, you could lay her on the ground for all she'd care now."

She had yelled at Grant, and then she was instantly sorry, and this had brought on a new round of tears.

Natalie had cried every day up to the funeral, and she cried as she dressed in Grant and Aimee's guest room, putting on a black dress because she didn't have to make a decision about it.

Someone already decided you should wear black, you see.

She didn't think she had any tears left, just an incredible sadness and the beginnings of rage.

She walked to the dresser mirror and stood quietly, knowing that Grant and Aimee were waiting downstairs, worried. Natalie shook her head, as if she could erase the memory of what had happened. She looked up and saw her face for the first time in days, the pale blue eyes, red with bags under them, the short blond hair, the black hat and veil that Aimee had given her.

Steph's dead, and what the hell can I do about it?

I've seen too many bodies already, some of the guys were beginning to talk, even before this. Too many trips to Disneyland last year. And Grant knows that I've grown weary of seeing too many young boys and girls with the slack faces of death, barely teenagers, lured into a battleground for a drug called crack before they could really calculate the cost.

Too many trips to Disneyland last year. Disneyland, the Happiest Place on Earth.

But can I find out who killed my sister? Can I? Can I find out who killed Stephanie?

Natalie shook her head again, a tiny beginning, a start to getting on with living, a purpose. She knew she needed to lock Stephanie away in a place, a corner of her mind where she could take Stephanie out to look at her a little less frequently than she had. Natalie returned to her question, not seeing the sad-eyed reflection in the mirror.

Can I find the person who killed my Steph?

Yeah, I can.

I'm a cop, a homicide detective, and a damned good one. Oh, there are plenty of officers who look better in uniform than I do. Loads of them who can give better speeches to the City Club or to the Rotarians. And a lot of them have more experience than I do. But if you have a loved one killed, hurt or missing, and you want to find the person responsible or want to find out who's lying—if you want to find out who fucked with your life—I'm as good as anyone.

Better.

I don't quit. That's how I got this job.

And I can tell in a heartbeat if someone's lying to me and how to get the bag of shit to talk and feel good about it while he's talking. I can find people who want to stay hidden so they can continue their violent, worthless lives. I can grab onto the infinitesimally small pieces of evidence that the Rotarian speaker overlooks and I can build a case with it.

If you want a killer, I can find him. I can.

I can hound him until he cries for help and when the time comes, I'll be there with the only hand he'll see.

Yeah, I'm a detective who can do it.

I can.

And I will find you, you bastard, with whatever it takes.

I can.

"Minnie Mouse?"

Natalie turned from the mirror, a new resolve working its way through her grief. She gave a quick glance back at her face in the mirror, touched the hat, and walked to the door.

Grant was waiting, his large face solemn and afraid.

Natalie reached up and put her arms around his neck, looked into his eyes, and gave him a kiss, lightly, on his lips. "Oh, Grant, it's gonna be all right," she said. "I'll be strong for both of us."

It's time to go see my Stephanie off and then to get to work. Yeah, I can do it.

Chief Kramer was in his dress uniform, blue with a lot of gold braid and stars.

"What's your best guess . . . what happened in there?" The chief looked out over the downtown area from his office on the fifteenth floor of the Justice Center. He had his back to the room, and he had one visitor.

The visitor cleared his throat. "She did it."

The chief stiffened, the reaction visible to the visitor. He spoke without turning around.

"Tell me."

"We found blood on the sleeve of the dress we believe she wore when she fired the fatal shot, high velocity impact spatter that can only come from a gunshot . . . "

"The blood?"

"Her sister's. A neighbor saw Sergeant Collins enter her apartment alone. And we have a lot of hair and fibers, although we had to send the lab work out, and they haven't started on—"

"What about Natalie's hands?"

The visitor shifted his weight backward and cleared his throat, wishing he could end this. "Uh, Chief, we didn't conduct any tests on Sergeant Collins's hands to check for blood spatter. We—"

"Why the hell not?" Chief Kramer turned and glared at his visitor, and then resumed his stare out the window.

"Well, uh, she was taken to the hospital, and she's a decorated veteran, and, hell, I don't know why it wasn't done. We—"

"The gun."

"We have the gun," the visitor said, relieved that they were on to something else. "We have a gun registered to her, the gun that was used and found in the room."

"Why would she stage the scene?"

"We don't know, other than that she's a pro, and thought she could get away with it. She must have been emotional, distraught, arguing with her sister . . ."

This brought another glare from the chief. "Prove it," he said flatly. "You know how she performs under pressure. Hell, that U.S. Bank shooting, we don't have many officers who could have made those kinds of pressure decisions, let alone survive it."

"Chief, the evidence is there. We *can* prove it. She did it."

The chief leaned forward until his forehead touched the glass. He stayed that way for over a minute, not moving. Finally, he straightened. "Rumors?" he asked quietly.

"I've heard two. The most prevalent one, of course, is that two men broke into her apartment and killed her sister. Most of the officers are mad as hell, tearing up the streets looking for suspects matching the composites, particularly the bearded man. A few of the officers are starting to think that someone in the apartment complex should have seen one or both of them. The shots were reported at eleven fifty-seven, and there are a lot of people around at that time on a weekend night. Hell, this city is full of nightlife and dinner clubs, with the streets full at midnight. I've even heard that Sergeant Collins caught her sister in bed with a man she wanted, and—"

A stare from the chief stopped the visitor.

"Who knows about this?"

"You do, me and my investigators."

"Homicide knows?"

"No. Some of them suspect that something isn't quite right, but they don't know of any of the evidence. We were on the scene too fast and relieved them of the duty."

"You tell no one, and report to me, and me only, and that's an order."

The visitor left, walking quickly through the outer office. The chief's secretary wrinkled her nose as the elevator door closed.

Chief Kramer stood at the window for several minutes. Hell of a way to spend your last couple of years on the job. Sergeant Collins had been a fine detective, a fine officer. He was a good chief, a strong one, a chief whose leadership had brought an end to years of turmoil and lack of direction in the bureau. The stress of the job had taken its toll on a fine police sergeant, and for him to survive, for the good of the bureau, Chief Kramer would have to stand by as she was destroyed.

As Chief Kramer walked to the elevator, he realized he was thinking of Natalie Collins in the past tense, as if she were already gone.

There were others who were also planning to destroy Detective Sergeant Natalie Collins.

One man knew who, but he didn't know why.

Two

The day was warm, the sun coming through scattered clouds. *Rain later*, Dan Harris thought as he looked to the west. He was sitting on a bench above the marina on the Willamette River, along the seawall and directly across from the gate that led to Natalie's apartment.

She's got to come home some time, and I'll be here.

The memorial for Stephanie was held in All Saints Episcopal Church in southwest Portland. Natalie held up better than she thought she would, and even though it wasn't an official funeral for a member of the Portland Police Bureau, there were a large number of blue uniforms in the church. They were friends and fellow officers who had worked with Natalie during the past fourteen years.

Natalie sat between Grant and Aimee in a family alcove, in the front part of the sanctuary. Grant had his arm around her. Natalie was very much a take-charge person, but for the past three days, she had been held in the inertia of grief. Grant and Aimee had made all of the arrangements for the memorial and had insisted that Natalie stay with them.

I'm all alone now, Natalie thought suddenly.

All alone.

Mom's been dead for years, and Daddy two years ago. And I can't tell them.

During the past three days, Natalie's grief had passed from sobbing into a feeling of incredibly heavy sadness, both for Stephanie and for herself. Her sister's life had been a fast track of three marriages to look-alike successful men, men who (Natalie believed) had loved Stephanie, but Steph was looking for the next new love almost before the honeymoon was over.

At age thirty-two, when Stephanie's engagement was broken to what would have been her fourth husband, she ran to Natalie, asking if she could live with her until she could figure out if she could do anything with her life other than look for a husband.

Natalie had quickly agreed, knowing that Steph needed a constancy in her life now, some stability. Five months ago, Steph had moved in. It seemed to Natalie that her sister had at last seemed to find the happiness that had eluded her for years. Stephanie was beginning to rely on no one but herself to make her happy. Natalie and Stephanie both had great hopes for the future. During the past two weeks, Stephanie had talked of getting her own apartment, but neither was in a hurry to have her move out.

One night a few days before Stephanie died, they sat up late and talked, looking out over the river, watching the boats and brightly lit bridges.

"I don't want to move just yet," Stephanie said. She was curled up in a recliner, drinking hot chocolate. "Okay if I don't?"

Natalie had looked over at her younger sister and smiled. "Sure, I'm getting used to having you around."

"You know," Stephanie said softly, "I've never told you how much I admire you, how much I always have, your—"

"Yeah, right," Natalie grinned. "I'm a lowly cop and you've been all over the world, visited royalty—"

"I'm serious! I traveled with someone else, always with their money, with their agenda. All I ever did was act the part of a pretty wife. But you, I envy you, Natalie, and—"

"Oh, quit," Natalie said, laughing, holding up her hand for Stephanie to stop.

"No," Stephanie said softly, "I've always admired you, your confidence, your career, your position as a sergeant and detective . . . and I've never told you that."

"Oh great, my Marilyn Monroe look-alike sister tells me how great I am. A homicide detective, working nights and weekends, looking at dead bodies."

"If I'm Marilyn, you're Jamie Lee Curtis, short hair, carries a gun. You ever see her in *Blue Steel* or in *True Lies*?"

Natalie nodded, laughing, thinking that maybe Stephanie might just find out more about Stephanie after all, instead of losing herself in a new husband.

And now she couldn't do any of that, and Natalie was surprised to find that her sadness was giving way to the beginnings of a powerful rage.

Whoever did this is going to pay, she thought. But if Natalie had known then what the cost would be, just how bad it would get, and how many would die, she would have dropped her gun and badge off at the Justice Center, said to hell with the pension, and taken a vacation on some Pacific island with no forwarding address.

Natalie listened to the chaplain talk about Stephanie as if he were talking about someone Natalie didn't know, a stranger. It couldn't be Steph. When it came time to stand, Grant held on, lifting Natalie to her feet.

"Grant, I'm all right, I . . ." and then her knees buckled and he held on, tighter.

"I'm here, Minnie Mouse," he said, his concern for Natalie tightening his face. "Just lean on me."

Natalie did, and she later realized that she had been leaning on Grant for the past three days. He had done everything, arranged for the service, picked up some of Natalie's clothes from her apartment, and notified Stephanie's former husbands.

When the memorial was over, Natalie entered the sanctuary and greeted friends and officers and some of Stephanie's coworkers at the band where she had worked. Natalie stood there with Grant and Aimee, part of her not willing to participate and believe in what she was doing, not wanting to admit that Stephanie was gone.

My poor baby sister is gone, and I'm gonna find out who did it, and why.

Natalie walked through the chapel, stopping to talk to those she knew, wanting now more than ever to be away from this place, wanting now to get the hell back to work, to look for the two men. Even though she had given a detailed statement to the detectives at the hospital during the early hours of Saturday morning, there were a lot of unanswered questions.

Who killed my Stephanie? Why? Who is the other man, the bearded one, and why was he there?

As soon as I get back to work, I'm gonna get some answers, Natalie thought. *I'm gonna find out who did this, and why.*

She stood outside the church with Grant and Aimee, lingering, talking to the last few people to leave. Stephanie was to be buried in the same cemetery as their parents and there would be no graveside services.

"Too much for me," Natalie had told Grant.

Too soon for Stephanie.

"Grant, take me to the Justice Center."

"Natalie, you sure your want to . . ."

"Yeah, it's time I found out who killed Stephanie."

Three

Natalie's appointment to the homicide section as a detective meant to many police officers that she had reached the top of her profession. The work was interesting and it paid very well. She was challenged and worked with some of Portland's best and brightest. She had to deal with messy scenes from time to time that were gross with human bodies, but she was able to detach herself from most of the worst. When it got too bad, when she found she couldn't live with what she saw, she would take a few days off, fly to the Disneyland Hotel in Anaheim, and spend some time in the Happiest Place in the World.

Portland, the gem of the Northwest, a city built on wooded hills where the Willamette and the giant Columbia rivers converged, was possibly the most livable city in the country. The city drew some of the best theater the country had to offer, and the city's symphony was thought by guest conductors to be one of the finest. The fresh and imaginative jazz musicians in Portland made those in the East and Southeast appear drab, retired. The Mount Hood Jazz Festival was attended by hundreds of thousands of music lovers each year, and the Portland Rose Festival was a city-wide Disneyland for kids and adults, with the Pacific Fleet in attendance on the bank of the Willamette River (just downriver from Natalie's apartment), the Rose Festival Parade, and the formula one races at Portland International Raceway. The slopes of the nearby Cascade Mountains and the Willamette River Valley boasted some award-winning wineries.

The city was more than livable. By Californian and Eastern standards, Portland was a small city.

By the time Natalie was assigned back to homicide as a sergeant, the city had changed. This gem in the Northwest had a deadly undercurrent of gang warfare rivaling that of any city. It was almost as if the Los Angeles gangs came together one day and said, "Hey, look up there at that land with no gangs and lotsa potential."

And so they arrived with their colors and their deadly drugs for sale to Portland youth. For every Crip chapter that arrived with guns and crack, a corresponding Blood gang would suddenly arrive with more guns, crack cocaine, a hatred for rival gangs, and a promise of money and power for youngsters. The police and the community were at first disbelieving and then frustrated as the number of gang-related deaths went from a couple a year to a couple a weekend.

Northeast Portland became a battleground. On one particularly bloody weekend, a two-month-old baby was shot in a drive-by shooting (the shooter got the wrong house).

By the time Natalie had finished her first year as a detective sergeant, homicide, she had grown weary of looking at the dead eyes of boys, barely teenagers, lured into a battleground they didn't really want or understand. Someone had to find the shooters. After a homicide, the survivors continued with their lives, and very few people cared if the cases were solved or not, or if justice prevailed. As Grant often told her, someone had to work for God.

Natalie went to Disneyland twice last year.

After the memorial for Stephanie, Natalie insisted that Grant drive her downtown to the Justice Center where their offices were located. They rode up in the elevator in silence, Natalie holding Grant's hand as she had held her father's, not so many years ago. She looked up at her friend as the doors opened and saw the age the past three days had put on him and she loved him then with a fierceness that surprised her. Hell, Grant should have been fishing somewhere in the Cascade Mountains or taking one of his grandchildren to the zoo. He stayed out of loyalty to her, she knew, and because he was damned good and didn't want to let go yet. He had been eligible for retirement for almost five years now.

Gretchen, Natalie's secretary, gave her a hug as they walked into the reception area. Natalie and Grant entered the squad room, a large room filled with desks and ringing phones. Most of the detectives were in, and Natalie felt as if she were coming home. She thought for the first time since Stephen had been killed that it would somehow be all right. With the help of the detectives in this room, she would be able to take on anything.

The talking stopped as they entered, and she stood there, as awkward as the first day she'd entered as a new detective.

"Well, what's this?" Natalie demanded. "You'd think all the crime stopped, what with all the silence in here."

Kirby, the newest member of the team and the one who looked as if he belonged in high school and at times made Natalie feel incredibly old, was the first to speak.

"Hi, gorgeous," he said, and he came up and put his arms around her. She blinked back tears, and then tried a grin. She pushed Kirby away, and gave him a real grin.

"Sarge to you, detective," she said, and then pulled him close. "Thanks," she whispered.

Kirby squeezed her and then turned around. "Hey, you old guys," he said, "time to get to work; Sergeant Collins is here."

"Old," Grant snorted. "*Old guys!* Hell, leftover bread's older'n you."

"Yeah," Thompson said from his desk. "I got mold in the lab older'n you."

"And smarter," Eldredge said, throwing his arms around Natalie.

Kirby stood there, grinning, as Grant steered Natalie to her office. She walked behind her desk and slumped in her chair as Grant closed the door. Natalie looked out over the squad bay.

"You're right kid; what you need is to go to work."

Natalie nodded.

Her team. They were great, and they would be the ones to find Stephanie's killer. Of that Natalie was certain.

She fiddled around with papers on her desk, and after a few minutes, she began to cry.

The windows to the study overlooked the sandy beaches of Florida's Gulf Coast. The newspaper clippings were out of place on the desk in the study, the otherwise neat desk littered with newsprint, the white stucco walls of the Spanish-style house covered with clippings as well. Those closest to the window were yellow and curled where the sun had done its work. On the wall across from the windows, there was a floor-to-ceiling bookcase, and newspaper clippings were hung without regard for aesthetics, taped on book spines, covering titles of the classics. If it were not for the headlines that shouted in the quiet room, it would look the work of a child, a display of preschool artwork on a refrigerator.

Victor Bramson sat at the desk, cutting an article out of *USA Today*. He had drawn a circle around the article with a red pen, highlighting the names of the article with a yellow felt pen. He looked at the picture accompanying the article with grim satisfaction.

Another one. He had found another one.

The burden of his task didn't get him down—there could only be so many who were likely to share his secret—and he would get another one. He glanced out the window, not seeing the beautiful day outside, thinking about airfare, schedules, and planning a trip itinerary to go and do what he must.

He held the clipping and turned on his computer, waiting until the colorful array of symbols came up on the screen. He brought his modem on-line and looked at flight schedules, planning the most secure route from Florida to Portland. He looked at the article he had just clipped out, the highlighted name of Natalie Collins, a detective sergeant of homicide. The article contained the story of her sister's death and mentioned that Natalie was one of the few female officers in the country to hold that position.

A survivor.

He read the article for the fourth time in the past hour. The fact of her survival thrilled Victor Bramson. He trembled, thinking that the intrusion by the insignificant man was meant to be. It was a strange and wonderful happening. Natalie Collins again survived when she shouldn't have.

I have to find out why. I must know, and then she will die.

Bramson pulled an article from the stack of paper on his desk and looked at the picture of a young man in a football uniform. James Anderson had grown up in the projects in South Florida, and he had come back from the dead. James had been in an automobile accident that had left him without a pulse or respiration. Even though he had critical injuries, he had been revived in an ambulance, and now he was playing football again.

A survivor.

There were other articles on his desk, circled in red, the names highlighted.

A young girl in San Antonio.

There was so much to do.

Outside, the Florida sun was making the temperature climb to the nineties at midmorning. In the upstairs study of the beach house, the light from the computer screen lit up the white face of a madman.

You will all die before me.

"What do you mean, I can't see the reports?" Natalie demanded angrily. She threw the paper she had been reading on her desk. "This office investigates homicides, right?" She rose from her chair and continued, without waiting for an answer. "We are going to find the person who killed my sister, and I want to see the evidence."

"Calm down, Minnie Mouse," Grant said. "You, of all people, should know that you can't be a witness and be involved and have your own unit investigate it." Natalie's office door opened.

"Natalie."

"Huh?"

"Join me in my office, just for a minute?" Captain Mitchell said. Mitchell, the detective division commander, stood in the doorway to her office, his back to the squad room, and waited for Natalie to join him.

The squad room was silent when they walked out. Kirby and Eldredge looked up as they walked past, Kirby giving her a smile and a wink.

The message from Captain Mitchell was brief: "Be here tomorrow for an interview with Internal Affairs."

Grant and Aimee's attempts at cheering Natalie up during the evening didn't work.

Now I have to fight the killer and the department too, Natalie thought.

She went to bed and cried into her pillow, giving in to the rush of emotions that she couldn't control. During the early morning hours, her sorrow turned to anger. She slammed her fist into her pillow and sat up, fighting for the control she had been able to use in the past. She had always been able to get through tough situations with humor.

One thing's for sure, she thought. *I'm not going to take much bullshit from Internal Affairs. I'm going to find the killer. Oh, yeah—I can.*

Wednesday, September 20

The Collateral Witness

One

Dan knew that it was dangerous for him to stay outside the apartment, but it was the one sure way to find the detective sergeant. Each time someone walked toward him on the sidewalk, his heart picked up a few beats. He had been sitting on the bench along the seawall for the third day, waiting.

The marina was active below him, sailboats and day cruisers coming and going on the river, the owners taking advantage of the warm fall weather. Dan opened the copy of the *Oregonian* he carried with him, looking again at the color picture of Detective Sergeant Natalie Collins. He had just caught a glimpse of her on the night of the murder, her then-pale face streaked with tears, the gun she held demanding most of his attention.

The picture in the paper showed a young woman in uniform, a woman with short blond hair, an intelligent face, and bright eyes. There was a picture of Stephanie in a gown. There was a picture Natalie Collins receiving a medal of valor for her part in arrests of bank robbery suspects.

Daniel McClellan Harris waited, looking at the boats below him to pass the time, watching the gate to the apartment where Detective Sergeant Natalie Collins lived. He waited as he had on the past Friday night, a stranger out of place. His shoulders slumped feeling the failure of the last meeting.

Why was he looking for her? What does she know? Does she know enough to stay alive?

Natalie had been in the Internal Affairs office on several occasions, usually to answer questions or to make an inquiry about an officer that she supervised. Captain Mitchell had assured her that there was nothing to worry about. This was a follow-up interview to the shooting, the death of Stephanie.

Natalie was wearing tan slacks and a navy blazer with a white blouse. She stood outside the door to the Internal Affairs office, nervous at the wait. It was ten a.m. when she opened the door. She felt the fatigue of the last few days pulling on her, the sleepless night with a fitful half an hour's sleep in the early morning.

These guys gonna catch him? No way. Me and my guys will have to do it.

"Natalie, come in," Lieutenant Derry said, ushering her to a chair in his office. "You know Sergeant Nichols."

Natalie nodded to Nichols, who was seated next to the lieutenant's desk.

"Well, let's get started. We don't expect this to take long—just a few questions." He smiled. Natalie returned the smile, more of a grimace, holding her purse in her lap, her stomach working against her will, churning.

She told them her story again, how she had walked home the four blocks from the taxi, how she had talked with Mr. Barker at the door of the deli, looked at the man with the beard on the seawall, and then went up to find her sister dead.

When she got to the fight, her voice grew husky, and she stopped for several minutes, the men quiet, waiting for her to continue. She described the fight in a monotone, all the way to when the medics arrived.

She sat, waiting.

Derry spoke first. "Natalie," he said softly, leaning forward in his chair, "Natalie, we found some of the people who were in the area last Friday night . . . some of the people who were around when Stephanie was killed, neighbors, Mr.—"

"Mr. Barker, the deli owner," Natalie said, looking up. "I talked to him, did he see . . ."

Derry held up his hand. "No."

". . . see anyone running, leaving my apartment?"

"No. In fact, he didn't see or hear anything. In fact, no one heard or saw any other person in or around your apartment." Derry leaned closer. "Except you, Sergeant Collins. You were the only person any of your neighbors saw or heard during that time period."

Natalie drew back suddenly, sitting up straight, her checks growing hot. She looked at the men in the room as the realization of what Lieutenant Derry was saying struck her. Her jaw slackened.

They think I did it . . . they think I killed Stephanie!

A sudden rage hit her, the injustice of it all, Steph killed, she herself almost killed, fighting for her life, and then the funeral, and then to have her story disbelieved by members of her own agency. . .

She started to get up, thought better of it, and sat back down quickly. Tears formed at the corners of her eyes, and she angrily blinked them back. She tried to speak, but what came out was a growl.

She swallowed rapidly, willing herself to wait until she had her thoughts formed.

"You don't believe me, do you?" she said in a hoarse whisper.

"We didn't say that," Derry said, "we just—"

"Bullshit!" The force of Natalie's yell made Derry flinch and surprised Natalie as much as it did them. "Did you gentlemen forget what the hell I've been doing for the past fifteen years, or do you think that I'm some kind of token skirt in detectives?" She glared at Derry, started to stand up, and then as her legs found strength, she jumped to her feet and clenched her fists.

"Huh?" Natalie yelled. "Do you really think I don't know what the fuck I'm doing out there, that I've been just some female in a man's world, hopping a ride on the good ol' equal opportunity parade every time a promotion comes around? *Well, do you?"* She glared down at them, a hatred of what was happening surging through her, a hatred foreign and hot and startling in its intensity. "Aww, what's the use?" she muttered, threw up her hands, and turned toward the door. She stood there, shaking, trying to stay in control, the emotions of grief, anger, hatred, and an incredible sadness at the lack of support washing over her, each fighting for prominence. At last, she turned around and faced the men.

"Have you gentlemen," she asked quietly, "have you gentlemen looked over my record as an officer and sergeant of this department?"

Derry nodded.

"Then you know about the bank business?"

"Yeah, we know of your record," Sergeant Nichols said. "We know of your record, not just from what we have read in your file, but from talking to your officers. They, quite frankly, think you walk on water and would follow you anywhere, and I don't blame you for being pissed." He pointed to Natalie's chair. "Let's work on this."

Natalie sat down again, still shaking. It was a fine speech Nichols made, and she would have said the same thing in his place. Gain cooperation, put the suspect at ease.

Natalie directed her question at Nichols.

"What's the problem? What doesn't add up?"

"Your story," Nichols said.

"Why?"

"We don't have any evidence of anyone else being there," he said, holding his hand up to ward off another outburst from Natalie, "and,"

Nichols continued, "we have evidence that suggests that you were the shooter."

Natalie shook her head slowly, disbelieving what she was hearing, shaking her head, thinking of seeing the man on the seawall, of finding Stephanie, of the fight, of the aftermath. Scenes flashing into her head.

She stood again, shaking her head from side to side, a jumble of emotions rocking her body, not able to keep the tears back now. She knew she had to get out of here before she began sobbing, the incredible fatigue of grief combined with no sleep and the absurdity of the statements making her weak.

She looked at each of the men before she spoke.

"I know evidence," Sergeant Natalie Collins told them quietly. "Do you really think I would leave something around so someone would find it if I were the shooter, and my . . ." And then her head drooped, as if it were suddenly carrying a heavy weight. She felt her knees grow weak and she didn't know if she could stand.

"My sister," she whispered. "Do you really think I would shoot, murder my own sister?" she hissed. She didn't wait for an answer. "Gentlemen, this interview is over."

"Sergeant Collins," Derry held up his hand again, and Natalie ignored it and stood up, clutching her purse, wanting to hit them with it, wanting to hit someone, something.

"Am I under arrest?" Natalie asked.

"No . . . of course not," Sergeant Nichols said.

"My apartment, is it still being held as evidence?"

"No, it was released this morning."

Natalie walked to the door and left them standing there. She grabbed the knob and turned around, leaving her hand in place.

"Make no mistake about this, gentlemen. I know how to investigate a homicide as well as anyone can, better than most, and I *will* find the bastard or bastards who killed my sister." She spoke fiercely, determined, and with a controlled anger now. She suddenly thought of her father then, willing herself strength from him, and it was her dad who gave her the parting words.

"It will be up to me to find the killer, 'cause you gentlemen couldn't pour piss out of a boot with the directions written on the heel."

She walked out and left the door open, knowing that departmental procedures required her to cooperate with an internal investigation. They wouldn't be quite as quick to suspend her with her record and medal of valor, but in the end, she knew that they would have to. She took the elevator down, breathing hard, as if she had been sprinting.

Why are they doing this to me—my own department?

She left the elevator at a jog, passing officers in the hallway, one calling to her.

"Hey, Natalie—"

She ran past them, wanting to get outside before the tears came, tears more from frustration than loss. She walked downtown, toward the park, without a destination in mind. After a few blocks, her thoughts turned to the real problem.

Who are these men? Why me? The one man knows the other—of that I'm sure—but who were they after? Me? Yeah, they were waiting for me—the killer could have fled before I got there. And the other man, he was waiting for the killer—he didn't even care about me, he was there for the killer. What the hell's going on here? Who are they?

Natalie walked back to her car and got in, thinking about what she was going to need from her apartment.

* * *

Dan saw the uniformed officer as he came around the corner by the deli, walking toward him, looking up at the apartments. Dan pulled his paper up, hiding his face as the officer stopped in front of the gate. The officer, a kid in his mid-twenties, looked around uncertainly, and then leaned against the fence, looking out over the river.

I've got to get out of here, Dan thought. He wanted to run, to flee, his heart hammering in his chest. He stood up and started to walk north along the river. The sidewalk would take him to the Tom McCall Riverfront Park in two blocks. The officer was too close, ten yards away. Dan turned and looked back at the cul-de-sac, and saw Natalie Collins come around the corner on the sidewalk. She was walking fast, purposefully, and she didn't see the officer until she was almost to the gate.

Dan stopped, holding his paper up, watching them from a half block away. He walked to the rail by the river and leaned against it.

Natalie stopped short of the gate when she saw the uniform. *They sure didn't waste any time, did they?* she thought bitterly.

"Sergeant Collins? I was told to give this to you," he said, giving her a letter. She tore it open and read the brief note from Lieutenant Derry. He was requesting that she bring in her badge and I.D. card and surrender them to the department. She had been taken off administrative leave and was being suspended, pending the outcome of a hearing. She opened her purse, her fingers shaking, and found her badge case, with badge and I.D. inside. She put them in the envelope, then thrust it at the officer.

"Give this to Lieutenant Derry. He needs it."

When the uniformed officer left, Dan looked up at the apartment, waiting to go up the steps.

Two

Natalie stood at the window and looked out over the river, much as she had done the night Stephanie died. Stephanie's room waited behind her, like a vulture waiting for movement to stop.

Dan's new haircut left him feeling naked and exposed. It had been almost two years since his hair had been this short, but with his beard gone, short hair, and sunglasses, he didn't look anything like the artist's picture of him the *Oregonian* carried on the front page. He was counting on his anonymity to get him through the next few minutes.

He was certain there were other ways to do this, to learn what he could from Natalie, but he couldn't think of anything better at the time. Going to her door was a tremendous risk, not for himself, but for any life he might have, and he felt he had never been this close before to getting his life back and to killing the man who had destroyed him.

He waited on the sidewalk below the condominiums, trying to look like a man waiting for a luncheon date, glancing at his watch, looking at the floating restaurant below him.

He waited until he had a chance to get inside the gate, a woman holding several bags and fishing for her key at the same time.

"I'm going up, too. Let me help."

He walked up behind the woman, passing her as she went to her door, knowing that she could identify him later if things turned to shit. He watched the detective's door for a minute from a half floor down, waiting for something to happen. In the end, he just walked up and dropped the envelope on the mat in front of the door, rang the doorbell, and walked quickly down the stairs without looking back. He opened the gate and walked to the seawall. He flipped open his prepaid cell phone and pretended to make a call, scared, waiting for the door to open.

What if she doesn't answer the door?

Natalie absently packed a bag, a large, oversize cloth bag with a shoulder strap. She rolled up jeans, cotton blouses, socks, and tennis shoes. She didn't need to dress up where she was going. The doorbell rang as she was finishing up. She stopped moving, standing beside her bed. Her heart pounded. She jerked her head toward the door, the paralysis caused by fear unusual and disturbing. She had lived with fear, had embraced it hundreds of times. But to be paralyzed by it . . .

A week ago, she would have answered her door without a second thought, especially in the daytime. She glanced out her windows at the river, and then moved slowly to her purse on the chair.

My gun—I'll get my gun and then we'll just see who is at the door.

As she opened the purse, she felt a knot of panic twist her stomach. Both of her guns had been taken as evidence by the department, a standard procedure, and she was left unarmed.

The door. Someone was at the door.

Natalie knew that she had entered the period of time when grief had to be worked out by herself. Family and friends had gone back to jobs and their own families after the funeral. She wasn't expecting anyone, nor did anyone know she was home. And a friend or coworker would have called first.

She waited, her inactivity making her heart pound harder, her palms grow clammy, cold.

"This is bullshit," she whispered to herself. *If the killer's here,* she thought as she moved to door, *I'll rip his face off and send him home to Jesus for what he did to my Steph.*

The drapes were drawn on the window by the door, so she couldn't see the front sidewalk and stairway. She walked quietly, carefully to the door and raised on her toes (and wondered, not for the first time, why the security peephole was installed for someone six feet tall instead of five foot two).

No one was there.

"Who is it?"

No answer.

She opened the door.

No one.

She hung onto the edge of the door, the adrenaline rush gone, suddenly feeling weak, tired.

She saw the envelope as she was closing the door.

Natalie looked at the plain white envelope, thinking that she was being foolish about being in her place, that no one was out there at her door, that the envelope had been there and she just missed it before. *This doesn't have anything to do with Stephanie or me,* she thought.

She stared at it and held it up to the large windows as she kicked the door shut. There was a note inside.

She pulled the note out by the corner, out of habit more than anything, her mind in an evidence mode, thinking that anything she did from now on would be directed toward finding Stephanie's killer.

She read the message, feeling her insides crawl up into a queasy ball as the content of the writing hit her. The message was scrawled with a pencil on a plain white sheet of paper.

Call me—you have two minutes.   541-555-9898
I know who killed your sister.
No cops or I'm gone.
I know who killed your sister.

What the hell does this mean? The number was probably a phone booth, with the number 9.

Natalie was scared, dead scared.

What the hell did you get into, Steph?

She dialed the number.

When the phone rang, Dan snatched it up, knowing that he would have only a few seconds to convince the detective that she should meet with him, that they could help each other, and he ended up talking too fast.

"Meet me in one minute."

Idiot, Dan thought, *she'll know I'm close and trap me.*

"Who is this?" Natalie asked, her voice raspy, hoarse.

"I know who killed your sister," Dan said, thinking that the woman would hang up.

There was a slight gasp at the other end, and then a quiet voice said, "How do you know?"

"Because I was there."

"There?"

"I had a beard. The other . . . the other person had a mask."

"One minute where?"

"At the restaurant," Dan said without thinking, and looked at the sign above a restaurant across the sidewalk. "Sigmond's Chowder House."

Jesus, Natalie, you don't meet informants alone, never, ever. Especially the first time. You always have backup, and this person is probably the murderer.

She dialed Grant's number and after four rings, she quit, nervous now, knowing that she would have to run out of the door in a few seconds.

She pressed the disconnect and dialed again, standing in the window overlooking the river, not looking at the water this time, straining to see over the condos for a look at the seawall.

"Homicide."

"This is Natalie," she said in a rush. "Who's in?"

"Uh, Natalie, they're all in a meeting, they—"

Natalie hung up the phone and ran out the door, snatching her purse from the couch, thinking that this was possibly the last thing she would do, meet an informant without a gun. How did the old saying go? "Like bringing a knife to a gunfight."

She ran down the stairs.

My God, she's beautiful, Dan thought, realizing then that he hadn't gotten a very good look at her on Friday night, when he was otherwise occupied with staying alive. She had changed from the slacks she had on when she came home, and was wearing blue jeans and a green sweater. Her stride was athletic, wary. Dan was standing near the seawall, watching the front door of the restaurant.

Natalie stopped at the entrance to the Chowder House, looked around, and went inside. Dan walked fast, entering the restaurant behind her. He stood just inside the door, letting his eyes adjust.

Shoulda checked for a back way out, he thought, *but it's too late now.*

There were a dozen wooden tables, with park benches for seating. Natalie was at the counter, talking with a kid in a white apron. There were no other customers. Natalie turned and looked at him, and Dan moved to a table at the end of the room.

God, she looks young, he thought, *like she's twenty-five*—even though he knew from the paper that she was thirty-seven. *She doesn't recognize me, my beard is gone.* He looked at the front door, and took a deep breath. He spoke to her from his seat.

"Natalie Collins?" he said, his voice louder than he intended in the small restaurant.

She jerked her head around and looked over at him. The kid at the counter handed her a Coke, and she stopped there, staring.

She walked toward the table and then stopped, staying several feet away, standing between him and the door.

The mask—he was the one with the mask!

But even as she thought it, she knew that she was wrong.

"Hey, lady!"

The call came from the counter. Natalie jerked her head around. "I need some money for the Coke." The kid behind the counter waited while she counted out the change. She turned and looked at the man sitting at the table. This time she walked closer. She noticed his clothes for the first time: expensive tan slacks and a navy polo shirt, dark-brown penny loafers. He was overdressed for lunch at a riverbank deli. He had a newspaper in front of him.

"Who are you?"

"I was at your apartment the other night, I . . . uh, had a beard." Dan touched his face and then let his hand drift down. Natalie stood and stared at him, a flush creeping up into her face. She saw the black eye, the puffy cheek with the Band-Aid.

"We need to talk," Dan said quickly, "and I'm not here to harm anyone. I just want to find out why this is happening . . . and—"

"*You* were there . . . at my apartment."

Dan nodded.

"But why?"

"If I *knew* why the man with the mask was here, in Portland, I wouldn't need to talk to you . . . or to anyone from homicide."

Natalie remained standing, staring at Dan.

"Who are you?" she whispered, her face tight.

"As I told you that night, my name is Dan." He spoke carefully, evenly, with no apparent emotion. "Please, sit down," he said, pointing to the bench across the table from him.

Natalie hesitated, knowing that she should have at least called Grant, or even a uniformed patrol officer. This was stupid, really stupid. It would have taken her ten seconds to place a call to patrol. Natalie looked around then, at the empty deli, the kid who served her Coke somewhere in the back. She was alone with this stranger who said he knew the killer. The man with the mask—was he here as well? Or was this actually the man who shot Stephanie, the man who wore the rubber mask?

She glanced around again, trying to see past the counter into the back room.

Stupid, oh, God. I'm really stupid. Gonna get another gun from Grant. Today. The strange man's voice made her jump.

"I didn't have to come here," he said, "I could have just drifted away. And," he said, louder now, "you could have called and there could be some of your police friends outside right now. So, who's taking the risk? We have to talk." He opened his hand and gestured to the seat across from him.

Natalie stood there, looking down at this man who said he was in her apartment, this smooth-faced man who looked harmless and a little sad. She sat down, holding her purse in front of her on the table, like a shield.

"Okay, I'm here, so talk."

Dan took a deep breath and began. "A little over two years ago," he said quietly, "I was living the American dream. I had a house, a mortgage, a wife and . . . and because of this man with the mask, the man who killed your sister . . . " He stopped and looked down at his hands, and when he began again, his voice was barely a whisper. "Because of this—this man—I have lost everything and have lived as a fugitive, as you will soon, and I have hunted this man with the mask for almost two years."

Natalie saw Dan's eyes turn down when he mentioned "wife," and she knew that her first impression was right, a man with sad eyes.

If she had known then where this would take them, of the evil they would see and confront, she would have said, "Fuck the pension, bring on the indictment," and she would have taken her chances in court. If she had prevailed in court, she would have gone to Disneyland and worked in a McDonald's concession stand for the rest of her life. A place where no one ever dies.

Three

The Multnomah County District Attorney's Office is in the old country courthouse, a gray stone building, six blocks from the riverfront parks, across the street from the courthouse. Senior Assistant District Attorney Charles Sims sat in his office with his back to the window and listened to the evidence being presented. He had his hands in a praying position, touching the bridge of his nose. He was practicing for a state circuit court judgeship, and if the current administration stayed in the statehouse in Salem, observers thought he might just make it.

Sergeant Nichols finished with his evidence, presenting it to Lieutenant Derry, Assistant District Attorney Charlene Harter, and Sims.

When Nichols stopped talking, they all looked at Sims, waiting for the hands to come down, and for him to speak.

When he started, he spoke softly, so those in the room had to strain to hear.

"You've got enough for an indictment," he said, "so go find her, now, when she's emotional about losing her badge and being suspended. She'll confess, and we'll move for a deal on first-degree manslaughter, calling it a tragedy, an emotional aberration on the part of a decorated veteran. That way," and he paused to look at each person in turn, "that way, we all win." He nodded at Nichols, dismissing him, and the Internal Affairs sergeant gathered his material and he and Lieutenant Derry quickly left the room.

"Can you believe it?" Charlene Harter told Sims. "Can you believe that a homicide cop would make up such a bullshit story?"

Sims sat and looked at her.

"What if she's telling the truth?" he countered.

"If she tries to take that story to court, we'll jam it down her throat," Harter said.

"I wouldn't want to be her, in any event," Sims said. "If she's telling the truth, there's someone out there trying to kill her. If she's lying, as you say and as the evidence suggests, she'll spend a long, long time in jail."

He shook his head and stared out at the river. "No, I sure wouldn't want to be Detective Sergeant Natalie Collins."

"Take three detectives and find her," Lieutenant Derry told Nichols. "We need to talk to Ms. Collins." The fact that Lieutenant Derry no longer referred to Natalie Collins as Sergeant Collins was not lost on Sergeant Nichols. As he walked to his office, he thought that he sure wouldn't want to be Natalie Collins.

No way.

"That's a Stone boat," Dan said.

"Looks like it's made of wood to me."

Dan glanced at Natalie then, and smiled. It felt good, and he realized later that it was the first time he had smiled in a long time. They were leaning on the metal railing along the sidewalk, looking over the river, at the boats in the marina.

"I know it's made of wood," he said and grinned. "I mean, this beautiful sailing sloop below us was made at the Stone Boat Yard in Oakland sometime after the turn of the century, and it's a beautiful, classic boat. And," Dan added, "it's made of wood."

"You know boats?" Natalie asked, looking at Dan for the first time as if he were a real person.

"I used to, in another life." They stood like that, shoulder to shoulder, looking at the water. Looking at a boat that was built long before either of them was born. The teak wood glistened on the deck, ageless, beautiful.

"The story I've told, Sergeant Collins, is—"

"Natalie. Call me Natalie."

"Okay, Natalie. The story I've told is accurate and truthful, and I've been going crazy trying to find a way to prove what I know about this man, and lately, I've just been trying to kill him. If you believe what I have told you is true, and if it means you can prove that he was the one that killed your sister, will you help me find him?"

And when we find him, I'm gonna kill him. Dan thought.

He looked at Natalie, looked into her eyes, and knew the answer even before she slowly nodded. They turned and looked at the water again, and then Natalie suddenly brightened, as if a switch had been turned on.

"C'mon," she said starting for the steps that led down to the marina, to the docks. "Let's go look at the old wooden boat, the Stone one."

Dan stayed on the railing, and when she saw he wasn't joining her, she returned.

"You want to look at it or not?" Natalie stood there, her hands on her hips, waiting.

"There's no way out of the dock except for that one stairway," Dan said, nodding at the stairs. "I don't want to go into a place where there is one way out, at least until this is over." He looked at Natalie. "We'll look at the boat when this is over."

She shrugged her shoulders. "At least you're thinking positively."

She was right, Dan thought. This was the first time he had dared to think of a future. There was, at least for the moment, someone to share the horrible knowledge with. Someone who might possess some answers as to why the killer had picked her.

They walked along the sidewalk, slowly, along the seawall, being passed by bicyclists, rollerblade enthusiasts, and people enjoying the sunshine. As they got to the corner, Natalie turned uphill, toward Front Avenue. She stopped and opened the door to Barker's Deli. Dan followed and watched as an old man came rushing up and gave Natalie a hug, shaking his head then patting her cheeks. They looked at Dan, their arms round each other, Dan standing just inside the doorway.

They look like a grandfather and granddaughter, Dan thought, Natalie looking like a college coed, with her green sweater and jeans. Dan was becoming increasingly aware of just how beautiful she was, of her bright and fun personality that came through even with the nature of their meeting.

Natalie motioned Dan forward and he walked up, glancing around the room, picking out the back room where there was a delivery door—a way out—and the other patrons—a younger couple in the far corner, involved in each other, and two men in suits with a sales catalogue spread on their table. No cops.

"Dan, this is Mr. Barker. He takes care of me; and Mr. Barker, this is a . . . Dan, a friend."

The deli owner took Dan's hand and shook it once, and then put his arm around Natalie.

He seated them by the window, overlooking the river.

"Natalie," Mr. Barker began, nervous, pain in his face, "I'm so sorry, dear, about our dear Stephanie . . ."

Natalie put her arms around his waist and gave him a hug. The white-haired deli owner turned away, saying that he would bring them what they needed. He returned with two bottles of Corona beer, each with a lime in the top, and left them alone.

Natalie thought of the strangeness of it all, sitting with a man who knew the monster who killed her sister. Four days ago, she had almost shot Dan.

Dan saw them first, knowing who they were the instant they walked round the corner of the deli. Natalie was talking, telling him about how she would be able to use her homicide people to help them solve this thing. She stopped when she saw Dan's face, his frozen posture, and then she turned to see what he was looking at. Two men on the sidewalk.

"Friends of yours?" he asked quietly, still staring out of the window. Natalie could see his pulse in his neck.

Natalie nodded. "I know them, and yeah, they work for the bureau." She had worked with the tall one on a robbery detail three or four years ago. Palmer—Barry Palmer. The other one, Natalie was beginning to know well. Detective Sergeant Nichols.

Dan rose, calm, not taking his eyes from the two men. "Get a room at the downtown Hilton," he said, "and use your name. You'll be okay for one night. I'll call you later."

He stood and left the table without another word, walking purposefully to the side door, not looking back at Natalie. He hesitated, looking for the men, and slipped out the side door. Natalie could see him walking quickly up behind a group of businessmen, looking as if he were part of their group. She caught one more glimpse of him as he walked along the sidewalk by the seawall, walking toward the downtown area.

"Everything all right, Natalie?"

She jerked her head around, her heart pounding, looking into the concerned face of Mr. Barker.

"Yeah, uh, fine, Mr. Barker. Listen, could we go into the kitchen and talk?"

The restaurant owner stood and grinned. "My house is yours, just follow me." With that, he turned, still talking, telling Natalie that she should come by every day for lunch. Natalie picked up her bag and looked at the Corona bottles on the table. She picked up the almost-full bottle that Dan had been drinking out of, carefully touching it near the top, and took it with her to the kitchen.

"Mr. Barker, can I have a paper sack?" She poured the beer into the sink, still holding it carefully by the top. She kissed the white-haired restaurant owner on his forehead, and smoothed the wrinkles on his face with her hand. "I'll be fine, really," she told him, knowing that he would still worry. She took his arm and they walked to the door that way, arm in arm, neither of them speaking.

"Natalie, if you need . . ."

I'm fine," she said, holding Mr. Barker at arm's length. "Really. I am." She went out through the delivery door, holding her sack.

Okay, smart guy, she thought, *let's find out who you really are.*

By the time she found out who Dan was, it was too late. She was on the road with him, on a bizarre journey where nothing was as it seemed, where the hunters became the hunted.

Four

Victor Bramson switched off the computer, leaving the room in darkness. He had worked all afternoon on his search and now that the sun was going down over the Gulf, he would go outside. He walked along the hallway outside his office and down the stairs. He put on a windbreaker and straw hat, ensuring that the last of the sunlight wouldn't touch his pale skin.

He walked on the beach below his house, staring west over the waters. The tide was going out, and he was able to walk another hundred yards straight out from the bank. He walked around a clump of seaweed, the raw smell of decay sharp and lingering. The shock of his discoveries hummed through him as if he had touched a bare electrical wire.

Four hundred years, maybe more. I'll be the most famous man who ever lived. The most powerful.

It was cooler now, the clouds over and the Gulf reddish with the sunset, the sun a faint light on the water, drowning far out in the Gulf of Mexico. Victor Bramson could not have imagined living in any other spot, his research on aging first taking him to Miami and then to the coast, the coast discovered by the early Spanish explorers.

You will all die before me!

The words thundered in his chest. And they had died. Mother and grandmother. His mother and grandmother had taken him to Miami when he was a young boy, living in a stucco duplex near Miami Beach, surrounded by the white hair of residual humanity. Years later, his longevity studies brought Victor back to Miami, and his first clients, all over one hundred years of age, eventually died. Some were excited about his work, looking to extend indefinitely the time until their last breath.

Victor learned to assist others in his search for answers. He assisted them in what he believed was their search for death. He had been driven by questions: what fails first, and why do we die? Even though life expectancy had doubled in the last century, Victor's century, he knew that the doubling was primarily a result of the eradication of childhood diseases. The genetically programmed cellular atrophy at certain ages meant that people would live to be seventy or eighty.

He stopped his walk, standing at the edge of the surf, his back to his house a quarter mile distant. He stretched, knowing he would watch a similar sunset one hundred years from now . . . two hundred years . . . three hundred.

You will all die before me.

Victor published some of his studies in medical journals. Some of his findings would never be published. His private journals of what the elderly had to tell him were too important to share. They had much to tell him, and he had much to learn. Cellular growth and rejuvenation, retarded cellular atrophy were written about in his journals. *I can do that now, I can stop the cellular genetic coding of destruction. The power!*

Victor waved his arms around, knowing he had the secrets the Spanish explorer Ponce de León was looking for, not the fountain of youth, but the secrets of long life: a very long life, an unending life, out to four hundred years now, and getting longer with each bit of knowledge Victor gained.

He stared at the waters of the Gulf and imagined himself on the ship with Ponce de León on that day of discovery, a Sunday in 1521 A.D.

It was morning.

The wooden ship rose on early morning swells, the captain in his cabin impatiently waiting for daylight. He sailed from Puerto Rico to the east coast of the island he named Florida in honor of the Easter Sunday he discovered the land, through the Keys, to the Gulf waters. He still believed that the land he saw was an island, and this was the place he had been seeking for almost thirty years, since the second voyage of Columbus.

The ship creaked and groaned as it jerked lightly into the wind, pulling on its anchor. The deck watch turned uneasily. The crew was sleeping in the fo'castle, and the watch sleepily waited for his relief.

The door to the captain's cabin was suddenly flung open, startling the watch. The captain was dressed in reds and golds, in his finest cloth. He walked silently to the rail and looked at the dark shore, waiting for the sun to hit the trees. He stood like that in the slight wind, oblivious to the jungle growth, the reds, whites, and oranges of flowers. Birds of all colors and sizes flew in and over the trees and beach.

A paradise of sand, sun and mineral waters that would turn back time . . .

The captain suddenly pushed away from the roll and turned, yelling for the mate to assemble the men for the boat to go ashore.

This would be the trip, the day he would find what he had wanted, needed . . . the water of the fountain.

They launched the boat, the captain in the front. As they approached over the bar, the beach that had been a cacophony of sound, became suddenly silent. As they rode the last fifty feet of swell to the beach, a flock of arrows replaced the birds and roses up from the jungle like an angry swarm.

The oarsmen tried to fight against the tide as they beached, their eyes bulging with the sight of naked bodies running from the jungle across the sand toward them.

The captain leveled his short rifle and fired, still standing in the front of the boat. The second boat beached now, and more shots were filed. The arrows hit the boats and bounced, one striking the captain in the right calf, the arrow burying deep in the flesh. Ponce de León cried out, cursing, as they retreated to the safety of the ship.

Victor Bramson grabbed the calf of his right leg and dropped to his left knee. The pain was intense, and he grabbed the muscle, massaging it with his fingers.

I found it, not you, Ponce de León. Not a fountain of youth—a passage into the next four centuries, and you couldn't even survive an attack.

Power. Wealth.

You will all die before me.

Bramson shuddered. He got to his feet and started back on the dark beach toward the house, limping, favoring his right leg.

You will all die before me.

Five

"Both of you come to the bench," Judge Felicia Hernandez said, her exasperation showing through her judicial demeanor. Detective Grant Birnam sat in the back of the courtroom, watching.

Defense attorney David Attinger grinned at the judge, his jowls shaking. He was large for a youngster of thirty-five, waddling as he walked up to the bench. He wore a green plaid jacket with shiny sleeves, a white shirt, and brown corduroy pants.

"Your Honor," he said, making *honor* sound like a word with four syllables, "Your Honor, my poor client here is being unnecessarily slandered by Mr. Sims."

"I'm going to make sure the state doesn't trample over your defendant's rights, even though this is his—help me out here, Mr. Attinger—fourth or fifth time being caught removing items from a house that he doesn't reside in."

"Allegedly from a house, Your Honor. The prosecution hasn't proven that yet, and…"

Assistant District Attorney Sims rolled his eyes up until the irises seemed ready to disappear into his skull and shook his head.

Judge Hernandez held her hand up again, glared at Attinger, and he shut up, not wanting to piss the judge off more than he usually did. He started again when the judge didn't immediately fill the silence.

"Your Honor, the defense would like to ask for a recess. My client's a sick man."

"Yeah, you betcha he's sick," Sims broke in. "A sick mother of a burglar," he added under his breath.

"He has a very bad toothache, Your Honor, and I hardly think, Your Honor, that a man with an impacted wisdom tooth can participate in his own defense. Just *look* at him, Your Honor." David Attinger waved his arm toward his client.

And Her Honor did. She looked over the heads of the two attorneys and glared at the defendant, who indeed did look like he had a swollen jaw.

"Looks miserable," the judge said. Attinger nodded with a grin. "But he has looked miserable every time he had a trial and I found him guilty." Sims was grinning now.

"In fact," the judge said to herself, "almost every defendant who comes into my courtroom looks miserable."

Attinger looked back at his client, who indeed did look miserable. He jumped when the judge banged her gavel down, inches from Attinger's ear.

"Court is recessed until Monday morning at ten a.m." She turned to the newly impaneled jury, and began her instructions. "You are not to discuss this case . . ."

Grant sat in the back and watched the show. It seemed to him that he had spent half his career in the court. A homicide detective does three things: looks at bodies, interviews witnesses and writes reports of the interviews, and waits and waits and waits and then testifies in court. As the jury filed out, Grant lurched to his feet, his bulk swaying, and stood aside as Sims walked by, tugging at his moustache. The prosecutor gave Grant a funny look and then was gone.

Attinger! Christ, Grant thought. *I can't believe that I'm actually going to him.* But the man was a fighter, a scrapper, and it didn't matter to Attinger if he had a pissant client who lied to his attorney, to the cops, to his mother, judge, jury, and his parole officer. Attinger defended all of them with wit, with a crazy unorthodox style, and he didn't take cheap shots. Grant walked up the aisle as the defense attorney shuffled his papers and legal pads into a stack. A deputy handcuffed Attinger's latest client and they disappeared through a side door.

They were alone in the courtroom when Attinger spoke without turning around.

"Got your call," he said. "Been curious why a big-city dick like you would call me, especially when we don't have a case going."

"I needed some elixir," Grant growled, "some snake oil . . . and I thought, now who would be likely to have some?"

Attinger turned and smiled up at the large homicide detective. "Why, you want me to minister to those poor unfortunate souls you railroad . . ."

"Arrest."

"Yeah, whatever you call it."

Grant shook his head.

They grinned at each other and shook hands.

"I don't need elixir, Davey," Grant said softly, serious now, "I need a damned good attorney, not a suit, one who ain't afraid of a fight."

"You?"

Grant shook his head. "No."

"I wondered when I got your message . . . you want me to defend Detective Sergeant Natalie Collins on a murder charge."

Grant nodded. "Everybody know what's coming down?"

"Everybody with his ear to the ground. Word is she's gonna be charged with the death of her sister."

"That's what I hear as well, but I'm not in the loop on this one, I.A.'s doing the investigation."

Attinger whistled again, louder, higher in pitch, dry. He picked up his briefcase and walked past Grant. "Then break out your plastic, big-city dick, We're gonna have dinner and adult beverages at the most expensive place we can find while you tell Davey the Savior all about it."

Six

"He's using his left hand," Gardiner said, looking at the Corona bottle under a large magnifier.

"Huh?" Natalie looked up from the notes she was writing.

"The prints on your bottle, they are from the left hand of your man. I can see at least ten points on his left ring finger print."

Dammit! What other obvious things didn't you notice, Natalie? She said to herself. Dan had been holding the bottle in his left hand and she just hadn't paid attention. And this Dan was smart and observant. *I'll just bet that he knows what hand I use*, she thought. Was he left-handed, or was . . . and then she had a chilling thought. It reminded her of an old police officer technique . . . drink coffee with the hand you don't shoot with. In theory, your right hand was always free. Your gun hand was never encumbered. *Is that what he was doing? Keeping his gun hand free? Was he that good?*

Natalie was in the Portland Police Bureau's Criminal Detection Laboratory, located on the twelfth floor of the Justice Center. Lab technician Gardiner was one of the best, and he and Natalie worked together on several cases. This was a rush job, she explained to him, and he began examining the bottle as soon as she gave it to him. Natalie was betting that Gardiner hadn't been informed of her suspension.

"How long ago do you think the prints were left on the bottle?" Gardiner asked, still looking through the magnifier.

"Thirty minutes."

Gardiner looked at Natalie out of the corner of his eye, and then back at the bottle.

"Thought you told me this was a homicide case," he said turning off the light.

"It is." Natalie smiled at him. "Sure wish I could tell you more, Terrance. But rules are rules."

"Yeah, right. I thought the rumor was that you were on leave or something."

"Just for a day or two more, Terrance, and then I'll be back. I just don't want this one to go stale."

He nodded, lifting the bottle by forceps, sitting it on another table. "Want me to try for saliva?"

Natalie nodded. A DNA match would be better than prints, but there wasn't a huge database in the DNA files, nothing like the fingerprints that had been collected in the last forty years. "How soon can you AFIS the print you have?"

"I'll get it ready today and send it out."

AFIS, which stands for Automated Fingerprint Identification System, took less than a day to match prints on file, a task that had taken weeks in the past.

"Terrance, will you be a dear and call me as soon as you learn something, and, no, better yet, route this to Grant, Detective Birnam, in homicide."

"Oh, and Terrance," Natalie said as she walked to the door and turned to look back, "be a dear and don't tell anyone but Grant about the results of our visit today, okay?" She blew him a kiss and was gone.

Seven

Grant walked into Jake's Restaurant with Attinger trailing, the restaurant beginning to fill up with the five o'clock crowd. A bald, tall and thin maître d' wearing black, reminding Grant of someone out of a horror film, greeted them with a smile. Grant remembered that he had worn his best suit today, which was why he merited such approval from the macabre maître d'.

"Two for dinner, gentlemen?" he said, his voice trailing off and his mouth turning down when he saw Attinger's rumpled and shiny jacket, his scarred and battered briefcase looking like a vintage sample case used by a career vacuum cleaner salesman.

"Yes, later. Put us down for dinner in an hour or so. We got some drinking to do. Name of Grant."

Attinger followed, looking around at the décor, brass and oak and ferns, and at the boisterous younger crowd. "Bet that guy would seat you where the fuck ever you wanted if you had American Express Platinum," he said, grabbing a handful of olives from the bar as they walked by, "but you better keep your Citibank Visa in its holster until the dinner's over. That bald guy, the one with the menus, glad he's not serving us." Attinger threw the olives in his mouth and chewed noisily.

The attorney ordered a double scotch. "The best you have," he told the waiter, leaning back in his chair, his jowls moving and shaking with the destruction of the olives.

"Didn't know you drank," Grant said dryly, as their drinks came.

"Don't usually," Attinger said. "but this is a special occasion . . . you're buying."

Grant watched helplessly as Attinger ordered one and then another tray of escargot.

"You gonna have dinner on top of that?"

"Of course," Attinger said, sounding wounded. "I need my strength if we are going to do this. Anyway," he said, wiping his lips and then his beard with his linen napkin, "anyway, why did Sergeant Natalie Collins pick me?"

"She didn't."

Attinger's eyes came up as he took in this new piece of news.

"You don't drive a new BMW," Grant said, "and you don't play pitty-pat tennis like those young attorneys who are afraid they'll lose a point."

Attinger nodded, garlic butter on his chin. He made a careful show of placing the last snail on a piece of bread and making it disappear in his mouth.

"I like a good fight, Grant, and this is going to be the best show in town." He took another sip of his scotch, and held it up, admiring it in the light. "For scotch this good, I should sell out and do divorces and bankruptcies, or maybe I should specialize in environmental law like those new puppies coming outta law school."

"How original," Grant said. He leaned forward toward the attorney. "But Davey, you'd be very bored."

Natalie waited until after five to leave the lab so that the majority of the workers at the Justice Center would have already left for the day. She didn't want to run into anyone who might be looking for her, and most of the officers and secretaries who worked in the building knew her. When she made it to the street, she found a cab.

"Beaverton," she said, leaned back in the seat, and closed her eyes. She tried to concentrate on what to do next, on where she was going, but her mind was a jumble of facts and ideas, all competing for her attention.

I've got to go to Beaverton and see Aimee and Grant. First things first.

Stephanie. No, I can't think of you now.

This man who saved me—

You mean, said he saved you, Natalie.

Her mind raced through the events of the night Stephanie died, and then she knew that Dan had indeed saved her life.

I'm going to stay with him, Natalie thought, *I'm going to use him to find the killer. And I know what to do then.*

Aimee came out to meet her when the cab entered the driveway. "We've got to stop meeting like this," she told Natalie, and walked her to the house, her arm around the younger woman.

"Where's Grant?"

"He called and said he was eating dinner with your attorney."

"My attorney? I don't have one yet."

"It seems as if you do now," Aimee said grinning.

"I need to call him," Natalie said, and punched in Grant's cell number.

They stood in the living room and looked at each other, knowing that some things were changing, and they would never be the same again.

"I have to leave for a while, you know," Natalie told her.

Aimee nodded, perhaps understanding what Natalie had to go through much more than Grant did. As they waited for Grant to call back, Natalie hugged Aimee and stepped back, looking at the woman she had loved as much as a daughter can love a mother, for as long as she could remember.

Her cell phone rang, and Natalie snatched it up.

"Minnie Mouse," Grant bellowed, causing her to hold the phone away from her ear.

"Grant, I'm with Aimee."

"I *know* where you are," he yelled, "I called my house."

Natalie heard the loud voices of a happy hour crowd behind Grant.

"Grant, what are you doing with an attorney?"

"Not just an attorney," Grant said, "Davey Attinger."

"The Courthouse Louse? Grant, how could you?"

"Because, whether or not you will admit it, he's the best at what he does. He wins and he fights and you don't like him because he beat you," Grant said, feeling light-headed from the whiskey. "And he beat you fair, and you know it, Minnie."

"Yeah, if you say so, Grant," Natalie said, smiling. "You been next to a whiskey bottle, Detective Birnam?"

"I've made a nodding acquaintance with one tonight, Minnie. How soon can you meet with Davey and me?"

"Can't for a while."

"And why the hell not?" Grant thundered again, causing Natalie to jerk the phone from her ear.

"'Cause I'm leaving," Natalie said.

"You stay the fuck there until I get home!"

"Grant, what kind of talk is that to use on a lady, and your sergeant, your supervisor, your—"

"Bullshit, Minnie Mouse, I want—"

"Grant."

"For you to stay—"

"Grant."

"What?"

"Retain the Courthouse Louse. I'll sign a check, leave it with Aimee." Natalie hung up, grinning at Aimee. "Your hubby says 'Hello,'" Natalie said, and they both laughed.

Natalie called a cab, and as they waited, she asked Aimee to take her to Grant's gun collection. Aimee led Natalie to their bedroom, where Natalie selected a Beretta 9mm pistol from Grant's gun case, and with it, three fifteen-round magazines.

Where you're going, Minnie Mouse, you're not going without a gun.

Aimee looked on, concerned, but she had lived with Grant's career, and then with Natalie's, for many years.

They stood in the living room, looking at the street, waiting for the cab to take Natalie away. When the cab arrived, Natalie tucked the gun in her waistband and pulled her jacket over it, easy with the gun like the veteran she was. From the street she looked back at Aimee in the window, and years later she remembered Aimee that way, her beautiful long gray hair glowing in the last of the day's light, her face showing wrinkles of concern and love for the daughter she never had.

* * *

Grant tried to finish his prime rib, picking at it, knowing that it would be futile to try to catch Natalie at his house. She had already left.

"She wants to retain the 'Courthouse Louse,'" Grant said, watching the attorney grin as he heard Natalie's name for him. "She wants to retain you to defend her if she is charged with murder," Grant said, "and I'll get a check to you tomorrow."

Grant pushed his plate away and told Attinger of the events of the evening Stephanie was killed, as related to him by Natalie. He talked about what he had heard of the evidence: the gun used, the blood spatter. Attinger's eyes glowed as he heard of the statement made by the bearded stranger.

The Courthouse Louse was shaking with excitement as he ordered yet another scotch. A bizarre case, a real mystery, and this time with a real client to take to the jury, one he didn't have to dress up and dust off like he did the others. This one would have the jury in tears. They'd be ready to hang the judge, the prosecutor, and even the damned court reporter if they picked on her.

"I've got some contacts in the District Attorney's office," Grant said. "We should be able to find out what they're up to."

"I have contacts there, too," Attinger said. "But have you considered they might bring someone in, a special prosecutor, if they decide there is too much conflict of interest here? They might have someone from the Attorney General's office in Salem, a staff attorney from the Department of Justice, someone good enough to get the job done, but someone politically expendable in case we prove she didn't do it."

Grant nodded.

"The D.A.," Attinger continued, "the D.A., he can't lose. If the prosecution prevails, he will say that his office regrettably had to defend the community and prosecute a bad cop, and if we prevail, he'll say that his office didn't want to prosecute her in the first place, a fine officer like that, but they had to go with the evidence."

Grant watched as Attinger pushed his plate aside, ordered another scotch, and began scribbling notes on a legal pad, already lost in the fight, stopping only to take a sip of the scotch Grant was buying. When he filled two legal pads and part of a third (and emptied two more doubles of Chivas), he stood up.

"Got a lotta work to do, gotta clean my calendar, and oh, big-city dick," he said to Grant as they were leaving. "This meal is not part of the retainer."

Grant sighed. "I wouldn't have it any other way."

Eight

Dan sat in the lobby of the Hilton Hotel, pretending to read the daily *Oregonian*. He was dressed casually, wearing dark gray slacks, and a light gray cotton sweater. He was sitting in front of a potted plant, the equivalent of having his back to the wall in the middle of the lobby, the branches spreading out over his head. It was comforting.

He sat with his back to the elevators, the main desk to his right, his small leather bag beside him like an obedient dog.

He preferred lobbies to rooms at certain times of the day. Rooms were frightening. He had seen people die in hotel rooms. You were more anonymous in a lobby than in a room. People walked by and didn't see you. The pulse of the hotel had quickened, the rhythm picking up with the evening rush.

As it was, he almost missed Natalie Collins. She was in through the main doors, following a group of conventioneers, and she had approached the desk before he saw her. She looked good in the crowd, her short blond hair making her look twenty, wearing jeans, white tennis shoes, and a white blouse, covered by a jean jacket. The jacket bumped on her left side as she walked, and Dan smiled grimly.

The lady was armed and kept it close, not in the bag where she couldn't get at it.

She carried a large bag, approaching the desk with a swinging walk, with a confidence that was missing earlier that afternoon.

She's had time to prepare for his meeting, not startled like today . . and if this were a setup, would she check in? No, probably not, she's too curious, and they are after her now. No cops at the desk in the last two hours.

Natalie laughed at something the clerk said, her laugh musical, as if she were checking in to meet a lover. She gathered up a key and walked toward the elevators, swinging her bag.

Dan waited for five minutes and walked to a house phone, suddenly afraid, not wanting to go on with it, thinking he should run away from here as fast as he could, pick up Angel, and go somewhere.

If it's a trap and they want me, I'm had.

He picked up the house phone before he could change his mind.

"Natalie Collins's room, please."

"Ringing."

She picked it up on the first ring.

"Yes?" Her voice was small, almost shrill, childlike.

"Natalie."

"Yes?"

"I'm in the hotel," Dan said, looking around, knowing that if he were set up, they'd know now, and people would be scurrying around looking for him.

"Room 680," she said, and the line went dead.

He waited until a group left the lobby bar, men wearing convention name tags, a computer company of some kind. Computer nerds, on their way to getting drunk. Dan got into the elevator behind them, not liking the confinement, but fearing the stairway more.

"How far you going, buddy?" The man by the buttons was large, his hair shaggy and all one length, his suit wrinkled as if he didn't care.

"Seven," Dan said.

"Hey, John," said one of the men in the back, "I think that redheaded bartender liked you."

"Naw," the large man said, "besides, she wasn't much to look at."

"Yeah, but she had nice tits."

The distance between us is so large, Dan thought, the strangeness sinking in, the conventioneers going to dinner, drinking, letting the booze talk; and me, I'm going up to discuss a killing.

He got off on seven, and took the stairs down to six, careful, wary. He walked to the door of 680 and looked around the empty hallway, carrying his paper and bag. He knocked before he could change his mind.

Everything you've learned on the road you're throwing away to go into this room, he told himself.

He knew that it could be a trap, and probably was, that Detective Sergeant Natalie Collins had plenty of time and certainly the connections and reason to want him to take a trip downtown, and Dan wanted to turn from the door and run from this place.

Then she was standing there, in the open doorway, her hand under her jacket, looking up at him, anxiety in her face. She smiled, and backed away from the door.

Dan entered, holding his paper with his left hand, ready to throw it and run if he saw another person, his legs trembling. He glanced in the open door of the bathroom to his left, and then quickly around the room. It was a small suite, with a king-size bed, a sitting area with a couch and chairs, and an oak dinette set by the window. The drapes were open, and he could see the lights from an office building across the way.

"Okay to sit by the window?" She didn't wait for his reply, and walked to the table and sat in the chair on the right, curling her leg under her, her right hand still grazing her side.

Dan walked over to the table, looking down at Natalie, wanting to run out of the room.

"I'm here for one reason," he said softly, "and that's to find the person who killed your sister . . . but I can't, no, I won't go downtown with you or anyone else, not willingly. Okay?"

Natalie nodded. "I'm about to be indicted for killing Stephanie," she said, "and—"

"That's absurd, but not unexpected."

Natalie looked up at him, startled. "How did you know?"

"I know him, and how he works, and we need to declare—."

"A truce."

"Yes, we need to work together," Dan said, sitting across from her, placing the paper carefully on the table, his legs still weak from the fear of being caught. Natalie got up and opened the door and looked into the hall. Nothing. When she returned to the table, she saw Dan removing clippings from the folds of the paper, clippings about her, some new, and some ancient history.

"For some reason, he went after you," Dan said, looking at Natalie, at her waistband, "and you won't need your gun. I only want to harm one person, and he's not here." He smiled, willing himself to relax, knowing that he had to relax to get through this.

"Who is he?"

"I'll get to that, but we've got to find out why, the key is . . . why us? What ties us together? So I have been reading about you," Dan said, carefully placing the clippings on the table.

"Tell me about you first," Natalie said.

"Okay, but if I can convince you that I saved your life, and that I didn't kill your sister, can we have a truce, can you not use that gun in your belt, can you relax a little?"

"Okay, truce." Natalie stuck her hand across the table, and solemnly shook Dan's hand. She grinned.

Jesus, Danny Boy, she's grinning at you.

Dan smiled, his lips pressed tight together.

"You call that a smile?" she said, grinning again. "That's pathetic. Tell me about yourself and this man."

"Two years ago, he killed my wife," Dan said, and across the table the grin faded.

"How do you know that?"

"I caught him at it."

"Like Stephanie?"

"Sort of, and he got away as I came home."

Dan looked at the table, thinking of a time that seemed a hundred years ago. When he spoke, Natalie had to lean forward to hear him.

"And then one day, the strangest of things, I saw him again—"

"Where?"

"I saw him on TV. He was part of a story on aging. He was right there on the television in front of me." Dan stopped, his voice a whisper, looking at the table, not seeing it. Natalie leaned forward until they almost touched.

"He was right there on the TV, right there in front of me . . . the same man, the same mannerisms." Dan was shaking, his eyes were closed. "The same face. He was part of a panel of people who studied longevity."

"Did you go to the police?" Natalie whispered, her face still close.

"No, by then it was too late." Dan looked up at Natalie, looked at her face, the small wrinkles at the corners of her eyes.

"By then it was way too late," Dan said softly, "because—."

"Because they already thought you did it," Natalie finished for him.

She suddenly realized she had just thought of the police as *they*. Her profession. She sat up straighter, looking across at Dan.

"What happened when the police thought you did it?"

When Dan finally answered, he said simply, "I ran."

I've come a long way in a week, Natalie thought, *from a detective searching for murderers to sitting in a hotel room with a strange man, a man who knows Stephanie's killer. The strange thing is, I'm not afraid of this man, I have a gut feeling that he's telling the truth, and I'm comfortable with him. It's all just so . . . bizarre.*

And Dan McClellan Harris began his story, a story about a killing and a dangerous and evil man, a story about a journey to catch a killer, only to be too late time and again, finding only the killer's work. He told of a journey that took him to Portland for Stephanie's death, weaving a tale with some parts left out, some embellished for effect.

After twenty minutes, he stopped and got up from the table. He pulled the plastic cover from a glass and filled it with water from the bar, thinking about what he had just told a total stranger. A cop. It scared him to talk about it, but at the same time, he felt better. He had never told anyone about the killings. Who would have believed him?

Oh, yeah, Detective Sergeant Collins, I can tell you a lot about this man, and I can tell you all about me, and I will tell you some, just enough to catch a killer, but never about Angel, not about us. Not ever.

Dan walked around the room, and stopped beside the table, looking at the street below, the street black and shiny, lights glistening in the early fall rain. He saw a blue-and-white police car moving through the traffic below him, its overhead lights painting the buildings red and blue, a flickering transient color, moving silently without its siren, the lights speaking about people with problems out of control. Natalie's voice brought him back to the room.

"You've been reading about me," she said. "What's so interesting in the paper?"

Dan sat down and looked through the articles. He had, Natalie saw, a lot of clippings, some of them copied from microfilm. *He's been at the library checking up on me.*

"You've been a busy woman," Dan said. "A detective sergeant in homicide, a police officer for fourteen years. A medal of valor recipient, a result of your handling a bank robbery gone bad, and—"

As Dan continued, Natalie coldly thought about the worst day of her life.

Gone bad? Gone bad is something that happens when you leave the cottage cheese out on the counter. Gone bad is what happens to some kids. This wasn't a robbery gone bad, this was evil, this was terror, and this was death for three customers of the bank. And for two bank robbers. And I spent two weeks at the Disneyland Hotel drinking fruity things with lots of booze in them, wiping the blood off my hands. Gone bad . . . hell, Dan, or whatever your name is, this was a bank robbery from hell.

Natalie sat there and listened to Dan telling her about her career, about what he had leaned from the *Oregonian* newspaper. If she closed her eyes, she knew she could smell the burnt gunpowder, a smell that lingered in a closed room like no other.

Gunpowder and blood. Stephanie. Stephanie, and oh, God the bank.

She shook her head. "Let's not talk about me anymore. Why don't you tell me where we can find this bastard who killed my sister?" Dan looked up from his clippings.

"Florida. Tampa Bay area." His voice was firm now, confident. This he knew about.

"When do we go?" Natalie whispered.

"Tomorrow, in the morning," Dan said, "before someone decides to look for you." He gathered up his clippings and copies, placing them carefully inside the *USA Today* paper. He got up and walked to the door, turning to face Natalie. "Be ready at six. I'll call. Don't go back to your place for any reason."

He opened the door and looked at Natalie for several seconds, and then closed the door softly behind him.

The look on Dan's face stayed with Natalie after he left, a haunted look of pain and of evil remembered, a look that made Natalie wonder what he had really gone through these past two years, and what he had seen.

Nine

In many parts of the south, the dead are "buried" above ground. In Florida, the spit of sand created by the convergence of the waters of the Gulf of Mexico and the Atlantic Ocean, the dead are interred in cement tombs, with caskets inside. The tombs, looking like large cement caskets, are stacked one on top of the other in orderly piles, with roads between, like a large, open warehouse.

Victor Bramson drove his car through the cemetery, his headlights flashing on the cement tombs. He thought they looked like frozen loaves of bread. White tombs with large cement lids, stacked higher than his head.

When he got far enough in, he turned off the ignition and lights. When his eyes adjusted, the graveyard became a contrast of white and dark. An almost full moon made the white cement tombs glow with a fluorescent quality. The places in shadow were black. He got out and walked, carrying what had become the tools of his trade: a new piece of rope, a glass cutter, and a knife. He was wearing dark slacks, deck shoes, and a dark sweatshirt. As he left the car, he caught a sudden scurrying movement in his peripheral vision, something moving on a tomb beside him, at head height. A faint skittering, scraping sound accompanied the movement.

Beetles. Dark beetles, scurrying in the crack where the lid fit over the tomb. He stopped to watch, peering closer in the dark, watching the antennae floating, a waiving, searching for food. As he watched, he put a name to the beetles. A common name. Cockroaches. A very ancient form of life. He watched them for a few minutes, the insects unaware of his presence.

He walked on again, feeling good, the pain in his right leg a distant thing, a pain that was with him when he walked. This was going so well this time, this one in Florida, and so near to home. He found his way through the maze of coffins. When he came to the edge of the cemetery, he continued on, into a residential area, pools of light surrounded by shadow. He walked for several blocks, the streets lined with palm trees, a middle-class section with stucco sides and two-car garages. After two blocks, he turned into an alley without breaking stride and stopped in a shadow.

Victor Bramson stood by the darkened window, a thrill going through him now that he was here at last. He held his tools in his right hand, not expecting to use them tonight, but he liked to be ready if he needed to be. He preferred the warmer climates and weather. He rarely had to break in to see and speak to his search—people left their doors and windows open and unlocked in the summer, as if it were somehow safer if the wind could blow into their windows. In the summer, they talked to their neighbors more, went out more, were not as territorial or insulated in their capsules. In the winter, people could detect intruders more easily, with a change in their artificial environments caused by the slightest noise or wind current.

He especially liked the early fall night in Florida, in this residential area in Broward County, just outside the city limits of Fort Lauderdale.

For most people, it is frightening to go through the dark and walk upon another's property, a front lawn, a driveway—a violation of privacy. When we walk uninvited upon a back lawn, beside a house, where people are sleeping, or eating, unaware of our intrusion, our hearts beat louder, faster, our steps quicken so we can reach the street and get off the property before we are discovered. To walk around a darkened house, a house that does not belong to us, makes us nervous, scared; we are violating the property trust.

For Bramson to go inside a strange house uninvited was a thrilling experience.

For most of the squirming amoeba who inhabit this country, he thought, *to go in is unthinkable.*

To go inside, when you are looking for something to steal, is exciting. To go inside, when you are looking for a person to kill is monstrous—and exciting. And I need the information. No one knows who I am.

Few people move easily in strange houses, in the dark. I am one of them.

I have a purpose, a much more noble and necessary purpose than petty theft. I am going to live forever.

You will all die before me.

The thrill of waiting in the dark, the thought of being inside, in someone else's house, a strange house. The object of his search—his victim—will be sleeping.

The one in Portland was a worthy survivor, and she must be interviewed.

I must stay on target, he reminded himself.

He went inside to watch.

The room was not a surprise, with posters of football players on the wall, young men in silver and black uniforms. The chest on the young man rises and falls, rhythmic. James, the football player.

Gotta come back in the daytime, might be missing too much at night. He reached out and touched the bare shoulder, lightly, his senses alive, hearing each night creak and groan of the house, and the breathing of others in their safe beds.

He brushed the shoulder once more, promising to be back. James's skin was gone, the shoulder a white clavicle.

You will all die before me.

Ten

Natalie sat at the table and looked out the window, staring at the lights of the cars on the street below. She stayed there for an hour, her mind racing with the deaths and killings Dan had just told her about.

She rose and took her clothes off, slowly, folding her jeans and blouse and putting them on the end of the bed.

Damn! I still don't know if I'm doing the right thing, she thought. *Dan (if that's his real name) knows a lot more than he's telling me, but there's something about him, something sad, and I trust him, even though I've only met him two times. No, three.*

She walked to the bathroom in her bra and panties, thought about taking a bath, but realized she was too tired. She brushed her teeth vigorously, looking up at herself in the mirror, grinning, trying on several faces with a foamy mouth, a tactic that usually cheered her up, but it wasn't helping tonight.

She placed her bra on top of her clothes on the bed and pulled a T-shirt from her bag. She left the drapes open and turned the lights off, getting into bed, suddenly lonely. The room felt empty after Dan left.

Natalie Collins drifted off to sleep in a strange bed, sleeping in a hotel in a city she knew so well, feeling like a stranger in a foreign city, hoping she wouldn't dream about things she had seen and done. Her dreams, when they arrived, were not as bad as some, but she couldn't get away with a night without death.

In Natalie's dream she saw old Joe Louis, the retired Joe Louis, working the front door of Caesar's Palace in Las Vegas, greeting the patrons. The one-time best-in-the-world boxer shook the hands of vacationing gamblers. He was dressed in a tuxedo, working the night shift for the dinner show crowd.

"How ya doin'? Pleezed to meetcha."

"Hey, ain't that Joe Louis?"

And then Joe Louis turned to Natalie, who had been standing just behind the boxer, and Joe said, "What about your retirement, Natalie ol' girl? You gonna go down there to Disneyland, down there where people don't die?"

"Yeah, Joe, I'm gonna work in the Happiest Place in the World. Gonna go down there to Anaheim, or maybe even once in a while to Orlando, wear a little uniform, and carry a broom and dustpan.

"Keep the place clean.

"Be around little kids all day.

"Nobody dies at Disneyland, Joe."

It didn't seem strange at all to Natalie that Joe Louis had passed on some years ago, and that they couldn't be having this conversation. Joe was retired, that was all, just like Natalie was going to retire . . . no more death . . . dying not allowed.

"*So pleezed to meetcha.*"

Natalie woke with a jerk, thrashing, kicking her covers, the dream so very real. She sat up groggily, half expecting old Joe Louis to come strolling out of the bathroom, wearing a rubber mask.

Death.

I've seen enough, thank you very much.

She slid her legs over the side of the bed and swayed to her feet. She stumbled toward the bathroom, knowing with a certainty that she was going to take the trip with Dan.

I have to do this one thing. I can't wait here to be indicted and sent away without a fight.

Death and dying. So very pleezed to meetcha.

If Natalie had known then just how bad it would get, she would have cheerfully gone back to looking at bodies, or said, "To hell with the pension," and headed for the Happiest Place in the World.

Thursday, September 21

Journey into Shadowland

One

Grant's knees were weak and his stomach felt as if a camel had crapped in it, but he didn't want any of the others to know that he had been drinking most of the night.

Oh, right. Who you gonna fool, you big-city dick?

At seven a.m. the detectives were all there, waiting at their desks and they knew why he had called them for this early morning meeting. Grant couldn't remember the last time he'd seen Eldredge and Thompson this early in the morning, unless they had been up all night.

Eldredge, at fifty a veteran police officer and homicide investigator, had been raised in Portland's northeast side, in the ghetto, Eldredge broke away from the street, educated himself, and became a police officer. People on the street trusted him, and what's more, so did Natalie.

Kirby, at thirty the youngest detective, a brilliant police officer. At times Grant thought they had grown up on different planets, with extreme differences in lifestyle, dress, and music. Assigned less than a year ago, Kirby had already proven himself to be an able investigator and a good cop. Grant suspected that Kirby was truly in love with Natalie (*Hell, we all are,* he thought) but with the different women Kirby brought to functions, it was hard to tell.

Thompson, a forty-five-year-old workhorse.

Gretchen, their secretary.

Richard Greene sat at his desk and waved to Grant. Greene, in his late thirties, was a competent, studious, analytical detective. A trusted detective.

"Glad you could all make it so early," Grant said. "I don't think I've ever seen Kirby this early in the morning."

"Yeah, and where's the coffee, Grant?" Kirby said. A look from Grant caused him to stop and sit down. This was not the time to joke.

Grant got up and sat on his desk. "We've all heard the rumors. Natalie is about to be indicted for the murder of her sister."

"Man that's a bunch of bullshit," Eldredge said, "and we all know it."

"What I'm going to propose," Grant said, "is that we don't sit around and let I.A. fumble around and come up with some evidence that points to Natalie so they think they have their case won. What we're gonna do, we're gonna help Natalie investigate this crime."

Grant looked around the room. "And I need to know right now if there's anyone here who can't do that. And that's all right, because nobody's assigned to do this investigation, and if I.A. finds out, we're gonna be in deep shit. However, I will take the heat for it, because I'm the senior person here, and we will become investigators for Natalie."

"You gonna draw a line in the dirt with your sword like that guy did at the Alamo, or what?" Kirby asked, standing up, grinning.

"Kirby, sit down and shut up," Grant said.

"Yessir." Kirby sat down.

"We're all in, right?" Eldredge said.

"Okay," Grant said. "We're gonna start small, but there are some other people in this division who would love to help Natalie and help us, and we will include them as we get going. The other option is that we pool some money and hire some private detectives to help Natalie."

"Would you want a private detective to investigate a crime you've been accused of?" Kirby asked.

"Not me," Eldredge said, "and I know some good ones."

"Kirby and Eldredge," Grant said, "I want you both to go back over Natalie's apartment. I.A.'s released the crime scene, and they are thorough—hell, we trained a couple of them—but they didn't find everything. They couldn't have; they don't do this that often. I've got a key to her place, and I want you guys to go over that place until you know every hair, and I want every piece of evidence there is to get from that apartment. I even want photos, and I will decide later where we will send the evidence we find."

"Do I have to work with Eldredge, Sarge? The guy's a walking brain stem," Kirby said, a nasal whine in his voice. He laughed.

Grant glared at him.

"Do I have to work with Junior, Sarge?" Eldredge said, getting out of his chair. "He always wants to go by the high school and drive reeeeel slow, so he can wave at his girlfriends."

"Yeah, you gotta work together," Grant said seriously, "and if you find something, call me and I will seize everything. Hell, I'm eligible for retirement, anyway. No sense you guys getting your peckers whacked this early in the game."

"Captain know about this?" Eldredge asked, leaning back in his chair.

"You see him here?" Grant retorted.

"When do you want us to start?" Kirby asked.

"Yesterday. Get some real cases to take with you when you go out the door so it looks as if you're doing something, for Chrissakes. Thompson, find out everything there is to know about Stephanie, in case she was the target. Greene and I will look at evidence and look for the two bushy-haired strangers."

"What you want me to do, boss?" Gretchen asked. She had worked in homicide as long as anyone could remember.

"I want you to make these yahoos check in with you every hour," Grant said, "and if we need to get in touch, call us. You will know where we are twenty-four hours a day for a while. Let's go."

Kirby started to walk out.

"Where you going now, puppy?" Eldredge asked.

"I never come to work this early, even on payday. I need to come back at my usual nine a.m. so nobody gets suspicious. Besides, I have to say good-bye."

"Good-bye?"

"Yeah, I left someone under my covers, and I need to go home and see for sure who it is."

"I'd better go with you and check her ID, see if she's old enough," Eldredge said dryly, and walked out with Kirby.

Later that day, they found something at Natalie's apartment, and no one in the squad knew what it was. Later, much later, when the puzzle came together, it made sense. But the detectives did know one thing with a certainty: Natalie didn't put it there. It was bizarre. "Spooky," the detectives said. "Frightening," they said when they found out what it was all about.

Two

Natalie angrily threw off her covers and sat up quickly, turning on the light. She had been awake for the past two hours, trying to sleep after the dreams.

The bedside clock said 4:30.

I've got to go on the road, she thought. *I need to do this one thing, and there's nothing else to do. If there was some other way . . .*

Natalie took a shower and got dressed in her jeans and a bright red cotton top. She looked out the window at the deserted streets below, still wet with rain. From her bag, she pulled out a baseball cap, put her Beretta in her waistband, and pulled on her jacket. She left the hotel swinging the bag, feeling better almost immediately, walking in the fresh air and light rain. She walked two blocks to an all-night restaurant and ordered coffee and toast.

"I'm the only one who knows who he is." Dan's statement from the night Stephanie was killed filled her mind. *Oh, yeah, I'll be waiting for your call.*

Natalie was in the lobby a minute after Dan called her, a few minutes after six. The hotel was beginning to wake up. The counter positions were all occupied and a few early risers were already checking out. Dan was sitting on a couch in the middle of the lobby, reading a paper under a large plant. As it was, Natalie almost missed him. *He has a knack for looking like part of the scenery,* she thought. Dan was wearing tan slacks, a white sweater, and a brown leather jacket, looking like a businessman about to take a day off and play. A successful businessman, she thought. His clothes were expensive and new-looking, not the thing you expected someone on the road to wear. She sat down beside him.

He looked over the paper at her.

"Hi," Natalie said brightly. "Where'd you stay last night?"

"Here, of course," Dan said, returning her smile. "I didn't want to have to go too far for our meeting this morning."

"You stayed in the same hotel?"

"Sure, I didn't think anyone would look for me here. You ready?"

"Yeah, I love to travel to warm and exciting places."

"Well," Dan said, picking up his bag, "Florida this time of year is warm, and this certainly should be exciting. Just drop your key off. Your room has been paid."

They walked out then, not hand in hand, but looking like lovers leaving the hotel, each carrying a bag large enough for overnight.

Dan waved for a cab, and from the back he gave the driver Natalie's address.

"I thought you said to not go there," Natalie whispered.

"That was yesterday," Dan said. "Get what you need for a week, and do it in a hurry, and," he added, turning to her, "we need to get your car."

Mount Hood was turning pink in the east when they arrived. The cab stopped at the end of the cul-de-sac and they got out, Dan carrying his small bag. The door to Mr. Barker's deli was closed, and it was dark inside. Dan looked at the marina, wanting to get a better look at the sailboats, but there was no time.

"If your department is looking for you, will they start on a Thursday morning?" Dan asked. He waited as Natalie opened the gate to the stairs.

"No. It's too soon. They don't know what to think today, but it won't take them long." She swung the gate open and they entered the terraced stairway, passing doors to apartments, the landscaping and planters making Dan think of a walk through a greenhouse.

My third time here, and I've never noticed this, Dan thought. *I was a little busy the last two times I was here.*

The damage to the front door had been repaired, the new wood unpainted. "How long will we be gone?" Natalie asked.

"Pack for a week, casual, sweats and clothes for a hot, humid climate."

He walked to the windows. Mount Hood filled the sky to the east, the sun coming up around the south side now. His anxiety was mixed with an emerging excitement. He was going home.

After all this time, I'm going to see my Angel.

"That's why I rented this apartment," Natalie said, coming up behind Dan. "I love to stand here and look at the mountain, and the city lights and river when it's dark."

Dan nodded. It was a great view. The mountain. The river, and the boats. Most of all, the boats. *The Stone boat is gone,* he thought. *A boat I should be on.*

Natalie's car was in the underground garage. They took the elevator from inside the complex, and Dan followed as Natalie walked to her car. She stopped beside a beige Ford Explorer, a four-wheel drive, four-door utility vehicle.

"This it?" he asked, surprise in his voice.

"Yes," she said, unlocking the driver's door and pushing the electric door locks so Dan could get in. Natalie threw her bag and a suitcase in the backseat, and Dan did the same.

He ran his hand over the leather seats. "Nice."

Natalie dove out of the cul-de-sac, accelerating up Front Avenue, toward the business district.

"Where to?"

"Airport."

She entered the freeway and accelerated rapidly, crossing the Willamette River on the Interstate 5 bridge, driving fast and confidently. She glanced over at Dan, who was holding onto the door.

"Scared?"

"Nervous."

"Why? I'm a good driver. I used to chase people on these streets when I was in uniform."

"You want to take a chance and meet some of your fellow officers this morning?" Dan asked.

"Uh, no," Natalie said, and slowed to fifty-five. "Where we flying to, Florida?"

"That's where we will end up," Dan said.

Natalie concentrated on driving at the speed limit the rest of the way to the airport. She was beginning to see just how adept Dan was at eluding those who wanted to find him. She glanced at him again, looking at the clean-shaven face, the strong chin.

Sure hope you're doing the right thing, Minnie Mouse.

She touched the gun in her waistband, reassuring herself.

They made it to the airport in ten minutes. Dan directed her to the No Parking zone in front of the terminal and they stopped.

"Now where?" she asked.

"Follow me." Dan walked to the cab stand and talked to the driver of the nearest cab. He waived to Natalie, and put his bag in the rear seat.

"Downtown," he told the driver as Natalie got in and gave Dan a strange look. They sat together in the back, neither of them speaking until Natalie couldn't stand it. She leaned over and whispered into Dan's ear. "My Explorer will be towed faster than you can pick up a hooker on Eighty-Second Avenue."

"That's the idea," Dan said. "When they really start to look for you—"

"They will run my license plate and find that my car was impounded at the airport. Smart, Danny Boy, but I thought we were going to Florida."

"We are," he whispered.

"We walking?"

"Amtrak," Dan whispered. He looked into her eyes from inches away, and then he smiled. "You may know this city, and may be a good detective, but you have a lot to learn about the ways of the road . . and besides," he whispered, "I hate to fly." He turned to the driver.

"Can you find us a good place for breakfast within walking distance of Union Station?"

"You saw her yesterday?" Grant asked, his voice rising at the end.

"Yeah," Terrance said. "She brought in a beer bottle, said she was working on something, wanted prints off of it. I called to tell you that AFIS has a reply. The prints come back to a Daniel McClellan Harris, from—"

"I don't care where he's from. What kind of bottle is it?"

"Corona."

"Corona, the kind the young puppy attorneys put fruit in?"

"Yeah, that kind, and there's something else—"

"Great, just great, but what the hell was Sergeant Collins doing in the lab yesterday?" Grant was talking to himself as much as asking the question. What the hell was she up to?

"Hey, I don't know, okay? She said it was for a case, but the AFIS hit has caused all kinds of hell to break loose."

"What way?" Grant growled.

"The print, the left ring finger I lifted from the bottle, the guy it belongs to is wanted for murder in Maryland. The Maryland State Police are going nuts."

"I'll be dipped in shit?" Grant yelled, pounding his fist on his desk. "Where the hell did she get the bottle?"

"She didn't say, but I'd say she just got it. The bottle was cold and there was still fresh foam in it when she brought it in."

What the hell you up to, Minnie Mouse?

"Who else knows about this print result?" Grant asked.

"You, me, the AFIS operators, and the Maryland State Police."

"You get any reports yet?"

"They're faxing a summary now, a Sergeant Plenard."

"You in the lab, Terrance?"

"Yep, got here early to go over some reports before the rest of the munchkins get here."

"Stay there. Talk to no one about this. I'll be right there." Grant hung up, then bellowed, "Thompson!"

Thompson looked up from his desk, where he was reading background information about Stephanie.

"Let's go. Bring your research. We may be a while."

Oh, Minnie Mouse, my little stub-nosed cutie—a fresh bottle of Corona with the prints of a killer on it. What the hell you doing, Minnie Mouse?

The high marble ceilings of Portland's Union Station echoed the yells of children and the sounds from the tracks outside. The exterior of the old station had been refurbished, with a new brick façade and sidewalks to make the building look like what it was, a mixture of old and new. Inside, though, the station was a trip through the past—a railway station made of marble. The voice over the loudspeaker bounced off the ceiling and came back at them, a rolling overtone of sound.

Dan paid for the tickets and learned that the Coast Starlight, the connecting train, would be a half hour late, and the Empire Builder, the train that left Portland and journeyed across the northern part of the United States to Chicago, would wait for the coast Starlight. They had two hours to wait.

"I need to be gone for an hour," Natalie said as they sat on a bench. "A personal thing."

Dan stood up, gripping his bag. "Let's go," he said, and started for the door. Natalie ran to catch up, carrying her bag.

"You don't have to go with me on this one," she said as they walked outside. A blue-and-white Portland Police car was coming into the circle drive as Natalie looked for a cab. She turned her head and stood behind Dan, hoping she hadn't been seen, her heart pounding.

This doesn't feel too good, Natalie, weird, hiding from your friends, thinking like, like what? Acting like a fugitive, that's what.

They walked on past, Dan between the car and Natalie, and got into the first empty cab in line.

"Parkrose Cemetery," Natalie said.

Natalie had taken the route through the cemetery hundreds of times, through the oak and fir trees, to the large area of lawn where her mother and father were. Now Stephanie was there, too.

Natalie directed the driver through the maze of roads. Dan got out with her when she told the cab to wait.

"I need to be alone with my family," she said, her mouth tight, fighting tears, and she started off without looking back.

Dan stood beside the cab and watched as Natalie walked away, down a grass-covered knoll, walking around the grave markers, looking more like a little girl as the distance diminished her size. She still walked with the swinging walk he had seen in the hotel last night, girlish yet athletic. She didn't look thirty-six. He suddenly thought that he hadn't had a normal relationship with another person for over two years; there hadn't been a time when he could just sit down and converse with another human being with trust—and truthfulness—or anything approaching love.

This detective with her fears of death and her bright outlook was the first person who even came close to knowing who he was and what he was running from.

You just like her because you told her your story, because she hasn't had you arrested yet, because of this great catharsis, you fool.

Dan shook his head. No. He'd seen people react to Natalie. They didn't just like her, they loved her. He watched as Natalie slowed her walk, her knees bending, now a staggering walk. She stopped before a headstone and drew her arms up around her chest, hugging herself. She kneeled and then leaned her head against the headstone. From over a hundred yards, he could see her body shake with sobs.

As Natalie leaned her head against the cool surface, the names of her parents etched on the smooth stone, the tears came steadily. Her tears ran down to the rough parts of the carvings, making the light gray a darker color. She shook, the tears falling in a stream off her chin. Natalie felt so terribly alone. Her parents, her sister, and now her department were denied to her.

Oh, Daddy, now what am I gonna do? Our Stephie's dead, and I have to go away. I don't even know if it's the right thing, but I have to do something, don't I? I just don't know if I'll be back. Stephie's over there, no marker yet, I thought something with Minnie and Mickey on it, you think?

Natalie stayed there until she was dry, no more tears left, and when her knees ached, she got up and looked around. It was as if she had fallen asleep outside, in the sun, and had awakened to wonder where she was. She looked in the direction of Stephanie's grave and decided against walking there.

"I'll get him for you, Steph," she whispered, her lower lip quivering. She walked slowly to the cab. As she approached, Dan held the door open for her. Natalie got in, and the cab started to move.

"Whaddya think, we're in a library?" Natalie said. "They can't hear us, so we don't have to whisper." She smiled, tried to laugh, and couldn't.

"We have an hour," Dan said quietly, looking at her, seeing the pain in her smile.

I've been pitying myself for so long that I don't see anyone else, he thought. He touched Natalie's hand and she looked up.

"Where to now?" he asked.

"I need money," Natalie said, and then added to the driver, "Union Station, but I need a money machine first."

They had thirty minutes to go when they got back. The station was crowded now. Natalie and Dan had to weave their way through travelers to get to the center of the building.

"I'm going to call Grant," Natalie said, and Dan nodded, following her through the crowd, heading for the far wall. She found a quiet bench, and dialed Grant's cell phone with Dan's prepaid phone.

Grant didn't answer, so she texted him and entered 66--9-1-1. This code never failed to work, one she and Grant had used for years. The two sixes were for the letters on the phone dial, MM, for Minnie Mouse, and the 911 meant emergency. Grant would know that she had called him from the number that would show up on his phone. Grant would know it was an emergency. Natalie looked at the graffiti on the walls above her, old carvings scratched out and replaced by a new generation. The phone rang.

Dan turned from looking at the crowd and looked at Natalie.

"Grant."

"Where the hell are you girl?"

"Public place."

"I *know* that, but *where?*"

"Grant, there's no time. Have you—"

"Natalie, listen to me," he said, urgency in his voice. There was something else there that scared Natalie.

Grant was afraid. She didn't know that Grant was capable of fear. He was afraid for her and that scared her even more.

"We got the print analysis from the lab. AFIS made a match. The damned bottle was a cold one, the lab told me, and Natalie, for Chrissakes, where the hell are you?"

"Grant, I'll call you again and soon. Just tell me."

"Natalie," Grant said, talking fast, trying not to yell, "the prints belong to a subject by the name of Daniel McClellan Harris, and he's wanted for the murder of his wife in Maryland." At the end, Grant was fairly yelling again, and then he lost control. He screamed into the phone.

"Minnie Mouse, for Chrissakes, don't do this to me! Where the fuck are you?"

Natalie held the phone away from her ear and stared at Dan. He had his back to her, looking out at the lobby. Who the hell was this Dan? He said that the man who killed Stephanie had killed his wife. What the hell was going on? Natalie touched the handle of her gun and looked at Dan. Was he the murderer? Was he a victim? Why was he here? Why had he saved her life? She wanted to, needed to believe him, but she felt the trust slipping away. She heard a loud sound coming from the receiver in her hand. Grant. He was yelling into the phone.

"Grant?"

"Natalie, where the hell are you?"

Dan tapped on Natalie's shoulder, pointing toward the track side of the lobby. He mouthed, "Let's go."

"Grant, I'll call you later, tonight, and —."

"Natalie, Godammit!"

"Grant, listen to me," she said urgently, "have you read the reports yet with the case?"

"No, but—"

"Get them. Read them. I'll call, I'll keep you posted. And Grant, I love you, love to Aimee. Trust me." Natalie said it all in one breath, and then she flipped the phone closed. She picked up her bag, giving Dan a blank look. She took a step toward the doors and stopped.

"You coming, or you gonna walk to Florida?" Natalie elbowed her way through the crowd and out onto the asphalt apron by the tracks. Dan followed, watching her push her way out the door, her purposeful strides making her seem much bigger than she was. She stopped and dug her ticket from her bag, showed it to a ticket agent, and followed his outstretched arm to locate their train.

Whatever she had heard on the phone didn't make her happy, Dan thought. He hurried to catch up.

Guess I'll have to tell her what really happened—and soon.

Three

"Dammit!" Grant slammed the phone down and yelled for Thompson. He grabbed his coat and lurched for the door, and then stopped. *Christalmighty!* He turned around and looked at Thompson, who was still seated at his desk. Thompson was shaking his head. Grant walked back and put his coat on the back of his chair.

If she's flying, she's long gone now.

He dropped in his chair and slumped down. His inability to act, to do something positive to help Natalie was maddening, and he knew he would have to do something soon or he would literally explode. He was saved from some very unpleasant thoughts by Gretchen, who was calling his name from the door.

"Grant."

He swiveled around and faced her, still slumped in his chair. She was holding a thick stack of papers, maybe seventy-five sheets or so. "You want this? It's from the Maryland State Police."

Grant lurched out of his chair so fast she took a step backward, into the doorway. He jumped across the room and snatched the papers from her, getting an evil look from their secretary.

The top paper was a fax cover sheet, with the Maryland State Police logo on the top. The sheet was signed by a Sergeant Plenard, with his phone number and a note that said, "Call ASAP" on the bottom. The cover sheet was followed by sixty-two pages. *Jesus, this is the biggest file I've ever seen sent by fax,* Grant thought. Most were a few pages, and usually when there was something this large to send, the other agency mailed it. Grant flipped the page over and began on the second page.

The heading said that it was a summary of the Daniel McClellan Harris/Jacqueline Cooper Harris homicide that took place on October 28, almost two years ago. Grant read the report for thirty minutes, not looking up when Thompson asked if he wanted him to stay. Grant said, "Stay," without taking his eyes from the page. When he was finished, he was confused, scared for Natalie, and more than a little shaken by what he had read.

What the hell was Natalie doing? Was she with a killer—one of the men who was in her apartment? And what the hell was the AFIS hit all about? *She's been conducting her own investigation.* Grant had heard some background noise, a terminal, a loudspeaker, like the airport.

He sat back and looked around. Thompson was still there across the room, sitting at his desk. Grant rubbed his eyes and picked up the phone to call Sergeant Plenard.

When I'm done talking to him, he's gonna be as confused as I am.

As the phone rang, he thought of what he had read. He believed Natalie—there was no doubt in his mind that the events happened the way she said they did. There had been two men in the apartment that night, and one of them was named Daniel McClellan Harris, from Maryland. And the man had been charged with the murder of his wife. Some of the evidence was so damned similar to Natalie's case, he didn't know what the hell was going on. Natalie was usually right about her instincts. About people.

What Grant didn't know, couldn't know, was that he would set into play a chain of events that would make Natalie a fugitive, and every law enforcement officer on the East Coast would be looking for her and her companion.

Four

The giant snake could feel the vibrations of the prey, closer now, crouching, fearful. Although the snake could not hear, the sense of sound was transmitted by the floor of the cage, and it quickly sensed the movement through its entire length.

The prey's rapid heartbeat, a miniature, arrhythmic drum roll, exposed its fright, its all-consuming terror. The snake felt it, smelled it, and raised its head, the black strips sweeping back from the unblinking eyes giving it an even more menacing look. The eyes, covered by transparent lids, did not see the prey, didn't need to.

The snake's tongue suddenly flicked out, catching the trail of the prey. Receptors in the tongue sent messages to the Jacobson's organ in the roof of the reptile's mouth, and a chemical reaction aroused the acute sense of smell. The thirteen-foot boa constrictor weighed sixty pounds, and hadn't eaten for a month. The snake had lived in the cage for almost a year, in the tank below the window, in the Spanish-style house with the red tile roof, north of Clearwater, Florida. A pet.

A pet belonging to a monster.

The snake and the prey were left alone in the dark. The boa was a nocturnal hunter.

The prey, in its terror, never moved from the glass side of the cage. The boa moved slowly, steadily, and in the end, didn't wrap around the prey, didn't have to. With a quick movement, the snake shifted its body and pinned the prey. It didn't take long for the prey to suffocate. The snake ate the prey whole, unhurriedly, its saliva covering the skin of the prey, a ritual that took place once or twice a month.

It was dark. No one witnessed the end.

*   *   *

The brake lights flashed in front of him and the car swerved, causing Victor to brake hard and jerk the wheel, the antilock brakes giving him the control to miss.

"Idiot!"

Victor Bramson swerved back into the right lane and slowed even more, shaken and brought back to reality. It was now full daylight, the early morning sun glaring off the Gulf waters to his left. The car that stopped in front of him, a red sports car of some kind, was slowing for a hot dog stand that had been set up at the freeway exit. The vendor, a young girl of about twenty, was wearing a string bikini. The bikini had a small patch of cloth in the genital area, with a waist string, connected to the patch by a string running up between her buttocks. "Butt-floss bikini," the native Floridians called them. *The driver of the red car must be a tourist,* Bramson thought, *to stop so suddenly.* The two men were ordering now, with silly grins on their faces.

He had driven the two hundred fifty miles from Fort Lauderdale in just four hours. He was almost home, driving north along the Gulf Boulevard, on a narrow spit of land that had Boca Ciega Bay on his right and the Gulf of Mexico on his left. The city of Saint Petersburg was to the east, and Clearwater was north.

He made it to his house in Crystal Beach in another twenty-five minutes. He pulled into the garage to the beach house and triggered the remote for the garage door. The garage was remarkable for the absence of rakes, shovels, lawn mowers, and the collective accumulation that infests garages the world over. Victor Bramson's garage had finished, textured walls, painted white, and except for the Honda Accord he drove in, the garage looked too immaculate, sterile.

He turned the key off and sat in his car, unmoving. The young man in Fort Lauderdale would be ready soon. It was important that he take him at the optimum time. He got out of the car, and walked to the door that led into the house. From the inside, the view of the Gulf was breathtaking. The usual cloud buildup in the afternoon often put on a spectacular show.

Inside, the floors were tile on the lower level, with hardwood on the second floor. The house was U-shaped, with a swimming pool in the middle of the U. Bramson didn't use the pool, and he was certain that no one else would, either. The area below the pool sloped down to the ocean.

Bramson walked through the living room to the stairway by the front door, and then went up to his office.

On the wall of the stairway, there was a large painting of an ancient sailing ship running before a storm, a large square-sterned sailing vessel of the 1500s. It was a painting of Ponce de León's flagship. A wooden bark.

In his office, Victor absently picked through his mail. He held a letter up to the light, a letter with the return address of the American Institute of Longevity in Chicago, Illinois. He threw the envelope in a pile and made a sound that could have been a laugh, but was harsh, brutal.

Those fools. They think that with their puny experiments into genetic manipulation to extend life they would catch me. Never. They will be studying their ways to extend lives in worms and fruit flies until they themselves drop over dead.

You will all die before me.

There was a glass tank under the window in the living room, a terrarium that was a full thirty feet long, with built-up rock and sand. Victor approached the tank and peered through the glass, looking for his baby.

"Oh, there you are, darling," he said, his delight at finding his pet in his voice. "Come on out and see me," he coaxed. He reached behind him and removed a large glove from a desk, a thick glove made of Kevlar.

The snake did not move, its tongue testing the air.

Victor reached into the cage, carefully putting his hand down, waiting for the strike. The rabbit was gone. He started to move his hand down toward the snake, slowly, grinning, anticipating what was to happen.

The snake struck so quickly, so powerfully that it knocked his hand into the side of the cage. The power and force stung, and Victor jerked his hand out, smiling now, thinking that he should quit this deadly game before got hurt, but he couldn't resist.

The snake was seventy-eight years old. And this species had a normal life span, at the outer limits, of thirty years.

Humans. How long do they live, in their squirming, yeasty crawl to stay alive? Seventy-five, eighty, sometimes ninety years. It was absurd, and yet so simple. The masses of crawling amoeba, whose lives are remarkable only to themselves, fight with their last breaths to keep their miserable selves alive. And for what?

Victor took the glove off and placed it on the desk, looking at the snake. The fact that she outlived her natural life limit by a factor of two made her more valuable than all the human masses of yeast combined. She held the key to the future. *A key I have*, Victor thought.

You will all die before me.

The studies now going on in other parts of the world suggest that humans can live to be up to four hundred years old. Or longer. And I have the secret. And a few others. A few others strategically placed in the world to thwart me.

But not for long.

He sat down at his desk and began to look through newspaper clippings he had saved for his research.

I know the secret. And in four hundred years, while I still live, I will control the secret, as I do now.

The others are just too focused on the wrong set of facts, The studies must take into account the intangible factors of accident, failure, and disease.

He picked up another clipping and held it up to the light, studying it, looking at the picture. Miranda Hernandez, of San Antonio, Texas.

She knows way too much, and I have to find out what it is and how she found out. A twelve-year-old. They can be just as dangerous as the full-grown ones. First the football player in Fort Lauderdale. Then the woman in Portland. Then Miss Hernandez. I'm getting close, and I have all the time I need.

They will all die before me.

Victor Bramson made his plans, excited, not wanting to wait. Fly to Fort Lauderdale this afternoon and get it over with. Give the final exam to the football player.

And then the first getting-acquainted trip to San Antonio to visit the young girl. She might have more knowledge and power than some of the old ones.

And the one in Portland. She'll tell me what she knows before I kill her.

Five

The Amtrak Superliner car had twenty-five passengers, a fraction of its capacity. Natalie walked up the stairs to the upper level where the seats were, and took a window seat on the left side. She put her bag on the floor in front of her. Dan followed and took the aisle seat.

Natalie leaned back in the seat and closed her eyes. *I'm really doing it*, she thought, realizing that the journey would change her life forever. But she knew that she couldn't stay in Portland and wait for the inevitable.

It was one thing for Dan to hint to me that he was accused of killing his wife, and for me to deduce that he was accused of it. It's another thing altogether for Grant to tell me that Dan is wanted in Maryland for murder; that the machinery of government had decided that Dan had killed someone and had put out an arrest warrant for him.

I want to believe him. I need to believe him, so I can believe that Stephanie wasn't killed because of me, because of my work. If Dan were truly a victim as Stephanie and I have been, then the last two years of his life would have been an incredible nightmare, a man on the run, man who had lost the person he loved and then was accused of it.

Natalie glanced over at Dan. He was leaning back in his seat with his eyes closed.

"Have tickets ready, please." Natalie looked up to see the conductor, a tall man with a round blue cap and dark blue jacket, at the front of the car.

If Dan were a victim, he could indeed be a fine man whose life had been destroyed, a man who now only wanted to destroy the man who killed his wife. If he were not, if he were part of a sick and sinister conspiracy to kill Stephanie and then me, then he might have a go at it again.

Natalie shook her head. *No, I've worked this job too long*, she thought. *I think he is who he says he is. And it must have been a very lonely journey for him these past two years.*

She glanced over at Dan and then looked at him as if she were seeing him for the first time. *He must have money or access to a lot of money. He wears expensive slacks, sweaters, jackets, and he wears them well, as if he's used to them. It could be part of his disguise for traveling on the road, but he would still need money to do that. His face is so much different than the first time I saw it.* Dan had a strong face. He was a handsome man.

Dan's hair had receded to the middle of his head, was light brown, and neatly trimmed. He looked to be in his early forties, and although she didn't know it, Dan had looked much younger two years ago.

I need to know him better. He's done something most people could not or would not do—he has tracked a killer, and by his diligence, by his skill, he saved my life. Natalie opened her eyes.

"You ride trains much?"

Dan opened his eyes and looked at her. "Yes." He closed his eyes again.

"Aren't very talkative today, are we?" Natalie asked.

Dan sat there with his eyes closed.

"Well, I want you to tell me everything about yourself, Mr. Daniel McClellan Harris." She said his name clearly, enunciating each syllable, and it got the desired result. Dan's eyes jerked open, and he stared at her.

"How did you get my name?" he whispered fiercely.

"It's a long story," Natalie said, "but remember, I'm a detective, and a damned fine one."

"The phone call," Dan said.

Natalie nodded. "Yes."

"But I don't understand," Dan said. He looked bewildered. "I never gave you my name. How did you get my full name?"

"As I said, I'm a detective. The beer bottle in the deli, I took it and found your prints on it . . . your left ring finger." Natalie reached down and took Dan's left hand in hers. "This one," she said, pulling his finger up.

"Your tickets, please," a voice said above them. The train was moving now, slowly crossing the Willamette River on a black steel bridge. At another time, Natalie would have marveled at the beauty of the city, the sparkling water far below, the river surrounded by parks and buildings, snow-capped Mount Hood rising up out of green misted forests like a white monolith.

Natalie dropped Dan's hand and took her ticket from her bag. Dan was looking at his hand as if it had betrayed him. "Dan," she said, "your ticket." She nudged Dan, and he continued to stare at his left hand.

"Your ticket, sir."

"In the bag," Dan said absently. Natalie pulled Dan's bag to her lap, found the ticket, and gave it to the conductor.

"All right, you folks all the way through to Chicago. The train is not very full, so you folks let me know if you want to change seats." He walked on by them.

"The bottle in the deli. I got your prints from it and had them sent through AFIS."

"What's ayfus?" Dan asked.

"AFIS is an acronym for Automated Fingerprint Identification System," Natalie said. "The print we got from the bottle was on a computer in the AFIS system, and we got a match on Daniel McClellan Harris, who incidentally is wanted by the Maryland State Police for the murder of his wife. The Maryland State Police in Baltimore would very much like to talk to you."

"Yeah, I just bet they would," Dan said bitterly. "So what are you gonna do with me now?"

"Why, we're going to Florida," Natalie said brightly.

"You want to go to Florida with me after you know this?" Dan shook his head. "Aren't you afraid," he asked softly, "that I will attempt to kill you on the way or after we get there?"

"Nope."

"You're truly not?"

"Nope. I've made up my mind," Natalie said, smiling. Her voice was light. "I've made up my mind about you, buster," and she tapped him in the chest with her index finger. "And don't be so morose, for now for the first time you have someone who believes in you, and I don't know why, but I do, I do believe you . . . and I believe," she said in a whisper, "that you saved my life." Natalie picked up his left hand and held it close.

Dan blinked back tears, and he was afraid to talk.

"If we are to defeat this man, this thing, you must tell me everything." She turned and looked closely at him.

"Everything. Everything about yourself. Because somewhere in your background and mine is the key to what links us together. We have to find that. Then we'll know how to get the son of a bitch who killed my sister and your wife.

"And," Natalie said, "it must feel good to have someone who you can talk to, someone who believes you. Right?"

Dan's lower lip quivered.

Ohmigod. I guess I'm getting too serious here, Natalie thought.

"Hey," she said, turning to face her new partner. "What kind of work did you do before all this, Dan?"

Dan sat there.

"I know," Natalie said, looking at his bald forehead. She slapped her hand to her forehead, pulling her hair back. "You were a Rogaine poster child?"

No response.

"Or, you were a model for the Hair Club for Men?" She laughed. This time Dan grinned at her, self-conscious.

"Hey," Natalie said excitedly, poking at Dan with her finger. "You hungry? I'm starved."

"Me, too," Dan said.

"It talks. Let's see if they have some food in this joint." She stood up, short enough to stand fully under the overhead. They walked forward, Natalie lurching as the train swayed, bending her knees. As they progressed to the lounge car, she got better at anticipating the train's movements. The lounge car was a domed observation car on top, with a stairway in the middle of the car to the lower-level snack bar and lounge.

They were leaving Vancouver, Washington, racing east along the Columbia River. "We're reaching track speed," Dan said, standing behind Natalie. The train rocked and lurched, and Natalie swayed back into Dan.

"How fast is that?" Natalie asked. "We seem to be going fast, way too fast."

"Track speed for Amtrak is seventy-nine miles per hour," Dan said, and started down the stairway. At the bottom, the snack bar was to their right; there were booths and tables on their left. A woman was standing at the counter, and a small girl about four was behind her, swinging on a metal rail. She was wearing a white summer dress with pink flowers, and had black curly hair.

"Janie, stop that," the woman at the counter said without turning around. The girl hooked a leg over the bar and tried to pull herself up on top as if she didn't hear her mother. She looked up as Dan and Natalie walked down the stairs.

"Can't get . . . up here," she said, looking at Dan, gritting her teeth.

"Need some help?" he asked, leaning down over the girl.

The woman at the counter turned around "Janie!" And then to Dan, "I'm sorry she's in your way. Janie! Get down!"

Janie appeared to not have heard her mother. Dan reached down and lifted her to the top of the bar and she grinned up at him.

"Thanks. Now I'm tall as Mommy."

"You sure are," Dan said, grinning back at her. He picked her up off the bar and set her lightly on her feet beside her mother.

"I'm sorry," she began, "she's—"

"A cutie," Dan finished for her.

They ordered croissant sandwiches and beer at the snack bar, and sat at a booth in the back. Natalie watched the Columbia River roll by as Dan started eating. He reached for the beer bottle and then stopped, looking at Natalie.

"I don't need another print from you," she said, picking up her sandwich, realizing how starved she was. She took a huge bite, watching Dan's eyebrows go up. Her gun was digging into her side, and she put the sandwich down and reached for it, carefully putting it into her bag, turning her body so no one could see.

"Does this mean you're not going to shoot me with it?" he asked, looking over his sandwich at her.

"Well, not now, anyway."

They watched the river as they ate, entering the Columbia River Gorge as they finished, the mountain towering above them, cliffs covered with mist from waterfalls.

"Why Amtrak?" Natalie asked. "Why not travel by plane?" She stuffed the last bit of her sandwich in her mouth.

"A lot of reasons," Dan said. "It's a good place to hide, to think, a good place to be on the road. Nobody looks for you here. Most train stations are dilapidated and run down, not very many police. You go through more scrutiny at airports, you have to check your bags, and," he took a swallow of beer, "shall I go on?"

"No," Natalie said laughing.

"And," Dan said, looking at her, "you don't travel by plane. A plane takes you from place to place. You travel on foot, on two wheels, on a ship or train, but a plane, to go on a plane is not traveling."

"Were you a Rogaine poster child?" Natalie grinned.

Dan grimaced, and put his hand up to his balding head.

"I did lots of things," he said. "I had a business in New York, in the stock market when I was younger. I made some money, and then I moved to Maryland, to my hometown, and built boats."

"Boats?"

"Yes, like the wooden sailboat we saw in the marina near your apartment. Sailboats. I built boats with my hands."

Natalie leaned forward, looking at Dan. "You know so much about me, tell me about you. Where did you grow up?"

"Chesapeake Bay area. On the water. My dad was a waterman. He fished, crabbed, harvested oysters, anything that was in season and paid."

"You worked on a boat?"

"I helped Dad until I graduated from high school."

"Were you a nerd in high school, like now?" Natalie asked, winking at him.

"Not then, but I suppose it would seem so now, to someone as young as you."

"I'm not young," Natalie protested, "I'm ancient."

"A grandmother."

"A great-grandmother," Natalie said, "I'm sorry, tell me about yourself; I'll be quiet."

That's not possible, Dan thought, not unkindly.

He had grown up on the banks of the Chesapeake Bay, Dan told Natalie. His parents had both grown up there, both from families of watermen, and for much of his life, Dan thought he would be a waterman like his dad. When he was eight, his father built him a sailing dory, and Dan spent his free time sailing in the Little Choptank and Trippe bays. He played football for Cambridge High School, across the bay and south from the U.S. Naval Academy at Annapolis. As he grew older, he wanted to live in the big cities and get away from small-town life. And he did. University of Maryland, and then on to New York. The stock exchange years were good to Dan. He met and married Jacqueline Cooper there, and they went home for a visit. He fell in love with the bay again, the quiet small-town life, the wind off the water, the boats.

He took Jackie sailing and told her what he wanted to do. He wanted to raise their children on the bay, he wanted to build boats—to live in a small town again. To his surprise, she agreed. They were both tired of the city, the hectic schedules, and Dan could work with his hands again.

They had been back on the bay for two years when Jackie was murdered.

Natalie had listened quietly, watching Dan as he talked. He stopped and looked out the window. He took a sip of his beer, now warm and flat. "The bay is such a big part of your life when you grow up on it," he said quietly, "and when I moved back, I knew that I would die there."

"You're a real person," Natalie said, touching his hand. "Thank you for sharing that with me."

"Yes, Natalie Collins, I am a real person . . . and I had a real wife, and it seems . . . it seems so long ago." Dan took her hand in his and looked at her. "In the last few days, I've felt as if I could get a life back, talking to you, listening to you tell me that you believe me—" Dan stopped, his eyes watering, and he looked away, out the window at the moving scenery, the Columbia River and the cliffs.

Natalie squeezed his hand, thinking that there was something missing here, that she had forgotten something. And she remembered how he had been with the little girl at the snack bar, a little one who had been sitting across from them in a booth with her mother. Children. Of course, Dan was a daddy. That's why he was so good with her.

Better than me, since I don't have any kids and am not likely to. Steph either, and we weren't particularly comfortable around them. Dan, he has kids.

"You have kids, don't you, Dan?" Natalie asked, stilling holding his hand. He looked from the window at Natalie, and the tears came then, nodding, yes, and he put his head down on the table, his body shaking. The tears rolled off his cheeks, hot onto the table. Natalie reached across the table and put her hands on the back of his neck, touching him. And before she could think about it, she suddenly slid out from her seat and slid in next to Dan, the woman and small girl looking at them. She put her arms around his shoulder, and then pulled his head into her chest, putting both her arms around him as he shook, silently crying.

"Mommy, why is that nice man crying?"

"Shush, be quiet, color your book."

"I'm gonna ask him, 'kay Mommy?"

"No."

They stayed like that until long after Dan stopped crying, the arms around him the first human touch he had felt in way too long. When he thought he had his emotions under control enough to look up, he took Natalie's arms and loosened them. He pulled his head up and opened his eyes, looking into hers from inches away.

"Thanks," he whispered.

"Sure," Natalie said brightly, unsure of her own emotions now, not wanting to think about what she'd felt while holding Dan. This was supposed to be a quick trip to find a killer. A business trip.

"Mr. Man." A little voice came from Natalie's side. Dan looked up to see the little girl with dark curls and brown eyes standing at Natalie's elbow.

"Janie, come here." Her mother reached for her.

"It's okay," Dan said. He leaned across the table and took her hand. "I was crying because I have a little girl like you, and I haven't seen her in a long time."

"Why don't you go see her?" Janie asked.

"I'm going to see her now," Dan said. And he would. The killer could wait. He would see his Angel if it was the last thing he did. Even if for a little while. Feeling better than he had in a long time, Dan got out from the booth and ordered two more beers for them. They had a lot to discuss.

"Who's your favorite actress?" Natalie asked. She returned from the snack bar with another beer and sat across from Dan, folding her legs on the bench seat.

Dan took a sip of beer. "Ellen Barkin."

"Ellen Barkin? Why her? How long have you been out here on the road?"

"You ever see *The Big Easy*?"

Natalie nodded.

"Sexy, that's why," Dan said matter-of-factly. "She was very hot in that movie. Who's your favorite actor?"

"That's an easy one—my Kevin."

Dan gave her a blank look.

"Kevin Costner, you fool. You see him in *The Bodyguard*?"

"No."

"*Robin Hood*?"

"Oh sure, I saw him in *Robin Hood*. Which one was he?"

Natalie leaned over and punched him in the arm, and stared dreamily at the window. "When he licked that arrow, I fell to my knees."

Dan laughed so loudly and suddenly that the bartender at the other end of the car looked up at them. He laughed until his stomach hurt, feeling better than he could remember. Natalie grinned and reached across and held his hands, grinning, a good and silly feeling.

Now I'm going to see my daughter, Dan thought.

He should have known it would be extremely dangerous to see Angelina. Dangerous for everyone.

Six

"**Why** do I have to carry this damned thing?" Kirby lugged the large evidence collection kit up the stairs to Natalie's apartment. The kit contained implements for collecting, examining, and preserving trace evidence.

"I don't mind your bitching as long as you still do the carrying," Eldredge said.

This un's real bad, Eldredge thought.

Since Sergeant Natalie had joined their unit, she made their job more bearable. Her delightful, bubbly outlook on life was enough to send most of them into fits of laughter, particularly when she first started. And most of them felt protective of Natalie.

I certainly do, he thought.

Eldredge had been in this business a long time, having grown up in Portland. He played football for Portland State University on a scholarship, and started with the Portland Police Bureau twenty-eight years ago.

He loved the city, the wooded hills, the Willamette River and Columbia River a part of the city. The deaths didn't affect him the way they did Natalie. Oh, he knew she'd been having problems lately. They all knew it.

He put the key Grant had given him into her door. They went in and Kirby put the case down.

"Where you want to start?" the younger detective asked. They stood there and looked around.

"You been here before, Eldredge?"

"Once at a party. You were here, dumbshit."

Eldredge walked over and opened all of the blinds. "We start with his trail, where Stephanie's killer was. We know for sure that he entered, was in the bedroom, Stephanie's bathroom, the hallway, the living room. So we're gonna—"

"Check every room," Kirby said, sighing.

"You got it, puppy. You start high in the living room, the kitchen area. I'll start with the bedrooms, and then we'll switch and do the entire thing again. Then the carpets. We'll do the carpets together."

Kirby photographed the entire interior of the apartment before they started. With the photos, Natalie might be able to tell if something were missing or out of place, and they knew it might be easier for her to do so with photos, instead of actually being in the apartment.

Kirby left for some coffee and returned. Eldredge continued in Stephanie's bedroom, Kirby in Natalie's. Kirby sat on her bed and stared at the dresser, looking at the objects on top of it.

If she was your target, you were in here. Weren't you, you son of a bitch? You found Natalie's gun in here. You had to look at where she slept, where she lived, at her personal things. And did you take something, asshole? Did you take something from our Natalie?

He stared at the figurines on the dresser, a collection of Walt Disney characters. They were all there: Mickey Mouse, Pluto, Goofy, Donald Duck and the other ducks, Tigger and the other Winnie the Pooh characters, characters from movies, *The Little Mermaid, Snow White, 101 Dalmatians.*

Hell, I couldn't tell if there were a dozen or more of the little guys missing.

"Kirby, get your ass in here!" Eldredge yelled from Stephanie's room. "And bring your camera."

Kirby saw Eldredge lying on the carpet in Stephanie's bedroom, looking at the nap of the carpet with a large magnifying glass.

"What?" Kirby asked.

Eldredge didn't answer right away, just grunted.

Kirby knew that Eldredge had heard him, that it wouldn't do to ask him again. The older detective took a pen from his pocket and carefully placed it on the carpet, the pen becoming a pointer so Kirby could find the object. Eldredge got up slowly and handed the magnifying glass to his partner. "Take a look for yourself. There, on the carpet."

Kirby took the magnifying glass and lowered himself to a prone position, on the side of the bed next to the window, a place where Natalie said they were fighting. The ball point of the pen looked as thick as a baseball bat in the magnifying glass, the carpet fibers looked like saplings.

On top of the carpet, suspended, like a mountain climber suspended in a hammock, was a gray object the size of a dime. Only it had imperfect, serrated edges, and what the hell was it?

Kirby stood up.

"The hell you think it is, Eldredge?"

"I don't know for sure, but we're taking it."

The piece of evidence they collected that day was unremarkable by itself. But Kirby was right—the killer had to have looked at Natalie's private things, he had to have been in her bedroom.

Had to take something, didn't you?

And what they found took them on a journey as well.

Seven

"**Stephanie** Walker was not sexually assaulted, nor was she killed in a manner to suggest sexual attack, either by an organized or disorganized killer." Lieutenant Derry stepped up to a large display pad and wrote "2. No sexual assault."

The line above it read, "1. Killed at home."

"How is that evidence?" Sims asked. Derry and Nichols were going through the evidence again. They were assembled in the District Attorney's private conference room. Lieutenant Derry was at the front of the room, writing on a large display pad.

"Most women killed in a stranger-to-stranger contact are killed as the result of a sexual fantasy, and are killed by men. If we are to believe Natalie's story, her sister Stephanie was killed before Natalie arrived home. There was no evidence of sexual assault, and while that is not evidence, it is arguable that there was no assault because there was not a man there as Natalie has said.

"Number three," Derry said, "she has no witnesses to the alleged assault or fight. No one heard anything." He wrote it on the pad. And then he wrote in succession:

4. Natalie's gun used to kill Stephanie
5. Apparent staged scene
6. Majority of homicide victims know their assailant
7. Natalie's dress had high velocity blood spatter on the sleeve
8. Blood spatter is Stephanie's blood
9. Sergeant Natalie Collins is an expert pistol shot, and she missed two men?
9. Didn't make herself available for interviews as ordered

"Well," Sims said writing on a pad, "we've gone with less and convicted. I think we're ready for grand jury. I have no doubt that we'll indict Ms. Collins for murder."

Eight

"**If** I were any happier, I'd just shit," David Attinger muttered to himself as he entered the waiting room of the district attorney's office. *I have a real case, my client's missing, and the D.A. wants to talk, thinks this is a winner.*

Attinger was dressed in what he called his felony tweeds—a green corduroy jacket from Sears, the elbows showing the wear of the lunch counters around the courthouse, looking more like something out of a transient's trousseau than from an attorney's wardrobe. His best slacks were five dollars away from Levi's, and his shirt, well, at least he had his white shirts cleaned and pressed at the laundry. His tie came from the rack at the Goodwill store, and his shoes were the newest hiking boots he could find in his closet.

Attinger had his own ideas about appropriate attire in the courtroom, the trenches, as he liked to call it. He knew it pissed off the attorneys in their thousand-dollar suits if he beat them, and he did often enough to make it profitable. He was not of the same fraternity, and it was a double blow for the establishment lawyers to lose to someone who dressed as he did.

"Good afternoon, ladies," he said to the three receptionists as he approached the counter. Two of them pretended not to notice. The third looked up, grimaced, and then looked down at her desk.

"I have a meeting with the Most High Assistant District Attorney of Multnomah County, Mr. Sims, and I'm sure if you would alert him of my presence in the building, he would have you send me right in."

A door opened on the side of the waiting room, and Sims waved to him, smiling, as if he had just heard a private joke.

The games are beginning, Attinger thought.

"Boy, don't you look nice," Attinger said.

"Hell, David," Sims said, shaking Attinger's hand, "transients dress better'n you. Come on in." Sims winked at the receptionists, and the two men entered into the labyrinth of hallways and offices. Attinger knew it well; he had been an assistant district attorney for two years, and had prosecuted cases with Sims, something the assistant D.A. would like to forget.

Sims made introductions and waved Attinger to a chair.

"You gonna indict Detective Sergeant Natalie Collins, or what?" Attinger said as he sat down.

"I've always admired your directness, David," Sims said. "If you could bring her in, well, we could probably clear this all up."

"She's on vacation," Attinger said. "And, while we are on the subject of bringing her in, I must tell you that she has retained me to take care of any legal matters she may have while she is recovering from the loss of her sister." He looked around the room at the others. "Any contact with Detective Sergeant Natalie Collins of any kind, particularly while she is a suspect in a criminal matter, will be made through me, and only me."

"Suspect?—why David, we just want to talk with her, and—"

"Don't bullshit me, Sims," Attinger said quietly. "You folks are about to indict her and we all know it. But you better have all of your gear in one bag or we'll take her record and past achievements and service to this city and jam it up your ass."

"David, David," Sims said, pulling his hands down and turning to face the attorney. "We just want to talk with her, and David, you'd better be able to produce her when she's indicted."

Attinger got up from his chair and walked to the door. He turned at the door and looked at the three of them seated in the room. "Put the word out to your henchmen, detectives. Detective Sergeant Natalie Collins is on vacation. Any contact with her, and I mean *any*, will be through me. And if you should feel so foolish and show a willingness to waste the state's money on an indictment, let me know, and I'll produce her. And if you're thinking about getting this over in a hurry, forget it. I will enter a plea of not guilty for her if she's charged. Good day, gentlemen."

Attinger closed the door softly and stood in the hall.

Didn't go too bad, he thought, wondering how he could get in touch with Grant to get another one of those dinners. He lumbered down the hall to find the detective.

I could get used to those dinners, but what the hell are we gonna do for a defense?

Nine

He's up there, all right, James Anderson thought, looking up at the stadium seats. There was indeed a figure there, the only one on the east side, with a ball cap and sunglasses. *A football scout up there coming to see me.* With the scout up there, it was impossible to concentrate, and he missed the call.

"James, wake up," Foster, the quarterback called. James brought his head down into the huddle. "Ninety-seven green right, on two," he said, trying to sound older than he was. James walked up to the line of scrimmage and flanked out to the right. His heart was pounding with the call, and he resisted a look up into the stands to see the man who had sent him the note. He listened to Foster call the cadence, trying to concentrate, but it had been oh so hard to think about anything else since he had received the letter in the mail this morning.

Me, a junior, and the scouts from major college teams are already looking at me. At a practice scrimmage, no less.

He wanted to tell everyone, but the note said to keep it quiet for now, and it was all he could do to not tell his friends.

On two, the quarterback received the ball from the center, and James surged forward with the line, running past the first defender, a school friend wearing the red practice shirt of the defense. He cut hard left at ten yards and slanted across the middle, looking back as he made his cut, the ball coming, high up, the wind in his helmet a distant thing, and he timed his jump perfectly, coming down and stopping dead, letting the corner back run past him, and he raced for the end zone, eighty yards away. When he had the corner beat by five yards, the coach blew the play dead, but James kept running anyway, showing the 4.0 speed he was known for. In the end zone, he resisted spiking the ball, glancing up at the stands as he ran back to the huddle.

He grinned. *Be driving a Porsche 911 in four years,* he thought. The rest of the practice was given over to drills, and the man in the stands was gone by the time the team headed for the showers.

James stripped off his gear and was into the shower in seconds. The note said to meet after practice, and he would be there in two minutes flat. He ran into the parking lot, carrying a gear bag, his hair still wet.

There. Across the street. By a car. A sedan of some kind. James had a flash of disappointment that the man was not driving an SUV hybrid. The man in the sunglasses who had been in the stands was wearing a white shirt and dark slacks, the baseball cap of the Tampa Bay Buccaneers.

Victor Bramson watched as James Anderson approached, his excitement mounting, thinking that this could be one of the important ones. He looked more energized than he had in his bedroom a few nights ago, certainly more animated. He watched the way the young athlete's bones came together, the way his skeleton moved so gracefully when he walked.

You will die before me.

He held his hand out.

"James," he said warmly. James Anderson stopped on the sidewalk and held out his hand, grinning. Victor took the hand and then put his arm around James. "James, I'm Dennis Baxter from Miami, and I'm so very glad to finally meet you. We've been watching you, you know, and we have big plans for you." James nodded, unable to stop grinning.

"James," Victor said, looking around, steering the football player to the passenger door of his car. "James, as you know, we're not supposed to talk to you until your senior year, but, well, you know, we thought we'd get something going a little early." He grinned. "You don't mind, do you?"

"Uh, no way."

"Well, get in, we'd better take a little ride, get away from the school so we won't be seen. Okay with you?" He held his hand out. "And James," Victor said, "I'd better have the note I gave you."

They drove west, out of the residential area and away from the school. Victor asked James about the plays he had seen, and soon the football player was talking, punctuating his sentences with his hands, showing a catch, a run.

They took Highway 41 west out of Miami, James not seeming to notice, wanting to impress the football scout from one of the best college football programs in the country. Victor nodded in the appropriate places and drove into the Everglades. They passed pine islands and saw grass marshes, mangrove forests and swamps. After thirty minutes, James stopped talking and looked around.

"Uh, Mr. Baxter, where we—"

"Relax, kid, we're gonna turn around right up here. I think I can tell the coaches that you will work out just fine for us." Victor smiled. "Tell me about your speed, your sprinting regimen." As James started talking, Victor found the road he wanted, a dirt track that led to a mangrove thicket. James turned around and looked at the paved highway they had just left.

"Have you home for dinner," Victor said, "just need to take a leak." He looked over at the product of his search, at a young man who would die before him, a young man who would tell him very soon what he needed to know. As he came to the thicket of trees, he drove in along a track and stopped when the car could no longer be observed from the highway. He suddenly thought of the other search who got away from him, the police sergeant in Portland.

Remember the lessons from Portland. Don't let him get away. The woman will come next, the woman who thought she was so smart and so good. She will die before me. The man, the man who saved her is of no consequence. He is not the one I want. She is. Just like James.

James got out to join him, looking at the marshes as Victor stood in front of the car. The mangrove thicket ended in a watery marsh, the water and green stretching as far as they could see. Up close, in the water and grasses, were several gloating logs where the mangroves had died and fallen into the water.

"Holy shit, man!" James said, almost a shriek, pointing toward the marsh.

"What is it?" Victor came around to stand beside James, and they stood there, looking at the marsh, the sun making the water a blazing reddish reflector.

"That big log, it just crawled up on the bank over there." James pointed. "Let's get the fuck outta here," he added starting for the car door.

"That isn't a log," Victor said. "That's an alligator." He looked at James. "But you're okay, they don't move very fast, and," Victor made a show of looking at his watch, "it's time to get back." He slowly removed a large lead-filled leather tube from his back pocket.

"Sure okay by me," James said, and turned to open the passenger door. Victor hit him in the back of the head then, hit him with the leather lead-filled sap.

"James, can you hear me?" Victor asked the question quietly, twenty minutes later. The young football player moaned.

"James."

His eyes flickered, and then opened. He looked around and closed his eyes again, trying to bring his hands up to his head. He couldn't. Something was holding his arms. He opened his eyes again. This time they stayed open. He was seated in the passenger seat of the car, the seat belt around him, his hands tied behind his back, his feet and legs secured to the floor with a rope that went under the seat.

"Wha you doin'?" he said thickly. His head hurt, throbbed in the back, and the fear came up so fast he couldn't swallow.

"I'm not going to hurt you if you answer my questions," Victor lied. "But if you don't tell me what I want to know, I'll feed you to those logs out there." Victor turned to face his quarry.

"Do you understand?"

James nodded, his stomach squirming, churning, the fear turning the saliva in his throat to hot acid. He haltingly guaranteed the man that he would tell him everything he wanted to hear.

They talked about survival, about how a young man survived a sure death when the others he had been with didn't. They talked about the life of James Anderson from his earliest recollection to the present time. What Victor learned about the life of James was enough to let him know that he hadn't wasted his time. James did contain some of the secret, and it was now way too dangerous to leave him alive.

When Victor was done with him, it was hours after dark. James sat bound up in the passenger seat, looking out at the darkness, while Victor made notes, the dome light inside the car giving him a weird sense of security. A cocoon. A womb.

Victor took his quarry by surprise again, waiting until James turned to the side, and then hitting him as hard as he could with the sap.

The football player's body sagged against the shoulder harness. Victor got out and unhurriedly walked around to the passenger side. He pulled James out and stripped the body of clothing. He put the clothes in the rental car, and then picked up an arm and pulled James's body along to the edge of the water, hearing the logs move when the body splashed into the marsh.

The logs came alive then, splashing toward the body as Victor walked back to his car. In the darkness, the logs grew snouts with long teeth, snouts that opened wide, thrashing, coming faster toward the food.

El lagarto, the lizard, or Alligator mississipienis, *descended from crocodiles living two hundred million years ago. Fascinating creatures,* Bramson thought.

When he was certain the alligators had found their food, he checked the area with a small flashlight, making sure he didn't leave anything behind that would identify him. He threw the clothes into the water and was rewarded with an accompanying movement toward him.

When the alligators were finished, James would be among the hundreds of teenagers in south Florida who dropped out of sight. Victor drove back onto the road and drove west, toward the Gulf of Mexico.

He smiled.

If the girl in San Antonio does as well as James, I will have a good week.

And then on to Portland for some unfinished business. The woman in Portland in the apartment, she shouldn't have been there. The other one is the one I want, the cop.

I need to ask her some questions about survival.

Ten

Grant Birnam sat at the table and looked at the lights across the river, sipping whiskey and water, waiting for others. He was at the floating seafood restaurant on the Willamette River, near the marina just below Natalie's apartment. The restaurant was a popular spot with the up and coming, oak and brass and large indoor plants surrounding the bar.

The restaurant had windows on three sides, giving the diners a view of the boats in the marina, the river, East Portland, and Mount Hood in the daytime. The lights from East Portland shimmered on the black water. *I should get up and call Aimee*, he thought. At nine-thirty on Thursday night, the restaurant was nearly empty, the dinner crowd gone.

"Hey, boss, what we drinking tonight?" Kirby asked, and he sat down beside Grant. He was wearing an old hooded sweatshirt, an expensive leather jacket, and jeans. Kirby looked around the room as he sat down. He knew what effect he would have on any unattached females in the room.

"Whiskey and water," Grant said. Eldredge sat across from Grant. "Thompson will be here in a minute," Grant said, "but why the hell did you want a table for ten?"

"Because there will be more of us for dinner than you had originally planned. In fact," Eldredge said, turning around, "here come some now."

They walked past the reservation desk in a group, talking as they approached. The six detectives from homicide stopped at the table and stood in front of Grant. Justin Falk was in the lead, a mid-forties detective, tall, wearing his ubiquitous charcoal suit. With solid gray hair and an urbane air, he was the dean of the homicide detectives, having been assigned there for almost two decades. Grant looked up, scowling.

"Grant, we're in," Falk said, and then he took a seat next to Eldredge, across from the detective sergeant. The others with him nodded in agreement with Falk, and took seats around the table. Jane Brady, at thirty-two, was the youngest detective except for Kirby. She had shoulder-length dark hair, was quiet and efficient. She walked around the table and sat next to Grant. The others were veteran police officers with at least a decade of police experience. Dennis Koch and his longtime partner Galen Pitman, and Duayne Olson and Frank Elliott.

Pitman and Koch grinned at Grant and the others as a waiter came for their drink orders. When the waiter left, the detectives started talking.

"How'd you know?" Grant asked Falk.

"Shit, man, we're detectives," he said. "Besides, I told Kirby that we were starting our own investigation and he said that we had better work together or there would really be hell to pay. And Jane found out that Kirby was in the office at seven A.M. this morning, and when she called me, we knew something was up."

"Only time Kirby's up at seven A.M. is if he's taking a piss," Eldredge said dryly.

"He ain't been in at seven since he got drunk on Friday night and left his paycheck in his desk," Falk said.

"Hey," Kirby said, "you guys quit pickin' on—."

"All right, hold it," Grant said, holding up his hands. "You're in, and Kirby's buying drinks."

Kirby protested, but they didn't hear him.

They ordered dinner, and as they waited, Grant told them what his team knew so far about the shooting in Natalie's apartment, the death of Stephanie, and the pending indictment.

"Looking at Natalie's account of what happened that night," Grant continued, "we should think that the second man there, a man named Daniel McClellan Harris, saved her life. We don't know why he was there, and since he has been identified, we know that these people are not local."

"How'd we come up with that name?" Koch asked.

"Natalie gave it us," Grant said. He told them what he knew about the case.

"You mean our Minnie Mouse is traveling with this Dan guy?" Jane asked.

"It looks that way," Grant said. "But what I've been asking myself all day is, what is the link between the killer, Dan Harris, and our Natalie? There must be something there. And who the hell is the killer?"

As dinner arrived, Kirby and Eldredge talked about their findings in Natalie's apartment. "We lifted prints all over," Eldredge said, "and took hair samples from where the men fought in the living room. We reenacted the shooting, and looked at the angles. Minnie Mouse should have been able to hit the witness if she had wanted to."

"And we found this," Kirby said, placing a sealed plastic bag on the table.

"The hell is it?" Falk asked, holding the bag up to the light. "Looks scaly or something."

"Our lab says it is organic, a substance that belongs to an animal of some kind, but they don't know what," Grant said. "Kirby and Eldredge are going to the federal fish and wildlife lab in Ashland tomorrow. They identify exotic animals from all over the world in their lab, sometimes with blood or tissue samples."

As they finished dinner, Grant made assignments. Jane Brady and Justin Falk were going to conduct a thorough canvass of the apartments around Natalie's apartment. They were going to start after dinner, to find out who was up at the time Natalie came home. They would do it again on Friday night.

Koch and Pitman were going to work on the background of Daniel McClellan Harris. They were going to find out who he was and what he had done, from the day he was born to the present. Olson and Elliott were going to assemble evidence, reports, and find the dress Natalie wore to the concert on the night Stephanie was killed. The dress was in the evidence room, but they would find a way to get a look at it, Grant said.

"Oh, I forgot to tell you. Natalie has retained David Attinger as defense counsel," Grant said.

"Christ, why'd she get that weasel?" Jane said.

"Well, at least he's an attack weasel," Grant said. "Let's go to work."

On the way out, Eldredge grabbed Kirby by the arm. "We better get some sleep if we're gonna drive six hours one way to Ashland tomorrow."

"Oh, didn't I tell you?" Kirby said with a grin. "I rented a plane. We're gonna fly down to Ashland. Less than two hours."

"I ain't flying with you or anyone else, Kirby." Eldredge's face had turned a pasty white.

"Sure you are, partner," Kirby said. "I'm a good pilot, had my license since college."

"Shit, you ain't even old enough to get into college," Eldredge said. As they left, Kirby said something to the elder detective that decided it for him. He agreed to meet Kirby at the local general aviation airport in nearby Hillsboro at six the next morning for the flight to Ashland.

What they found in Ashland didn't make sense, but it did make it more bizarre and frightening for Natalie.

And chilling—much more chilling. Something out of a horror story, Kirby thought later.

Friday, September 22

The Homecoming

One

The train rocketed at track speed, the interior of the cars darkened in the early morning hours while the passengers slept. They were somewhere in northern Montana. Natalie was awake, listening to the clatter of the wheels, an occasional crossing alarm with the bells rising in pitch and then falling immediately as the train sped away. Other than the flashes of light at the crossings, there was darkness outside. They could have been on another continent, another planet.

Dan lay sleeping in the seat next to Natalie, on the aisle, his face relaxed in sleep, the only relaxed pose she had seen on a man she had now come to know as a gentle and kind person.

At their first meeting in her apartment, Natalie had seen a madman, a grizzled violent attacker. Earlier in the day, she had seen Dan shed years of hurt and solitude, opening up to the little girl, Janie, spending part of the afternoon reading and playing with the four-year-old. Natalie had thought of kids as curious things, creatures that others cleaned up after and spent their entire paychecks on. She had a biological clock that she had convinced herself had long ago wound down, and kids remained an oddity, like exotic pets that other people owned. *And,* she had told herself, *I have my career.*

Some career you have now, Minnie Mouse. You couldn't even handle the death and dying when your career was wonderful. Before Stephanie's death.

Across the aisle, Janie and her mother were sleeping, the little girl curled up with a blanket and a ragged stuffed animal of undetermined species. Janie had argued with her mother about sleeping, and had finally agreed to when Dan had told her of the games they would play when she awakened.

"Night, Dan. Night, Natalie," she had told them, and had gone to sleep, looking at Dan. A four-year-old without a father, her mother had said.

Dan's daughter, who does she have now, and don't you wonder what she's like . . . but you know, don't you, Minnie Mouse, if she's like him, she's quite wonderful.

Natalie stared at her reflection in the window, and tried making a face at her reflection. The smile was flat, and she grimaced, trying to smile again at the sad face, but it didn't work, and she turned away when the sad face was too much for her to see.

Oh, you've made a fine start in your investigation, Minnie Mouse, haven't you? Running around the country with a man who was in your apartment the night Stephanie was killed. Intuition? Hunch? Doesn't mean much if you're wrong. Doesn't mean much if you don't find the killer. Doesn't mean much if Dan isn't who he sasy he is.

He saved your life.

Maybe, but so what?

Natalie leaned back and reclined her seat, growing tired of the sudden introspection, a pastime she rarely engaged in. Better to be funny and a jokester. but look at where it got me, she thought bitterly. Dan had been asking about the bank, something he read about in the *Oregonian* articles. He asked about the significance of it before he went to sleep. He said that he had read about a medal of valor, and the paper referred to it several times when they mentioned her. When she had looked at him the last time, he didn't ask again.

The bank.

"Beautiful Oregon, with the most per capita bank robberies of any state, and you never enter a bank without your gun, Minnie Mouse," her training officer had told her. In the eighties, most of the bank robberies were committed by the cranksters, the speed freaks, the dopers wound up on methamphetamine, called crank, or speed. Now, most of the robberies were committed by children on crack. *Let's decriminalize dope. Sure, be glad to, Minnie Mouse, if only someone would tell the criminals.*

These guys don't look like they came out of a crack house, Minnie Mouse.

Gunpowder and blood.

It was a day that had destined her for bigger and better things in the department, if that made sense. A day of death and dying. Natalie leaned back and closed her eyes, and she could almost smell the gunpowder and blood. And almost as soon as she had closed her eyes against the rocking of the speeding train, she was there again.

In the bank.

Death and dying.

So very, very pleezed to meetcha.

Gunpowder and blood.

The smell was staggering, sharp, almost acidic. The coppery smell of blood invaded her nose; lower, heavier, an organic smell, the smell of fear. The smoke came in at a higher level, more transient, as if it were not something to be smelled but felt, hot and scary.

The pain! My side hurts so bad, Natalie thought, *so bad that I can't move.* She looked ahead toward the end of the counter, wanting to look at her side but knowing that it would debilitate her even more. Finally, she had to look, keeping her gun pointed ahead, glancing down at her side. There was a lot of blood there.

She put her hand there, sliding in her blood. *I'm losing blood, gotta get to a doctor fast. The carpet is gray.* The thought bounced around in Natalie's head until she did look down at the industrial carpet.

"Gray and red now, folks," she muttered, and giggled, knowing that she had to stop, it hurt too damned much and she had to stop. *Why is it always gray in banks?* Three feet from Natalie's left side and out from the counter was a man in a blue blazer and tan slacks, a man of about fifty with some gray hair around the sides. He was lying on his back, staring at something on the ceiling, his eyes unblinking. He was staring through a mesh of pantyhose, the stockings used for something other than what the company had intended them. The hole in his forehead was almost dead center, and when Natalie looked at him and thought about it, she giggled again.

Dead center. Center punched you, sucker.

There was almost no blood around the hole, but the gray carpet beneath the back of his head was turning red now, and pink with cranial fluid.

Gray and red now, folks.

Gotta get a grip, there's two left and I'm between them and where they need to go. Surprised you, suckers. Your buddy wearing

*pantyhose on the wrong body part tried to shoot
me, so I center punched him.*

*Boy, Grant's gonna be pissed. I come in here
to cash a check and the guys with the pantyhose
on their faces shoot a woman running to the
door as I enter from the other side. The young
one in the back got spooked and shot her.*

*Christ! I'm really fucked up now, lying here
with a dead man, a leaking hole in my side that
hurts so bad,* and then Natalie squeezed tears
out of her eyes, blinking them open again and
staring ahead.

She caught movement to her left, and Natalie
saw a woman on her knees, bending over a small
child, a boy of about two, rocking back and
forth, the woman weeping, looking at Natalie
with a wild, horrified stare.

*She doesn't know who I am, what I am, saw me
shoot Mr. Pantyhose, center punch the sucker,
now all she sees is my gun. And if the other
two fellas who wear pantyhose on the wrong part
of their bodies come running around the corner
there to get outta the bank, Mrs. Wildeyes and
her baby boy are gonna join Mr. Pantyhose and
stare up at the ceiling tiles for a long time.
Course, they could see better 'cause they don't
have any pantyhose on the wrong body parts.*

Gunpowder and blood.

*Natalie held the Beretta up. How many rounds
did I shoot? Five, I think, shot five times,
eleven left. Gotta stand up now and see where
those two fellas are.* Natalie tried to push
herself up into a sitting position, keeping the
Beretta pointed toward the end of the counter.
She was behind a counter where people stood to
make out their transactions before going to a
teller. *They gotta come out soon, they can't
wait for the boys in blue to arrive, gotta come
out soon.*

She pushed herself up, the pain in her left side making her dizzy, her eyes swimming.

Up in front of her on the gray carpet, near the glass door to the street, a woman was lying facedown on the carpet, her leg curled under her, her dress up over her waist. She didn't have a pantyhose mask on, and she couldn't stare at the ceiling. If she was not dead, she would be soon, Natalie thought, looking at the large pool of blood on the carpet around the woman.

There were people behind the teller counter, maybe seven or eight, and that's where the other two with pantyhose in the wrong place ran when I shot Mr. Pantyhose. Probably some more bank customers behind me, although some made it out before they gunned down the woman who's staring at the gray carpet.

Gotta get outta here. These guys hear sirens, they'll wanta take their withdrawal and run.

Natalie wiped the blood on her left hand on her slacks, thinking that the Nordstrom Brothers should see her now. "If she gets out of this," they would say, "she'll definitely be in line for some new slacks." She glanced down at her side, knowing that wounds usually look worse than they are.

What about the guy on the floor next to you with the pantyhose in the wrong place? His wound doesn't look all that bad, hardly any blood.

Gotta move now girl, gotta move, Natalie thought, and she started to push herself back away from the counter.

A gunshot sounded. And then there were three more reports in rapid succession. The counter above Natalie exploded and one of the pantyhose men came into view, the small one in the gray suit, young looking, pulling the trigger. Natalie could see the brass ejecting from his automatic, looked like a .45, and she raised the barrel of the Beretta up as he rounded the corner and she pulled the trigger, shooting faster now, the gun jumping in her hand, timing the shots so as the sights came down, she pulled the trigger again, and the gray-suited man with the pantyhose on the wrong part of his body shot a wild round over her that hit the glass behind her and then the other one rounded the corner right behind the first, not seeing what his partner was shooting at, and Natalie fired shot after shot, as fast as she could pull the trigger, and then the slide locked back, the magazine empty.

Ohmigod! Oh, fuck me!

Natalie thumbed the magazine release with her right thumb, reaching for the pouch on her belt without looking, watching the second man with the pantyhose on the wrong body part fall away and out of her sight, his gun thumping across the carpet to stop at the feet of the woman who was staring at the gray and red carpet.

The empty magazine dropped out, and she slapped the full one in and reached up with her left hand, the pain in her left side making her cry out, and she pulled the slide of the Beretta back and let it fly forward, chambering a round from the fresh magazine.

Suddenly it was quiet . . . so quiet that Natalie could hear the ceiling fans humming in the teller area. Somewhere, not far off, a woman was sobbing.

The silence was harsher than the shots.

They waited in silence.

A siren far off. Someone coughed, away to Natalie's right in the teller area. Then it was quiet again.

Natalie tried to sit up, holding her side now with her left hand, holding her gun unsteadily in the direction of the second man with the pantyhose on the wrong body part.

Maybe the guy's just faking it. Maybe there's another person with them, Natalie thought, the pain making her dizzy.

She sat up, the room swimming in and out of focus. She looked to her left and the woman was staring at her, her look one of complete horror. Terrified.

Natalie looked behind her. A group of five or six bank patrons and employees were on the floor behind desks, all looking at her. Even the sobbing had stopped now.

Quiet.

The ceiling fan to her right pushed the gun smoke around swirling over them, the blades slowly revolving, eerie silent witnesses to the carnage.

Gonna puke, Natalie thought.

She heard more sirens and someone behind her talking on a phone.

I'd better tell them I'm here with the pantyhose men, Natalie thought, or the uniforms will never come in.

"Tell them I'm a cop," Natalie said, her voice loud in the silence. She saw movement outside the door where the woman was lying.

"Tell them I'm a cop!" Natalie yelled, holding her gun on the second man with the pantyhose. Her gun wavered, and she lowered it to the floor.

My side's all wet and I'm gonna die.

Natalie held her side with both hands, her blouse slick with blood, two of her fingers sinking into the wound in her side.

I'm really fucked up. Oh, my side is on fire!

And then she saw the pale blue uniform of the Portland Police Bureau beside her, the officer holding a shotgun on the men on the floor, the men with the pantyhose, and she felt hands on her, pulling her back, lowering her to the floor. As her blouse was being cut away, she saw a medic hold an IV bag above her, and she thought then that she might just make it, *But the medic looks pretty grim,* she thought.

She pulled the oxygen mask away as it was placed on her face, motioning for the medic with the IV bag to come closer to hear, and when he placed his ear next to her lips, she whispered, "Get my daddy, get my dad," and the medic nodded.

If I can see Daddy, I can let go. I can die. Oh, Daddy, it hurts. And then she saw them, her daddy and Stephanie on Main Street, U.S.A., Stephanie's ponytail bouncing as she ran after Mickey Mouse.

Two

Natalie jerked awake, the dream just out of her consciousness, leaving her with a vague, uneasy, paranoid feeling. She knew she had been dreaming of the bank again, even though she couldn't remember specifics.

Gunpowder and blood.

The train was slowing, and she sat up and looked around.

Dan was gone. The sky was turning from black to gray in the east. She thought it was about five-thirty, as she looked around the car. Most of the passengers were still sleeping. She pulled her bag up from the floor, and found a makeup mirror. She grimaced at the weary eyes, and then tried on a smile.

Smile still looks bad, Minnie Mouse, and your hair's sticking up all over, maybe that's why Dan left. She grimaced, and then looked around to see if anyone else could see her. She grabbed her bag and felt for the gun, relieved that it was there. She swung out in the aisle, getting her sea legs again, anticipating the lurches of the train with bent knees. She went downstairs and found an open rest room and closed the door, with just enough room to stand in front of the sink.

She put her bag up on the counter and stripped her clothes off. In less than ten minutes, she had washed in the sink, starting with her hair. She carefully applied makeup, and put on a white cotton shirt and jeans.

She found Dan in the observation car. He was sitting in the domed area at the far end of the car, staring at the Montana mountains. Natalie stopped inside the door and watched him. They were alone in the car. *I'll bet he never even had a traffic ticket before this,* Natalie thought. He looked lonely, and later she remembered him like that, a man who'd journeyed for years alone.

A good man. A man I believe in, and God knows why. A man who knows children, who is running to find a madman. A man who got caught up in a madman's plans.

Maybe that's why I trust him; we both got caught up in a madman's plans.

She walked slowly toward the front of the car, toward Dan, swaying in time with the rocking of the car, the train at speed again. The large mountains of Montana swept by, but she knew Dan wasn't looking at the scenery. Natalie walked up and quietly sat down beside him. She began to think he wasn't aware of her presence, and then he spoke.

"Be snow here soon," Dan said softly, so softly that she had to strain to hear him. He continued to stare out of the window, his leather bag on the seat beside him, a silent and faithful companion to his travels. Natalie put her hand on his arm

"Morning," she said, looking at him.

"She needs me," Dan said.

"What?"

"She needs me. Angelina needs me," Dan said.

Natalie suddenly reached up before she could think about it and put her arms around Dan. "Her daddy needs her just as much," she whispered, squeezing him.

Dan didn't talk, afraid he couldn't. Natalie leaned over and kissed his cheek. Dan put his arm around her and they held each other, chasing demons away.

"Thanks," he whispered.

"You hungry?" Natalie asked.

"Always."

"Then buy a girl breakfast."

He grinned.

"Why wait?"

"I agree," Dan said. "Let's go wake up the cook."

"No, I mean, why wait to see your daughter? Let's get off the train and fly east. Today. You could see your daughter by morning."

Had she known then what she would see, what would happen to them, she would not have been in such a hurry to get East.

She would not have wanted to make the journey at all.

Three

"What're you doing? You're tipping the fucking plane!" Eldredge screamed. He grabbed onto the side of the seat with his left hand, pushing on the ceiling with his right.

"Relax," Kirby said, grinning at his partner. He was, in fact, "tipping" the plane. They were flying at 7,500 feet, south toward Ashland, in the valley between the coastal range of mountains and Oregon's Cascade Mountains. Kirby had started a gentle turn to the southeast. Out the window, they could see Mount Ashland directly south of them, and south of that, California's Mount Shasta.

Eldredge had been a pretty good passenger, Kirby thought, for someone who didn't like to fly. When they left the Hillsboro Airport at seven in the single-engine Cessna 206, Eldredge told his younger partner that he didn't hate flying, he just didn't think that Kirby was old enough for a driver's license, let alone a pilot's license.

Kirby was a good pilot, and since he had started flying in college, he had totaled over a thousand hours of flight time.

"Eldredge." Kirby looked over at his partner. Eldredge stared straight ahead as Kirby leveled the wings and made his final approach. For Kirby, it was like coming home. He had learned to fly in Ashland when he was a student at Southern Oregon State University.

"Eldredge, look at me."

"No."

"Eldredge, we're level now, and it's okay. Look at me."

The detective glanced over at Kirby, his face drained. "That's better, buddy, and besides, we wouldn't even be to Eugene yet if we drove. I'm gonna get you to like this yet."

Eldredge didn't say a word when they landed. They were met by the senior forensic scientist from the U.S. Fish and Wildlife Criminal Forensic Laboratory. He was a tall man in his forties, with short, sandy hair, and he wore jeans and cowboy boots.

He led them to a green van and held the door open.

"I'm Gary Kilpatrick," he introduced himself and shook hands with the detectives. "You boys cops, right?"

Kirby nodded.

"Not attorneys?"

"You wanta live long?" Eldredge growled, his body still weak from his fear of flying.

"Okay, just checking," the lab tech said. "You hear the one about the two attorneys walking down the street, and they see a gorgeous lady walking toward them, and one attorney says to the other, 'Boy, I'd sure like to screw her,' and the other attorney thinks for a minute, and asks, 'Yeah, outta what?'" Kilpatrick laughed and banged on the steering wheel.

Eldredge smiled. It was good to be on the ground again.

"Man, this is a new sucker," Kirby said, as they drove up to the lab. "And big," he added, as they got out of the van.

They stood in front of the new forensic lab the Fish and Wildlife Service had established in Ashland. The building was long, one story, painted white, a modern government building.

"The lab has three goals," Kilpatrick explained to them as they entered the building. "To identify the species in question, determine the cause of death, and to connect the suspect to the case." Eldredge handed the technician the piece of evidence and Kilpatrick held it up and looked at it. They waited as a lab technician made an entry into the evidence log.

"We're going to take this to the morphology section," Kilpatrick said as they followed him down a hallway. "We need to know what this piece of material is." They entered the lab, with a bizarre display of equipment and creatures. On one desk Kirby saw a baby alligator, on another, the bright wing of an exotic bird. "Endangered species," Kilpatrick said.

He removed the piece of material from the envelope and looked at it under a light, holding it up to his face, as Eldredge told the details of how they'd found it. He walked to a stereo-zoom microscope, and examined the piece. He pulled a reference book from a bookcase and examined the piece again.

"Part of a carapace," he said.

"Huh?" Kirby looked at the technician.

"Part of a turtle shell."

Kirby and Eldredge looked at each other, and Kirby shrugged.

"I'll take this to serology for a more positive ID, but I know what we have . . . a small piece of a turtle's shell. I can identify it visually and microscopically. We can identify it down to genus and species with a serology report, and with a DNA workup we can match subspecies and probably match it to someone's collection. How far you want to go with this?"

They didn't talk much on the flight back to Portland. Eldredge screamed only once, when they landed.

A turtle, Kirby thought, *a damned turtle. What the hell does it mean?*

Natalie and Dan would find out. In less than a day they would learn what turtles had to do with it all.

Four

"Auntie Susan?"

"What, Angel?" Susan Prader answered, not taking her eyes from the road.

"My daddy's coming home yesterday." Angelina said it so quietly, so matter-of-factly, that Susan glanced over at her niece. Her eyes flashed back to the road and she braked for a car trying to merge into her lane. Driving in morning traffic in the Baltimore suburbs was like driving in Mazatlan or Puerto Vallarta; he who hits, pays.

"Uh, no honey, your daddy's not coming for a while, uh—."

"No, really," Angelina said, her voice pleading, "I know he is, I dreamed about it tonight." Angelina seemed satisfied that her daddy was coming home, and she looked out the window at the Maryland countryside. They were passing the exclusive Pine Ridge Golf Course, on their way from their house to a private school. Susan knew she could not dissuade her Angel. At seven, when Angelina was convinced of something, Susan could do little to change her mind.

Angelina had lived with her Aunt Susan for the two years since Dan had disappeared. Susan knew how close Angel was to her dad, and she did very well for a seven-year-old who had lost her mother and then her father. Susan and Angelina had seen Dan every four or five months, each time a joyous and then heartbreaking event for all of them. It was impossible for her to know when her dad was coming home. Susan fretted as she turned into the school parking lot. She knew her Angel was going to be very disappointed. They hadn't seen Dan for almost six months.

I don't even know if he's alive.

She gave Angelina a kiss and hug and watched as her niece ran into her school, her pigtails flying out behind her. *She's so pretty she makes my heart ache,* Susan thought, *but Dan coming home, how can that be?*

Susan Prader, Dan's older sister and only sibling, was fifty-three, eleven years older than Dan. She had three grown children and was a widow. Her life in Baltimore had been turned upside down when Dan's wife was murdered. She now had a daughter to care for when her most important functions before had been her bridge game and her garden.

When Dan called that afternoon, it was her turn to be surprised. How could Angelina have known?

The call was brief, a few seconds long. "Meet me tomorrow noon, same place," he said, and hung up, afraid of a trace. *The police did look pretty hard for him after he escaped,* Susan thought. She went about making her plans, becoming more paranoid now, wanting to do everything humanly possible to ensure she and Angelina were not followed to the meeting.

"My daddy's coming home yesterday."

Angelina had been juxtaposing words, especially words referring to time, since her mother died and her father left her.

How could she have known?

Five

When the train stopped, Natalie jumped off into the chilly morning air, wanting off the train and some fresh air, no matter how cold. They were in Havre, Montana. The conductor said it would be a thirty-minute stop for a crew change.

The wind-chill factor must be thirty degrees, Natalie thought. They were in the mountains, the big country of Montana, but she didn't have time to admire the scenery. A deli cart met the train, passengers crowding around it to purchase items the train commissary didn't carry. Natalie passed them.

She walked to the side of the terminal. Dan dropped off the steps to the train and followed, carrying his bag. At least he had the sense to wear a jacket. Natalie shivered and flipped open the phone, her jacket in her bag below the phone. She dialed Grant's cell and put her emergency number in.

Dan opened his phone and punched in his sister's number. When his sister answered, he felt a jolt through his body. A person who loved him without question was on the line.

He told her about the meeting and hung up.

Natalie held her phone, holding her bag, knowing that Grant should have called back by now.

"Natalie." Dan stood beside her.

She turned and looked at him, impatient.

"Natalie, we need to leave the train now. We're flying east."

She looked at the phone and shrugged, willing it to ring. She looked up at Dan and grinned. "You live out west much, partner?" she asked.

"Why?"

"Finding a plane in Havre, Montana, might be tough."

Dan pointed to a large building a block distant, with a two-story-high sign on the roof. The sign said "Casino."

"See that sign? That means you can gamble here, the closest to Reno you can get, legally. There's an airline flying in and out of this burg, and we'll find a way. We need to be in Maryland by noon, tomorrow."

"Really?" Natalie grabbed his arm and they walked toward the brick building that proclaimed itself a casino.

"Yes, and I do know something about traveling. You've been in Portland too long."

They took a cab to the airport, and to Natalie's surprise, several airlines were represented there, with a flight leaving for Chicago on United Air in thirty minutes.

Gambling in Montana! Who would have thought?

Dan stood back as she paid with her credit card, figuring that even if she had been indicted, they wouldn't start looking for her in earnest just yet.

"What's the name on the other ticket?" the agent asked, typing their reservations into his computer.

"Dan, uh, Dan Collins," Natalie said, and turned to look at her new relative.

"Luggage?"

"Carry-on," Natalie said.

"Okay, Mrs. Collins, you're booked to Chicago, and then on to Baltimore this evening. Have a nice flight." He handed her the tickets.

Dan placed his bag on the security conveyer, the guards watching a screen as it passed through the X-ray machine, looking for weapons. Natalie placed her bag behind his, and she heard a beep as the man in front of Dan activated the alarm when he passed through the gates. Her stomach churned and she leaped past Dan, grabbing her bag off the conveyor just before it passed through the X-ray machine.

"Natalie, wha—."

"I'm not feeling well," she said, clutching her bag to her chest. She spun around and walked away, increasing her speed as she reached the hallway.

Dan watched as Natalie sprinted around the corner and out of sight, the security guard watching as well. Dan smiled, thinking that Natalie was being herself, as he had come to know her. *Unpredictable, in a nice way, and alive. Vital. And very attractive,* he told himself. *What are you doing, Dan Harris? Thinking about a woman? God, it's good to feel alive again after all this time.*

And he did feel alive, for the first time in the last two years, and it was due to meeting Natalie, to being around her. It was also due to the action they were taking, the planning for a future. He was finally doing something with another person who believed him.

And we are going to see my Angel.

Dan was so nervous and excited that his stomach was churning.

Natalie hit the rest-room door in full stride. Once inside, she locked herself inside a stall and sat down, shaky. She reached into her bag and pulled the Beretta out, holding it in her hand. Without giving it more thought, she removed the magazine, pulled the slide back, ejecting the round in the chamber, and then she removed the slide from the pistol. She removed two loaded magazines from her bag.

She flushed the toilet, wrapped the slide in tissue paper, and deposited it into the wastebasket before she left the rest room. Outside, she put the grip and magazines into different trash cans, and walked through into the security area.

"You okay?" Dan asked when she joined him, concern on his face. He was getting used to her sudden moves, but this one surprised him. They didn't need extra scrutiny by the police.

"I had to get rid of something," Natalie said, and then told him, his face turning white when he heard about the gun.

"Hey, don't worry, Daniel, I'll protect you." Natalie punched Dan lightly on the shoulder. She smiled, and he returned the smile.

But I sure don't feel like smiling, Daniel old boy, I sure as hell don't. I have a feeling we're gonna need that gun, and now it's gone. A very bad feeling.

Later, when Natalie thought about this, she wished they had taken Amtrak all the way to Baltimore. At least she would have had her gun then, when they needed it.

And they would need that gun as much as she ever had needed a gun in her young life.

Six

"**What** do you mean, they don't know where the prints came from?" Lieutenant Bill Norton asked. "This sounds like bullshit to me," he told Sergeant Plenard. Norton walked around his desk and picked up a report on the Portland contact. "Someone in Portland Police Bureau runs Harris's prints, they get an AFIS hit, and then they tell us they don't know how they got the prints?" He threw the report back on his desk.

"I called the homicide sergeant back," Plenard said. He looked in a notebook. "A Sergeant Grant Birnam. He said that the prints were sent to the lab by a Sergeant Natalie Collins, and that she's on vacation. Birnam says he doesn't know how she got the prints or where they came from."

"Fantastic."

"Something else, boss. I called back and asked for Sergeant Natalie Collins, and I got transferred around and was finally told she was on leave, not on vacation, on leave." He looked up at the others in the room.

The lieutenant stopped his pacing.

"What kind of leave?"

"I don't know."

"Well, find out. It could be important. The first contact we've had from Mr. Harris in two years, and we get this kind of shit." Lieutenant Norton walked to his desk and picked up a legal pad. He sat down and made some notes, and then spoke without looking up at the others.

"I want to start a surveillance on the daughter and sister. Who did that last time? Foster? You're on it, starting in the morning. Early. Live with the sister. You were sure that Harris had been contacting them all this time, right?"

He made other assignments, hoping this time they would capture a person who had escaped from their custody two years ago.

"One more thing. This guy knows this area. He grew up on the bay. If he comes back here, we will get him. We won't do this forever, so stay sharp. This guy's still a burr in the director's ass.

Seven

"**Relax,** you," Natalie said to Dan. He was sitting on an aisle seat, Natalie in the middle. Their seatmate had been sleeping since they taxied out. They had been in the air an hour and Dan had gone to the rest room four times. He was ready to lurch up again when Natalie put her hand on his arm. He looked at her and gave her an uncertain smile.

"I'm trying," he said, and slumped back down. "It's just that . . . I haven't seen my baby in . . . so long." He turned to Natalie, remembering, smiling. "If you only knew her..."

"I will, you can count on it, buster." She put her arms around his waist, and snuggled into him. *He's a darn good daddy,* she thought, remembering how Dan was with the little girl on the train. *The best daddy.*

"You think Angelina will still lover her dad?" Dan asked, his voice back to normal now, his eyes closed, his cheek on Natalie's head.

"Of course, silly."

But what about you, Minnie Mouse? What the hell is going on here? You falling in love with a fugitive? This man has touched you like no other. You want to mother him, love him, you'll probably fall in love with his daughter, and admit it, you want to do wild and bawdy things with him.

Yeah, I do.

You gonna, Minnie Mouse?

Yeah, probably.

Natalie snuggled deeper into Dan's neck, smelling him, feeling his warmth. She reached up and pulled his arm around her, and started to drift off.

And at age thirty-six, at an age when she thought it had passed her by, Detective Natalie Collins (homicide) was falling in love.

Dan hadn't flown into Baltimore-Washington International since before the death of his wife. As the plane slowed and entered the pattern, he could see the lights from Annapolis off the left wing; the dark places were the Chesapeake Bay. He could feel his excitement in his stomach. He tried to look over on the right side of the plane, to where he knew his family home must be, across the bay and a little south from Annapolis, but all he could see was darkness. He resisted an urge to get up and lean across to see the lights of the small town of Cambridge, where he'd played high school ball. The "fasten seat belt" sign came on. *Oh well, bad idea. I want to look like a tired traveler,* Dan thought, *not a returning fugitive. But Angelina, my baby, is here. How do I know what's better, take a prison sentence for my wife's death, destroy my life, or go on the run?*

Natalie shifted and murmured as Dan straightened up. *And what do I do about this person? She's lovely and strong. A fighter, and she likes me. I think she's feeling the same way about me as I feel.* He shook his head. *No. Nothing's going on. You just haven't allowed yourself to feel in so long, you don't know what it is like. This is nothing. Two people thrown together in a time of need for both of them.*

They had flown from Havre to Chicago, and then on to Baltimore, where they were scheduled to land at 11:50 P.M., and they should be on their way into the city by one in the morning.

Natalie woke up and looked over at Dan, giving him a hug and a smile.

As the landing gear bumped down and the plane angled into a steeper descent, Dan shook off the feelings of fatigue and stretched in his seat, bringing his hands up above his head. In the cabin of the plane, people were stirring, picking up their nests, getting ready to get off the plane. Better wait for it to land first, folks, Dan thought. And then he had a wild thought of the plane heading straight in, and those bags the woman across the aisle was gathering up would be scattered all the way to D.C. He shook off the thought and brought his arms down. He ran his hands over his face, feeling the stubble of two days. *I look a lot like I did when I left here,* he thought. *No beard to hide behind now. Maybe it's as it should be, looking like the fugitive I am. Hope the airport police aren't looking for me, because if they are, I look like the same Dan Harris who ran two years ago.*

They sat in their seats and talked while the other passengers stood in the aisle, the interior of the plane bright now with all the lights on. The airport was busy at midnight, with baggage trucks and planes swirling around on the pavement outside, a noisy dance of people and machines. Dan pulled Natalie toward him and whispered, "Let's walk off with a group and get a cab."

She nodded.

They walked up the ramp and into the concourse, Natalie shouldering her bag, looking tired. As they approached the security gate, she hooked her arm in Dan's and they passed by, the police busy with screening for an outgoing flight. Dan knew they were looking at him, and he tried to relax, and not let his paranoia create a problem. When they reached the lower level, Dan found a phone by the exit door, and called for a hotel reservation. The airport, in one of the oldest cities in the country, a city of nearly one million inhabitants and close to the nation's capital, was busy at all hours, and this night was no exception. Natalie stood beside him and watched the crowds moving along, thinking that airport crowds were no different from any other people with a place to go in a hurry.

Natalie held onto Dan's arm as they walked along the row of cabs in the upper drive area. Dan saw the bus he wanted and led Natalie toward it. As they got on, Natalie whispered, "Where we going?" Dan didn't answer, giving the driver their reservation number. As they walked back through the aisle, he leaned over and whispered back, "The hotel with the name on the front of the bus."

Natalie swung into a seat in the middle of the bus on the right side and Dan sat down beside her. "What hotel is that?" she said, just above a whisper.

"You will see," Dan said. Two more passengers got on, and the bus started away from the terminal. Natalie had her nose pressed to the window like a little kid, and Dan watched her. "Have you been here before?" he asked.

"Is there a Disneyland here?"

"No."

"Then why are we going?"

PART TWO

I would rather be ashes than dust!

I would rather that my spark should burn out in a brilliant blaze than it should be stifled by dryrot.

I would rather be a superb meteor, every atom of me in a magnificent glow than a sleepy and permanent planet.

The proper function of man is to live, not to exist.

I shall not waste my days in trying to prolong them.

I shall use my time.

JACK LONDON
1876-1916

Saturday, September 23

THE REUNION

One

The bus entered the freeway I-295 and drove northwest toward Baltimore's downtown area. Even though it was after midnight, the traffic seemed heavy to Natalie. As they entered the freeway, she leaned against Dan and put her arm around his shoulder. She might have dozed, she thought, for in a few minutes she looked up and they were in a lighted area, the lights from the buildings bright.

"Look." Natalie pointed out to the right of the bus. "That's the U.S. frigate, the Constellation," Dan said, looking at the towering masts of the ship. The bus turned in to a driveway, and Natalie stared at the ornate facade of the Harbor Court Hotel.

"Pretty fancy, Mr. Dan," she said.

He picked up his bag and Natalie followed him out of the bus and into the lobby. Uniformed attendants and high ceilings said old money.

"This cost more than Motel 6?" Natalie whispered, as they approached the desk.

"More in terms of money," Dan said, and smiled. Natalie winced as he presented her credit card. He signed the register, Mr. And Mrs. Dan Collins. Natalie stood on her toes and looked over Dan's shoulder, her arms around him. She had a rush of happiness, wanting the bad things about the trip to go away, to spend some time with this kind and gentle man.

The ceilings were high, ornate, the carpet thick with a rose pattern in it, the attendants erect and imperious. *You know it's an expensive place,* Natalie thought, *when the people working here act as if they have some of the old money, too.*

They rode up an elevator that made creaking noises, Natalie searching for the date on the permit. She didn't question Dan as he opened the door to a single room, a vast suite with two large beds. The view of the harbor was breathtaking, and Natalie stood by the window and looked at the ships.

"A little like the view from your apartment, don't you think?" Dan asked, walking up beside her.

"Well, there's water in both places," Natalie said. "But why this?" She waved her hand at the room. "Why this expense for one night?"

"Because the police don't show up here as often as they do at the cheaper motels. And some of them in Baltimore must be seeing my picture often." He walked to the window and stood behind Natalie, looking over her, staring out the window.

Natalie looked up at him, seeing that he was somewhere else.

"How close are we to her?" she asked softly.

"What?"

"Angelina."

Dan didn't answer for a while, and then he said, "Close. So close to my . . . " and he stopped, his emotions so jumbled, and the guilt for leaving her hit him then. Even though it wasn't of his doing, his daughter surely didn't understand that.

"She's here, with my sister," he finally said. He looked down at Natalie and slowly put his arms around her. He looked out then, and began talking.

"I won't be able to sleep tonight. I have to touch her, to feel her, to hold her." Dan continued to talk, to tell her of his memories of his baby daughter, who thought her daddy was the greatest in the world, of her brightness, her shrill laughter. His voice grew husky, and the tears came again, Natalie thinking of his strength, of his love for his daughter. She pressed against him, and held his arms with hers.

I love him.

The thought was out before she could stop it, think about it.

And neither of them knew just when it was that the holding changed from a comfort hug to something more, and Natalie turned and put her arms around Dan and reached up and kissed him, pressing her body into his.

Two

Susan Prader closed her book and turned off her bedside light. She could see the light from Angelina's room shining across the hallway floor. She put on a robe and quietly entered the hallway, twisting the cloth tie on the robe as she approached Angelina's room. *How could she have known her dad was coming?* Susan asked herself. *She hasn't seen him in months.* Susan's heart was breaking over the ordeal caused by Jackie's death.

She loved her brother Dan. He had always been her little brother. Even though they had grown up separated by so many years, they had always been close.

She loved him fiercely, and part of her life was destroyed when Dan's life was as well. She would do anything for him, would have done anything for him, and she knew that by taking Angelina, part of Dan's life was saved. Susan's own children were grown and pursuing careers. When her husband died, Dan had been there for her, taking care of the details that she and the boys were not able to cope with.

She was old enough to be Angelina's grandmother, and she loved her as much as a mother and grandmother combined.

When Dan had been arrested for the murder of his wife, Susan had been there for him, taking Angelina in with her. She had enrolled her in a private school, and had done everything to make Angelina's life a pleasant one.

When Dan had escaped, Angelina was five-and-one-half years old, and at that time the child had told her aunt that her daddy was going to find the bad guy who killed her mommy.

Susan didn't know how she could have known, and they didn't see Dan for three months. At that first covert meeting, Dan's appearance had shocked Susan. Angelina was afraid at first, but then, when she knew it was her daddy, it didn't matter. He was disheveled, had a matted beard, and his hair was dirty and stringy.

He smelled like cheap wine and vomit. He had been wearing the same clothes for a long time. He had been riding the roads to kill the pain, and he told Susan that only the thought of his daughter kept him from killing himself.

For the first meeting, Susan and Angelina had met Dan out along the Conrail line, in a deserted hobo camp, a place that Susan didn't know existed so close to her home. When the meeting was over, she put Angelina in the car and came back and hugged her brother, his clothes and odor making her skin crawl. As much as she loved him, Susan had the only harsh words she had ever had with her brother.

She had told him that he was not her brother anymore, and that if he wanted to find this man, he couldn't do it from a hobo camp. She promised him she would take care of Angelina. "But if you want my help," she told him, "you'd better become Dan, my brother, again."

And he had.

The next meeting, and successive ones, they'd met at the Baltimore Zoo in Druid Hill Park.

Three months after the meeting at the hobo camp, they met again. This time Dan was wearing a beard, but it was trimmed, and he was wearing nice clothes. Susan had power of attorney over Dan's not inconsiderable finances, and she had transferred his money around enough times, making transfers by Western Union, so Dan could pick it up on the road.

Susan looked in Angelina's room from the hallway. Angelina was sitting up in bed, her pillows propped up. She was reading, unaware that her Aunt Susan was outside the door.

After the first trip to the zoo to meet her father, Angelina had begged Susan to take her back to the zoo the next week.

Susan had resisted until her Angelina started crying, and then she had given in. It was the worst thing she could have done. The first hour at the zoo, Angelina waited for her father by the giraffe corral, and when he didn't show up, she began searching for her father's face in the crowd.

Susan convinced Angelina to have lunch, and they did, Angelina excited, waiting for her daddy. Susan tried to tell her that this was not a meeting time for her daddy.

Angelina refused to believe it. They stayed at the zoo until closing, with Angel running, crying, from one exhibit to another, until Susan had to pick the sobbing child up and carry her to the car.

The next time Dan called, Susan didn't tell her niece until they were on their way to the zoo.

Angelina looked up and saw her Aunt Susan standing in the doorway. She grinned at her aunt and patted the bed. Susan went over and sat beside the child, putting her arms around her niece.

"Auntie Susan, I'm too excited to sleep."

"Angel, how did you know your daddy was coming?"

"I don't know, but I just did," Angelina said.

"Well, let's turn off your light and get some sleep, so you can see your daddy tomorrow." Susan gave her another hug, and then pulled away. "Do you want to sleep with me?" she asked softly.

"No, I'll be fine." She hugged and kissed her aunt. Susan tucked her in, turned off the light, and walked back to her bedroom. The few words she had heard her brother speak today had helped her. This ordeal had taken its toll on her as well. Dan had sounded more confident, more positive than she had heard him sound in a long time.

Maybe he had found some evidence, something he could use to get someone to believe his story.

Three

The men outside in the car parked down the street made a note in the log, and one of them spoke quietly into a radio microphone. The man speaking into the mike looked at the other man who was in the driver's seat.

"I don't know about you, but I hope we catch the bastard. He sure as hell screwed up my Friday night."

"Hell, probably the entire weekend," his partner said.

"It's time."

He nodded, and the driver removed a metal object from his pocket. He flipped a switch on the metal object, and the passenger spoke into the microphone again.

"Signal's on. You read it?" he said quietly.

"Affirmative, we have a strong reading."

Both men opened their doors quietly and got out, shutting the doors without a sound. They approached the house where Susan Prader and her niece, Angelina Harris, were sleeping. The first man carried a small metal object in his left hand. It was about the size of a package of cigarettes, was painted black, and was affixed to a powerful magnet. Attached was a small black antenna, with spirals in it, resembling the antenna to a cellular phone. The object was a transmitter, commonly called a "bird dog" unit. It sent out a powerful signal that enabled the vehicle to which it was attached to be tracked.

While the stocky man holding the transmitter watched, his partner walked up to the garage doors of Susan's Prader's house. He motioned for his partner to join him, and they both walked around the side of the garage, into the darkness. It took them less than a minute to open the side door with a set of locksmith's keys and enter the garage. The Volvo 840 wagon was the only vehicle in the garage. Other than the Volvo, there were some gardening tools on a bench, two boxes on the floor, and two bicycles, one a pink child's bike, and the other an adult's mountain bike.

That was it. No skis, no boats, just the car.

It took less than thirty seconds to put the transmitter under Susan Prader's car and quietly leave the garage.

Back in the car on the street, the passenger talked into the mike. "It's on. Got a signal?"

"Still strong. Wherever the car goes, so shall we," the voice said.

"It might be morning," the passenger said as they moved off down the street.

"We'll be here if it moves. Wherever she goes, we go."

Four

Grant threw the paper down in disgust. He immediately leaned forward and picked it up again. He sat in his chair in the living room in the early hours of the morning, a single lamp lit, a glass of whiskey, a large tumbler that had once been full, on the table beside him. Aimee was upstairs in bed, crying, he was sure, thinking about Minnie Mouse.

Minnie Mouse. Jesus, Natalie, where the hell are you, and what the hell are you doing? He didn't know what worried him more: that someone would have the balls and stupidity to indict her for murder, as the headlines of the *Oregonian* proclaimed, or the fact that she was off into the unknown with a man who was wanted for murder.

But is he a murderer? Maryland State Police say he is, but you don't, do you, Natalie?

And guess what, Grant, you grizzled old detective, you don't think he's a murderer, either.

He reached for his glass and drained it in one long pull. *Time for bed. We got a hell of a fight ahead of us.*

One hell of a fight.

Five

Dan and Natalie stood by the window, their arms tight around each other. Natalie pressed herself against him as she leaned up and kissed his neck. Dan gasped, surprised by the suddenness, the fierceness of her kiss. She put her cheek on his neck and held onto him, pressing her body against his. The emotions of the past few days, the thought of seeing his daughter again, the trust Natalie seemed to have in him . . . made it difficult for him to speak.

And he knew she did trust him.

She had made up her mind that he was a good person, that he was telling the truth, that he was a trusting soul, and she threw herself into their new partnership with a fierceness of her own, a purpose. She was quite unlike any person Dan had ever met, with her comedy, her own pain and ghosts, and her spirited fighting ability, an ability to fight and fight back in any situation she found herself in. Dan knew she was unique. The doubts of the past years surfaced again.

How could she love me? She's only known me for a few days.

He reached up and pulled her hands down from his neck.

"Natalie," his voice hoarse with emotion, "Natalie, Natalie, I . . ."

"Dan, you don't have to say anything," she whispered.

She reached up and took his face in her hands.

"Dan."

He stood still.

"Dan, I know you need me, and I . . . I'm falling in love with you." There, she'd said it.

Dan looked intently at her, his face inches from hers.

"Tell me," Natalie said. "Tell me that you are feeling the same things I am."

"I am," Dan said. "It's just so damned hard, after so long on the road."

Natalie pulled his face down and kissed him, and when she kissed him, she pressed her body into his, her breasts pushing into his chest. Dan felt himself falling, as if from a great height. When their tongues touched, he kissed her fiercely, hungrily, as if he couldn't kiss her enough. When he held her, he swayed slightly back and forth.

He felt alive, his body aching, and he trembled with emotion for this woman he had saved, who in turn had saved him and was making him a real person again.

He felt himself grow hard pressing against her, and he involuntarily pulled back, embarrassed by his need. Natalie sensed this, and pulled her arms from his neck and put them around his waist, pulling him tighter to her, now beginning to rub her body against his.

Dan gasped and moaned and took his lips from hers. Natalie reached up and grabbed Dan's arm, looking into his eyes, leading him to the bed. She forced him to sit, and then put her hands on his chest and pushed him over backward, grinning at him.

"Natalie, I don't know why we . . . "

"Ssshhh." She put her finger to her lips and grinned at him again. She jumped on top of Dan, straddling him, pinning him with her knees, and put her hands on his hands, pulling them out to the side. She was flat on him then, kissing his neck, his lips, his eyes. Dan thought he would explode.

Natalie had been engaged twice, and had come close to marriage, but she had never felt anything like this – so intense, so right.

He's what you need, Minnie Mouse. He's what you have needed for a long time. You must help him not to be afraid now.

They undressed each other slowly, lying, then sitting, and it was she who helped Dan when their clothes were off. She rolled over on her back.

Dan was awestruck by her beauty when he lowered himself on top of her, breasts round and beautiful, her thin waist, her athletic legs.

She pulled Dan overr on top of her and guided him into her. Natalie gasped when he entered her, the beauty and pleasure of it more than she could stand, realizing in the back of her mind that Dan had yelled as well. She wrapped her legs around his waist and pulled him deeper into her, and before she knew what she was doing, she moaned and screamed into his ear, "I'm coming," like it had never happened before, wondering, *This soon, why this soon?* She came again, a continuous shuddering climax that was foreign to her and absolutely wonderful. She wrapped her legs tighter around him, whispering and then urging him, "Come Dan, come, my darling."

When he did, she came again. He had his eyes tightly closed, whispering her name, and at last he slumped down on her and she wrapped her arms around him, saying his name again and again.

They lay like that for a long time, whispering and touching each other, caressing.

Natalie let her fingers trail over his body, and she felt him grow hard again. This time she lay quietly as Dan took over their lovemaking, moving slowly at first, and then with more urgency.

Natalie woke sometime in the early morning and looked at Dan as he slept beside her. She marveled at how she loved this man. Minnie Mouse and the balding poster child. So improbable. So possible.

Death walked.

Natalie shivered, holding Dan closer, marveling at how human touch could shut out the darkness.

Six

If he stood still, Victor could feel a slight breeze coming off the darkened swamp. In the blackness of the night, he waited by the water's edge. When he first heard the noise, it sounded like a single-engine airplane, far off. The water muffled the sound, and the wind brought slight bits of it to him, off and on. He strained to look into the darkness to locate the source of the sound, but he couldn't see anything.

After a minute, the sound grew steady and louder. Victor saw the wake before he saw the machine, the water shining white in the dim starlight. The phosphorescent wake straightened and headed straight for Victor. He often marveled how the driver of the sled could find his way in the dark, how he knew where he was going. The machine making the wake was an ungainly hybrid between an airplane and a boat. The driver sat in front, up high in a seat he was strapped into. There was an engine behind him, an engine on stilts with an aircraft propeller behind it.

A swamp sled.

The engine slowed, the murmur coming down to an idle, the wake overtaking the sled. The sled rode the swell created by its own wake, and the operator turned on a light. He expertly docked the sled on the small beach just in front of Victor.

"Turn off the light," Victor said, as the driver killed the engine. The driver ignored him and unbuckled his seat belt. That he had a seat belt in the first place was strange: the sled was filthy with grease, stains of undetermined origin, mud, old oil cans, trash, and reeking organic matter on the bottom of the sled. The driver didn't look any cleaner than the sled. The man looked middle-aged, but Victor knew he was in his early thirties. He was wearing the same coveralls he always did, the dirty brown color of the swamp long since obliterating the original color. He had on a dark rubber raincoat, patched with duct tape and held together with wire. His face was covered with a month-old beard, and he had what looked like an entire package of leaf chewing tobacco in his mouth, covering stumps of what once had been teeth.

"Billy," the driver bawled, and a younger, thinner version of the driver jumped down from the other seat, a copy minus the beard and raincoat.

"Comin' Dad."

"Billy, get those bags ready," he growled, and jumped onto the sand bar with Victor. Victor was used to seeing the man's skeleton, to seeing the boy's as well, thinking that the boy was a product of a union between the man and his daughter. He watched as their skeletons moved within the filthy clothing.

They will die before me.

"How many do you have?" Victor asked, looking past the skeletonized driver, looking at the sled and its cargo.

"A dozen smallish ones, half that many mature ones. You said you wanted big ones, but they're getting harder to find. Let's see your money."

"First I see the merchandise."

The driver turned and held up his hand, yelling at Billy, "Leav'm on the sled."

Victor reached inside his jacket and pulled an envelope from an inside pocket. He had to play to this game each time with this creature conceived in a petri dish and he did it calmly. The man delivered. Victor handed the money over to the sled driver.

"It's all there," Victor said. "Five hundred each and a thousand dollar bonus for being here on time." He had just handed the sled driver ten thousand dollars.

The sled driver looked up and squinted at Victor. He nodded and yelled at Billy without turning around. The younger man started to pull burlap sacks from the sled, sacks that moved and thrashed.

Victor opened one, looked inside, holding the end to the light. He replaced the tie and carried it to the van. The driver watched, not offering to help. Billy followed, carrying sacks to the van. As they were getting the last few into the van, Victor quickly jerked open a bag and examined the contents.

He walked over to the sled driver. "There's one dead, and I didn't order dead merchandise." The friendly game had gone on long enough.

"So what," the sled driver said, spitting tobacco within inches of Victor's boot. "It's hard enough to find these and not get caught catching them, and it's not my fault you think one's dead."

Victor grinned. "Okay, no harm done, compadre, I kill them anyway, make soup out of them and trinkets out of the other parts." It would be too much for the swamp rat to comprehend if Victor were to tell him how useful the cargo really was, or what he did with it. As Victor grinned, he knew that he would need the swamp rat only one or two more times. When he had no more need of them, he would sink the rat and his offspring with their filthy boat.

The swamp rat climbed aboard the sled and started the engine, waiting for his son to push the boat away from the sand bar. Victor shut the doors of the rented van and climbed in the driver's seat, watching as the sled went up on plane, speeding away. He waited until it was out of sight, the only evidence of its passing a distant droning.

He backed around and left the sandbar, the headlights cutting the dark on the sandy road, the sacks settling down in the back, the movement stopping.

This might be all I need, he thought.

Then I'll come back and finish the swamp rat and his offspring anyway, just because.

There was something Victor Bramson hadn't counted on when he started his research; he found that he liked killing.

He wasn't sure when he realized he was different, that he was beginning to see the bones of his patients. The old ones were first, the ones he studied, the ones he counseled. They were so easy. Everyone expected his patients to die, and that's what they did. They told him their secrets, how they lived so long. They told him the best secrets when he helped them end their lives.

When he had to look for survivors, he found that he liked that as well. He learned a lot in those years, a lot about himself. He found that it didn't make any difference to him in the least, the crawling, puling amoeba, the squirming humanity that rose up like yeast, writhed, died, was ultimately replaceable with millions of other crawling, squirming, yeasty amoeba, all indistinguishable from those who had gone before and those who would replace them.

Squirming, crawling, yeasty oatmeal.

If they all died tomorrow it wouldn't make a nickel's worth of difference to the outcome of his studies, of his life.

They are the living dead anyway.

San Antonio in the morning.

You will all die before me.

Seven

Natalie opened her eyes and moved her head from side to side, looking over the dimly lit room. She turned on her side and thrust her leg across the bed, getting comfortable and starting to drift off again. She reached out and touched cool sheets where Dan had been lying.

Motel room – where am I?

She raised her head up and looked around. The events of the late evening came back to her then, the warmth of their lovemaking, the closeness of Dan.

Dan.

Gone.

Natalie rolled over and sat up.

Dan stood there, wearing briefs, looking out the window, the lights from the harbor highlighting him. As she watched, she realized that she had awakened without a dream of death and dying for the first time since Stephanie's death. *Dan. How different he looks from the first time, when he had his beard and wild eyes.* She looked at his muscled arms and legs, the brown hair, and imagined his brown eyes looking at her, questioning and then loving.

Natalie held the bedspread with one hand, and ran her other hand over her breasts, remembering what Dan had done hours earlier. Her nipples were growing hard, and she was amazed at the strength of her reaction when she thought of Dan. She had dismissed the thought that there might be one right person for her; the men she had known in the past had always been less than what she wanted.

I'm not willing to settle for okay now. I know what I want – who I want.

"Dan," Natalie called to him, softly.

He turned and looked at the bed and smiled.

"Dan, come to bed and tell me about it."

"About what?" he said as he walked over to her.

Natalie held the covers up and slid over, Dan looking at her body. He got into bed and lay down beside Natalie. She put her arms around him and gave him a hug, touching him with her bare breasts. She could feel him grow hard.

"Can't sleep?" Natalie asked, running her hand over his chest, looking into his brown eyes.

"No," Dan said, "I was thinking of the morning."

Natalie slid her hand down to his groin, to his underwear, and rubbed his hard penis out the outside of the cloth. He groaned.

"Are you going to keep those on for the rest of the night, sir?"

Dan shook his head.

"Can I help you off with them?" And she did. As she straddled him, a wild thought raced through her head.

Death and dying. Gunpowder and blood.

She pushed it away and thought of Disneyland.

Dying not allowed.

And she lost herself in Dan; took him inside her, riding him, holding onto his arms, lowering herself down on top of him, whispering his name, whispering "Love you," to him, over and over again, smiling at her love for him, shuddering at her climaxes, urging for him to come inside her, wanting all of him, pushing away the bad thoughts as she fell exhausted on top of him.

"Natalie."

"Hummmmm?"

"Natalie, I love you."

"Was that so hard to say?"

"I never thought I'd be saying it again. But I do, I love you.

"I know. I love you too."

"Natalie."

"What?"

"What are we going to do?"

"'Bout what?"

"The fact that we are both wanted for murder."

"Oh, that. I thought we would get jobs at Disneyland under assumed names, take Angelina with us, put her on rides all day, live in an RV, okay?" She snuggled under his arm.

"Okay, but do you know the best part of all?"

"Hummmmm," Natalie said sleepily. "Make it quick, buster, I'm in for some more sleep." She closed her eyes and snuggled closer.

"The *we* part. I'm not alone anymore."

"Me either," she murmured, "and you can't get rid of me."

Dan could barely hear the last part. Natalie was sleeping.

He looked down at her and marveled. *She's so beautiful, and so wonderful.* He pulled the bedspread up higher, and held her. And when he didn't think it would happen, he fell asleep, holding on.

As it turned out, it was a good thing, for it would be a long time before either of them slept again.

Eight

Susan glanced in her rearview mirror again for the tenth time in as many blocks. Was that brown car the same one that had been on her street? She looked again and didn't see it, not relaxing, just as worried.

"Aunt Susan?"

Susan Prader glanced over at Angelina, and then back at the road. They had just left her house in the Pine Ridge area, northwest of downtown and outside the beltway that circled Baltimore, and they were now only a few blocks from the beltway.

"What, honey?"

"Aunt Susan, do you think my daddy will still have his beard?"

"I don't know, honey, but we'll soon find out." *God, I hope he makes it,* she thought, wondering what she was going to do if Dan didn't show. She glanced behind her again. The brown car was closer now, and there were two people in it. *Dammit!*

Susan increased her speed, the traffic not too heavy now at eleven a.m., and she took advantage of it. She pulled in behind a truck in the left land and slowed down, the entrance to the beltway, eastbound, just ahead. With a sudden impulse, she floored the accelerator and swung left around the truck, and then cut in front, missing the bumper by inches. She jerked the wheel again and the Volvo wagon swerved onto the on ramp to the beltway. The truck driver hit his brakes and Susan saw a flash of movement in the cab, the driver waving his arms.

* * *

"What the hell's she doing?" Sergeant Ames screamed, slamming on his brakes, letting the truck go by him on the right. The Volvo disappeared in front of the truck. He jerked the wheel and pulled in behind the truck, now past the entrance to the beltway.

"Bullshit bullshit bullshit!" he screamed, pounding his fist on the steering wheel as they went under the beltway. He looked for a way to turn around as his partner told the rest of the surveillance team that they had just lost her. "She's eastbound on the beltway," he said, and he heard a unit a half mile behind them copy their call.

Susan grinned and patted Angelina on the head, her niece looking up at her as if she were a crazy driver. "I almost missed the turn, honey, and we can't have that today." She looked in the rearview mirror as she accelerated onto the beltway, choosing a lane to the left of middle, speeding up to seventy, putting some distance between her and the brown car. She didn't think they had made the turn.

They hadn't, but two other cars entered the beltway a quarter mile behind the white Volvo wagon.

"This is J-410, I . . . I think I see them just ahead, approaching the 83 turnoff." *Damn, she's not letting any grass grow.* Detective Busey floored the accelerator, moving to the left lane, passing cars, trying to keep the white Volvo wagon in sight. He announced his position again to the rest of the chase vehicles.

Sergeant Ames came over the radio. "J-410, stay with them, and watch her lane changes. She either doesn't know where she's going, or she's aware of us."

"J-410, copy," Busey said. "She's got to be aware of us, or else she's a maniac." He urged more speed out of the unmarked car, then picked up the mike and said quickly, "Looks like she's taking the 83 freeway toward downtown."

"Not far now, honey," Susan said. The Baltimore Zoo at Druid Hill Park was up ahead, two miles. By the time they had traveled one of those miles, two of the surveillance vehicles had taken positions behind the white Volvo wagon.

Angelina grinned, and leaned forward against her shoulder harness, looking at the familiar signs for the zoo.

My daddy's coming home yesterday.

Nine

"**Dan,** look," Natalie said excitedly, pointing at the huge zoo gates. She was trying to keep Dan preoccupied enough so he wouldn't sprint to the zoo. Distract him.

But he was distracted enough. He was going to see his baby very soon. They had eaten breakfast at the hotel. A taxi brought them to the zoo a full hour before the scheduled meeting time.

As they walked up to the line that had formed behind one of the ticket windows, Dan was suddenly apprehensive. He felt out of place, as if he were a visitor from another planet. There were throngs of people, families, mothers and fathers with children, teenagers, standing in line and congregating at one of the gates.

This was a Saturday, and probably one of the last Saturdays in the fall when it would be pleasant enough or warm enough to spend the day at the zoo. It was a beautiful day, the leaves starting to turn colors on the deciduous trees, with the temperatures promising to be in the mid-sixties.

Dan and Natalie stood in line, Natalie with her hand in Dan's, excitedly looking about, chattering, saying something about zoos being the next best place to Disneyland. Dan had a similar thought. *Animals are there for children and we are all children. And here we are, waiting to see a daughter I should have been able to tuck in every night. And the rest of these people here are more worried about mortgages and putting braces on kids' teeth than staying alive and out of jail. Strange.*

The distance between us is so vast, those here with ordinary lives, and me wanted for murder. So vast.

His heart ached. His hands needed to hold his baby daughter.

She's a five-year-old, the age she was when I lost her for good.

As they moved closer to the ticket booth, Dan began looking around, looking at the crowd, looking in the direction of the parking lot, looking at people walking from the large lot to see if he could see his baby girl. He knew they were early, at least an hour before the meeting time, but Susan and Angelina would be early as well.

Natalie saw Dan's apprehension grow, saw him begin to look around, carefully at first, then his movements jerked as he looked in haste for his daughter. She grabbed his right arm with both of hers and gave him a hug. He smiled at her and put his arm around her shoulders. He continued his search of the crowd.

Dan got their tickets and they walked inside, moving with a group of people past the big cat exhibit. They walked down the path by the food stands, clowns, wide open grassy picnic areas. Dan held Natalie's hand and led them through the crowd. He stopped when they got to the giraffe exhibit.

He found a bench and sat with his back to the giraffes, watching the path they were just on, the one from the main gate. Behind them, inside the fences, was a large pasture made to resemble an African veldt. There were at least a dozen giraffes, half of them mature adults, sixteen feet high, and some smaller ones in the enclosure. Dan turned and watched their graceful, curious gait, and Natalie sat beside him.

"When we first decided to meet at the zoo," Dan said, "I picked the giraffe exhibit because it was Angelina's favorite. We went to the zoo when she was three and four years old and she would watch the giraffes for hours. She would stay until we made her leave." Dan looked at Natalie and then quickly back to the sidewalk.

"She would run to this bench and stand up and look over the top of the fence. Her eyes were so alive, and she would watch for at least an hour.

Dan grinned, looked at his hands, then up the sidewalk. "She would have the silliest grin on her face as the giraffes walked."

He pulled Natalie's arms around him and she whispered, "I love you, Dan."

"I love you too."

Dan caught a flash of color on the walkway in front of them, the slight downward slope letting the little person pick up speed, caroming off people in the path, a flash of green that burst into the open area in front of them and launched itself at Dan.

"*Daaaddee!*" Angelina struck her father in a full run as Dan was standing up to see what the noise was, realizing that it was Angelina, turning his head toward the sidewalk as she struck him. He threw his arms up and around her, falling back onto the bench, crying, saying her name over and over again.

Angelina wrapped her arms around his neck, calling to him, "My daddy, my daddy, my daddy."

Dan was aware of his sister walking up, and Natalie stepping back beside Susan.

When Susan approached the front gate with Angelina, the girl had run from her, into the crowd of people. Susan tried to follow, and lost Angelina in the crowd.

"Angelina!" Susan yelled, but by then she had already lost sight of the green jumper. She hurried on, maneuvering around parents with strollers and excited children, praying that Angelina was going to the giraffe exhibit. She got there just in time to see Angelina hugging a strange man.

My God, it's Dan, and he looks better than he has in years.

Susan stood back, watching her brother and niece crying, and she started to cry with them, tears running down her face, ruining her makeup, and she didn't care.

We have to find a way to keep them together. We must convince the authorities that Dan isn't a criminal.

She became aware that the woman beside her was also watching Dan and Angelina, watching intensely, her lower lip quivering. *They must be together.* Dan's bag was on the bench, next to a flowery cloth bag.

A meeting had never been like this before for Dan – so intense, so emotional. He'd always been emotional when he saw his baby daughter when he'd been away, but he was also depressed and disheartened about his situation.

Dad had such a jumble of feelings: love for his daughter, sadness at what he had missed – *my baby is now a little girl* – and he put the anger away. He was crying openly, kissing Angelina, whispering, "My Angel."

But a seven-year-old can be intense for only so long.

"Oh, Daddy, I'm so very, very glad to see you," she said. She sat up suddenly, keeping her arms around his neck, looking closely at his face. She put her hands on his cheeks and patted them. "Daddy, you shaved your beard," she said excitedly.

"Yes, honey, I shaved it just for you," Dan said, drying his eyes on his sleeve. He smiled at his daughter, keeping his grip tight around her, and said, "You're a big girl now, and so tall."

Angelina jumped off his lap and told him, "I've grown this much, Daddy, and I have so much to tell you." She jumped back on his lap.

"I just bet you do, honey." He made a resolution then to not be separated from his daughter ever again.

"Auntie Susan, look," Angelina said, Daddy shaved his beard."

"I see that, honey."

Dan looked at Susan and pulled her down and felt her arms around him. She wiped her eyes on the back of her hand and he knew she would think of her makeup running all over her face. "It's good to see you, big sister," he said softly. Susan stood up and kept her hand on Dan's shoulder and introduced herself to Natalie.

"Susan," Dan said, "this is Natalie, and she is going to help me out of this trouble. She believes in me, and we are going to fight this together." Dan put his hand out for Natalie.

"I knew when he talked with me yesterday his voice was different," Susan said. "You must be the change for the better."

"I don't know about that," Natalie said, "but I have a very special reason for believing in Dan. You see, he saved my life."

Dan felt the emotion of the last few minutes, and he struggled for control. He squeezed Natalie's hand tighter.

"Daddy, who is that lady?" Angelina pointed at Natalie.

"Honey, this is a very special friend of Daddy's." Dan knew he wasn't doing so well with introductions, but he was with the three people he loved most in the world.

"Hi, Natalie. My daddy's come home."

Dan let Natalie's hand drop, and watched as Natalie kneeled down in front of Angelina, and whisper in her ear. Angelina straightened and said, "Are you and Daddy going to get married?"

Natalie laughed.

Susan came up and put her hands on Natalie's shoulders, and Dan felt his throat grow tight. He was saved by Angelina asking, "Hey you guys, is anybody hungry?"

"Where the hell did she go?" Sergeant Ames yelled at his partner. He jerked his handheld radio up and began to give instructions. A voice came over the radio. "Uh, we lost the girl at the front gate."

Ames made assignments: 9L90 and 93 were to take the lower areas, the big cats and then the elephant exhibits, 9L85 and 91 the avian cages. He made the rest of the assignments quickly, looking at the map he'd gotten when they entered the zoo..

"She went to the right, boss," Ames partner said. "Let's go down there."

"No, we're gonna stay by the front gate," Ames growled. *We need to get this guy today. We will. This fugitive is so close to jail he can taste the food.*

Dan carried Angelina as they looked for a place to eat. He followed Susan and Natalie, watching as the two of them chatted, arm in arm.

"What shall we eat, Angel?"

"Hot dogs."

"Okay, a hot dog coming up."

"No, Daddy, I want hot dogs."

"More than one?" Dan couldn't stop grinning.

As Natalie and Susan walked toward the main gate, Natalie glanced at Dan's sister and appraised the clothes, the athletic walk. *She's very fit for someone in her mid-fifties. She dresses as if she's going for an afternoon gala event at the country club,* Natalie thought, not unkindly. She could tell that Susan deeply loved Dan and Angelina, and she knew that Susan must have put her life on hold for her brother and her niece. Natalie felt Susan's arm around her, and she felt for the first time that things might turn out okay. They might be able to have a life. They came to the intersection of the path to the elephant exhibits and the birds, and stopped.

"What do you mean, Dan saved your life?"

"A man broke into my apartment and killed my sister," Natalie said, her voice growing soft as she thought about that night. "Dan had been following the man, the person he thinks killed his wife, and . . ."

"Jacqueline," Susan whispered,

"Yes, the man who killed Jacqueline. Dan came in while the man was trying to kill me and he chased him off. He saved my life, but it was too . . ." She stopped and caught her breath.

"I'm sorry, honey," Susan said. She put her arms around Natalie.

"We're looking for the same man," Natalie said. "We're not sure why or how, but the man who killed my Stephanie also killed Dan's wife."

"Hot dogs!" Angelina yelled behind them, and Natalie turned to see Dan grinning as he came up.

"She wants hot dogs," Dan said, and Natalie held her hand out to him.

Natalie laughed and looked at Angelina as the child pointed at an outdoor restaurant. Natalie led Susan to a table in the back, as far from the sidewalk as she could find. Dan and Angelina ordered.

It's crowded, Natalie thought, so we should be safe.

She was wrong.

When Dan returned with a tray of hot dogs, Angelina was holding a stuffed giraffe by its neck, and promptly sat on her dad's lap.

"I knew my daddy was coming home yesterday," she said, her mouth full. Natalie looked at Susan, and then at Dan.

"I don't know how, but she knew you were going to be here today," Susan said.

"Yesterday?" Natalie asked.

"Temporary, the school psychologist said. A wish for a better time, the using yesterday and tomorrow for today. Not to worry yet, he said."

Natalie glanced around, knowing that something didn't seem quite right. She looked at Susan. "Do you think you were followed?"

"Maybe," Susan said. "I might have been, but I must have lost them."

Natalie turned her chair and looked out over the sidewalk. "Can you recognize any of the officers who followed you?"

"No, I don't think so."

"Natalie should be able to spot them," Dan said. "She's a homicide detective from Portland."

Natalie looked at Susan and saw the older woman appraising her with a slight grin. She reached over and patted Natalie's hand. She stood up and walked over to Natalie and hugged her. Natalie grabbed Susan's arms and held on, liking the warmth and caring in the hug.

Susan pulled back and looked at Natalie. "Why can't you just go to the police here and tell them that it's all a mistake?"

"No, we can't do that, Susan," Natalie said. "At least, not for a while."

"I don't understand."

Natalie took Susan's hands and pulled her down to sit beside her. Natalie leaned close, their faces inches apart.

"This guy's slick," Natalie said quietly, just above a whisper. "We don't know why he killed my sister, but I think he was after me. We think he killed Dan's wife and we don't know why. But he arranged the evidence to look like I killed Stephanie, much the same as he did at the scene of Jackie's death. He's slick. And we are going to get him, but for right now, we can't be caught."

The look on Susan's face was enough for Natalie. She put her arms around Susan again and hugged her. Natalie told Susan that it would be alright, that she believed in Dan, and there were those who believed in her. As Natalie pulled away, she thought, *I just hope you're right, Minnie Mouse.*

Natalie took a bite of her hot dog and looked at Dan and Angelina, thinking of how painful it must have been for Dan to be separated from her. Angelina was chattering about her school, her friends, about knowing that her daddy was coming home. A beautiful girl, with Dan's eyes. Natalie leaned forward and whispered, "Susan."

The older woman looked up over her cup of coffee.

"Susan, how are we going to separate them today?"

Susan shook her head and shrugged her shoulders.

"We can't stay here very long," Natalie said, watching as Angelina rested her head on Dan's shoulder. Natalie reached for Susan's hand and held it, looking at the sidewalk. She watched the ever changing crowd of people flowing by, babies in strollers, moms and dads with kids, teenagers with hair so strange to her world, and men in suits.

Susan suddenly squeezed Natalie's hand.

"What is it?"

Susan didn't answer, just stared at the sidewalk.

"Police?" Natalie whispered.

Susan nodded.

"Where?"

Susan pointed at the sidewalk. "The man with the radio."

Natalie watched as a man in a tan suit spoke into a radio, almost close enough to hear what he was saying. *He isn't looking this way yet, but he knows what he is looking for.*

Natalie reached across the table for Dan's arm, touching him, getting his attention, keeping her gaze on the man she was sure was a detective.

"Susan, do you know what they look like?"

"I think so, a couple at least."

The man turned, his gaze sweeping past them, and he moved past them and stopped, looking.

"Can you lead them away from us?" Natalie asked.

"I can sure as hell try," Susan said, "but what are we going to do with Angelina?"

Natalie looked at Dan and his daughter, and knew that it would be a noisy, tearful separation if they tried something now.

"We'll get Angelina to you later. Lead them away from us and Dan and I will take her with us for now."

Susan quickly hugged them, and then whispered to Natalie, "You're a keeper, my dear." Susan looked at them, and walked toward the direction of the police.

Natalie turned to look as Susan walked directly in front of the man in the tan suit. She saw his startled reaction and then the crowd closed in and she was gone. Dan picked up Angelina.

"They will be calling others to help, you know," Natalie said, her stomach turning over. *It's either the hotdog, or the prospect of the chase.*

Natalie pulled Dan along behind her and walked toward the front gate, slowing, thinking about where the police would put someone. *They'll be out front for sure, at least I would be.*

"Daddy, I have to go to the bathroom," Angelina said. Dan put her down on the sidewalk and Natalie took her hand.

"Can I take you?"

"Sure, c'mon Natalie, let's go."

In the restroom a woman was changing the diaper on a small, squiggly baby. Angelina entered a stall and Natalie waited outside. Angelina buttoned the top strap of her jumper as she came out. She caught Natalie's arm.

"Nat'lie."

"Yes, honey."

"Why are those bad men after my daddy?"

Natalie stopped and sat on the bench, pulling Angelina down beside her. Her stomach did a slow roll, not knowing what to say.

"They aren't bad men, Angelina. They're just doing their job, and they think -."

"That daddy killed mommy?"

Natalie's heart did a flip-flop now, feeling a wave of emotion pass over her. *First Stephanie and now Angelina. Gunpowder and blood. And I can't get away from death.*

She put her arms around Angelina. "No, honey, your daddy didn't kill your mommy, we know he didn't."

Angelina slowly nodded. "Are we gonna find the bad guy so Daddy can come home?"

"Yes, honey, we are, your daddy and I, but we can't let the police find out where we are until we do."

"But you're a police, aren't you, Natalie?"

"I am, and soon they will believe me."

Angelina pulled away and smiled. "I can run very fast."

They hugged each other and walked outside. Angelina skipped up to her dad.

She has the trust in the goodness of the future – the complete trust of a seven-year-old. A very beautiful seven-year-old, with my Daniel's eyes.

Susan walked as fast as she could, threading her way through the crowd. She wanted to lead the police on for as long as she could, letting Dan and Natalie and Angel make their way out of the zoo. She smiled at the thought of Natalie, a young, vibrant woman. *A woman for Dan, and for my Angel.*

"Mrs. Prader!" The voice came from close behind her. Susan didn't turn, but walked faster, brushing by people, past the bench where Dan had been sitting, past the giraffe exhibit.

"Mrs Prader!" A hand grabbed her shoulder, pulling her back, forcing her to stop. Susan suddenly turned to face the person who had so rudely stopped her.

"Sergeant Ames," she said, smiling.

The homicide detective turned red, clenching his teeth, the frustration evident on his face.

"Mrs. Prader, where is your brother?"

"I don't know, I thought you boys were looking for him."

"And where is your niece?"

"She's here at the zoo, here with friends, and I'm out for a stroll."

Ames pulled his radio up and spoke urgently. "He's not here, check the exits."

"Daniel didn't do it, you know," Susan said. "You're looking for the wrong man."

Ames blew out a breath in a long sigh. He motioned toward a bench, and Susan followed him there. He waved two officers off, a man and a woman, and they hurried on toward the front gate.

"Even if he didn't do it, Mrs. Prader, he needs to turn himself in. You must convince him, because all the police from here to San Francisco know is that he is wanted for murder. And most of the people we get murder warrants for actually did kill someone. What I'm telling you is that police officers will be very careful with your brother and they will take any movement as an extreme threat." He turned to face Susan. "Do you understand?"

"I do, and I think that Daniel knows that as well, but he didn't do it, and he will soon be able to prove it. You know where I live, Sergeant?"

"I know the address."

Susan walked down the sidewalk, looking at the people sitting on the lawn across from the giraffe pastures. *I hope you are safe, brother. And now Natalie and Angelina, with you. Please keep them safe.*

But if she had known what would happen to them, she would have called Sergeant Ames back and helped the police find Dan.

At least then they would have all been safe.

Ten

"**Okay**, here's what we'll do," Dan said. He kneeled down and put his arms around Natalie and Angelina. He pulled them close, their faces touching. With their backs to passersby, he thought they would look like a family in a huddle, deciding which exhibits to see first. He looked around at the front gate.

"Hey, nice family," Natalie said, speaking what Dan suddenly thought. She surprised him by kissing on the lips. Angelina kissed him on his cheek.

"Stop that, you guys." Dan grinned in spite of the tenseness of the moment.

"Why?" Angelina giggled.

"Really want us too?" Natalie asked.

"Yes," Dan said. "No, I mean, this is what we need to do. You think you can go with Natalie for a few minutes, Angel?"

"Okay, Daddy, for a few minutes."

"Good girl. Natalie, there's a shopping center just down from the entrance of Druid Hill Park. I'll meet you in the restaurant on the north end. It's gonna be easier if we don't go out the front gate together. Now get going."

Natalie grabbed his face and kissed him again, longer this time, and Dan felt himself losing his resolve to leave them. She rubbed his face and said, "Be careful, Dan."

"Love you, Daddy."

Natalie walked around him hand in hand with Angelina. She stopped and turned back. Dan saw what had made her turn.

"There's a detective there, blue windbreaker, on the west side of the gate," Natalie said. "If they catch you, don't fight them, Dan. All they know is that you are wanted for murder, and they won't take any chances. If they catch you, I'll find the killer and we will get you out."

Dan nodded. "If I get caught, get to Susan. She'll help you." He turned to face the gate as Natalie and Angelina walked away, Natalie with her bag slung on her shoulder and holding Angelina's hand, saying something to make Angelina laugh, and he soon lost sight of them in the crowd. He caught a flash of green by the front gate and then they were gone.

So was the man in the blue windbreaker.

Dan had to resist the urge to run after them, to grab Angelina and Natalie and never let them go, to grab them and run and keep running. And he had to resist the urge to stand there and cry.

Time to get moving, Danny boy.

Detective Eric Stattler stood by the main entrance, looking at the endless waves of people coming into the zoo. *Christ! Everyone in Baltimore must be coming here today.* Sergeant Ames thought that the wanted subject, Daniel Harris, was coming to the front gate, but shit, he hadn't even been seen yet, just the sister and her niece. *Where the hell else would the sister take her niece on a Saturday? To the fucking zoo, of course. The guy we want is probably in Mazatlan with a tan and a half dozen Mexican girlfriends to take him to the beach.*

"L-90." Stattler pulled his radio form his pocket and answered.

"L-90, go ahead."

"See anything at the front gate?"

"Lotsa people coming to the zoo," Stattler replied, not being able to resist the remark, one that he would pay for later.

"L-90, I'm sending more people your way, and look for the girl."

"L-90, roger."

Look for the girl, roger, Boss. Shit, I wouldn't be able to see her if she walked in front of me, the way the crowds are starting to form outside the gate. What's she gonna do, leave just after she got to the zoo?

Stattler did look at the exit lanes, and thought that it was a stupid waste of time, since no one was leaving this early.

Dan walked laterally to the main entrance, going to the far end of the gates. Damned few people going home. His legs trembled with the thought he might get caught. His forehead and scalp broke out in a sweat. A single drop rolled down his cheek as he walked through the gate. Once outside, he walked past the lines of people forming in front of the ticket booths, and started across the cement apron toward the parking lot. He made his way to the end of the lot, his destination the gardens, large trees, and underbrush of the park.

Dan looked around, hoping to see Natalie and Angelina, thinking that he could join them before they made it to the restaurant, but they were not in sight. He breathed a little easier and turned toward a cab parked at the end of the parking lot.

This was almost too easy.

Detective Stattler decided that he needed to be closer to the exits, and he moved that way, knowing that the entire exercise was a waste of time. He approached the exit gates through the crowd, looking at Dan, watching as the fugitive walked through the gate and out of the zoo. *The guy there, probably going home to watch football, the lucky bastard, dropping his kids off at the zoo. Jesus, he's the right height, the right face, hell it could be him.*

Stattler jogged toward the gate, touching his shoulder holster to reassure himself his gun was there. He jogged up behind the fugitive as the man made for a taxi.

"Harris?"

Dan turned and looked over his shoulder as he heard his name. The man with the blue windbreaker was jogging up behind him. The man looked at him and Dan saw the recognition in his eyes. Without another thought, Dan turned and ran, putting his head down and pumping his arms and legs, holding his bag in his right hand.

He sprinted across the parking lot, running for the grassy area and the woods behind, hearing a shout and knowing the man was only steps behind him. He ran in front of a tour bus, startling the driver into slamming on the brakes, hoping the detective had to wait for the bus.

He didn't, and if anything, he was closer. Dan sprinted across the grass, the woods only fifty yards away, and he glanced behind him.

The detective had slowed and was talking on his radio, still running. Dan's lungs burned, but he was still too scared to feel much, his breathing coming fast, his heart roaring.

He reached the woods and entered a path at full speed, running downhill, sliding on leaves, hearing the footsteps pounding behind him. He took another quick glance over his shoulder and he tried to run faster, the cop ten yards back.

I'll be in jail before Natalie and Angelina have time for a snack in the restaurant.

The cop was gaining, and Dan jerked back around to face downhill. He tripped over the branch and fell headlong, throwing his bag and his hands in front of him, banging his knee on the way down, and then he was hit from behind. The detective landed on him and drove him down, the air painfully exploding from Dan's lungs.

"Give it up, Harris," the detective yelled as he grabbed Dan's wrist. Dan went limp and held his arms out in front of him, his face in the leaves.

"Hold your right hand up."

As the detective brought the handcuff down, Dan turned on his side and saw the detective's gun hanging from his shoulder holster. Without giving himself time to think, Dan jerked the gun out and stuck it into the detective's stomach.

"Get off of me," Dan ordered, keeping the gun tight against the man's stomach.

"Now!"

Detective Stattler raised his hands and rolled back on his heels, his forehead visible with sweat. He didn't say a word.

"Stand up, all the way," Dan said, holding the gun in his right hand, staring at the detective. Stattler stood up, holding the handcuffs in his left hand.

"Handcuff one wrist," Dan said and Stattler did, still saying nothing. Dan could see the fear give way to anger, and he knew he didn't have long or the detective would jump him, and Dan knew he couldn't shoot.

But the detective didn't know that yet. He ordered the cop to put his arms around a medium sized tree.

"Handcuff yourself around the tree."

Stattler didn't move. "Do it yourself, you son-of-a-bitch."

Dan raised the gun and pointed it at the detective's head.

"What's your name?"

"Stattler."

"Well, Detective Stattler, either handcuff yourself, or I'll pull the trigger."

Stattler put his arms around the tree and fastened the handcuffs, glaring at Dan. "You won't get very far, Harris."

"Maybe not," Dan said, and he removed the magazine from the pistol Stattler had been carrying. He pulled the slide back and ejected the round from the chamber and placed the magazine and pistol in front of the tree, out of Stattler's reach.

"Tell your friends I didn't do it," Dan said, looking at the detective. "Also tell them that I'm not armed, that I'm looking for the man who killed my wife, since you guys haven't bothered to find him."

Dan heard sounds of people yelling in the park, near the entrance to the trail. Stattler looked back over his shoulder.

"L-90, what's your location?" Dan searched for the radio, following the noise, and found it under the leaves, in front of them on the trail. He picked it up and pushed the talk button.

"L-90," he said excitedly and in a rush, "he's going back inside the zoo, front entrance, repeat, *front entrance!"*

"You bastard," Stattler yelled and jerked at the handcuffs. "He's here, over here!" he screamed. The sounds from the park faded and Dan turned off the radio. He dropped it near the gun and picked up his bag.

"Detective Stattler, you take care, you hear?"

Dan jogged down the path until he came to Druid Hill Avenue. He crossed the road and entered the shopping center, knowing that they would not have much time before the police came out in force. He thought about what he'd done and realized that he couldn't have done it much differently without someone getting hurt.

He thought about the gun then, wondering if he should have taken it, and he knew he had made the right decision.

In the early hours of the morning, he would have given a great deal to have that gun again.

Eleven

Victor Bramson was in the passenger boarding area of the San Antonio International Airport, waiting for his flight. He was able to wait patiently, ignoring and disdaining his fellow passengers. He spoke to and took notice of others only when circumstances forced him to. He sat with his briefcase on his lap, primly locked. There was a low level of excitement running through him, not visible to others.

I almost have the answer.

In his forty-fifth year, Victor Bramson believed that he would take his body from beyond the limits of cell life, to current unknown limits, that he would live for four hundred years—longer than anyone now living, or their great-great-great-great-grandchildren.

This ability wasn't something he would share or wanted to share. He knew of the power a single person could have with a life five to six times longer than current limits.

There was one unknown, and with the knowledge he was gaining, that unknown factor would be his to control. People were so stupid, he thought. In the times of the Roman Empire, the average life expectancy was twenty-eight years. During the early nineteen-hundreds, in the United States, the average life expectancy was forty-nine years. It is now approaching eighty years, and in Japan, now, for women it is over eighty years. We aren't really extending our lives that much, he knew, but rather we are eradicating childhood diseases. A man of fifty a hundred years ago could expect to live to be seventy-two. And part of the equation had to do with accidental deaths.

Why do some people live through catastrophic events and accidents, and others die? Why did some men go through battle after battle in wars, and others die their first time out?

He was close to the answer. A tangible, transferable method of survival. He had spent a lot of time on airplanes, and he knew that if they crashed, he would survive. He had talked to those who had. And it wasn't luck, it was knowledge, subliminal knowledge that he had extracted.

You will all die before me.

The attendant called his flight. He rose and took his place behind the line forming to board. He was unaware of the family in front of him, using only enough energy to locate the attendant taking tickets. He was flying to Houston this evening, then on to Tampa International, and then home.

He looked up as the attendant reached for his boarding pass, a tall woman with brown hair, the blue suit and red scarf hanging loosely on her skeleton.

You will die before me.

Twelve

"Can we listen to some ZZ Top or something? This supermarket music is getting me down." Natalie grinned and waited for Dan's response. She was driving, with Dan and Angelina in the back seat together, where they could duck if they had to. Dan had found Natalie in the restaurant and they had immediately left, taking a cab to a car rental, where Natalie had used her credit card to rent a car. Two hours and three stops later, they were driving northeast on Highway 95, about to enter Wilmington, Delaware.

"ZZ Top, huh?" Dan said, reaching forward and grabbing Natalie's shoulder. "You nervous?"

"Oh, not at all," Natalie said, watching the road. The traffic was getting heavier as they approached the city limits of Wilmington.

"We just leave Baltimore with every, uh, every—." Natalie looked in the rear view mirror at Angelina. The seven-year-old was snuggling on her dad's shoulder, her eyes closed.

"We leave Baltimore with every police officer in the northeast looking for us," she finished.

"I like to leave with friends watching out for me."

"We are going to run out of home towns, leaving the way we do," Natalie said. She glanced behind her again. "How's the punkin doing?"

"She's fine. I think she's doing better than we are. She's with her daddy."

In the end they decided to take her with them, arranging for a meeting with Susan later. Natalie had argued that it would be too risky to meet Susan now, that they would be putting Angelina in danger if they were apprehended. Dan had stopped twice and tried to call, but each time he tried, there had been no answer. The second time they stopped for a phone, he made plane reservations. They would be flying out of Philadelphia, another thirty miles north from Wilmington.

Natalie drove with Dan and Angelina dozing in the rear seat, thinking about how far she had come in the past nine days, about how her life had been changed forever by one murderous bastard.

And you aren't any closer to finding him, are you, Minnie Mouse? You've been a cop for almost fifteen years, and you know, you fucking know that you and Dan will have to find this murdering bastard and bring him in or kill him. Before he gets you—or Dan. Hell, he's got us already; look at the shit we're in.

Kill him. Before he gets our Angelina.

Natalie followed the signs for Philadelphia International, and pulled up to the rental car return lot. The sun was going down and she sat there and waited for Dan and Angelina to wake up.

We're gonna have to change our tickets, she thought. *Can't go to Oregon just yet. We gotta go check this guy out. Get Angelina to a safe place and then go to Florida. Yeah, I can do it.*

They ate dinner at the airport, Dan growing more worried about Susan, calling twice during dinner. "She's still not home," he said, sitting down beside Angelina.

"She's fine, Daddy Aunt Susan's fine. She's just out late 'cause she doesn't have to take me with her."

Natalie left the table and called Grant, dreading the yelling she was going to hear. He should be home, it was 10 P.M. in Portland. He answered on the first ring, Natalie holding the phone out away from her ear as she told him who was calling.

A woman dragging a large bag stopped to look at her as she winced and held the phone out as far as it would go, a voice bellowing from the small speaker. Then the yelling stopped.

"Natalie?"

"Please don't yell, Grant."

"Natalie, where the hell are you?"

"Philadelphia."

"Phil—what?"

"Grant, I'm in Philadelphia, at the airport. Grant, listen, I love you and I'll be home soon."

"Okay, Natalie, how's this—and I won't ask you again what the hell you're doing in for chrissakes Philadelphia, Minnie Mouse, but-."

"Grant."

"What?"

"Grant, I'm going to hang up if you don't slow down and listen. Okay? Grant, I will be home sometime tomorrow. Will you meet me?"

"I'll try, Minnie Mouse, but all Hells' broken loose here. The D.A.'s looking for you, as well as the I.A. The brass from the Maryland State Police have been raising hell about the fingerprint and we haven't been able to give them good answers. You need to come home—now." He stopped, out of breath.

Natalie slumped in her seat. She was tired. Tired of death, tired of running around the country.

"Grant, can I talk to Aimee?"

When Aimee came on the phone, Natalie told her of her plan to get back into Portland without being arrested. If nothing else, Natalie wanted to walk into the police bureau under her own power, to pick and choose when she would appear in court.

"Don't tell Grant," Natalie said. "We'd be putting him in a spot." Grant took the phone.

"Minnie Mouse, you know anything about turtles?"

"Turtles, Grant? No. You gonna raise them or what? Keep them as pets, make soup—."

"No, just listen. Eldredge and Kirby took a piece of something they found on your carpet to a fish and wildlife forensic lab, and they told us it was from a turtle, probably a rare sea turtle. Mean anything?"

"No, only turtles I know were a rock group from the past, no real live turtles."

"Be careful, Minnie Mouse."

As Natalie and Dan and Angelina boarded a flight to Tampa, she thought about the strangeness of Grant's information. Before the night was over, no one thought it strange. They saw things so frightening that they forgot about the turtles.

They slept on the plane, awakening when they landed. In the Tampa airport, Dan carried a sleeping Angelina to the rental car desk, feeling as if he were going to spend the rest of his life in airports.

They got a map of the Tampa, Saint Petersburg, Clearwater areas at the rental car desk, and Dan carried Angelina outside the terminal, Natalie carrying the bags. As agreed upon, Natalie drove. Natalie didn't want to think about what might happen if they were stopped with Dan driving.

The warm, humid air hit Natalie as she walked out of the terminal, a change from the cold rain of Portland, and the coolness of the night in Philadelphia. There was thunder coming from the Gulf, bumping and growling, and even though the sky was clear above them, a promise of rain was on the way. They got in the car, a blue Ford Taurus four-door, and this time Dan got into the front seat, putting his sleepy daughter in the back.

Angelina looked around as she got into the car. She fastened her seat belt, and curled up on her jacket.

"Night, Daddy. Night, Natalie."

"Good night, Baby," Dan whispered.

As Natalie started the ignition, she looked in the mirror, glancing at her greasy hair and face with makeup long since washed off. She felt as if she had been in her jeans for a week, instead of one day.

Dan reached over and squeezed her hand.

They didn't make it back to the airport.

Thirteen

For Victor, flying home was not the tired, dreary journey it was for some travelers. He had projects at home, his studies, his life, his plans.

The plane slowed and tilted downward, beginning its descent from far out over the Gulf of Mexico, beginning a landing pattern that would take most of a half hour.

Home to his survivors.

He removed the blindfold and carefully folded it. He reached for his briefcase under the seat, put it in his lap, and sitting very straight and proper, he opened the latches, first the left and then the right with precision. He placed the blindfold in it and carefully snapped the latches. He sat that way until the plane landed, his hands folded on the briefcase.

You will all die before me.

The Beach House

One

Tampa Bay opens at the south end to the Gulf of Mexico, running north from there in the shape of a claw, with the city of Tampa forming the web of the claw. The peninsula extending south from Old Tampa Bay has the city of Saint Petersburg to the south, and the city of Clearwater to the north. Natalie drove across the north part of Old Tampa Bay in the dark, on the Courtney Campbell Causeway, and entered the city of Clearwater. They continued west for five miles to Clearwater Bay, and then north, up the coast. Just south of Tarpon Springs, Dan told her to slow down, and peered through the windshield for the turn. When he saw it, he motioned for her to turn left, toward the beach. The sign said Crystal Beach.

The road took a turn to the north and paralleled the beach, with houses on both sides of the road. They passed small, weathered beach houses and new monstrosities, some with lights on.

The house sat apart from the others, off on a bluff of sand, with the short wide-bladed grasses surrounding it in a natural turf. Natalie caught a glimpse of the front as they passed a break in the brush. The thick growth of magnolias and jasmine completely obscured the house from the road except for the driveway. The driveway was a sandy track, leading around the house.

There were no lights on when they drove past.

"Is that it?" Natalie whispered.

"Yes."

"You're sure?"

"Yes."

The house stood silent, waiting in the dark. The bluff on which it stood was overgrown with vegetation, and the house was visible from the Gulf, a hundred yards up from the high tide area on the beach. Brush formed a hedge on the street, and the house was visible from the break in the brush where the driveway entered the street.

"How do you know that's the one?" Natalie whispered, peering through the windshield of the rental car at the dark house.

"It's his house. I have followed him here."

"But it's so dark," Natalie said. She watched the house.

"He must make a lot of money in the aging business. That house is worth a bunch, maybe a million or two," she said.

"He does well," Dan said. "He has expensive hobbies."

They sat staring at the dark house, with the lights off at the entrance to the driveway. The clouds from the thunderstorms out over the Gulf of Mexico were moving closer, obscuring the moon and most of the sky, the waves shining white as they broke on the shore behind the house. *I'm sure in the daytime it will look different,* Natalie thought, *but now it looks spooky, the windows dark and watching.*

The house was designed like an old Spanish estate, Natalie saw, with two stories, at least in front, with balconies surrounded by black wrought iron coming out from the second-story windows.

The outside was beige stucco, the roof red Spanish tile. Natalie looked for house numbers and couldn't see them.

"Dan, I don't like this," she whispered. He was staring at the dark house. What Dan had in mind scared her, and she wasn't completely sure that they were at the right house. She had once gone on a search with other officers, looking for drugs. The house was in north Portland, an area taken over by gangs and their wars. They approached the house and yelled, "Police with a search warrant," and kicked the door in, only to find an old lady in a rocking chair, throwing her hands up in the air, scattering the Christmas cards she had been writing.

The real drug house was across the street, the address one number greater than the house they hit. The drug dealers were on their front porch watching the cops hit the wrong house. And since the warrant had the address and description of the little old lady's house on it, they could not then walk over to the drug house and search for drugs.

It's so easy, Daniel my love, to get the wrong place, and what're you gonna do? Walk in and say, "Oops, I'm sorry, I burglarized the wrong house, see I'm looking for your neighbor, the killer, the one who killed my wife and Natalie's sister." And the homeowner would say, "Oh, that's okay, the killer lives across the street, real nice guy if you don't cross him."

They watched the house, waiting, straining to see movement.

"I don't think he's home," Dan said.

"It's a big house, how can you tell? He may be on a balcony in the back, looking at the ocean, and we wouldn't know."

"I'm going to look," Dan said, determined. "I'm not going to do anything to him, just going to look. Besides, no one's home. And I know that there will be something in that house that tells us why . . . why Jackie and why Stephanie. Why us."

Dan looked in the backseat at Angelina. She was still sleeping, curled up around her jacket. Natalie reached back and removed Angelina's seat belt and slowly stretched the child out on the seat.

It was dark in the car, and Natalie could barely see Dan. She grabbed him and held his face, kissing him.

"I love you," he whispered. "Let's back the car out of the driveway and down that way, by the brush. You should be able to see part of the house from there." He pointed behind them, to a spot at the corner of the lot.

Natalie turned the engine on. It seemed loud in the night. She backed up along the brushy hedge in front of the house, going north up the lane. She stopped, thirty feet from the driveway. Dan pulled a dark jacket from his bag and shrugged into it in the car. When he opened the door, the interior light blinded Natalie, and she whispered, "I love you." Dan nodded and slipped out, shutting the door and putting Natalie and Angelina back in darkness.

As soon as Dan was out, Natalie rolled her window down and whispered, "Dan!"

He came around the front of the car and stopped by the window.

"Thirty minutes, Dan, or I'm coming to look for you."

"I'll be back by then," Dan said.

When he reached the break in the brush at the driveway, the darkness swallowed him. As Dan went out of sight, the first raindrops fell, slowly at first, then faster and bigger, smashing into the windshield, making it impossible for Natalie to see the hood.

She looked at her watch. One-fifteen A.M. *You'd better get back here Danny Boy.*

Two

When Victor Bramson traveled, he took his briefcase and a small carry-on bag. He never checked his luggage, allowing him to get into and out of airports as quickly as possible. When he flew into Tampa, he took the shuttle to long-term parking, and was on his way home by one-twenty.

Dan walked slowly toward the house, the wind and rain making it harder to see, his eyes tearing. The rain was coming harder now, soaking through his jacket. He walked beside the paved driveway, ready to dive into the brush if he saw anyone in or around the house.

It looked deserted, the wind and blowing brush making the house look uninhabited. But he knew that was not the case; he knew that the killer lived here.

And I know that you keep something in the house that tells of your visits, something about your occupation, you bastard, a memento, a keepsake from the dead.

With a crackle and roar, he saw lightning zap down out of the thunderhead over the Gulf, momentarily drowning out the rumble of the surf behind the house. The rain opened up then, soaking Dan and blinding him. The vague shape of the house was just ahead, and as he got closer, he stepped on the driveway, walked up to the garage doors, the main part of the house on his right. Standing in close to the door, he was out of the wind, and stopped for a moment to let his breathing and heart slow down. He walked to his left to the corner of the garage, and looked along the side. The wind and rain hit him again as he peered around the corner of the house, looking toward the surf. The garage was about forty feet deep, and then the land dropped off to the beach.

Dan touched the corner of the house, feeling the cold sides of the adobe walls, touching the house as if it were alive, an entity. An enemy.

Suddenly he was afraid, the fear coming up through his excitement, making him weak. Whatever was in this house was not for anyone to see. Whatever madness it contained should stay locked away from all other eyes. He forced himself to move then, before he ran back to the car. He stepped out into the wind, along the side of the garage, heading for the back of the house.

The rain stung his eyes, and he shielded them with his left hand, his right touching the wall of the garage. He walked in the wet, sandy dirt, slowly, until he came to the back end of the garage, the white tops of the surf visible now in the blackness, about thirty feet below and sixty yards out from the house. Behind the garage Dan walked toward the main part of the house, the upper story visible now. There was a large balcony on the back of the main part, on the second story, extending the length of the house.

Dan came to the end of the garage, and he saw that the house was built in a U shape, with the opening toward the Gulf, the single story garage forming one side of the U. As Dan came to the open courtyard in the back of the house, he strained to see.

Movement. There, in front of me.

The pace of his heartbeat jumped up a notch, and then almost stopped when he saw the movement in the courtyard, movement low to the ground in the dark, as if someone was crawling.

"Mother of God," he muttered, his voice shaky, his knees weak, the coldness of the rain forgotten. He wished then he had taken Detective Stattler's gun, damn the theft and the armed fugitive fear it would create. He'd never wanted anything as badly as he wanted a gun right then. He resisted the urge to run, his body and mind screaming for flight, and the movement stopped, up by the front of the U, and then resumed, coming toward him, slow and low to the ground

*   *   *

"Nat'lie?"

Natalie turned in the seat and reached for Angelina.

"What, honey?" She found Angelina's hand and leaned through the opening between the bucket seats, putting her arm around Angelina. Angelina reached up and touched Natalie's face.

"Do you love my daddy?"

"Yes, Angel, I do." It was more official, less frightening, now that she had told other people, more permanent somehow. *I love him. He's a good man, your daddy.* "Here, come on up here." Natalie moved over to the passenger side, and helped Angelina through the seats, pulling Angelina onto her lap.

They put their arms around each other. Angelina snuggled with Natalie, putting her head on Natalie's chest. *God, I could love this child,* she thought, a strange and wonderful feeling, caring for a child.

In her job she had always seen other people worry about their children, grieve for them. Parents sometimes knew that she didn't have children, and knew that she couldn't possibly understand the depth of their fears and worry.

Natalie put her cheek down on top of Angelina's head.

"That's good, Nat'lie."

"What, honey?"

"That you love my daddy."

"Oh, I do, Angel, and how long have you been awake?"

"I heard you talking to Daddy, and then I woke up." Angelina pulled her head up and looked around the darkened car, trying to see out the rain-streaked windows. "Where are we?"

"We stopped to see someone, a person your daddy wants to check up on." Natalie felt Angelina stiffen, as if a jolt went through her body.

"The man who killed Mommy?" Angelina asked, her voice going shrill at the end, the fear coming into the car a visible thing. Natalie tightened her grip on Angelina, holding her, wanting to ease Angelina's fears, not able to keep the fear out of her own mind. She realized then how little she knew about the workings of a seven-year-old mind, how little she knew about how fast a child could think and internalize the problems of the adult world.

"He's just looking at the house, honey, the man's not home."

Angelina relaxed a little, putting her arms around Natalie's neck. "I love you, Nat'lie." The unreserved, total commitment of a child, her mind made up without worrying about how long she had known Natalie, as an adult would.

"I love you, too, honey." Natalie gave her a hug.

"Nat'lie?"

"What?"

"Where we going yesterday, when Daddy comes back?"

"We're going back to the Tampa Airport, and then to my house to meet your Aunt Susan."

That seemed to satisfy Angelina, and she put her head down on Natalie's chest again, her arms around the person she and her daddy loved. They sat in the car like that, not able to see the house in the blackness of the night through the trees and brush and rain, Natalie becoming more worried with each passing second about what Dan was doing and why he wasn't back yet.

What're you gonna do, Minnie Mouse, if he doesn't come back?

Dan froze, hugging the wall of the garage, watching the movement in the dark. He could stay here by the corner and wait for whatever was coming for him, run back to the car, or cross the opening of the U to the far side and see if he could find a way inside the house.

He started forward, keeping low, and discovered that there was a low cement wall across the U, forming a kind of pen. The movement was inside the enclosed area, with a cement and tile deck surrounding the pen.

Dan watched the shadows at the other end of the courtyard, halfway now across the opening, and with sudden blinding speed and a series of grunts, the shadow moved in the courtyard and ran straight toward Dan. He yelled and started to run for the other side of the house, his feet slipping on the sand-covered tile. He fell down hard, next to the pool.

The reptile hit the wall with its snout, the impact causing a louder grunt. *Hit the wall right where you were. Jesus, Danny Boy, it hit the wall right there.* Dan shook and raised his head up, looking over the wall, looking into the eyes of the largest alligator he had ever seen. In the darkness he could make out the large flap of skin rising up over its eyes, the large snout and scaly back. The length of the alligator stretched away from the edge of the pool back into the dark.

The thing's twenty feet long!

Dan's skin crawled, thinking about what might have happened if he had crossed over the wall and headed toward the house. In the low light he could see that the courtyard was divided, with movement in the area next to the alligator's area. Smooth shapes, moving.

Large turtles, a few moving slowly, the convex shapes of their shells making bumps on the sand of the courtyard.

Dan heard a noise behind him, toward the beach, and he moved, running for the far side of the courtyard, reaching the corner of the house, under the upper deck. Without stopping, he grabbed a support for the deck and began climbing a smooth pipe, wet with rain. He jumped as high as he could, climbing, slipping on the pipe, reaching for the lip of the deck. He thought of what was waiting for him below, images of alligators waiting below the pipe, and caught the lip with his left hand. He pulled himself up, grabbing the wrought-iron railing and getting a knee up on the deck. He dropped over the railing and lay on the deck, breathing hard.

When he could move, he looked below the pipe at the sandy ledge above the beach, beyond the wall.

Nothing. No alligators. Maybe they'd left. He shuddered, thinking about the ultimate watchdog.

Dan got to his feet, crouching, looking over the railing at the surf, the rain slowing. The thunderstorm was moving away to the south, leaving broken parts of clouds behind, the sky clearing. He saw that there were houses on both sides of the house. Both houses were secluded like this one, separated from their neighbors by a wall of trees and brush. Lights were on in the one to his left, or south. The other house was dark. Dan turned and walked along the deck, trying doors and windows as he came to them.

The second door he tried was unlocked. He tried to look in through the glass door, and found he couldn't see through the curtain. He entered quickly, shutting the door as soon as he was inside.

*   *   *

Natalie stared at the digital clock, straining to hear sounds of Dan coming back. *One fifty-five, and he's still not here. What the hell you gonna do, Minnie Mouse?* Angelina had fallen asleep in her lap, the seven-year-old exhausted after the draining events of the day.

I've got to go for him, we just can't leave him here, but what the hell am I going to do with the pumpkin? She didn't know, but she knew she had to do something soon.

She stared at the clock.

Dan stood inside the door, keeping his hand on the door handle to orient himself, the room completely dark. He was standing on carpet. He thought he was in a bedroom, but he couldn't tell. He opened the door slightly and turned to the room, the dim light from outside giving it shape. He could make out the outlines of a bed, a dresser, and an open doorway that must lead to a bathroom. Probably the master bedroom.

Dan decided to leave the door open, and walked carefully, slowly across the room to a door. He listened at the door, his ears ringing with the pounding of his heart. He slowly turned the knob and opened the door inches, pressing his face into the opening. He saw a hallway with a railing, open to a great room below, the balcony going around two sides of the U.

There were rooms off the hall, with closed doors. Further down, toward the front of the house, Dan could see a stairway that led down to the great room. He opened the door and stepped into the hallway.

Three

Victor Bramson drove north out of the city limits of Clearwater, minutes from home, driving by rote, the windshield wipers the only company, the road deserted. He looked forward to getting back home. Tomorrow he would study what he had learned from the newest search and plan for his trip back to San Antonio. The thought excited him. He was close to having all the information he needed to sustain life.

Survival, no matter what.

You will all die before me.

Dan entered the hallway from the end closest to the beach. He looked along the hall toward the stairway at the other end, and walked quietly in that direction until he came to the next door. Keeping his eye on the stairway, he slowly tried the knob and opened the door an inch, then peeked inside.

Nothing. A room used for storage.

He moved slowly across the hall to the railing and looked over, at the great room below. There was a massive chandelier, a wood and metal thing that had a rustic, Spanish-explorer look. He could see dim shapes of chairs and couches. There must be a kitchen under the walkway or one of the bedrooms.

Nothing. No light. No sound. No movement.

Dan started again toward the stairs, trying a door on his left. It opened into a long, rectangular room, an office, with a desk and worktables. He closed the door and walked to the stairs, resolving to come back and thoroughly search the office. He started down, slowly, into the darkened lower room. When he reached the bottom, he realized he was looking at the front door, with its side windows. He couldn't make out the car with Natalie and Angelina parked on the other side of the brush and trees.

Get out, Danny Boy, get out while you still can. Get in your car, hug your girls, and get the hell out.

He ignored the inner voice, a voice with what he was sure was very good advice, and started for the back of the house on the ground floor. He walked slowly, placing each foot carefully, holding his hands out in front of himself like a newly blinded person.

He stepped on something between the great room and the kitchen, something round and soft, something that moved under his tennis shoe.

Dan's skin grew an instant rash of bumps, his hair rising on his head, and he almost yelled, flinging his right hand out to keep his balance, his equilibrium lost to fright. His leg quivered.

His hand hit the shade of a lamp, and it scooted off the small table it was on and fell to the tile floor with a very loud crash.

Dan stood completely still, not putting the weight back down on what he had stepped on, and he listened.

Nothing.

The boa constrictor had felt the vibrations of Dan's passage beside the garage, and tracked him with sensors unknown to us, tracked Dan's movements around and then through the house. It had waited on the floor for the man, unafraid and in anticipation. When Dan had stepped on the boa in its midsection, it adjusted slightly, moving in a slow undulation to bring its head back around toward the intruder.

Dan took a large step, reaching beyond the spot where he had stepped on the mysterious soft thing. The boa's head passed behind Dan, its tongue flicking, taking a sample of the environment for analysis.

Dan moved on into what he thought must be the kitchen, toward the courtyard, not seeing the large reptile behind him. He moved closer to the back wall, toward a room with more light. The clouds were breaking up, and there was a quarter moon with a few stars to light the room through the windows that faced the courtyard. Dan walked to the kitchen and stood there, looking out, seeing the shiny shells of the sea turtles. He could better see how the courtyard was divided now, with the sea turtles occupying one half of the area. The other side, the side with the alligator, appeared to be empty. The gator must have found a way out.

Great, just what the hell I need. Better be careful on your way to the car, Danny Boy.

Dan shivered.

He walked to his left and saw the shape of a door going to the garage. He opened it and looked into the blackness. He felt along the wall for a switch, and turned it on, the room exploding into brightness.

A workshop. A laboratory, with sinks and benches, computers, and equipment he couldn't identify. He walked to a large piece of equipment with a small stool in front of it, and read on the side, "Scanning Electron Microscope."

A laboratory. What the hell for? He quickly looked around and found nothing of interest, except for what looked like turtle shells in the corner. *Carapace,* he thought they were called, not shells. Some were intact, and some were in pieces.

He left the room quickly, turning off the light, and stood in the dark, waiting for his eyes to adjust. When he thought he could see enough, he started forward, and walked into a chair, the scrape on the floor loud, sudden. He walked carefully back into the living room and found the stairway, and walked up to the office, careful where he put his feet, thinking that he didn't want to know what he had stepped on the first time he had gone through the room.

I don't have anything yet. I have to find out why, why did he pick us?

Dan had a chilling thought. *Where is he going next?*

Dan fumbled around the wall with his hand, and found the light switch. His discovery frightened him badly. He picked up a newspaper clipping, from *USA Today,* and read the first part of the article.

"You son of a bitch," he muttered strongly, angrily. "You evil son of a bitch, I'm gonna kill you." His knees shook.

"Angelina."

"Mmmmph."

"Angelina, honey, wake up."

"Don't want to," she mumbled, sleepily.

"Angel, this is Natalie . . . wake up. I need to go look for your daddy."

Angelina raised her head from Natalie's shoulder, looking around. The rain had stopped and she could see the shape of the trees next to the car. She sat up, looking wildly around, the movement easing the pain in Natalie's shoulder and tired arms. Natalie thought later that a part of parenthood she had previously been ignorant of was the muscle cramps and joint pain associated with holding a loved one.

"Where's Daddy, Nat'lie?"

"He's in the house, and I need to tell him it's time to go. I want you to stay here in the car where it's warm."

"Don't go, Nat'lie." Angelina drew her arms tighter around Natalie's neck.

"Honey, I have to go and get your daddy. I'll be right back."

"I want to go, too, I want to go with you."

"Angelina, listen to me," Natalie pleaded softly, holding Angelina's cheeks. "I need to run up to the house and get your dad, and you need to do your part and stay here for just a few minutes. See the clock?" Natalie pointed to the clock. Angelina nodded.

"It's now two oh five. You watch it and I'll be back by the time it says two oh nine. Okay, honey?" She gave Angelina a squeeze.

"Okay, Nat'lie, but I'm scared."

"I know, honey, but I'll be right back, I promise." Natalie reached into the backseat and found the stuffed giraffe. "Here, hold her, and think of what we should call her while I'm gone."

"Betsy."

"What, Angel?"

"I'm going to call her Betsy."

"Hi, Betsy," Natalie said, and lifted Angelina onto the console between the seats. She opened the door and whispered, "I'll be right back." Angelina nodded, holding Betsy up to her face, her arms wrapped around her stuffed giraffe, looking at the clock. Natalie waved. She remembered Angelina like that, sitting very still in the car, looking small and afraid, holding her giraffe, staring at the clock with big eyes.

Alone.

You never leave children alone.

Angelina reached out quickly and locked the driver's door, and moved around the car and locked the rest of the doors, then returned to her seat, holding the giraffe. When the clock reached 2:07, she began to cry.

Natalie took the driveway, walking straight up to the house, wanting a gun so badly she would have taken on the Tampa Bay Buccaneers to get one. Well, maybe not all of them, she thought, and giggled in her fear.

I'm so scared I would love to see the Buccaneers right now, she thought. She was experienced in tense, scary situations, but this was not the usual scary situation—without backup, without a gun, and even without being right. She was trespassing. And scared to death. As she reached the front of the house, she turned and looked at the hedge. She thought she saw movement between the hedge and the house, low, close to the ground. She looked harder, straining. She didn't see anything, and continued to the front door.

Four

Dan gripped the article and sat down at the desk. An article about a plane crash in Colorado, a commuter plane with twenty-eight people on board crashed in the mountains, and the only survivor, an eleven-year-old boy, walked out of the mountains with no injuries.

What the hell's going on here?

Dan picked up other articles, articles circled in red ink, with names highlighted. He read an article, a story about a baby surviving a six-story fall from an apartment in Queens, with no apparent injuries, according to the paramedics. In another one, a woman escaped unharmed from a flaming freeway crash. A young football player in south Florida was knocked out and had no pulse or respiration, and then sat up and began talking again, with no apparent damage.

There were stacks of war stories, stories about survivors who never should have made it. A thought of Dan's uncle flashed through his mind. His uncle Jeffrey had gone through the entire Pacific island campaigns with a Marine unit, a unit that was decimated on several beaches, and Uncle Jeffrey had made it through without a scratch, only to die in a hunting accident ten years later.

An article about a man who was riding in a C-47 plane carrying paratroopers, when he found himself floating under the canopy of his parachute, the plane having blown up. An article about a police officer being shot twelve times and surviving, shooting three of her assailants.

Ohmigod, Natalie.

My Jackie.

Dan fell back in the chair and closed his eyes. The connection was . . . what? That the killer sought out survivors of bizarre events, events that should have had no survivors, and killed them?

Why?

Natalie the survivor in the bank shoot-out. Jackie surviving a plane crash in New Jersey, but that was years ago. Before I even met her. If that's the connection, why? Dan threw down the articles, and pushed them off the desk. He looked around the room. On the wall by the door he saw a map of the United States, with markings on the map, like a pin map the police might use to show crimes. Dan got up and walked over to the map, looking at the dots.

There was a dot in Portland.

One on the Chesapeake Bay.

Natalie and Jackie.

There were many more dots.

Anger, buried for a long time, came up in Dan, hot and unchecked. He ripped the map off the wall in a spray of thumbtacks and threw it on the floor. He looked around the room, and walked quickly to a file cabinet beside the desk. He jerked open the top drawer and began to throw out files, flinging them against the wall. When he emptied the drawer, he jerked open the second one and threw out its files, pulling the drawer out when it was empty and hurling it against the wall.

The clang was sharp and loud, and Dan stopped and looked around. He went to the desk and picked up a journal, ready to throw it, to smash something else, when he stopped and looked at the cover. It had a date on it: January 1995.

He opened the journal and began reading, an account of a search. A killing of a survivor. He sat down slowly.

An alarm sounded, and stopped.

Dan froze, holding the book open, not moving. The alarm sounded again, and then rang continuously.

The doorbell.

Someone was ringing the doorbell. Dan held the journal and walked to the door, hitting the light switch as he did so, looking down the hallway at the stairs. At the bottom of the stairs he could see a shape in the glass by the front door, a shadow.

Natalie?

He took the journal with him and walked to the top of the stairs and started down, his left hand trailing on the wall. The doorbell stopped and a small shape looked in the window beside the door. Even in the dark Dan could see it was Natalie, and he trotted down the stairs and called out, "Natalie!"

He opened the door and saw Natalie there, jumping back, fear in her face. She was soaked, her sweatshirt clinging to her, her hair plastered to her head. When she saw Dan, she grabbed him and they held onto each other, Dan holding the journal in one hand.

"Dan," she whispered loudly, "we have to get out of here."

"Natalie, I've found it, I know why the bastard is going after you. And Jackie. *I've found it.*" He held the journal up for her to see.

"Dan, we have to go. Angelina's alone in the car."

The shriek of an alarm made them both jump, Dan turning to look inside. Natalie saw the flashing light beside the door and the numeric pad, something she had missed when she began to ring the doorbell.

Damn!

Dan pulled her face up, inches away from his. "Natalie, go back to the car, now! I'll join you in a minute, I *have* to go back."

"Dan, come with me!"

"*No!* I'll be right there, go!"

Natalie turned and ran, chased by the shrieking of the alarm. Dan turned to enter the door and stopped short, his legs quivering. The largest snake he had ever seen was moving toward him, between him and the bottom of the stairs.

"Boy, I hope that thing isn't hungry," he said, the sound of his voice scaring him even more, a shaky, scared voice. Without thinking, he ran at the stairs, jumping over the slow-moving boa, running for the landing in the dark, stumbling and going down, holding the journal. He was up instantly. The screaming of the alarm gave him a sick feeling in his gut, knowing that the police were probably on their way, and whether they were caught or not depended upon how close a police unit was when the call went out.

Things you can't control, Danny Boy.

Thirty seconds. I have to get out in thirty seconds. He had watched a movie where bank robbers had a stopwatch, with one member of the team calling out elapsed time to the accomplices, knowing that there was only so much time before the police would arrive. *That's the way I feel now,* Dan thought, *a criminal with time running out.*

He jogged to the door of the office and entered, hitting the light switch on the way by, going to the desk and grabbing a handful of clippings, taking two more journals with him, grabbing some computer disks. As he turned for the door, he saw the map on the floor and picked it up, crunching it up, holding his booty to his chest, and ran out the door, leaving the light on.

Natalie made her way to the driveway, shivering, jogging as she hit the smooth surface, then slowing as she approached the road. The alarm suddenly quit, and Natalie stopped to listen by the trees, hearing only the soft rain on the leaves. The sudden quiet was more frightening than the screaming of the alarm. She turned and looked at the house, a light on in the upper story, and then saw a figure leave the front door, carrying something.

She waited, and saw Dan running toward her on the driveway, his form backlit by the clearing skies over the Gulf.

"Let's go," he whispered urgently, and ran past her, turning up the road for the car. As he made the turn, he stopped short, his heart seizing with fright. The dome light was on, and the passenger door was open. Natalie came up behind Dan and stopped beside him. From where they were, they could see Angelina's stuffed giraffe on the ground below the door, lighted by the interior light. There was movement next to the car, low, shifting, lurching movement, between the car and the brush, near the open door.

Oh Dear Mary, Mother of God!

A large shape was in the brush by the car—an alligator!

"Angelina!" Dan ran down the road, holding the papers and journals to his chest, screaming his daughter's name, loud in the silence after the alarm. He ran toward the driver's side of the car, keeping the car between himself and the alligator, running up to the car and looking in, praying that Angelina was in the car.

Dan jerked open the back door on the driver's side.

The car was empty.

He threw his bundle of papers and journals into the backseat, some of the clippings scattering on the ground below the door. Natalie was with him, looking for Angelina, calling her name. She heard it first, a soft cry, on the other side of the car, in the trees, next to the alligator.

"Daddy."

"Dan, she's over there!" Natalie yelled, going around to the rear of the car. Natalie sprinted into the brush and hooked around a tree, yelling for Angelina, and stopped, grabbing at brush to keep herself from falling forward. The alligator was coming through the brush, somewhere behind her, and Dan was on the other side, yelling, screaming. Natalie burst through the screen of brush that separated the front yard of the house from the road, and ran toward the driveway.

She ran right in front of the alligator, hearing the hiss and then the roar of the reptile, and she jumped to her left, into the brush, and fell down beside Angelina. She had rolled up into a ball, wet and shivering.

"Nat'lie, I'm scared." Angelina put her arms around Natalie's neck and hugged her so tight that Natalie couldn't breathe. Natalie struggled to get up, Angelina crying, and then Natalie was on her feet, holding Angelina with one arm, disoriented, staggering, moving away from the hissing.

"Dan, I've got her, get the car."

Dan continued to yell, and then stopped.

"Dan, get the car!" Natalie came out of the brush ten yards in front of the car, holding Angelina.

"Dan!"

The alligator came out of the brush, between her and the car. It turned its head and started for them. Angelina whimpered in Natalie's arms, and buried her face in Natalie's neck. Dan stood, frozen, watching the figures in the dark, then started forward, toward Natalie and Angelina.

"Dan, get the car!"

He jumped in the driver's seat and started forward, swinging into the road and around the gator as it started for Natalie and Angelina. As he got to Natalie, the gator was barely feet away, coming for them in that rambling, swinging gait of reptiles. Dan slowed and Natalie jumped on the hood as he stopped.

"Keep going," Natalie yelled. Dan took the car another fifty feet and stopped. Natalie hopped off, carrying Angelina in both arms, and Dan opened a back door for them. As Natalie slid in, she saw Dan's white, strained, and tear-streaked face. He was shaking. Natalie bent over, pulling Angelina in on top of her. Dan slammed the door and the interior was dark again.

"Daddy, I was scared," Angelina said. "That man scared me so I got out of the car. Then Nat'lie saved me." She kissed her savior. He started forward, turning on the headlights as he did so, the road jumping into light.

What man?

Dan looked in the rearview mirror, seeing Angelina and Natalie with their arms around each other.

"What man, honey?"

"Daddy, wait!"

Dan stopped. "What, honey?"

"Daddy, my giraffe, we can't leave Betsy." Angelina turned around and pointed at the rear window.

Dan backed up, fast, passing the stuffed animal lying in the road on her side, soaked with rainwater. He got out, looking around nervously for the gator. His legs were still shaky from finding Angelina gone from the car.

He put the Taurus in gear and started forward, passing the driveway to Bramson's house. He didn't see the car come up fast behind him. Dan thought later that Natalie must have seen something because she cried out just before the car hit. Natalie twisted around, and was slammed back into the seat, her head going back and into the rear window. Angelina screamed the slammed into Natalie, her head striking Natalie's shoulder and then Natalie's cheek slammed against the top of the child's head. Angelina yelled, "Bad man!"

Dan fared better, his body slamming back into the seat, and then forward, locking the shoulder harness. He instinctively slammed on the brakes, stopping both cars, then floored the accelerator, the car rocketing forward, the corner coming up fast, taking the corner almost flat out, the car sliding on the sandy soil, hitting some shrubs on the outside of the corner, and then they were shooting forward again, speeding down the lane to the highway at sixty, then seventy, then seventy-five miles an hour on a road designed for thirty.

He didn't think anyone was following them, and then he saw the car slide around the corner behind them, the headlights broken out, the hood crumpled. Dan slowed for the turn for the highway, looking frantically for headlights coming from the left and right, his brake lights out except for the one on the rear deck. He hit the paved highway at thirty-five, sliding across the road, wrenching the wheel, sliding toward the ditch on the wet pavement.

As he straightened out, he floored the accelerator, shooting forward, thinking then that he should stay and fight. But he had almost lost Angelina and Natalie once today through his stupidity, and he knew he had to keep going.

The car made the corner behind him, steam blowing out of the hood, and Dan knew that it would be a matter of minutes before the race was over. He crested a rise in the road in another half mile, and he could see the emergency lights of a police car coming fast, south of him, from the direction of Clearwater.

They were over the rise and out of sight and he never saw the car again. He raced forward, the dark waters of the Gulf of Mexico on his left, Angelina crying in the backseat, Natalie holding her.

When he looked in the rearview mirror, he saw Angelina with blood on her head. Natalie was holding her neck at an odd angle, and she had a gash on her cheek.

"Natalie, you guys okay?" Dan asked, his voice shaking.

"We'll live, Daniel," she whispered. Angelina was quiet, resting her head on Natalie's chest, her tear-streaked face white.

"Daniel?"

He glanced up in the mirror.

"You get your driver's license through the mail or what?"

"L. L. Bean."

"L. L. Bean doesn't sell licenses, you dummy."

"I know, they didn't give me one."

He thought he saw a smile on Angelina's face.

Dan turned his attention to the road, keeping the Taurus at eighty where he could. Five miles from there, he slowed to fifty-five.

This isn't over yet, Victor Bramson. Not by half.

He stopped at a 7-Eleven in Tarpon Springs, parking the car on a side street, coming back minutes later with a sack of sandwiches, sodas, moist towels, and crackers. Natalie lay on the seat with her eyes closed, Angelina holding her hand. He cleaned them with the wipes, putting some Bandaids on Natalie's cheek, looking at Angelina's head. He gave Natalie some aspirin, and Angelina some children's acetaminophen.

"What do you think, Natalie, stay on the coast highway?"

"I guess," she said with her eyes closed.

Dan had Angelina come up front, made Natalie as comfortable as he could in the back, worried about her neck, then he drove north. When they were both sleeping, he kept thinking that they had to get Angelina somewhere safe.

Victor Bramson controlled his fury, explaining to the police that he had accidentally set off his alarm, his broken car safely hidden in the trees across the highway.

"Thank you, officers," he said. He smiled at them, seeing their skeletal remains in uniform.

You will all die before me.

The key was the child—the child of a survivor, in fact, the child of two survivors. She would tell him everything he needed to continue.

The other two I will just kill, the man first. The meddlesome man first, quick.

Then the woman with the girl watching.

Then the girl.

You will all die before me.

Five

The sky was dark, and in the blackness of the night, Natalie could just make out her shoes and the pavement of the road. Her shoes flashed, white patches in the starlight. There were large, dark shapes ahead, rock formations or maybe buildings.

As Natalie ran, her Nikes made little patting sounds on the pavement. She slowed to a jog, continuing on, hoping there were no obstacles in the road. As she jogged, she saw that the shapes were buildings, lining both sides of the road, tall buildings with the dark and deserted shapes of a modern ghost town. The glass fronts of the buildings reflected what light there was, making the street even darker. The road was empty of cars and people.

Natalie was wearing a black sweatshirt with shiny silver lycra on her legs. Running clothes. She passed a large fountain with dry and silent waterspouts. The desert breeze came up behind her, scattering a newspaper along beside her, keeping time. Natalie was breathing harder than usual for a slow jog, her breath loud in her ears. A marquee loomed above her, a mute white giant with dead lights. She squinted up and could make out the black lettering on the white background. It said, "Caesar's Palace." The lettering was a full ten feet tall, and below it, in smaller lettering, "Wayne Newton—Appearing Nightly."

Natalie turned toward the building, and then looked up and down the dark and deserted street. Her heart was beating fast, almost too fast to count, and the hair on her back and arms stood out, her skin tight and painful. The fear came up and made her knees weak.

Las Vegas. I'm in Las Vegas, and this town never sleeps. She turned toward the front entrance, her stomach weak and churning, knowing that the last time she had been here the town was blazing with lights at four-thirty in the morning. The sidewalks were full of people on a weekend in a town that never sleeps.

Never.

There should be hundreds of cars and people here and the city should be using millions of watts of power to keep the lights going. Las Fucking Vegas could be seen from hundreds of miles in space, as bright as a new star.

Natalie moaned.

She ran on then, faster, down Las Vegas Boulevard. The Strip. Behind her, the new Treasure Island Pirate Village was dark. The British frigate, the H.M.S. *Royal Brittania*, floated in Buccaneer Bay, waiting to be sunk again by the pirate ship.

New Las Vegas. A glitzy road show for the families of the baby boomers.

Natalie glanced behind her. A large white skull floated in the dark, below the Treasure Island sign, part of the marquee for the village.

She ran on.

She passed the ruins of the Dunes Hotel, the darkened spires of the Excalibur ahead.

The wind picked up, moaning and whistling in the empty street. Natalie stopped in front of the new Luxor, built in the shape of a pyramid, a gleaming glass pyramid guarded by a ten-story sphinx. She walked toward the sphinx, the lion's body so huge it straddled a nine-lane loading area in front of the hotel. The waters in the lagoon out front were black, forbidding.

The voice beside her came with no warning, and she stopped, scared, with goose bumps on her legs.

"Natalie."

The voice was deep, a rich baritone, coming from a dark and very large person, a man dressed in a tux.

She jerked to a stop.

"Natalie, that you, girl?" the voice said, and then in a lower tone, "How you doin'? Pleezed to see you again." Old Joe Louis held his hand out and grabbed Natalie's, his hand warm and large, swallowing up hers, holding it gently.

"That you, Joe?"

"Yes, Natalie, it's me, still here greetin' the folks so they can lose their money." He looked closer at Natalie, and she could make out his face in the dark.

"I thought you were at Caesar's Palace, Joe."

"Was, Natalie, but I moved to the Luxor, a beaut, ain't it? You gotta keep up with the times, Natalie." He stood close to her in the wide street, looking at her.

"You got a journey to go on, girl."

"I know, Joe, who you kidding? I'm gonna go to the Happiest Place in the World, Disneyland, but you know that, don't you Joe?"

"No, Natalie, you got a journey to go on, and it's not to Disneyland, it's not to a place like that at all, and—."

"But, Joe, I don't want to go to any other place, I need the Happiest Place in the World."

"Natalie, listen to me, you've got to go back and take care of some things. Don't you think I don't know what's going on, girl, 'cause I do. They's all sorts of bad doings since I got this job here."

"But not for me, Joe." Natalie said, her voice breaking. "I've had to deal with too much, too much random, baseless violence, violence that doesn't mean anything to the animals who do it."

"Natalie, since I got this job here they done killed all those people in that restaurant in

San Ysidro, down there under the golden arches, that man who walked in there in Mickey D's with guns and killed and killed. A man with an assault rifle in a California schoolyard, a nut who thinks he's Christ in Waco, Texas. Oh Natalie, they's lots for you to do."

"No! I'm not going," Natalie said, , tears coming down her cheeks.

"Natalie."

She turned to run.

"Natalie, looka here."

And she turned to look and Joe had his arm around someone, someone smaller. Someone with long hair in a braid. Angelina.

Ohmigod, Angelina, and Natalie stopped to reach back for Angel, crying, yelling her name, the tears coming down, up close to Joe now, sadness in his face.

"You have to travel, Natalie, to take a journey, a journey you have to take alone, and you can't take anyone with you."

Angelina stood there, looking up at Joe Louis, and Natalie reached for her again, only to reach for air.

They were gone.

"Nooo!" Natalie screamed, and she ran toward the glass, the front door of the Luxor.

But they were gone.

Death and dying, gunpowder and blood.

Angelina was gone.

"*NOOooooo!*" Natalie screamed, swinging her arms, kicking her legs as she tried to walk.

"Natalie."

Dan's voice. What's he doing here?

"Natalie." His voice was louder now, his grip firm.

Natalie opened her eyes, saw the light coming into the car, Angelina stirring beside her. Dan's face was inches from Natalie's, wrinkled with concern.

"Natalie," he said softly. "Natalie, it's all right. You were dreaming." She stopped kicking and slumped down on her back on the rear seat. She reached up and pulled Dan down to her, his cheek on her wet face, feeling his weight, feeling his arms holding onto her. Natalie pulled him between the front bucket seats. She didn't want to talk, to think. She reached over with one hand and touched Angelina.

Natalie looked out at the gray dawn. She heard a steady rumble, a clacking noise, then recognized the shadows of moving boxcars that flitted through the windows. They were parked in a grove of trees next to a railroad track.

Death and dying. So very, very pleezed to meetcha.

Six

The next two days were a blur for Natalie, a period of resting and healing. They stayed in a motel in Tallahassee, getting Angelina back to being a kid again. Although Natalie had never been to Florida's capital before, she was in too much pain to sightsee, and stayed inside. Dan studied the journal and all of the clippings that had survived the trip, making notes and a list of questions and things to do.

Dan and Angelina were worried about Natalie. She was in a lot of pain with her neck. He thought she had hyper-extended it during the car wreck, and decided to take her t to the emergency room of the local hospital.

The doctor gave Natalie a neck brace and some pain pills, and both relieved her pain. Angelina and Dan made a big fuss over her, Angelina shadowing Natalie, doting on her, worshiping and loving her the unconditional way a seven-year-old can. She was convinced that Natalie had saved her life, continually asking Natalie if she could do anything for her.

Natalie dreamed again in the motel room, scaring all three of them when she woke up screaming. Dan called a very worried Susan, and they agreed to meet in Portland in two days.

They were traveling again, Dan getting them tickets from Tallahassee to Dallas-Fort Worth, and from there to San Francisco. Natalie had a plan to get back into the state of Oregon, and it didn't include flying into Portland International and into custody at the same time. She wanted to give herself up on her own terms and at her convenience.

Whatever happened would take place in Portland, a town she knew.

They flew across the country again, first to San Francisco, and then to Redmond, Oregon. Angelina had her nose pressed to the glass, watching the mountains. They rented a car to take them over the Cascade Mountains, a three-hour trip to Portland.

Come and get me, you son of a bitch. I'm home.

Victor Bramson did come for Natalie, but he wasn't just after her. He wanted the child.

Wednesday, September 27

The Gathering

One

They waited in their suite for their guests to arrive: Susan, dressed as if she were going to the theater at Kennedy Center; Angelina, her brown hair swinging in a ponytail, wearing a new red dress; Dan, wearing tan slacks and a brown cotton sweater, evidence of a shopping trip hours before; and Natalie, with neck brace in place and some strong Tylenol on board, wearing black slacks and a white blouse that glittered.

Dan couldn't keep his eyes off her, watching her, loving her.

At ten to six there was a knock on the door, and Dan looked at each of them, hugging his sister, Natalie, and Angelina. Natalie opened the door, and Grant and Aimee stood there, Aimee putting her arms around Natalie immediately.

"What happened to your neck?" she asked anxiously, walking Natalie into the room.

"She couldn't wait, Minnie Mouse," Aimee said, and Natalie went to him, Dan, Susan, and Angelina looking on.

Natalie kissed Grant, and put her arms on both of them, turning slowly, the neck stiff and painful. "Oh, Grant, I'm so sorry for making you worry."

"You should be, Minnie Mouse, and——."

"Hush up," Aimee said.

"Daddy, who's Minnie Mouse?" Angelina asked.

"I am, Angel," Natalie told her, and she introduced them. Aimee instantly fell in love with Angelina, asking her about her school, her family.

Natalie opened the door to another knock, and there stood the man she had once called the Courthouse Louse.

David Attinger was wearing the most awful mustard-colored plaid sport coat she had ever seen, missing a button in front, his dress shirt wrinkled and frayed.

"Well, the wandering princess returns," Attinger said, and walked into the room. Natalie rolled her eyes and followed him, giving Grant a dirty look, as if to say, "Grant how could you do this to me?"

"Uh, this is Natalie's attorney," Grant said, "and he has been working his tail off on her behalf."

"We're gonna be together in court, we're going clothes shopping," Natalie said, giving Attinger a grin. She walked over and carefully put her arm around him. "He may not look like much, folks," she said as she introduced him, "but he's mine."

Attinger looked around the room. "Pretty nice," he said. He walked to the bar and opened the cabinet, selected a bottle of Chivas, and asked, "We going to make this a working dinner or what?"

"I've called for a waiter," Dan said. "We'll eat here."

There was another knock on the door, and Natalie stood there looking at a small man in his sixties, with white hair and a white beard. He was immaculately dressed in a charcoal suit.

"I'm Dr. Morganstein," he said, looking Natalie over. "Sergeant Grant called me and asked me to meet you here. And you are?" he asked Natalie.

"Natalie," she said, and brought him into the room. "Doctor of what?"

"Medicine," he said, "and psychiatry is my specialty."

"I asked for him," Dan said. "He's going to help us decipher some things tonight."

They brought another table in from Susan's suite, and put it next to the couch. Susan and Angelina sat with Aimee. Grant, Attinger, Dr. Morganstein, and Dan were at the other table. Natalie sat back on the couch, slowly lowering her neck back against the rest.

"By now we are all familiar with the events Natalie told us about the night her sister was killed." Dan spoke loudly, so they all could hear. He looked at each one in turn, and when the doctor nodded, he continued.

"The man responsible for killing Stephanie and my wife, Jackie, is named Victor Bramson. I know that he has also killed dozens and dozens of ordinary people around the world, people like us." That stopped Attinger as he was raising a drink to his mouth. Aimee raised her hands to her face. Grant looked grim.

Angelina walked over and put her hand on Dan's shoulder, gave him a kiss, and sat down on the couch beside Natalie.

"I don't know when he started," Dan said, "but I believe it was some time before he killed Jackie, almost two years ago. He is very crafty, and smart, and he often arranges enough evidence at the scene to implicate a family member. Several people have been successfully prosecuted for the murder of someone they didn't kill, and at least one family member has committed suicide."

"Do you know why he's doing this, Mr. Harris?" Dr. Morganstein asked softly.

"Yes, and as I go along, that should become apparent."

"Can you prove any of this?" Attinger asked.

"With some work, I believe we can. On the night my wife was killed, I returned home to find a man leaving, and I struggled with him, not very effectively, and he got away. I was later charged for the murder of my wife, and I escaped from custody during the trial. If some of you think this was a romantic time, like *The Fugitive,* I can tell you that it was a time of despair and hopelessness, a time of deep depression, and if it had not been for my sister, my Angel, and Natalie, I would not be here now.

"I saw the man who killed Jackie, saw him on television one night, and learned that his name is Victor Bramson. I also learned that he is an authority on aging and longevity, and that he has become quite wealthy speaking on these subjects. He lives on the Gulf Coast of Florida, and he is a vicious killer. I have been following him for over a year, and was following him the night he killed Stephanie. I know why he killed Jackie, Stephanie and the others."

Dan got up and went to the writing desk by the bed. He picked up two legal pads and one of the journals he had taken from the house in Florida. He turned to face the group and saw their somber faces. Angelina had her head in Natalie's lap, her eyes closed, Natalie stroking her head.

"Doctor, before we leave tonight, I would like for you to examine this journal, and tell us something about the author, if it's possible." The doctor nodded. As Dan started back for the table, room service arrived with their dinners. When the waiters left, Dan started again.

"Victor Bramson believes that he will live for hundreds of years."

Attinger lowered his fork and stared at Dan. "No way," the attorney said, and then put a piece of prime rib in his mouth, looking up at Dan.

"Victor Bramson believes he has found a way to extend cell life, to reverse the effects of aging, to keep his body at its present age of fifty-one, to live for perhaps four hundred years. And, according to his journals, he knows that if he lives that long, he may well discover a way to keep his cells alive for another four hundred years. He believes he is a modern-day Ponce de Leon who has discovered the fountain of youth."

"So what? Why kill people?" Grant asked.

"Because, if I read his journals right, Bramson is crazy, certifiably crazy. Not a murderer who kills to satisfy sexual desires, for gratification like Bundy or Gacy, but a killer just as deadly. Bramson kills for knowledge. He kills to find answers to the one wild card he can't predict. He kills to find out why some people survive almost certain death, why some people are survivors."

"Why kill them?" Grant repeated.

"Because Bramson believes that these people will tell him, as they are dying, things they might not have otherwise known, that at the moment of death people know what's beyond and how they escaped death before."

"That's a pretty wild theory," Grant said. "What's the connection between you and Natalie?"

"My wife was one of the two survivors in a plane crash, a commuter plane that went down in New Jersey years ago. The other survivor was a ten-year-old kid named Gerald Goldson. I'm sure if you check this out, Sergeant Grant, you will find that the kid is dead."

"I intend to do just that," Grant said. He got up and walked to the writing table and made a phone call. "Where was the kid from?"

Dan looked at his notes.

"Middlesex, New Jersey."

Grant called the on-duty supervisor at the Kelly Butte regional dispatch center and asked for a computer message and phone call to Middlesex. "Get anything you can on a Gerald Goldson, born in about 1982, living in Middlesex." He sat back at the table.

"My wife survived the crash without a scratch, the Goldson boy with some scrapes, and all the rest of the passengers and crew died . . . all seventy-nine of them." Everyone in the room had stopped eating, looking at Dan.

"Natalie survived a shooting in a bank against three armed robbers, men who were better armed and who were shooting everyone who got in their way. Even though she was wounded, she survived." Dan took a drink of his coffee, now cold.

"And I found these in Bramson's study." He held up two newspaper clippings. "One is a short AP filler on the bank robbery, and the other a lengthy story clipped from *USA Today* about the plane crash. He kills survivors," Dan said. "And I have a complete list of names and hometowns from the other clippings I could find, stories about survivors. It shouldn't be hard to check." He looked at Grant, and the detective sergeant nodded, his face noticeably paler than when he'd come in.

"He kills survivors," Dan said softly "That's the key, he kills and kills survivors, and I was too late to stop him at least two times."

Natalie struggled up from the couch and put her arms around Dan while he was seated, laying her cheek on his head.

Attinger had stopped eating and was furiously scribbling on a legal pad, his fondness for food suspended only by his love of lawyering and a good fight. Grant got up and looked for another drink, pausing to give Aimee a squeeze on the arm. She smiled at him, her face as pale as his.

"You okay?" Natalie whispered to Dan.

"Fine."

"I love you," she said softly, kissing his neck, not caring that there were others in the room. She straightened up. "I have something to tell everyone," she said, looking around the room. "I love this man, his daughter, and his sister, and I want to be a member of their family."

"Me, too, Nat'lie!" Angelina yelled. She jumped up and clapped her hands and ran to Natalie, putting her arms around her waist.

"Me three, you darling girl," Susan said, smiling. Aimee took Susan's hands and held them, then turned toward Grant, grinning at him. Grant scowled.

"Oh, pulleeeze, could we get on with it," Attinger said, still scribbling furiously. "You get all sentimental on me, Sergeant Collins, and I might just puke, and then I'd have to double my fee."

"You puke, it certainly won't hurt your clothes," Natalie said loudly, "and I'll double the fee if you buy some presentable ones, you Courthouse Louse!"

The room broke out in laughter, Grant clapping Attinger on the back, the attorney still trying to write. The somber mood was broken, at least for a few minutes. Dan stood up and hugged Natalie and Angelina, getting congratulations and hugs from Aimee and Susan.

Dr. Morganstein was immersed in the journal, occasionally making a note in a small book.

"Hey," Angelina said, "who is Sergeant Collins?"

"Your new family member, you little Minnie Mouse," Grant said, bending over and putting his arms around the seven-year-old.

"Does this mean we're engaged?" Dan whispered to Natalie.

"Worse than that, buster," Natalie told him, turning her head slowly, giving Dan a kiss on the neck.

"Oh, Christ. We'd better call Sergeant Grant back. He leave a callback number or say where he was calling from?" The assistant supervisor looked at his screen and talked to the 911 supervisor. "Call up message ID#97889 and take a look. Someone's mighty interested in the Goldson kid."

Dan got another Henry's beer from the refrigerator. Grant followed.

"How many on the list you made?" he asked quietly. Dan looked at the man Natalie considered her second father.

"A lot, thirty-seven to be exact, but I lost some of the clippings looking for Angelina, and there were more there on the desk."

"I need a copy if we—." Grant's cell phone beeped, and he looked at the text message. Call the 911 center.

"I made a list for you."

Grant called, and when he flipped his phone closed, he stared at it and didn't look up. *Christ! What the hell's going on here? I'm getting too old for this shit.* He looked up to see Natalie watching him.

"Grant?"

"That was the dispatch center." They were all looking now. Even Dr. Morganstein looked up from the journal. "It seems that the ten-year-old who survived with Jackie Harris is missing, has been for two years. The F.B.I. wants to talk to me. They had Gerald Goldson's name flagged in the computer, requesting contact if there were any inquiries about him."

"He's dead," Dr. Morganstein said from the table.

Grant walked over to the window, looking at the street below.

"How do you know?"

"According to this journal, he is," Morganstein explained.

"Angelina, honey, why don't we go take a bath in my room?" Susan said, putting her arm around the little girl.

"Okay, night everybody." She got hugs from Dan, Natalie, Grant, and Aimee, patted Attinger on his arm and got a grunt in return, and shook hands solemnly with Dr. Morganstein.

"Can I go with you?" Aimee asked.

When the door closed, the room remained quiet, Attinger thinking, and making an occasional note, Morganstein reading, and Dan and Grant standing by the bar, Dan with a beer, Grant with a whiskey. Natalie sat on the couch with her head back, eyes closed.

"Doctor," Dan said, "are you familiar with the genetics, the chemistry and biology that Bramson's talking about in the journal?"

"Familiar enough so I can follow what he's writing about," Morganstein said.

"I think I have it down in layman's terms, Doc, and I want to talk about it. Would you fill in the gaps that are missing or correct me if I'm wrong?"

"Certainly."

"To begin with, Bramson's not going to live for four hundred years, or even half that long. Unless I've missed something, he just thinks he is."

"Correct," Dr. Morganstein said.

"But he may be on the right track, he is studying the right subjects and has some new ideas that might be of value. This is what he believes: that cell life is finite, and that this life can be extended with certain genetics, chemical compounds, and biological care. Bramson has studied the aging process for three decades, and has conducted extensive research with people in their seventies, eighties, nineties, and people over one hundred years of age.

"His research and speaking engagements have made him a wealthy man, and somewhere along the line he became convinced that he had discovered how to live a long time."

Morganstein nodded.

"But there was a wild card he couldn't control, the possibility of an accident that would kill him prematurely, even in his two hundredth year, and he felt he had to control that as much as possible. So he went looking for survivors, people who have for some reason survived when they shouldn't have, people with secrets to tell. Or so he thought.

"He started with a Vietnam veteran, a man who had been on several missions that he shouldn't have survived, a man who remained unscarred through three tours. And it almost ended there, because he picked one tough son-of-a-bitch. The man almost killed him, and Bramson decided that the Vietnam experience was too dated anyway, so he used newspaper articles for his research.

"Can you believe it? He reads about my wife's plane crash in *USA Today* and he fucking kills my wife?"

Natalie opened her eyes and reached for Dan, motioning for him to sit beside her. He put his beer on the coffee table and sat down, no one speaking, waiting for him to begin again.

"He followed research in several areas, watching closely the research in genetics, for instance, working with the notion that our cells are genetically programmed to atrophy after a certain age, depending upon the condition and age of the cell. He was mostly interested in the chemistry of cellular destruction. He cites research in his journal about the use of the drug deprenyl, a drug used to treat Parkinson's disease, where the drug actually increases the production of dopamine by the brain.

"Bramson was taking deprenyl . . . in large quantities.

"Bramson was also counting on—working on—the cell destruction that takes place environmentally, the destruction caused by ultraviolet rays from the sun. He knew that UV light is an oxidant, destroying free radicals in the body. He also knew that some species spend much of their lives in the sun, and also have long lives, such as some species of sea turtle. Did these creatures have a chemical, biological, or genetic makeup that countered the effects of UV light?

"He was looking for this. We found lots of sea turtles at his residence in Florida."

"We found a small piece of sea turtle shell in Natalie's apartment," Grant said.

"There were both live turtles at the residence in Florida, and pieces of dead ones. There were a number of turtle shells in the laboratory, both intact and crushed," Dan said.

"A false hope with the turtle shells, I would think," the doctor said.

"That's what I thought from reading the journals," Dan said. "But he's probably on to something there. From reading the journals, I know he's in contact with laboratories around the world, and with his knowledge and access to research, he could make it to one hundred twenty years of age."

Attinger got up and found the scotch. "This may be impertinent to question, but how did you get the journals and clippings and the tour of this guy's house . . . he invite you?"

Dan looked at Natalie and then started to answer, knowing that at some point he would have to talk about what he had done. But he would do it again, and again, if for no other reason than to have people finally believe in him, believe that he didn't kill his wife.

"Never mind, I don't want to know, at least not here with these other people present. I will represent you until we can find another attorney for you, as I have a potential conflict representing Natalie."

"There's something else, something from the house." Dan walked to the closet and removed the map from his bag.

"This was with the clippings," he said, spreading the map on the table. They all crowded around to look, looking at a map of the United States. There were dots clustered in and around most major cities. Several in the New York area. Miami, Washington, Baltimore. One on the Chesapeake Bay. Los Angeles, Denver, Seattle.

"Two in Portland," Doctor Morganstein observed.

"How?" Attinger asked.

"I've counted eighty-eight on the map," Dan said, "but the journal doesn't reflect whether these are actual visitations, or whether they represent areas where people have survived extraordinary conditions."

Dan thought about what he had just said. *Visitations. A strange word for a lot of killing of innocent people.*

They drifted away from the table. Attinger and Grant went to the liquor cabinet; Natalie and Dan sat on the couch, with the doctor at the table. Dr. Morganstein picked up the journal.

"I'd like to see everything that you have from this man, but I'm ready with a few observations if you'd like to hear them now."

Dan nodded.

"First of all, this is a very disturbed man. If this journal was written by Victor Bramson, he is affected by a paranoid delusional system that is monstrous. He wants to live forever, he sees himself as a modern-day Ponce de Leon, believing he has the knowledge and power to extend his life by a factor of six and more. And his delusion is that he can predict and therefore avoid the untimely death that may beset him by accident. The delusion is that he can obtain the secret of avoidance of death by causing the death of those who are survivors and listening to them at the time of their death."

Dr. Morganstein paged through the journal, marking a page with his finger.

"He writes about some of the things he learned from the victims, what he asks at the moment of death. He apparently believes that the victim will have some kind of insight into why they were spared, and some insight as to what will happen to them when they die."

Natalie moaned, and they turned toward her, Dan holding his arm around her on the couch. She had been numb most of the night, a combination of pain and pain pills, friends around her so she didn't have to think, and a feeling of safety. She hadn't even let herself worry about the pending hearing and the possible loss of her freedom.

She was just drifting, listening to the doctor's voice, when she had a sudden thought: *Did the bastard write about my Stephanie?*

"You okay? Dan asked, concern on his face.

Natalie turned to the doctor. "Is Stephanie in there, my sister Stephanie?"

"Yes."

She put her face in her hands, and shook her head, the pain from her neck adding to her sadness, and then to her fury. She spoke into her hands, the words indistinguishable a few feet away.

"What's that, Natalie?" Grant asked, walking toward the couch.

She pulled her head up and looked around. "I'll tell you all this much, the son-of-a-bitch who killed my sister isn't going to live to be four fucking hundred years old."

"My belief is," Dr. Morganstein said, "that the person who wrote this is very dangerous, a ruthless and cunning man who will stop at nothing to kill all of those who have read this, particularly Natalie and Dan, who he might believe took it from him."

"He knows we did, Doc," Dan said, holding up his hand to Attinger. "I know, I know all about witnesses, but you all know that I took this material from his house. He saw Natalie and me as we were leaving. That's how she got the neck injury, when he rammed us with his car."

"We probably can't use anything here," Attinger said, "either to acquit you or charge him." He smiled, thinking of tomorrow's battle. "I will, however, call you to the stand, and have you tell me everything about this, which will have the same effect on Judge Hernandez's mind as LSD. Boy, is she gonna be pissed, a straight-forward preliminary hearing blown all to hell with these wild stories."

Attinger stood, gathering up his pads, stuffing them in an old briefcase, a leather accordion type with the lock on top. "Night all," he said, and to Dan and Natalie added, "my office, eight A.M. sharp." Dr. Morganstein stood to go, motioning for Grant and Dan to step out into the hallway.

"I think he's losing control," he told them quietly. "The killing is becoming more important than the information he's getting."

"Is he going to be easier to catch, this way?" Grant asked.

"Possibly, but he is infinitely more dangerous. Good night, gentlemen."

Grant and Dan re-entered the room. "What was that you said, Natalie?" Grant asked abruptly. "What did you say to the press when they pulled you out of the bank?"

"I told them in the ambulance that I was so very lucky to be alive, that I thought I would live forever, after surviving the fight."

"When we get through this hearing," Grant said, "we will get our evidence on Mr. Victor Bramson. We'll get him to convict himself."

"How?" Dan asked.

"We'll stage a bizarre, frightening, obviously fatal accident, and have a person walk away from it, playing it up in the press. We'll make it an accident involving a single person, and have the survivor tell the press that as they were about to die, they realized that they couldn't, that they thought they would be able to live forever. They now have the secret."

After they made love, Natalie whispered, "Do you think Grant's plan will work?"

"No."

"What will we do?" She was weary and she hurt. "Can we get enough evidence against him to help us and convict him?"

"Maybe not. But you know what we have to do, don't you, Detective Sergeant Collins."

She nodded. *Oh, yeah, I know as well as you, Danny Boy.* "One of us will have to find him and kill him."

"We can't have a life together, you, me, and Angelina, unless we do, and I want a life with you, Natalie. I truly want one."

"Me, too." She snuggled, thinking about Dan's words, hoping the dreams wouldn't be too bad.

Gunpowder and blood.

One of us will have to find him and kill him.

Two

Bramson stood on the sidewalk in the rain, looking at the massive stone building, a product of fifties' architecture, columns, facades, frescoes. He traced the route he would take, walking around the corner to Eighth Street, and stopped short. A figure was crouched on a storm drain, steam from the sewers providing heat, a figure with several layers of tattered clothing.

"Got any spare change, buddy?" A face looked out from the rags, a face with grimy flesh, giving way to bone.

"No such thing," Bramson said, walking around the sidewalk denizen, thinking of the tools he would need tomorrow. It was colder here than on the Gulf Coast, the rain different, chillier. Not a place for sustaining life. Too cold. An inner voice chided him. *Adaptability is the key, Victor, adaptability. You could live here.*

He looked back at the transient, seeing that his entire face was a skeletonized version of what he had seen seconds earlier. He was in control again, and the thought that his power and knowledge had diminished was distant, ephemeral.

You will all die before me.

He walked through the downtown area, toward the river, waving at the two police officers in the white-and-blue car, seeing the bones of their faces and hands as they waved.

You will all die before me.

Thursday, September 28

Sacrifice

One

Natalie and Dan stood up as David Attinger entered the small waiting room. Natalie was wearing a navy blue suit with faint pinstripes, a white silk blouse, white nylons, and navy flats. A white foam neck brace made her movements jerky, awkward.

Dan wore a gray Armani suit with a light blue oxford shirt and dark tie. Natalie thought he looked wonderful. She twisted her hands together, waiting.

"The judge is ready," the lawyer said. He was wearing his best suit, a solid brown one that was now a couple of sizes too small for him, with a white shirt and a yellow tie. The shirt was straining to the point that Natalie was ready to duck if one of the buttons should let go, but it was a great improvement over what he had worn last night, and she told him so.

"David," she said, putting her hand on his arm, "I'm sorry for calling you a louse. I know you'll fight for us." His face was flushed with excitement and anticipation of what the day would bring, and he nodded.

"Natalie, David," Dan said, standing between them, putting his arms on their shoulders, "I will most assuredly be in jail by the end of the day."

"Most likely," Attinger said.

"And I could be as well," Natalie said, looking into Dan's eyes. "I love you, Daniel McClellan Harris."

"You, too, Natalie, and you look great."

"You lovers want me to ask the judge for a postponement, tell her you want to go pick out rings, or what?" Attinger asked, holding the door open.

The courtroom was packed with people and was so noisy, it seemed to Natalie that everyone was talking at once. As she walked to the defense table with Attinger, she saw Grant sitting with the other members of the homicide squad. Eldredge and Thompson, and even Gretchen, they were all there, and Natalie loved them for it. Her depression suddenly lifted, and she smiled and gave them a thumbs-up sign. Kirby waved and blew her a kiss, and Natalie blew one back, glancing at the bench. The judge hadn't entered yet.

Natalie walked past the prosecution table and on an impulse, stopped in front of Sims. She leaned over slightly, bending at the waist, until Sims looked up, looking at her neck brace. She smiled and stuck her hand out until he took it He gave it a shake, looked back down at his pad, and continued writing. Natalie took her seat at the defense table.

"All rise," the bailiff, Mr. Thomas Langley, called out.

"The Circuit Court of the State of Oregon, Multnomah County, is now in session, the Honorable Judge Felicia Hernandez, presiding." Langley banged his gavel down.

"You may be seated," Judge Hernandez said, in a clear and slightly accented voice. As the crowd was rustling down, Natalie looked at Felicia Hernandez. She had been in Judge Hernandez's courtroom a lot of times, and no one had ever thought of her as "nice," a literal translation for Felicia. She was fifty-five years old, and had fought her way to the bench, struggling through law school at a time when there were few women there, and fewer minorities. She was taller than Natalie at five foot four, and was forty pounds heavier, with reading glasses and short, dark hair. She was a good judge, and if the gallery or the attorneys doubted her toughness in her court, they wouldn't doubt it by the end of the day.

Attinger said Felicia was fair, had a sense of humor, and ran her courtroom like a Mexican mother ran her family, with no bullshit allowed. "I think she likes me," Attinger had told Natalie.

"I know both attorneys here today, and I don't expect any surprises. For those of you watching, it will be a long day, and I will tolerate no commotions of any kind in my courtroom. Our constitution allows for the public to attend this hearing, and I agree with that, but if any individual can't sit still without talking, coughing, laughing, or whatever, you won't be a part of the public attending this hearing."

The courtroom was very quiet. The reporters in the front row scribbled on their long, narrow tablets. An artist for the *Oregonian* was seated in the front row, on the aisle, holding his pad up at an angle, sketching Judge Hernandez, something for the paper tomorrow morning.

"This is the time set for the preliminary hearing, *State of Oregon v. Natalie Collins,* with a charge of Murder in the First Degree. Through an agreement reached with the D.A.'s office and Mr. Attinger, we will be holding this hearing instead of the usual grand jury process. Mr. Sims, is the state ready?"

"The state is ready, Your Honor."

"Do you have any prehearing matters?"

"Your Honor, I would ask that the court exclude witnesses."

Judge Hernandez looked out and spoke to the courtroom. "If there are any witnesses or potential witnesses in the courtroom, you will be excluded from the courtroom at this time, and will remain in the immediate area until you are called."

Natalie looked around at Dan, who was seated in the front row behind her with Grant. Grant whispered something to Dan, and he got up and walked toward the doors at the rear of the room.

Dan walked out, looking for Susan and Angelina. His daughter had insisted that she be allowed to go to the court, and everyone objected but Natalie. She wanted Angelina there, and Susan agreed to take her. They had been standing in line since eight A.M. and then found a seat in the back when the doors opened.

Susan waved from a seat by the wall in the far right corner. Angelina saw Dan and stood and blew him a kiss, a tall man in a charcoal suit turning away from her as she waved.

"Mr. Attinger?" Judge Hernandez called.

David Attinger stood up. "The defense is ready, Your Honor, and I have a prehearing matter that I need to discuss with you, should take a minute."

"Here or in chambers?"

"The court is fine, Your Honor. May I approach the bench?" Hernandez waved him up, waving to Sims as well.

"Well, David, it's your show," the judge said as he walked up to the bench.

"I know this is unusual, Your Honor, for the defense to call witnesses in a preliminary hearing. However, I have a witness whom I just located and talked with last night for the first time, a witness who will testify that another person killed Sergeant Collin's sister, and that he was with Natalie when she struggled with the killer. The anonymous, collateral witness that Detective Sergeant Natalie Collins told the police about that night."

Judge Hernandez stared at Attinger, her brows closing down over her eyes. Attinger thought he might have been a little too hasty to praise this woman; right now she looked mean and more than a little pissed off.

"This won't turn into a circus, Mr. Attinger. I'm going to let the state proceed, and then we'll talk about your 'witness,' or whomever you have, in my chambers. And the testimony from both sides had better damned well be relevant. We will not be wasting the court's valuable time with trivia or tricks." She looked at the Assistant D.A. "Mr. Sims, how long for you to present your case?"

"This morning should cover it, Your Honor, but we've seen Davey in action before," he said, hoping to include the judge in his view of Attinger, "and for that matter, the state doesn't care who his witnesses are; we have witnesses who will testify that Natalie Collins acted alone that night, that her story is just that, a story. The state has no objection, if, as you say, Your Honor, it doesn't turn into a Barnum and Baily production."

After glaring at Attinger for effect, Judge Hernandez dismissed them with a wave.

"Don't you think the neck brace is a little overdone, Davey?" Sims muttered as they returned to their seats.

If you think this is a circus, Attinger thought as he walked back to his chair, *you ain't seen anything yet.* He grinned.

Natalie watched as Attinger returned, her stomach churning, hoping the judge would allow Dan's testimony. When he grinned, she thought it looked hopeful.

"She hasn't said yet if he's in," Attinger said, and he leaned back in his chair to watch the show begin.

Deputy District Attorney Sims got right to the point. He stood and faced the judge, holding a legal pad with his right hand, his left hand on his hip, a workingman's pose.

"Your Honor, this tragedy is one that all of us wished didn't happen. A young woman died. Another young woman, a brilliant, decorated, and dedicated police officer, is accused by the police of killing her sister. Two lives destroyed, but the state of Oregon doesn't ask us if we like the defendant, the state demands that people be held responsible for their actions. In the course of their investigation, Your Honor, the police found evidence to lead them to believe that Natalie Collins killed her sister, shot her in a premeditated manner, and the state is prepared to display sufficient probable cause to show the court that Natalie Collins should stand trial for murder in the first degree." Sims sat down, looking at Judge Hernandez as he did so.

"Call you first," Judge Hernandez said.

Sims didn't waste any time. His first witness was the state medical examiner, who established that Stephanie Walker was killed with a handgun, a gun fired by a person other than Stephanie Walker. He testified that she had not died by her own hand.

Natalie sat at the table, looking at a pad that Attinger had placed in front of her. She had worked with Dr. Jack Dailey many times in the past, and she couldn't look at him, listen to him describe how Stephanie died. Massive trauma to the brain, death was instantaneous, due to a gunshot wound. Natalie wanted to yell at him, "So what, Jack, we know she's dead! You'd better do half as good a job when we get the real killer in the courtroom!"

"Any way at all this could have been a suicide?" Sims asked.

"No, as I have testified," Dr. Dailey said, "the gun was not fired by the deceased."

"I have no further questions for this witness, Your Honor," Sims said.

"Mr. Attinger, you may examine the witness," Judge Hernandez said.

Attinger rose up slightly from his chair. "I have no questions of this witness, Your Honor."

Sims called a neighbor of Natalie's, Mrs. Taylor, who told the court about hearing a crash, and what sounded like a shot, and that she had then dialed 911.

"How long have you known Natalie Collins, Mrs. Taylor?" Sims asked, his voice low and sincere.

"Ever since she moved in, two or three years ago." She smiled and gave Natalie a little wave. Natalie smiled.

"Has she been a good neighbor?"

"Oh my, yes, she has been wonderful. She's such a darling girl."

"Ever hear any problems at her place, other than that Friday night?"

"No...well, not until her sister moved in."

"Can you explain that for us?"

"Well, some time after her sister moved in, I heard them arguing, like they were yelling at each other."

"Could you hear what was said?"

"No, only that they were yelling. I could hear them over *Jeopardy.*"

"The TV show, you could hear them when you were watching TV?"

"Well, yes, but just that one time, in the summer."

"Mrs. Taylor, you said that you heard a crash, and then what sounded like some shots, is that right? How long after the crash did you hear the shots?"

"Well, they, uh, they were pretty close."

"Thank you, Mrs. Taylor," Sims said, adding to the judge, "I have no further questions, Your Honor."

Attinger got to his feet and smiled at Mrs. Taylor. "Ma'am, you have known Natalie for quite a long time, haven't you?"

"Yes, as I said."

"Has she ever done anything that bothered you?"

"Oh, heavens no. She's a great neighbor."

"When you heard Natalie and her sister arguing, could they have been talking loud?"

"Sounded like they were talking loud, yes."

Attinger felt he had done everything he could with Mrs. Taylor, and he sat down.

Sims called a succession of witnesses: Ambulance attendants, the first uniformed police officers arriving to take charge of the scene, crime-scene technicians, and detectives. He didn't take long with any one person, and Attinger didn't ask many questions. At eleven o'clock, Sims called his last witness of the morning, Lieutenant Derry of the Portland Police Bureau's Internal Affairs Division.

As he walked up and stood before the bailiff to be sworn in, Natalie felt herself shrink in her chair. It wasn't going to look good that she'd run out of his office, had refused to answer his questions, but there wasn't anything she could do about it now.

Susan thought of asking the nice detective if he was ill, he looked so pale and white, as if you could see through his skin in places. Unhealthy. But he didn't cough and was pleasant enough. *And the man dresses acceptably,* she thought. *A nice charcoal suit.* He leaned over toward her, leaning across Angelina, and said something.

"I'm sorry, what did you say?" she whispered.

"I said I think Natalie's going to be just fine."

Susan smiled. "I'm glad so many of her friends are here."

"We're close friends, and I hate to see her going through this," he whispered. Susan patted his arm, and he smiled.

"Lieutenant Derry, would you tell the court how you happened to become involved in the investigation of the shooting death of Stephanie Walker?"

"I was called by the homicide detective supervisor, Captain Mitchell, shortly after it was determined that Natalie Collins had been involved in the shooting." He looked at the judge and continued. "Any time a police officer is involved in any use of deadly force, my division conducts the investigation, and in this case, since Natalie Collins is assigned to the homicide division, her unit would not be allowed to continue the investigation."

"Tell us what happened when you first contacted Natalie Collins."

"I was informed that she was at the hospital. I sent a team of detectives to the scene of the shooting, her apartment, and I went to the hospital with Sergeant Nichols. At the hospital, we talked with Sergeant Collins for some time, and she told us that she had arrived home and found her sister's body."

"She said that her sister was already dead when she came home?" Sims asked, his voice rising at the end.

"Yes, and she told us she struggled with a man she found in the bedroom, and was saved by another man. She talked about fighting and then shooting at the men, and after a time the police arrived."

"Lieutenant Derry, what is wrong with Natalie Collins's story?" Sims asked. Attinger started to get out of his seat and make an objection, thought better of it, and sat down. Judge Hernandez watched him.

"Mr. Attinger, did you have something to add?" she asked

"No, Your Honor, not at this time."

"Lieutenant Derry?" Sims said.

"I went to the scene with other detectives, to continue the investigation. And the longer I was there, the more I became aware that the physical evidence at the scene didn't fit the events as told to us by Natalie Collins."

"What physical evidence?"

Lieutenant Derry went through the pieces of evidence that he and his investigators had found at the scene: the lack of signs of a struggle in the bedroom; the struggle in the living room looked contrived: the broken lamp, the smashed door frame; the gun used to kill Stephanie was Natalie's; the blood on the sleeve of a dress in the closet, high velocity blood spatter that could only have come from a gunshot wound; the dress belonged to Natalie.

"Lieutenant Derry, when you went to the apartment, were you looking for ways to disprove Natalie Collins's story?" Sims asked quietly.

"No. We were investigating the crime using the information she told us, that there were other people in the apartment who killed her sister. The facts in the apartment didn't fit her story, of"—and Derry looked at Natalie— "her story didn't fit the facts. And she missed."

"What do you mean, she missed?" Sims asked.

"She missed the bad guy who was supposedly in her apartment. This lady"—and he pointed to Natalie—"this lady is one of the best shots in the department. She has proven herself under fire in a bank robbery and defended herself against several people who were shooting at her, and she misses two unarmed men in her living room? I don't believe it. And when we tried to ask her about the events, she got mad and ran out of the room, refusing to cooperate with us or answer our questions."

"I have no further questions, Your Honor," Sims said, and sat down.

Angelina took Susan's hand and squeezed it. "Daddy and Natalie will do better," she whispered.

David Attinger stood up slowly, looked at the judge, and then at Lieutenant Derry.

"Lieutenant Derry, we've listened to your stories about what you found at the apartment. I would like to ask you, have you worked with Detective Sergeant Collins in the past?"

"Yes."

"How many times?"

"Several."

"Can you be more specific, cite some cases where you worked with her?"

"Several years ago I worked a burglary ring case with her."

"And what was the outcome of that case?"

"Several arrests were made."

"Did you evaluate Sergeant Collins then?"

"Yes, I believe so."

"Do you remember what you said at the time?"

"Not exactly."

"Didn't you write that"—Attinger looked down at his notes, before continuing—"didn't you write that, and I am reading from an evaluation you signed, didn't you write, 'Officer Natalie Collins is one of the most productive and professional police officers I have ever worked with.'"

"Yes, I wrote that."

"Lieutenant Derry, prior to this incident on Friday night, September 21 of this year, have you ever known Sergeant Collins to lie?"

"No."

"Lieutenant Derry, did you or any officer perform a Gunshot Residue Test on Detective Sergeant Collins's hands that morning?"

"No."

"Well, why not?"

"Because she told me that she fired a gun in her living room. According to her story, there should have been traces of GSR on her hands, even if she didn't shoot in the bedroom."

Attinger looked at his notes. *Good one, Davey, you dumb shit.* He continued. "Did you check her hands for blood?"

"No."

"Why not?"

"I was told that her hands had been washed."

"Isn't it likely that the person who shot Stephanie would have blood spatter on their hand?"

"Yes, it's likely."

"So the one test that may have excluded Sergeant Collins as the shooter wasn't performed?"

"No."

"Lieutenant Derry, do you know what dress Detective Sergeant Collins wore to the symphony that night?"

"No."

"What dress was she wearing when you saw her at the hospital?"

"A sleeveless black evening dress."

"During your investigation, did you interview anyone or otherwise find out what kind of dress she wore to the symphony that night?"

"A sleeveless black evening dress."

"Is your theory that she and her sister Stephanie struggled when she got home?"

"Struggled or argued."

"Isn't it stretching your theory a bit much to think she changed clothes, then struggled, or argued, then changed back into the sleeveless evening gown?"

Sims stood up before Derry could answer. "Your Honor," he said, "he's asking the witness for a conclusion, and I'm not even sure I understood the question."

"Sustained," Judge Hernandez said. "Ask a better question, Mr. Attinger."

"Lieutenant Derry, is there any evidence that Detective Sergeant Natalie Collins was wearing the long-sleeved gown that night?"

'Uh, I don't know."

"Is there any evidence that Detective Sergeant Natalie Collins was wearing that gown when her sister Stephanie was shot?"

"Well, yes."

"What?"

"It's her gown, and it was in her closet."

"Is there any physical evidence that Detective Sergeant Natalie Collins had her arm in the sleeve of the gown when Stephanie was shot?"

Lieutenant Derry didn't answer right away.

"No."

"I have no further questions, Your Honor." Attinger sat down, and Natalie put her hand on his arm.

Sims stood up. "I have a few questions, Your Honor. Lieutenant Derry, didn't you used to work in homicide?"

"Yes."

"In fact, didn't you supervise the homicide unit at one time?"

"Yes."

"How many death investigations have you been involved with, in twenty-five years of police work?"

"Hundreds."

"As the supervisor of the Internal Affairs Division, are you out to get Sergeant Collins?"

"No. On the contrary, we spent days in the neighborhood looking for any witnesses to what happened, looking for someone who saw the men Natalie Collins told us about. We didn't find one witness who told us they saw anyone run in or out, or lounge around Natalie Collins's apartment. We looked for evidence to support her story, but it wasn't there. Her gun was used, her dress was worn when the trigger was pulled. I wish it were different."

"I have no further questions, Your Honor." Sims sat down.

Attinger half rose from his seat. "I have no further questions for this witness, Your Honor."

Sims stood up. "The prosecution rests, Your Honor."

"It's eleven forty-five," Judge Hernandez said. "Let's break for lunch and be back at one-thirty. Court is adjourned until then."

*   *   *

The man in the charcoal suit stood beside Susan, in the back near the door, shielded from the front by the rush of people in the aisle. *There's only one person who knows what I look like,* he thought, *and he's not in the room.*

"I'll see you at one-thirty," he told Susan, "and I'll save your places for you."

Susan smiled up at him. "That's very nice," she said, thinking that Natalie's friends were indeed nice. *What a nice man. I need to tell Natalie about him.* She took Angelina's hand and they walked out through the double doors to the courtroom, waiting for Dan and Natalie.

The man walked out in a crowd, leaving the courthouse and walking to a rental car. There was much to do, and one-thirty didn't give him much time to prepare. The little one would have so much to tell him. So very much.

You will all die before me.

Natalie stood up, looking around at the crowded courtroom as people were filing into the aisles. As David Attinger put his notes in his briefcase, she tried to fight the depression that was threatening to engulf her, but it was hard to listen to yourself described in the context of evidence. *Hell, if I had been investigating the crime,* she thought, *I might have reached the same conclusions.*

How many times have I done that? How many times have I used pieces of evidence that seemed to fit, that I looked at in only one way? How many times have I been wrong about someone's life?

David said something, something about the afternoon. She shook her head.

"I'm sorry, David, what did you say?"

"I said, watch out, Judge."

"Oh." Natalie put her arms around him and looked over the courtroom, looking for Susan and Angelina.

Oh, yeah, Attinger thought as they walked toward the back, through the now empty aisle, *watch out, 'cause we're coming with everything we got in the P.M., and if Natalie goes to jail, it won't be for trying, 'cause I have a feeling you'll be there before her, Davey Attinger, Attorney at Law. Wonder how the food is there?*

"David."

"What?"

"What happens if we lose, if they don't believe us?"

They walked out into the hallway, and saw Susan and Angelina against the far wall, waiting. David waved at them, not giving Natalie an answer. But she knew the answer immediately. *This is bigger than us.* There were things you didn't tell your attorney.

Someone has to go to Florida and hunt him down and kill him.

Two

Natalie picked at her salad and listened to David Attinger tell them about the case Assistant District Attorney Sims put on. She didn't want to go back to the courtroom, to hear the evidence about how she killed Stephanie.

It's so unfair. I'm not even allowed time to grieve for Steph.

Not able to go to Disneyland, the Happiest Place in the World.

"They have the gun, and they have the sleeve of the dress. And that's about it," Attinger said, at the same time pulling a large mass of spaghetti from his plate and stringing it to his mouth.

Dan had reserved a table for them at an Italian restaurant two blocks from the courthouse. Natalie sat beside him, across from Attinger. Susan and Angelina were beside Attinger.

"That's more than we've had in some cases where we convicted," Natalie said quietly, looking at her salad. "The blood on the sleeve, why would he think of that? Blood spatter interpretation has convicted a lot of people, because it usually shows the defendant is lying, that the events couldn't have happened the way the defendant is saying they did. And that's what is making the case for them, the blood on the sleeve. It makes everything we say seem contrived."

She moved slowly, woodenly, the pain in her neck and back adding to her depression.

"We have your testimony, and Dan's," Attinger said, "and that's more than I usually get. And we have some points of law here to go through, the collection of evidence without consent, a warrantless search, the interpretation of evidence can go for us as well as against us. I'm going to argue that the evidence is there to support your story, and the judge will have to take that into account."

"And if she doesn't?"

"Then the judge will rule that there is sufficient probable cause to believe that you caused Stephanie's death, and the case will be set for trial."

"Will Natalie go to jail like my daddy did?" Angelina got up from her seat and walked around the table. She put her head on Natalie's shoulder and put an arm around her, holding her giraffe in her other hand. Natalie put her right arm around Angelina and leaned down as far as the neck brace would allow. Dan kneeled beside his daughter. *A child shouldn't have to go through this,* he thought angrily.

"I'll be fine, honey," Natalie whispered, looking into Dan's eyes from inches away. Dan didn't say anything. He winked at Natalie.

"Oh, so you're the one trying to cheer people up," Natalie said.

"Someone has to," Dan said. "The job's yours any time you want it back." He didn't know what bothered him more—the thought of Natalie going to jail, or her depression.

Attinger stopped eating, looking at the family, at Susan, and then at his plate. He picked up his fork and waved it at Natalie.

"If the judge puts you in jail, I'll immediately request a bail hearing, and we'll get you out."

"Angel," Dan said softly, pulling her arms from Natalie. Angelina held on tighter. She wanted to tell her dad about Natalie's friend who looked like the bad man, but he and Natalie had enough to worry about now.

"Angel, maybe you and Aunt Susan should go shopping this afternoon." He looked up at Susan, who nodded, her face grim.

"No!" I'm staying with Nat'lie." She tightened her grip on Natalie.

Their waiter approached, his pad in hand, forcing a smile, thinking that people should leave children home until they were eighteen. "Does anyone want any dessert?"

Three

"Mr. Attinger," Judge Hernandez said.

"Yes, Your Honor," David Attinger said as he was rising. The courtroom was full again, a low murmur of conversation causing the judge to look over the crowd. Natalie sat at the defense table, looking at her pad. They had left Dan waiting in a conference room, down the hall.

"Will the defendant be making a statement?"

"Yes, Your Honor, but may I approach the bench first?"

"Go ahead," Judge Hernandez said, sounding to Attinger as if she could become irritable without much provocation.

"Mr. Sims, you'd better come up as well," the judge said.

"Your Honor," Attinger said, "the defense has one witness, Daniel McClellan Harris. He has testimony regarding a person who we believe killed Stephanie. I would like the court to listen to a part of Mr. Harris's testimony in chambers, with the court's indulgence and permission. The testimony contains some very bizarre evidence, and I don't want to turn this into a media circus that—."

"Mr. Attinger," Judge Hernandez said tightly, "you've never minded turning my courtroom into a circus before, so why the change of heart now?"

Sims grinned.

David Attinger leaned forward and said in a whisper, "This will turn into a circus by the time it's over, Your Honor, but there are other things to consider here. We believe that one attempt has been made on Sergeant Collins's life, the evidence notwithstanding, and we are prepared to give testimony about the identity of that person, and it would be nice if we could give the police time to preserve some evidence that will be lost if those sharks in the front row put this in tonight's news." Attinger stopped and waited for the judge to digest what he had said. *She's giving that look again,* he thought, looking at the judge's round cheeks. *She's looking at me as if something just crawled out of a carcass.*

"Do you have any exhibits to offer?"

"No, just an interpretation of the evidence, such as Mr. Sims did for the state."

"I'm listening, Mr. Attinger. What will Mr. Harris say that will inflame the press if I have them withhold the name of their suspect?"

Attinger smiled, what he hoped was his most engaging smile.
"Your Honor, they will tell the court that the suspect is a man who
thinks he will live forever, or at least several hundred years, and that
the suspect is going around the country killing people."

Sims rolled his eyes up and shook his head.

Judge Hernandez looked at Attinger, Natalie Collins, and then at
Sims. "Well, if this is going to be a three-ring circus, I want you
gentlemen to remember I'm the ringmaster." She glared at Attinger.
"This had better be good, Mr. David Attinger, or you will want to trade
places with the defendant." She looked over the courtroom.

"This hearing will continue in my chambers for an undetermined
period of time." There was a groan from the press section. They
wouldn't be able to publish what happened in chambers. Judge
Hernandez stood up, wondering what the hell Davey Attinger had for
her now, but one thing was certain, it would be entertaining. She liked
David—he fought for his clients—but if he was pulling some shit in
her courtroom, she was going to crush his gringo cajones with her
gavel.

"I'll be back in a minute; I have to check on something," the man
told Susan as the judge was leaving. She nodded, smiling. *I forgot to
thank Natalie for having someone sit with us,* she thought.

David gathered up his notes, and winked at Natalie. "Better come
with me. The judge might hear some of your statement in chambers."

She waved a hand, her neck hurting to the point she didn't think
she could. *I'll have to take a pain pill soon,* she thought, *and I didn't
want to before I testified. It hurts now, it really hurts.*

"I'll be there in a minute, David," Natalie said.

The noise level in the courtroom rose immediately, as soon as the
judge was out of sight, people speculating on what was happening,
what was going to happen. Several people got up and entered the
middle aisle, leaving the courtroom for the rest rooms or a break.
Angelina sat next to her Aunt Susan, holding her giraffe up to her face.
Her stomach hurt. She wanted her daddy and Natalie to get out of the
courtroom and take her home. Any home, as long as they were all
there.

"Aunt Susan?"

"What, honey."

"Have you been to Nat'lie's home?"

"No."

"I want to go there, see what it's like."

The man came back, Natalie's detective friend. He picked his way past the people sitting on the same long bench, stopping as he got to Susan. He leaned down. "Dan wants to see Angelina, have her wait with him for a while." Susan started to get up. "Oh, no, sit still, I'll take her. You stay here. Those vultures waiting to get in will take our places."

"That's very nice of you."

"Anything for Sergeant Collins," he said, and motioned to Angelina, giving her a smile.

"Auntie Susan," Angelina said, standing up. The bad man. He was a bad man and she had to tell someone.

"Go on, Angelina, it's fine, this man is a friend of Natalie's. You're going to see your daddy."

Victor Bramson straightened up, his back to the front of the courtroom, his eyes on the double doors at the back. He held his hand out for Angelina, motioning for her as she walked in front of her aunt. He looked at the very fine, small bones in her hand, so white and fragile. Angelina hesitated, then took his hand, and they walked out to the aisle.

Angelina turned at the aisle and looked behind her at Natalie. *Nat'lie please look at us,* she thought, and then the man was pulling on her hand, smiling. And then she knew something that Natalie had known for years . . . even bad men could smile.

Angelina looked at her aunt, pleading with her eyes, not wanting to make trouble for Natalie because her friend was a bad man, thinking then it must be okay 'cause the man was taking her to her daddy.

Susan Prader smiled at Angelina. *She's really my daughter, too.*

She always remembered Angelina that way, being led away by the man she soon learned was not a police detective. If she had it to do over again, she would have screamed and attacked the man, yelling for help for her poor baby.

Four

"**Your** Honor," Attinger said, "we have a witness who substantiates what Detective Sergeant Natalie Collins told the police that night, that there were two men in her apartment and one of them killed Stephanie. This witness is one of the two men."

Judge Felicia Hernandez was seated behind her desk in her chambers. The chambers in the old courthouse had old oak and mahogany wood panels, bookcases with law books and novels, and a wet bar on the wall behind the desk. She had taken her robe off, now wearing a stylish black suit and colorful scarf. Attinger and Sims sat in large chairs facing the desk. The court reporter was in the corner, back by the bookcases. The judge gave Attinger a neutral look, but her message was threatening, a professional promise. She nodded at the court reporter to begin.

"This will be a part of the record. If there is no substance here, I will be suggesting to the D.A. that he look for a conspiracy on the part of Mr. Harris, and premeditation by Ms. Collins. I'm sure this will occur to Mr. Sims and others. You understand, Mr. Attinger?"

"Yes, Your Honor."

"I want to question him first, in chambers," Judge Hernandez said.

"I'll get him, Your Honor."

"I thought my daddy was in this building," Angelina said. They were going outside and down the steps of the courthouse.

"He's at Natalie's apartment, and wants me to take you there. You want to see her place, don't you?"

"I want to see my daddy." She tried to pull her hand away from his, and he held tight.

"We'll ride in my police car, and I'll take you right to your daddy." He led her to a parking area a block away, Angelina carrying her giraffe in her right hand, her left locked in the man's grip.

"This doesn't look like a police car."

"You know that detectives, like Natalie, drive ordinary cars, like this one, don't you? It's only a few blocks to where your daddy is." Victor Bramson looked around, unlocked the driver's door and shoved Angelina in, pushing her across the seat as he got in behind her. He held her with his right hand as he started the car and moved out into traffic. Down to the Willamette River. Then eight blocks to her riverfront apartment. Once she was inside, she was his.

And so were her secrets.

And no one would know where they were.

He needed quiet time with his search.

He saw her mandible drop down as she started to cry.

You will all die before me.

Dan entered the conference room and looked at the judge. He stopped as he approached the desk.

"I want to talk with you before we go into the open court," the judge said. "Are you familiar with Mr. Attinger?"

"Yes"

"This is Mr. Sims, the prosecutor. I'm going to ask you some questions about what you've observed, and this will be sworn testimony. Please raise your right hand."

Dan sat in a chair on the side of the desk, and faced Attinger and Sims.

"Mr. Attinger, where is Ms. Collins?" Judge Hernandez asked.

"She'll be here in a few minutes, Your Honor. She had to take something for her neck, but with your permission, we can start . . ."

Judge Hernandez nodded and looked at Dan. "Tell us your full name and what you know about this case."

Dan started with his name and former address. "Your Honor," he said, "two years ago I was building sailboats on the Chesapeake Bay. Prior to that I had a seat on the New York Stock Exchange, and I retired at the age of forty-one. I was successful, had some money, had a wife and baby daughter, and was working with my hands, crafting boats. And then my wife was killed, murdered, much the same way Natalie's sister, Stephanie, was murdered."

Dan looked down at his hands. He wanted to get through this without breaking up, becoming emotional. But then again, he was an emotional person, and it always affected him. He was still grieving the loss of his life. He looked over at the judge, who was listening intently.

"Go on," she said.

"I was accused of the murder of my wife, much the same as Natalie is being accused of the murder of her sister. During the trial, I escaped. Right now, Your Honor, I am a federal fugitive, wanted for the murder of my wife."

Sims was on his feet before Dan finished the sentence.

"Your Honor, this man's a murderer, and I want him locked up."

"*Sit* down, Mr. Sims," Judge Hernandez said coolly, and then added to her bailiff, "please bring a deputy in and have the deputy sit here to guard Mr. Harris. I'm not through with him yet. When the deputy gets here, give Mr. Harris's name to the police and have them run a check on him. At least we can see if he's telling the truth about that." She turned to Dan, her face tight and serious. "You may go on with your story, and it had better be good." She looked at Attinger with what he described later as two black laser eyes, eyes that could cut through the heart of a lawyer at ten miles.

"I didn't know, Your Honor," Attinger pleaded.

"If you didn't know, Mr. Attinger, Mr. Harris will get out of jail before you do." She turned to Dan. "Please continue, Mr. Harris. I'm through with my threats." As Dan began, Judge Felicia Hernandez muttered, "For now."

"I spent six months on the road, running, hiding in transient camps. And then I decided to do something about it. I found out who killed my wife, and I have been following him when I could for the past year. I was following him when Natalie Collins's sister was killed. I was the man who broke into her apartment and fought with the killer. I am her witness."

"And who do you think this killer is?" Judge Hernandez asked.

"A man named Victor Bramson, a man who lives in Florida and believes that he will live forever. A man who has, in addition to killing my wife and Natalie's sister, killed dozens of other people."

Natalie looked around the courtroom, waiting for the judge and the attorneys to return. The homicide detectives she had worked with were absent, probably working cases, she thought. They didn't have the time to sit in court all day unless they were testifying.

The press row was mostly empty, with reporters finishing their stories, using what they had from the morning's proceedings. Most of the gallery remained. Serious courtroom watchers knew if they left, they would not find a seat when court started again.

Susan and Angelina must be here, Natalie thought, and she got up. *Hell, I'm not in custody yet, and I may not be, so I can go where I want.* She started down the aisle, the courtroom suddenly silent, people watching her, some calling to her.

"Good luck, Natalie."

She continued walking, ignoring the faces turned toward her, the people staring. She was looking for Susan and Angelina.

There. Susan is standing, waving to me, in the back by the wall. Natalie walked down the aisle and sat down beside Susan. They hugged.

"I was at Dan's trial every day, until he ran," Susan said. "Oh, Natalie, the day he ran, the police thought I helped him, and they questioned me until evening, and I didn't even know he was going to go. Listen to me, going on. How are you holding up?"

"I'm doing okay, and you're very sweet." Natalie looked around the bench. "Where's the peanut?"

"Oh, she went with that nice detective you had sit with us, going to see her daddy."

Natalie's stomach flopped and churned.

"What detective?"

"The nice man who was sitting with us. I thought he was working with you, said he was, he left when the judge went out. About a half hour ago now."

"Susan, what did he look like?"

"I don't know, he was wearing a suit, a gray one, had brownish hair with some gray, kind of a tall, a nice man, and he—."

"His skin, did you notice his skin?"

"Well, yes, I did, but I don't see what this has to do with him taking Angelina to Dan. His skin was very white, you could almost see through it."

Natalie's face drained of color, and she stood up. "Susan, did he say anything else, about where he was going?"

"Natalie, what's wrong, what is it with him? You're shaking, child. The man said he would see you later at your apartment, so I thought it would be all right."

"Susan, find Detective Grant, or some of the others who were in the court today. Tell them I need help at my apartment. Call 911, tell them the same. Now!"

Natalie turned too quickly, and was rewarded by a stab of pain going through her neck. She pushed her way through to the aisle, and ran for the door, the courtroom buzzing. She slammed into the door, throwing it open, and ran for the stairs, not waiting for the elevator.

The son-of-a-bitch has Angelina, the son-of-a-bitch shot Stephanie, and the son-of-a-bitch is gonna kill Angel, and I'm not gonna let him!

She took the stairs at a run, throwing her shoulder into the wall to slow herself down, her neck screaming, the pain shooting down her back.

One flight.

Bottom floor.

Natalie ran off the last step, pumping her legs, her shoes smacking on the tile floor. She ran into a group of people standing by the door, hitting a man as he turned, putting her shoulder into him.

"Get outta my way," she screamed and straight-armed the man, the others in the group jumping back, startled. "Hey lady, watch out," one of them said. She hit the door and ran out into the rain, calculating the distance to her place. Twelve blocks or so.

I need a car.

She jerked her head, the neck brace twisting, the pain continuous now. With a yell she tore the neck brace from her neck, the Velcro fasteners ripping open as she grabbed it and threw it down.

She ran into the street, hearing a car braking, sliding on the slick asphalt. A horn blasted at her, and she turned to see a white Nissan slide up to her, Natalie putting her hand out on the hood as it came to a stop. There was a terrified woman, about thirty years old, behind the wheel.

Natalie ran to the driver's door, jerking it open, screaming at the woman, the woman too scared to speak. Natalie pulled the driver from her car, screaming, "Get out! Get out!"

Natalie slid into the driver's seat and slammed the door.

Oh, God, he's got Angelina, my Angel little pumkin Oh, God, he's got the pumkin.

Natalie slammed on the accelerator, the tires spinning, and she hit the car in front of her.

Calm down—gotta calm down.

She threw the lever into reverse, backed up, and drove onto the sidewalk, honking, yelled, "Get the fuck outta the way! Natalie pulled back onto the street, turned the corner wide, slid, sideswiped a car, and then she rocketed down Morrison Street, heading for Front Avenue and her apartment.

She held one thought: *Kill him—kill him—kill him.*

I'll kill the bastard with my hands if I have to, she thought, and when she suddenly realized that she didn't have a gun, she didn't slow the car at all.

"He visits his victims before he kills them," Dan said. They were all listening now, even the prosecutor. Sims tried to look bored, but if it wasn't true, it was a good story.

"He is attempting to learn if there is a formula to avoiding death by accident, why some people survive catastrophes when they should have perished."

"Your Honor, for Pete's sake," Sims said, standing up. "Harris—."

"Mr. Sims, sit down and be quiet," Judge Hernandez said, not taking her eyes from Dan. "Mr. Harris, please continue, I will tell you when to stop." Grant entered the chambers, telling the judge he was there to give the court the status of Harris as a fugitive.

"Later, Detective Birnam. Continue, Mr. Harris."

Dan started with his story, with the survivors. He told about his wife Jackie surviving a plane crash, and the Goldson boy. Missing. When he got to the part about Grant helping them, Sims threw his pen on the legal pad in his lap and crossed his arms. The only other sound in the room was the quiet movement of the keys on the recorder's machine as Dan talked about seeing Bramson on television, and knowing that he was the man who killed his wife.

Susan ran along the corridor, looking for the detectives Natalie had talked to earlier, not seeing anyone who looked familiar. *I've got to call emergency, tell someone.* She turned the corner and pulled her cell from her purse and dialed 9-1-1 with shaking hands. As she slumped against the wall she tried to get her breath, and the phone rang and rang.

"Nine-one-one, what is your emergency?" The operator's voice was crisp, efficient.

"I need help!" Susan yelled, her breath coming fast, blowing into the phone.

"What's the problem?"

"Amantookmyniece."

"Slow down and start over. A man what?"

"A man took my niece," Susan said, forcing herself to slow down, so she could think. Natalie's house. "Sergeant Natalie Collins said she needs help . . . at her apartment."

"What does she have to do with you needing help?"

"Sergeant Collins went to help my niece, at her apartment. She said to call 9-1-1 and tell you she needs help."

"What's the address?"

Susan felt her knees go weak.

"I don't know."

"We can't help if we don't know the address."

"It's Sergeant Natalie Collins's apartment!" Susan yelled, fighting hysteria.

Dan, I have to find Dan.

She dropped her phone and ran back down the hall, turning the corner, and running for the courtroom, her body sick with fear, tears starting to run down her cheeks.

Victor Bramson parked in the cul-de-sac, at the curb next to the deli. He got out and pulled Angelina with him, who was by now so badly frightened it was hard for her to walk. She clutched her giraffe in her right hand. They walked down the sidewalk above the marina, walking toward Natalie's gate, Bramson watching for someone to go in or out. Angelina stood with him outside the gate, shaking. The rain started up again, a few drops at first, the gray overcast threatening more and more rain.

"Oh, you poor thing," a woman said, coming to the gate from the steps inside, looking at Angelina.

"I'm visiting a friend," Bramson said, "and I guess he forgot to tell me about the gate."

"Let me get it for you," she said, stepping back out of the way as she opened the gate. "Better get the little one inside."

"I plan to do that right away," Bramson said, pulling Angelina into the terraced area. He started up the steps for Natalie's apartment.

"I want my daddy," Angelina whispered.

"In just a few seconds," Bramson said, and smiled.

You will all die before me.

Five

"**Get** outta my way!" Natalie screamed, slamming on the brakes, swerving around a slow car, hitting the corner and swerving onto Front Avenue, sliding to the opposite curb, the river on her left, jamming the accelerator to the floor. *Too much!* The car spun sideways, Natalie letting the pedal up and then slamming her foot to the floor again.

Ohmigod! I'm gonna be too late!

And then she had a thought that scared her worse.

What if they're not here, what if he took her to some other place?

Natalie kept the accelerator down, her speed going up through the sixties, then to seventy-five, in a forty-mile-per-hour speed zone. She passed a car on the right, swerving back in front, missing a parked car by inches, the rain and mist making it harder to see. She fumbled for the wiper switch in the unfamiliar car, and slammed her fist on the steering wheel when she couldn't find it.

One block. One more block to go.

Victor Bramson entered the same way he had before, silently, with Angelina watching. *The man said that Daddy was here,* she thought, but she wasn't sure, because he reminded her of the bad man. She held the giraffe in her left hand now, unaware that she had put her right thumb in her mouth, the thing that babies do.

Victor opened the door and pulled Angelina into the room after him. He shut the door.

"Daddy?" Angelina called, her voice quavering. *He's not here, oh, my daddy's not here, and the bad man has me, oh Daddy.*

"He's not here," Victor Bramson said, looking down at Angelina, saying out loud her worst fears. "Come on, I want to show Natalie's room to you."

Angelina stood there, looking at the counter across the room, not able to look up at the man. And then she whirled around and tried to run to the door, but a hand caught her shoulder, and the giraffe dropped, Angelina screaming, "Nooooo, help me!" She tried to scream again, until a huge hand covered her mouth.

"Come on," Bramson said. He picked her up and carried her down the hall. Angelina struggled, still trying to scream. "Stop screaming," he said calmly. "I have some questions to ask. We need some time to talk before Natalie comes home. Then, I'll take you to your daddy, okay?"

Angelina nodded.

Natalie took the corner wide, the car sliding into the right curb, the wheels slamming into the cement and caroming off, heading down the hill to the river, where the street ended in a cul-de-sac. There was a Pontiac in the turn-around circle, a no parking zone.

Please God, let that be his.

Natalie sped straight down toward the end, slamming on the brakes as she got there, the car bouncing off the curb at the seawall. She opened the door and was out and running, leaving the car there with the engine on. She ran on the sidewalk toward the gate, her shoes slapping on the wet cement. A man and woman in their twenties were at the seawall, holding hands, looking at Natalie.

"Call the police, I need help!" Natalie screamed at them as she ran toward the gate.

My key! I don't have my key, oh Christ!

She ran up to the gate and shook it and started to climb it, pulling herself up, her neck tearing in pain, her shoes slipping on the iron. She kicked her shoes off and pulled herself up on top of the gate. She balanced on top, and then vaulted over and down the other side, landing hard, her balance off with the injury to her neck.

The man and woman were still standing there, staring at Natalie.

"Call the police," Natalie screamed at them.

Natalie stumbled and fell forward to her hands, getting up and running up the terraced stairway, up two flights to her doorway.

A gun, I need a gun! There are no guns in my apartment. Both are in evidence. Oh, sweet Jesus, I need a gun.

Natalie stopped at her door, swaying, and tried the doorknob.

Unlocked! Her door was unlocked, and she hadn't been home in a week. They were here. She turned the knob all the way and pushed gently on the door, keeping her body to the side as much as possible. She pushed the door open a foot, looking into the living room. From what she could see, it was empty, and she opened the door another foot, silently.

Natalie stepped inside, carefully, quietly, moving her head to cover all the angles, all of the blind spots, and was rewarded by a pain shooting from her neck down her right shoulder and arm.

She closed the door, quietly.

There on the carpet, in the living room in front of her, was Angelina's giraffe.

Oh dear God. They are here.

And then she smelled it.

Gunpowder and blood.

Susan ran to the front of the courtroom, looking for someone in charge, looking for Dan, for the attorney, anyone. The conversation stopped a she ran up the aisle to the front, her movements frantic, jerky. People were turning to see who was running in the courtroom.

The judge was not back in the courtroom yet, nor were the attorneys or Dan. She went past the judge's bench and turned to the door the judge had used when she came into the courtroom. Susan took a look behind her at the court, and then entered the door.

"In his journal he talks about the ways he kills, and the questions he asks," Dan said. He took a sip of water, and continued. He had been testifying for several minutes without an interruption from the judge or either attorney. "Some look like accidents, with some he plays with the evidence, wearing the clothes of household members and planting them, always throwing suspicion on someone other than him, and, some—."

Dan stopped and looked at the judge. He looked at Sims and Attinger, weary now that this part was almost over.

I think she believes me, he thought. *No, I know she believes me, or at least she wants to, for Natalie's sake.*

"Some of the victims," he said, "just disappear, and are never seen again. In the journals I have read, he doesn't always tell what he has done with them, just what he asked them."

The door burst open behind the attorneys, and Dan looked up, staring at his sister, Susan, who stood swaying in the open doorway, her tear-streaked white face telling him things he never wanted to know. Susan ran into the room, running at the judge's desk, past Sims, and throwing her arms around Dan.

"Dan," she sobbed, "he's got Angelina."

Natalie walked quietly, quickly crossing the living room and going into the kitchen. *They must be in the back, and I'm going there in five seconds,* she thought, *but I won't be stupid about it. Oh, baby, hang on, I'm gonna be there.*

She looked in a cupboard where she kept her off-duty gun, knowing when she opened the door it would be gone, and it was. She grabbed two steak knives from a drawer and slid them into the inside pocket of her suit jacket. She took a heavy meat cleaver in her right hand, and a butcher knife in her left, and walked quietly around the counter to the hallway.

Both bedrooms were on the right of the hallway, with Natalie's first, and then Stephanie's room.

Gunpowder and blood.

Hang on, baby.

You'd better be quick and good, you bastard, or there won't be enough left of you to put in a trash compactor.

Natalie walked down the hallway, years of training and experience making her movements automatic, holding the knife in her left hand out to jab and parry, the right hand with the meat cleaver in a high striking position. She felt a rush of emotions, fear and rage for Angelina, and for her and Steph.

You bastard, I'm gonna do you.

You're in a real bad spot here in this hallway, Detective Sergeant Natalie Collins, especially if he steps out with a gun. It's all over, you with a knife.

Save the baby, you have to save the baby.

And then it happened so fast she didn't have time to think, just react.

Bramson stepped out at the end of the hallway, wearing a rubber mask. He brought a gun up, lining it up on Natalie's chest, firing, three times, rapidly.

Natalie, with no place to go, threw the cleaver as soon as he stepped out, throwing it hard without thinking. The first bullet hit Natalie in her left side, burning her, Bramson flinching as she threw the cleaver. The other two shots went wide, past Natalie and beyond, through the living room, where they shattered the large windows overlooking the river. The cleaver hit Bramson on the left side of his head, then stuck in the wall behind him, the blow driving him backward and down on one knee, his gun dropping, the rubber mask sliced where his ear would be, blood running down inside and outside the mask.

"You bitch, I'll kill you for that!"

Natalie switched the butcher knife to her right hand, the pain in her left side intense, raising her right hand to put the knife in throwing position. "No, I'm gonna kill you, you evil bastard," Natalie said coldly, and then yelled, "you're under arrest, get down on the floor, face down!" As she walked toward him, he suddenly lunged to his left through the open doorway into Stephanie's room and slammed the door.

"Natalie!" Angelina wailed from the bedroom.

Natalie walked into her room, and into the adjoining bathroom. The bath was positioned between the bedrooms, with access to either.

And Bramson knew it.

"Let her go, Bramson," Natalie yelled.

There was no answer. She yelled again, walking past the Disneyland souvenirs on her dresser. "Let her go, Bramson, and get out while you can!"

The gun! Jesus, Natalie, the gun is in the hallway!

She walked backward to the doorway and looked down the hall toward Stephanie's room. The gun was missing from the floor where Bramson had dropped it!

Natalie walked back to her bedroom and entered the bathroom, standing before the door to Stephanie's room. Bramson outweighed her by over a hundred pounds, and she knew that if it were humanly possible, she was going to kill him.

At least you bleed, you bastard!

Gunpowder and blood.

Natalie Collins entered the bedroom.

Dan stood up, staring hard at the judge, holding Susan. "Who has Angelina?" he asked his sister. What she told him made his blood go to ice.

"The man from Florida," she sobbed.

"How do you know?" Dan asked, trembling with fear and rage.

"Natalie told me, and she said that she was going to her place, where she thought the man took Angelina."

"Judge, I'm going to help my daughter," Dan said, letting go of Susan. He started for the door.

"Mr. Harris," Judge Hernandez said, "I remind you that you are in custody."

"I'll take responsibility for him, Your Honor," Grant said, "and we'll take the deputies with us."

"You——," Judge Hernandez said, and they were out the door, the deputies trailing.

Natalie pushed the door open with her left hand, holding the knife in her right. She stared at the blood she left on the white door, wondering for several seconds how it got there.

I get close enough to him, I'll buy him a headstone. I have to get close, to take away the gun.

She knew at close range a sudden knife attack could be more deadly than a gun, especially if he didn't have the gun ready, much more frightening, and almost impossible to defend against. She fought a wave of dizziness and pain.

"Come on in, Natalie Collins," the voice said. Natalie did a quick peek around the corner and saw him there, the mask gone, along with most of his right ear. He held the revolver in his right hand and pressed his left hand up against the bloody hole in the side of his head, his white skin turning red.

"End this," Natalie said quietly, grunting in pain, "end this and kill yourself . . . put the gun to your head and pull the trigger."

His eyes were bright with pain and madness. *I can't connect with him,* Natalie thought, his madness palpable, filling the room. Angelina sat on the bed in front of him, his left arm around her, loosely, possessively, as if he were holding a lover. She sat very still, looking at Natalie but not seeing, her eyes lifeless, catatonic.

"Let her go," Natalie whispered.

He lowered the gun, the barrel coming toward Natalie in slow motion, a fresh spurt of blood coming from the hole in the side of his head, the ear hanging down on his cheek like a grotesque organic earring. He shot once, and Natalie saw the gun jump in his hand, the round hitting the door frame beside her head, and he shot again, lower this time, the round hitting her, spinning her around, dropping her face down in the bathroom, her head hitting the tile with a smack.

Victor Bramson was up off the bed, taking Angelina with him, mumbling, "All die," Angelina walking woodenly, with the compliance of a child in an adult's world gone wrong. They went down the hall and out of the apartment, starting down the steps.

Suicidal? Oh, I'm not suicidal. I will live forever, you stupid, insignificant little person. The little survivor will tell me what I need to know. I'm the ultimate survivor.

He shuffled his feet, the evil dance of a madman.

Pleezed to meetcha.

Natalie stirred on the tile floor, pushing her hand out, sliding on the wet surface, the voice shouting in her head. She shook her head, wanting the voice to go away, wanting to sleep.

So very pleezed to meetcha, Natalie girl.

The voice came again, closer now, warmer, insistent.

Natalie pushed it away, wanting to dream of pleasant things, thinking about Disneyland, about Stephanie, seeing her ponytail bounce as she ran after Mickey Mouse.

Gunpowder and blood.

So very pleezed to meetcha, Natalie girl.

She saw Joe Louis, an older Joe Louis, in his tuxedo, standing by an iron gate next to the stairway to her apartment. He held Angelina's hand.

"You must go get her, Natalie girl, you must help her 'cause there's no one else."

He danced a step, a shadowboxing step, no longer in Las Vegas, looking back over his shoulder up the stairway. He walked down the stairs to the dock, standing there, looking at the water.

Angelina was holding his hand, looking up at him.

"C'mon girl, you can do it, you're the best, you're the can-do girl, remember? The baby girl needs you, only you."

Natalie pushed herself up on her hands, locking her elbows, the pain coming over her in waves, the scar tissue from her old wounds tearing with new ones.

"I made me the greatest, girl, I did it, I had heart.

"You have heart, Natalie.

"No time left.

"You can."

Natalie pushed herself up to a sitting position, pain slamming into her head, the bathroom spinning.

"I can't, Joe, it hurts too much!" She cried out, and cursed him again.

"You have to, Natalie, there's no one else.

"The baby will die"

Joe Louis pleaded with her, fading, and Angelina was gone.

The Willamette River, so sparkling blue in summer, was black under the gray, rain-filled sky. Victor Bramson shambled forward, across the sidewalk from the gate, and stood at the top of the stairs that led down to the river. Below the stairs, the dock to the marina ran out into the river in the shape of a T, forming a protective harbor. On the right side of the dock was the floating restaurant.

Bramson started down the stairs, pulling Angelina behind him. A woman approached the top as they started down. She had been looking over her shoulder, holding onto the handrail, talking to her lunch partner, another woman in her thirties. She was talking with her hands, animated, she looked up and saw the horror coming down at her and her face drained of blood.

Bramson's blood-crusted ear had dried on his cheek, looking as if he had glued it there, hanging by the lobe, blood still oozing out of the ear hole. The woman shrank away from him, from his madness, stopping on the stairway as he pulled Angelina along behind him. He didn't notice the women. When he got to the dock, he looked down at Angelina, surprise showing in his face, as if he were seeing her for the first time.

You are the one with the answers I need.

He walked out on the dock, past the floating restaurant, holding the gun in his right hand, pressing it against the blood-soaked side of his head, holding Angelina's hand. A waiter inside the restaurant stopped in the middle of the aisle and stared. "That man with the little girl has a gun," he said, causing the dour businessmen next to him to look out the window. Like a frightened school of fish, the patrons of the restaurant turned in a wave to look out on the dock.

When he reached the end of the dock, Bramson hesitated, and several people in the restaurant had the same thought—*He's going to walk into the river with her.* Instead, Bramson turned left, and walked along the dock, looking ahead.

At the end of the dock a blue-and-white thirty-one-foot Bayliner sport fisherman was tied up, its engine idling. The owner, forty-nine-year-old Charles Coburn, was on the dock, with his back to the approaching Bramson. He was taking the stern line off, getting the boat ready for one last ride before he pulled it out for the winter. He didn't hear Bramson approach.

Natalie got up on one knee, crying out, yelling, cursing Joe Louis. She stood, the bathroom spinning, and turned, jumping at the figure in the mirror, a bloody apparition with hollow eyes. Her white blouse was splashed with red, her hands streaked with drying black and red.

*   *   *

Bramson walked up behind the man and slowly lowered his gun, shooting once, hitting the man in the back of his head as he started to rise, the mist from his head spraying the dock. He was unaware of the audience in the restaurant, of appetites gone, the patrons standing in shock, the waiter on the phone. He swung Angelina in front of him and up and over the side of the boat, tossing her aboard, her head bouncing on the transom.

She lay very still, crumpled on the floor.

Bramson cast the line off and stepped into the boat, walking over Angelina without a thought.

Natalie pressed both hands to her side inside the suit jacket, her fingers pushing her silk blouse into a bloody oozing hole.

Oh Christ, I'm really fucked up. Gotta go, Natalie girl.

She stumbled into her bedroom, bent over, and hooked around the corner into the hallway, not stopping, using the wall for support, leaving bloody handprints on the white walls. She staggered outside and started down the terraced stairway, four steps and then a landing, four more, stepping sideways, holding her side, blood dripping on the cement, mixing with the rain.

The gate, I'll never get over the gate, oh, help me.

As she approached the bottom, she saw a man and woman enter the gate. The man held it open for her and shifted a grocery sack as he shut the gate. He closed the gate and they looked up at the same time.

Natalie shuffled down to them. Her neighbors, Mr. And Mrs. Martin.

"Help me . . . the gate," Natalie croaked.

He turned around and opened the gate, Mrs. Martin with her hands to her face.

Natalie didn't remember the walk down the stairs to the marina. She remembered the pain. She heard a shot as she reached the bottom and started out onto the dock, and she looked around at the restaurant and then the docks.

Up to her left, a blue-and-white boat was idling, a man stepping inside. A man in a dark gray suit, black with the rain. Bramson!

Natalie lurched along, trying to run, stumbling, her hand holding her side, keeping the blood in.

Bramson stood below the flying bridge at the controls, looking at the levers and knobs. He pushed the throttle forward, the engine changing from a burbling idle to a fast whine, but the boat didn't move. He looked at the controls again, looking for a gearshift.

Run, Natalie girl, you can do it.

She took her hand away from her side, the blood spurting out, her arms swinging wildly, her legs pumping, trying to sprint, weaving, running faster, now at the restaurant, flashing by the small group of men who had gathered just outside the front door, watching the Bayliner.

"He's got a gun!" one of them yelled, and then she was past them, turning down the left arm of the dock and sprinting now, screaming, blood trailing from her side, the boat drifting from the dock.

Bramson turned around as Natalie left the dock, surprise on his face as he pushed the gearshift into drive.

Natalie launched herself at the vessel, her body horizontal in a shallow dive. She hit the side and vaulted into the boat as the engine revved and the Bramson slammed the transmission into forward gear. The Bayliner suddenly shot out into the river, throwing Natalie toward the rear seat, her body narrowly missing Angelina in the back of the boat.

Dan put his head in his hands, sitting in the rear seat of the deputies' car with Grant, the car sliding and accelerating. "She can't do it," he said, shaking his head.

"What?" Grant leaned closer.

"I said, what can she do against him, especially without a gun?"

Grant stared out the window at the cars flashing past. "You don't know her very well, Dan, 'cause she never quits. Never. There's something inside her that won't let her. This guy Bramson will find out." Grant leaned forward and said to the driver, "Use the siren. We want him to know the police are coming."

I hope it's true, he thought, *I hope you can do it, Minnie Mouse, but Dan's right, you're gonna lose without a weapon.*

The unmarked police car slid around the corner and shot down toward the river, stopping in the cul-de-sac beside the Nissan Natalie had driven, Dan seeing the open door. He was out and running down the sidewalk along the seawall toward the gate before the car stopped.

As Dan ran down the sidewalk, movement on the docks below caught his eye, a group of people by the restaurant, a figure running, and from where he was, he could see the short blond hair, the small athletic figure in a navy suit, the skirt up around the waist. *Oh, Christ! She's running for the boat. Natalie!*

Dan turned and yelled for Grant, running for the stairs to the dock, seeing Natalie fly through the air at the boat as it shot away from the dock.

Natalie lifted her head up, seeing movement coming toward her and then above her, and then Bramson was on her, grabbing her arm. Natalie screamed with pain. He lifted her up and pulled her to the gunwales, Natalie screaming again, and reaching out blindly, grabbing, her hand finding Bramson's ear hanging on his cheek. She pulled, letting her weight go with it, and it came off in her hand, Bramson screaming, pulling back.

The boat was picking up speed, running at full throttle, bouncing across the water as it started to come up on plane. It veered toward the east bank, over a quarter mile away; at the same time, it was carried down river with the strong current of the Willamette. The Hawthorne Bridge was coming up, high above, downstream.

Bramson was on his knees, howling, glaring at Natalie, holding his head in his hands, blood coming from the ear hole. Natalie fell backward onto the seat cushion on the transom, and watched as

Angelina crawled past Bramson, crawling forward into the cabin area. Natalie tried to push away from the seat, waves of dizziness and nausea coming over her, her vision swimming, her body a spasm of pain.

Rest, I gotta rest, she thought, letting the nausea take over, bending over, retching, bringing her head up, seeing Angelina crawling into the cabin.

She'll die if you don't stop him, Natalie girl.

I can't stop him.

Yes. You have to, get up!

Bramson stopped howling and got to his feet, swaying drunkenly on the bouncing deck. Natalie slid off the seat and tried to stand, coming up on her knees, looking at Bramson as he came for her. She pushed herself up, using the seat for leverage, coming up on one leg, and then he hit her, hard, yelling over the engine noise below them.

"Die!"

He hit her again, and Natalie went down on the deck, moving, struggling through the pain to get up.

Gotta get up, gotta fight, Natalie, you don't win fights by lying down.

I can't, I'm losing, let me die.

What about the little pumkin?

Natalie struggled to her knees and was hit almost immediately.

Dan ran along the dock toward the restaurant, seeing people lining the windows, watching the struggle on the speeding boat. Grant followed with his gun out, the deputies trailing.

"Over there." Dan pointed to the boat, to the man lying on the dock. He turned to the crowd of people standing at the entrance to the restaurant.

"We need a boat," he yelled. One of the men in the group pointed. A forty-foot sloop was coming around the end of the dock, running on auxiliary power, putting out into the river. The owner was standing at the wheel, watching the river. Dan ran, waving his arms, yelling, and the boat veered back toward the dock, the owner bringing it in. As it came into the dock, Dan, Grant, and one of the deputies jumped on, the other deputy kneeling over the man lying on the dock. As the sailboat straightened out to follow the Bayliner, Dan could see figures moving on the back of the fishing boat.

It was too far away to tell who they were.

The sailboat on auxiliary power would never catch the Bayliner running at full speed.

The blow snapped Natalie's head back, her neck popping with excruciating pain, as if she had been hit with a machete. She fell forward and bounced on the deck. Bramson pulled on her left arm, pulling her into him, her face inches from his, all sanity gone now, putting his arms around her, and they moved to the transom at the rear of the boat, a grotesque parody of a lovers' dance, Natalie beating him with her right arm.

"Leave her alone." The voice was quiet, insistent.

"Dan, look." Grant grabbed Dan by the arm and pointed downstream. Dan had been watching the struggle on the boat, three hundred yards in front of them, the distance between the two boats increasing all the time, the larger boat faster, more powerful. Dan followed Grant's arm, watching as the Bayliner veered downstream, running in the middle of the river, headed for the massive support of the Hawthorne Bridge.

Oh, Christ! They're gonna hit the bridge!

They watched helplessly, as the blue-and-white boat sped toward the bridge support.

Bramson stopped, holding Natalie up in the air, holding her out in front of him, and then Natalie heard the voice again.

"You leave my Nat'lie alone," Angelina said behind them, and Bramson turned his head to look at the front of the boat, seeing Angelina holding something, lurching toward them, and then Natalie saw it.

A fire extinguisher.

Angelina was holding a red fire extinguisher, shivering, looking so very small and frail, holding it high up, holding it out in front of her as if it were toxic, and when Bramson turned, she shot him full in the face with white powder, holding the nozzle in his face as he dropped Natalie, his hands clawing at his eyes. He screamed, making a swipe with an arm, trying to hit Angelina. She jumped back, keeping the nozzle on him, holding the stream in his eyes until the stream ran out.

Bramson staggered to the front, toward the cabin, Angelina moving out of his way, dropping the empty canister.

Natalie stood, reaching for Angelina, and looked up at the bridge looming above them, the cement support directly in front of them, the boat running at full speed, and she knew they couldn't turn the boat, no time, and using strength she didn't know she had, she grabbed Angelina in her arms, and dove over the side.

The explosion struck Dan like a slap, the Bayliner rising up and crumpling against the concrete support as it hit it at full speed, exploding in a large spout of flame.

My Angel. Oh God, my Angelina!

By the time they got there, the debris from the remains of the Bayliner had gone on past the bridge, carried on the current. They took the sailboat under the bridge, slowly, looking at the water.

"Bring it around the other side," Dan said, crying, tears mixing with the rain on his face.

As the boat came around the east side of the bridge support, they saw some cushions and broken wooden pieces of the Bayliner floating down past them. The sailboat engine was at an idle, the sound of the cars on the bridge above them muted.

"Dad-deeee."

Dan and Grant turned to look toward the voice, looking over the debris.

"There!" Dan yelled, pointing to the east bank. Someone in the water. Angelina! The sailboat angled over, reversing against the current as they came down on the figure in the water. Dan jumped in as they got close, seeing Angelina holding a face out of the water on a cushion as he jumped. *They're both so white,* he thought. He kicked and swam over to his daughter, the shock of the cold hitting him.

"Help me, Daddy. Nat'lie's hurt very bad."

Grant and the deputy pulled them up, the deputy getting blankets from below. Grant bent over Natalie as they laid her on the deck, the deputy talking urgently into his handheld radio.

"Get this thing to shore," Grant yelled.

"What about the other one?" the boat driver asked.

"Fuck him, he's dead," Grant said, and then muttered, "I hope."

Dan took Angelina below into the small cabin, holding his daughter as they both shivered.

"Daddy," Angelina said, crying, "she can't die, she just can't, I love her too much." Dan cried with his daughter.

Natalie's lips were blue, her breath ragged and shallow as Grant bent over her, wrapping her in blankets, holding her bloody side. Her eyes were closed, her head back on the deck.

Her eyelids fluttered, as if she were dreaming.

There was old Joe Louis, standing on the shore, there on the east shore, out of the rain under the approach to the Hawthorne Bridge, holding hands with someone Natalie couldn't quite identify, someone smaller than Joe.

Joe waved.

"You did good, Natalie girl. You're a fighter, like me. A best-in-the-world fighter, a champion."

As she got closer, Natalie could see Joe's companion.

Stephanie, wearing a Disneyland sweatshirt with Minnie Mouse on the front, a Mickey cap.

"I want to go with you Joe," Natalie said, "please, Joe, I hurt so bad."

"Not this time, girl," Joe said, turning away, Stephanie turning with him, waving, blowing Natalie a kiss.

"You, Natalie girl, you gotta fight through the pain, you gotta get better, now you got a family to raise.

"You raise a fighter, someone who doesn't give up, like you and me, girl, and then you take them to Disneyland, the Happiest Place in the World, the place where no one dies."

Tuesday, June 18

Main Street, U.S.A.

Epilogue

Dan walked behind them, watching his wife and daughter make their way down the busy sidewalk. He was window shopping, strolling, keeping them in sight. They stopped and sat on a bench in the block ahead of him, under the shade of a West Coast oak tree, the temperature in midmorning already eighty degrees. Angelina was talking, her body animated, her hands waving, describing something. *She's growing so tall,* he thought. At eight, she was only a few inches shorter than Natalie.

He could see them laughing as he walked toward them, Natalie bending over at something Angelina was saying. Angelina jumped up from the bench and whispered to Natalie, and stood there with her hand on Natalie's shoulder, still talking. Natalie was holding her side, grinning at her daughter. They looked up and saw Dan and waved.

He loved to watch them unobserved, feeling as if he could project his love to them.

Protect them.

In the early hours of the morning he often wondered if we could ever protect our loves, if protection were a whim, a roll of the dice. He shook his head and smiled. This was a happy day for them, a trip they had planned for.

A trip they needed.

Natalie grabbed her cane as Dan came up to them. Angelina grabbed her hand, helping her up, doting on her. They had been inseparable since the time in the river. Natalie limped some, the limp not bothering her as much as the few gray hairs she had found this morning. Her yell from the bathroom had brought them running. They had laughed at her and she yelled again, plucking out gray until she laughed with them.

Gray is good, Dan told her. We want to grow old together, the natural order of things, to see our children and grandchildren grow up, and when our time comes, to die.

He heard a noise behind him, from the Central Plaza, the beating of a drum.

"Daddy, the parade! Look, Natalie!" Angelina pointed down the street, jumping on her toes, her ponytail bouncing. Dan walked up to them and took Natalie's hand. She smiled up at him and he saw that her eyes were wet. She was where she wanted to be, a place she needed to be. She was at her Disneyland, the Happiest Place in the World, a place for children, where no one ever dies.

Angelina ran down the sidewalk toward the parade.

The townsfolk of Newharbor, Oregon, would tell you that if you didn't like the coastal rain showers, wait for an hour and there would be another one, particularly if you were on vacation. The Newharbor *Sentinel* was published twice a week and carried some national news along with the meeting times of the volunteer firefighters' association.

Fourteen-year-old Jered Hamblin carried the paper in the rain for most of the year, and he conscientiously placed the papers in screen doors and on porches so they would stay dry. On a Tuesday in the middle of June, he was fighting a windblown rain, riding his bicycle up and down the hills of Newharbor, delivering the *Sentinel*. He rode down the long driveway, the overgrown brush almost touching the handlebars of his bike, and threw for the porch of the cabin.

Missed.

He got off his bike and retrieved the paper. He glanced in the front window as he threw the paper, the strange sight causing him to look closer.

News clippings. There were clippings taped up on the walls of the cabin. From where he was, he could see the red circles around the articles. He jumped back on his bike and rode down the driveway, thinking that customers could sure do some strange things with newspaper.

ABOUT THE AUTHOR

Enes Smith relied upon his experience as a homicide detective to write his first novel, *Fatal Flowers* (Berkley, 1992). Crime author Ann Rule wrote, "*Fatal Flowers* is a chillingly authentic look into the blackest depths of a psychopath's fantasies. Not for the fainthearted . . . Smith is a cop who's been there and a writer on his way straight up. Read this on a night when you don't need to sleep, you won't . . ."

Fatal Flowers was followed by *Dear Departed* (Berkley, 1994). "You might want to lock the doors before starting this one," author Ken Goddard wrote, "Enes Smith possesses a gut-level understanding of the word 'evil,' and it shows." Ken Goddard is the author of *The Alchemist*, *Prey*, and *Outer Perimeter*, and Director of the National Wildlife Forensic Laboratory.

Smith's work as a Tribal Police Chief for the Confederated Tribes of the Warm Springs Indians of Oregon led to his first novel in Indian Country, *Cold River Rising*. *Cold River Resurrection* is the second novel in the Cold River series. He worked as the Tribal Police Chief in 1994 and 1995, and again in 2005 and 2006.

He has been a college instructor and adjunct professor, teaching a vast array of courses including Criminology, Sociology, Social Deviance, and Race, Class, and Ethnicity. He trains casino employees in the art of nonverbal cues to deception. He is a frequent keynote speaker at regional and national events, and has been a panelist at The Bouchercon, the World Mystery Convention.

COLD RIVER RISING IS SOON TO BE A MAJOR MOTION PICTURE

Made in the USA
San Bernardino, CA
17 July 2014